Praise *for* *Dreamers*

"Take Annie, a fresh college grad from a traditional middle-class white family in Pittsburgh, stir together with Thomas, a handsome black man with baggage who's hell bent for theater success, turn them out in New York City awash in weltschmertz, drugs and the Civil Rights Movement of the 1960s, add a rich white sugar-lady who's been paying Thomas' bills in exchange for boudoir duty, sprinkle with innocent love and naked ambition, and you have a gripping novel served up by Margaret Murray. Brimming with truths of the heart and spirit, here's a unique coming-of-age love story you won't want to miss."

—Naida West, author, www.bridgehousebooks.com

Also by Margaret C. Murray

Sundagger.net, a novel

DREAMERS

An Interracial Romance of the '60s

by Margaret C. Murray

To Pat,
A fellow
Irish dreamer!
Enjoy.
"Margie"
Margaret C.
Murray

WriteWords Press
Sebastopol, CA

DREAMERS

A novel

WriteWords Press
Sebastopol, CA

ISBN: 978-0-9793573-1-2 (pbk.)
E-Book ISBN: 978-0-9793573-8-1
Library of Congress Control Number: 2011920633

Dreamers is a work of fiction. Whereas the neighborhoods of Pittsburgh and New York are real, as are the historical figures of the Civil Rights era, Thomas, Annie, and the other characters in this novel are fictitious products of the author's imagination. No reference to any real person is intended or should be inferred.

Printed in the United States of America
Cover Design: Charr Crail, www.charrcrail.com
Interior Design: WriteWords Press

For My Father

Acknowledgements

Thank you to my high school friends, Franny Pavone Jutras and the late Kathy Trebac Heller, for believing me to be a writer. Thank you to Sister Mary Noel Kernan, my high school English teacher, for speaking of me and literature in the same breath. Thank you to the late Professor John Hart of what was then Carnegie Institute of Technology for reading my folded-up "novels."

Many thanks to the Provincetown Fine Arts Work Center for awarding me the opportunity to begin *Dreamers*. Thank you, P-town fellows of '69-'70, for supporting my young writing.

To Lester Gorn of U.C. Berkeley Extension who forced me to rewrite. To the Squaw Valley Writing Conference for awarding me a National Endowment Award to attend the Screenwriter's Workshop. To the Rich & Famous Writers group: Amy, Dan, Nancy, Shelley, and Shirley. Thank you to John Brewer who saw Thomas better than I could and helped me navigate Pittsburgh after all these years.

Thank you to Josh Kamm for his impeccable editing. Thanks to my brilliant cover designer, Charr Crail. Thanks to Michael.

From all my heart, thank you to Jonas, Annemarie, and Chris who grew up with this book.

Prologue

I was in love with trouble. When Thomas touched me, I felt beloved. I felt intense pleasure just being in the same room with him. How beautiful his skin.

It all happened so long ago—in another lifetime, but still mine. The 1960s in America were another country. For some people, the '60s never happened. Black and white in Pittsburgh, Pennsylvania lived in different worlds in 1966—the year I met Thomas. It was three years after JFK sent out his Civil Rights message, when Governor Wallace of Alabama pledged segregation, "Now, Tomorrow and Forever," to prevent those colored teenagers from integrating Tuskegee High School. Medgar Evers had been murdered three years before and Freedom Summer had been over for two. Four little black girls had been bombed into shrapnel in a Baptist church in Birmingham. Urban inner city riots had erupted, even in Pittsburgh. Malcolm X had been killed in NYC and over 10,000 had rioted in Watts, California. LBJ had passed the Civil Rights Act. Martin Luther King, Jr. had already given his "I Have A Dream" speech.

I had my own dream and it began in Pittsburgh, the city where I was born, grew up, and live now. But I was not the only one! Thomas was a dreamer too—his assumed alias, Dreamer, was not only ironic. It was the truth. His place was in the sky with the stars. He loved the stars piercing all that open dark space. The only space that was big enough for him was on the stage he used to tell me. Thomas had a horror of small places, crowded rooms. He had a horror of being locked up like his brothers in the Pen he told me. I fed off his terrible stories—each one proof he cared enough for me to tell me the truth.

So here I am waiting at Pittsburgh International Airport in my shapeless, beige jumper to see Thomas again after forty years, but all I really see is that dissolute, stubborn, intense young woman who was me so long ago. They're even playing a Peter, Paul and Mary song over the airport loudspeaker. I sit stiffly in the back of a row of blue seats beyond the security area watching the Arrivals list on the US AirWays monitor, holding that first email and the second and third.

From: <thedreamer@gmail.com>
To: <annieryanlawton@yahoo.com>
Sent: January 24, 2008
Subject: the same annie?
Are you the same Annie who I met at Christmas in Pittsburgh in 1966? Do you play the violin? If you are, we know each other.
Write back,
Thomas

It took me three months to answer. After reading that email, I fell sick from Pittsburgh as if I'd eaten too much. What was it like to grow up then? Rivers and hills surrounded me. Hills were everywhere, hills were Pittsburgh, hills and rivers and bridges crossing them, and the great green trees bowing beneath the haze of summer sunlight, the cobwebs and mazes of bare branched trees in winter, fronting a backdrop of smog and sulfur flames from the steel mills, the furnaces still operating in the '50s and '60s. Pittsburgh housed all the neighborhoods of Europe, the Near East and Russia in miniature, one nationality predominant on each hill and each hollow, and you could find your own country from any one of 56 bridges.

When I ran beneath the old elm and maple trees of Schenley Park and Frick Park, I heard in the branches and fluttering leaves deep and sonorous echoes of pure joy, like the piano concertos of Brahms or Wagner's compositions. Music ran along the roots of the trees, not so majestic or exciting as Beethoven, whom my father loved, but more like slow-burning Mahler. As for me, second generation Irish-American, I ran ignorant and free, madly, wildly over the grass. Magic happened here under the trees, the magic of good and evil. The good I could feel in the pull and spring of my legs, my outstretched arms, as I ran. The evil was very old and long before my time, lurking in the black holes in the hills where the coal mines had been, but were now scars like dried blisters of deep sores, boarded up, blighting forever the hillsides on both sides of the Allegheny Mountains.

My father loved Pittsburgh more than he loved me. He knew its history when it was Fort Duquesne and George Washington came here as a surveyor in the French and Indian War. He could describe the nuances of Greek and Roman architecture on all the public buildings, columns and colonnades copied from Europe and paid for by steel barons. Dad knew about the rise of the steel mills, fights with the union workers, and, naturally, the ins and outs of Irish politics. When he drove me places, he could point out where the Irish neighborhoods began and merged with the Italian, where the Polish ghettos by the river crossed the Lithuanian neighborhoods along the railroad tracks, and the Episcopalian bankers lived in pseudo-English estates in Sewickley and the North Hills. As he drove me along the rivers, he talked about where the robber baron millionaires of the 19th century, Carnegie and Mellon, lived and died. Oh, he knew the rivers all right with their Indian names marking the time before the white men, before the French and Indian War and George Washington. The Monongahela cutting out the South Side and the Allegheny the North, both flowing into the Ohio at the Point. Dad knew the water high points and low, when the rivers flooded, how many barges went up and down in one year, and all the years since he was born in 1912 in Midland, a river town too. Yes, Dad knew all about Pittsburgh, but he never knew about me.

If only I had been Pittsburgh! I would not have needed to fall in love with one Thomas Find, aka Thomas Dreamer, the man I wait for at the airport today. And I the sorry fool of love. A poor dreamer as my mother would say.

I ran after him, all the way to New York City. Other than Central Park and the promenades by Battery Park, there are no trees in New York City, no real ground to walk on, just high rise buildings and concrete and tight hard corners framed by harsh wind. I have to forgive the lack of trees, the harsh winter. I have to forgive myself for following him. I have to forgive him for lying.

Lies are like lovers running away. You see them from the back as they disappear, or you see them in their absence, trails of dust where once your lover ran.

What makes one person lie and not another? What makes a person lie to one person, and not to another? You immediately think it's your fault when that person lies to you; something about you made the difference and allowed the lie.

My father lied to me too. How? What did he say? How did he betray me? Even today, my father long dead, I do not really know. Yet I feel betrayed. I loved my father. If you didn't count his prejudice and racism, he was a nice man, a kind man, a sweet erudite, cultured man, despite his Irish Catholic immigrant background, his family's rank poverty, his lace-curtain Irish pretensions to English aristocracy, his outright "balminess" as my mother described all the dreamy, unpractical Ryans.

Even now I don't know how to explain the anguish I felt trying to love my Dad. I can see him playing golf. He'd come home from one of those emerald green golf courses in the East End of Pittsburgh with this rare crooked smile on his pale worry-lined face. When I saw him holding his golf clubs and grinning at me, I felt twisted up inside. Why? Maybe I imagined how quickly his expression would change if he knew my thoughts or if he knew how angry Mother was at him for the pleasures he didn't share with her. I blamed him for her anger and I still torture myself with memories of how I displeased him and how disappointed he was with me.

But it was Dad who led me to that fated play, *Midsummer's Night's Dream*, though when I met Thomas on a snowy street outside the Pittsburgh Playhouse, it was midwinter, not summer, not like today. I wonder, is Thomas still so thin and quick? Does he lope and saunter still, swinging low to the ground like a coyote on those brown hills of Northern California I saw once while on tour with the Pittsburgh Symphony.

The play spoke to me—told my story, my dream. I wanted to be on center stage in a magical sparkling land where elves and fairies, queens and kings spoke exquisite poetry as they coupled in innocent, rosy beds.

What does love mean? I have a different answer now. Then my body was starving for a love I could only see as a color not my own.

Back then fear masqueraded as superiority as I spun my symphonic cocoon of classical violin studies at Carnegie Tech. I think of all those times I crossed the Carnegie campus to avoid the student-led demonstrations against the Vietnam War. I pretended not to see the police with their clubs randomly harassing or beating up on some outspoken student or assistant professor. I dismissed the anti-war movement as hopeless and the war as unstoppable, sure that Johnson and then Nixon would never change their horrific policies while people my age, boys I knew from the Catholic high school nearby, were being conscripted, were dying, coming back in black plastic body bags or, if they were lucky, fleeing to Canada. I could see them on TV any night. But I avoided TV. I avoided my parents when they argued about the war and McNamara. My father was a Republican, my mother a Democrat. But I was giving in to the enemy inside without knowing it.

Everything is different now. The young are a lot more cynical, including my own children. We were more innocent then, more hopeless and romantic. The whole world was changing. America was in upheaval and I was just a girl. All I really did was read *Soul on Ice* by Eldridge Cleaver and a few other books by iconoclastic American intellectuals. I thrilled to their cold, brilliant anger. I loved Cleaver's sexual diatribes against white men, misreading him as being my ally. Thomas too. Is that what they wanted? To trick me?

But here I am waiting for him to return. I can't believe it. If Thomas had been white, would it have been different? Does it make any difference in the end?

I heard that Eldridge Cleaver died penniless and destitute in Oakland, California in the late '90s. Did it make a difference to him? His whole career had been based on those hated differences.

From the moment I saw Thomas, he took over my life. I was submerged as if he were the sea and I the spawning fish. I wanted him at any cost. Or did I?

Sometimes I look up at the stars and think about how Thomas believed in them and wish I had that to console me. I wonder if he still follows the stars. I can ask him when I see him.

The monitor shows Flight 95 from New York arriving on time. He will be here soon. Or will he? I am terror-struck. I don't want to go back and yet I still want him.

Georgie G

When the trolley heading to downtown Pittsburgh crashed into the Impala, all of Momma's old clothes fell out into the snow. Momma's dresses, Christine-Marie's African robe, torn stained underpants, Carlotta's cracked girdles, and all the faded shirts with broken buttons.

Jeans without zippers, old sweaters, thin dresses, my yellow T-shirts from Homewood Junior High marked "Georgie G", socks with holes, matched socks, and unmatched socks.

Lorn's Marine pants and shirts from the last time he was home from Vietnam. Richard's sweatshirts that read:

Westinghouse High School
Basketball State Champions '57

Momma would clean the sweatshirts and send them on to Western Penitentiary whenever Uncle Richard needed one. In there for armed robbery, he be 36 when he gets out in '74, eight years from now.

John's blue stuff, colorless and thinner than paper, ripped to shits. Momma use it for rags now. John ain't been back in a long time. He was the youngest, the uncle closest to me. John left everything behind at the reform school in Latrobe when he run off. They shipped it home. How neat the stuff was packed: shirts, jock straps, pants folded like Kraft cheese slices in plastic wrap.

Betty and Karlene's brand new 36A padded bras from Woolworths fell out too. The cups were stitched into cones. My auntie twins were skinny and ugly but one good thing, they were both seventeen and not pregnant yet. Nobody could tell who was their daddy; Momma said the milkman, but who drinks milk?

My daddy, Thomas Find, the big star, he didn't leave no damn clothes behind.

Thomas

Rock hard, it broke him. Thomas Find heard those sirens. He saw the red lights. Ice dripped from the Christmas billboards on the streetcar over the wreckage while he waited inside the new 1966 Impala. Through the broken glass, the approaching conductor was distorted, two-dimensional, squared off, a uniform blue-black gash. There was no blood on the conductor's face and Thomas, holding his bleeding forehead, got angry. He expected somebody beside himself to be hurt too.

The conductor motioned them to get out of the car. Thomas pushed on his battered door but the lock had been crushed by the impact of the streetcar. The dislocated steering wheel pushed against his chest. Lana would kill him for this—her car was totaled.

"Try opening the window. Go on, open the window," shouted the conductor, a wizened white man with strings of gray hair blowing under his blue cap.

It hurt, slush dripped.

Two of his sisters, Christine-Marie and Carlotta, sat in the front seat crying and holding their heads.

"Hey, get us out a here," Georgie G yelled through the broken glass. Thomas winced at the unfamiliar sound of his son's tremulous high-pitched voice. It pained him how much Georgie G looked like his mother. He had Georgina's wide soft face, darker than Thomas' deep brown, and without Thomas' high Cherokee cheekbones and prominent nose. He felt the ache of hemorrhoids bothering him again.

"We didn't do nothing!" exclaimed Georgie G.

"We're so sorry, we just wanted to have some fun," cried Christine-Marie. "We didn't mean for this to happen."

"Hush," Thomas hissed in his best off-stage voice.

Their guilty voices made him mad too, as if it were their fault.

Several torn plastic baskets and bags of clean laundry had fallen over beside them on the back seat. There were socks on the dirty floor.

"Who's going to pick them things up again, I want to know?" yelled Georgie G. "I cleaned them once. I ain't going to do that shit again."

"Hush, boy," snapped Carlotta, "You think you can act so bad in front of your daddy. He don't like that sass, do you, Thomas? You hush or he won't come home no more."

"Hey, none of that. I did come home, remember. We'se all family, ain't we?" said Thomas, wincing at the whine he heard in his own voice. Funny how that jive talk he so painstakingly discarded came right back. It was as if he had never left Pittsburgh.

"He told you open the window," squeaked Georgie G, sitting between the twins, Betty and Karlene. His son. He was still a runt. Georgina hadn't expected him to live, Thomas remembered. Jesus, that was twelve years ago. Georgina was only fifteen when she had him and now she's gone.

"Hush, you, Thomas know what he said," hissed Carlotta.

"Knows," Thomas corrected her silently and then wanted to kick himself. Stupid fool habit, working to be white. "Shhhh," he hissed.

"Huh?" piped Georgie G.

Thomas tried the window again. The backward pull wrenched his arm. Ice dripped. Finally, the window broke. Glass fell over his arm. A few black men got off the streetcar and walked around between the wrecked Impala and the streetcar to examine the damage. It began to snow again.

"What'll they do to us, Thomas, I don't want to go to no jail," cried Carlotta. Two years younger than he, Carlotta should have been married and out of the house or in school. What was she doing and Momma taking care of her kids? But he knew the answer. She was working at an auto parts store, supporting the entire household, his son included. He himself had given nothing to his family in the last five years—until now, and look what happened.

"Don't be silly, girl," he replied in a quiet voice. "It was just an accident for Christ's sake. That goddamn streetcar ran the light. It's their fault. My God, only in Pittsburgh."

"Oh, Thomas, what'll we do?"

The conductor was trying to pry open the doors on the passenger side where the baskets of clean clothes had been but were now spilled over onto the floor. But the door wouldn't budge. Again the conductor pulled, this time shattering the window. He was holding a heavy metal rod. Glass spilled inside the car and the girls screamed as he smashed at the door handle with the steel rod.

"I want you all to get out of here as quick as you can," ordered Thomas. "I want you to get on home. Take Georgie G. with you, hear? And don't tell nobody about this. There's no cause for Momma to worry, you hear?"

"Yes, sir," said Christine-Marie, his favorite sister, the baby of the family.

"No, we won't, Thomas," Carlotta agreed.

The conductor put his hand through the broken window. "Come on," he said, pulling the back door handle. "Just lean over that way," he called out. He held out his hand to the girls cowering in the back seat.

"Get!" Thomas hissed at them.

Georgie G. hung back on the other side of the Impala. "Come on, boy," the conductor said, walking around to help him. There was more commotion in the street. Noticing the growing crowd slipping and sliding on the slush and ice, the conductor walked away, shouting orders to back off the broken glass on the street. As the conductor moved off, all the girls jumped out and ran away.

"Dad?" asked Georgie G in a quivery voice.

Thomas swung his head around to face his son cowering in the back seat.

"I told you to get home, boy!" he hissed. Then he saw the tears in his son's eyes. Thomas reached back and put his hand on Georgie G's knee. The boy was trembling.

"Hey! There. It's going to be alright. Hey, there. This here ain't worth crying about. Hey, don't I know. There, there," Thomas reached up and touched the boy's wet face. "You crying? Naw. Naw. You—your tears are…" Thomas searched for the right word. A line from a bad play he'd been in once came to him, "Your tears are precious to me."

As Georgie G wiped his face dry, Thomas caught his hand. "You hear that, son? This ain't worth nothing. You the one who counts. Now you open up that door and run like I tell you, hear?"

"Yes, sir," nodded Georgie G. "But I don't want to leave you with this mess."

Despite himself, Thomas laughed—a small, quiet, deep chuckle that continued until Georgie G laughed too.

"Son, I ain't staying around to clean up nobody's mess," Thomas said finally. "I'll be home before you know it. Now get. Ready?"

As he spoke, Thomas rubbed his hand on the cloudy window. By now there were two crowded 76 streetcars waiting behind the wreck in the blowing snow. Almost everyone inside the cars was black too. When he tried rolling down the window, it broke, spilling shards of glass on his lap. His finger began to bleed. "Ready?" he asked again.

"Yes."

Looking for the conductor, Thomas sucked at his finger till he felt glass on his lips. He spit the glass out the window. In his mind he saw thin dribbling bloody glass fall onto the streetcar tracks. Way down Second Avenue he saw the steel mills, flames burning sulfur into the windy, snowy night. The rivers, though he couldn't see them, were full of ice too.

"Now get!"

Cold wind rushed in as Georgie G pushed open the back door and fled. Thomas heard the crunch of his son's boots hitting the packed snow, but he didn't turn around. Instead he watched the cops arrive. Hearing the siren, seeing the red and blue flashing lights, Thomas clutched his gut to hold the fear still, like it was a rabbit and not the snarling rabid dog he felt inside him. Come on fool, he told himself, it's just another show.

Thomas made himself get out of the car and face the cops. Two of them, one white and one black. A head taller than anyone else, Thomas looked down at the cops, making himself impressive even in the blowing storm. He could feel himself tightening into the hard cold scare, high as the hawk. Hadn't felt it this bad in years. Must be coming to Pittsburgh done it. Borrowing Lana's car done it. He should never have let her loan him her car. He hadn't wanted to; he was going to go back home on the Greyhound bus, but she told him he'd make a bigger impression with her car—and then he remembered it wasn't even in her name. She had bragged about that—it was in her daddy's name, registered in Connecticut. The Man, an important official in some honkie town, Wallingford. What would her family say? C'mon nigger, you know what they'd say. But Thomas stopped himself from thinking more or feeling angry. He don't have time for that shit.

Why had he taken Lana's new white Impala? Guilt, he thought, and pride. Guilt that he was leaving her and pride to show off before the family he'd abandoned five years before. Sins Momma would never forgive him. Or had. Like she didn't forgive him for leaving Georgie G when he came home from Korea.

The white cop approached. One long string of red lights swung above them between telephone poles on the south side of the street, Homewood's left-handed Christmas card, off-balance and crude like so much here. A part of him was surprised to see the low-down, shit-poor poverty in Pittsburgh. That part was the dream that drove his career onstage. And then again, another part of him was not at all surprised, realizing that with his expectations, he'd bought into yet another example of that master-slave white propaganda. All those dreams were an entertainment, a drug to numb the injustice, like Elvis' latest popular poor white song, "In the Ghetto." Thomas had half a mind to sing it now. Spook everyone, ha ha.

Did the rats still crawl under the streetcars in the old lot on the corner of Hamilton and Frankstown across from the market advertising Duquesne beer and Wonder Bread? Thomas had counted the rats one day when he was about ten.

Look into the cop's eyes, blue in the Pittsburgh snow. Thomas started to smile.

"Goddamn rush hour traffic," said the cop, but not to him. Thomas clenched his jaw.

A tow truck driver came and the cops hitched up the Impala, blocking all the traffic on Tioga Street. The tow truck hoisted the front end of the battered car up into the air and all the rest of Momma's old clothes fell out of the plastic baskets onto the dark, wet, snowy street. Thomas felt as if he had been stripped naked. And all because of a goddamn accident, a fucking trolley. He shook his head in disbelief. And then he saw Georgie G running behind the tow truck, picking up the clothes. A skinny dog ran behind the boy, growling and shaking a torn shirt collar in his mouth.

"Get away," yelled the white cop.

"Fuck you," shouted Georgie G back. Thomas looked the other way, his gut tightening for the boy or for himself, he didn't know which. When he looked over again, Georgie G was gone and so were most of the clothes. He breathed a sigh of relief, feeling a rush of hope, like a small miracle, overtake him. Maybe it was going to be all right.

No time for that now.

The tow truck lurched forward, pulling Lana's Impala up the hill. As the streetcar finally began to move, people pushed their way up the steps into the warm, lighted car. Lana had something else now to hang over his head.

"Don't pay it no mind." Thomas could hear her joke in that fake black dialect she often affected with him, especially after sex. "I don't give a shit that you totaled my car, Tomboy." He hated that name. He could see her laughing, see her black pageboy hairdo swing around her pale peach face. "I'm just a no-account white girl, don't mind me." Her sarcasm made him all twisted up inside. He couldn't think things through. Lana was pure beauty and trouble. Like Georgina. They go together his momma told him when she learned about him and Georgina, who was only fourteen when they first made out on the torn seat of that abandoned car in the lot outside Forbes Field. They could hear the fans cheering the Pittsburgh Pirates.

Beauty and trouble. Lana was all that and more. An actress just out of Radcliffe, and before that, some exclusive private schools. He met her in a hole-in-the-wall theatre on the Lower East Side where he had a bit part. Rich, oh yes, a WASP from Connecticut. Almost immediately she seduced him and then asked him to move into her studio in the West Village. He was awed by it and her wealth, her careless abundance. Lana was dismissive of all the things he never had, which she had too much of. She was so available, too available, and realizing that, she treated herself like trash. He just couldn't believe his good fortune. But things changed mighty quickly when she took drugs, drugs he sometimes sold to get through the lean times, harmless drugs like pot at first. But soon she was telling him to find her the harder stuff, which he sold too, on occasion. It took him almost two years to get the nerve to leave her. He'd used this trip home as an excuse—he wanted to make a clean break, but he could see he'd ruined it by accepting her car.

And look at him now. A dangerously pure hatred welled up in him like vomit.

Several old men jumped back on the streetcar as it began to inch forward, the wind blowing their cigarette ash like red strings of dying embers in the piled-up dirt and snow. The cops, convinced he wasn't about to bolt, went back to directing traffic. Thomas stood alone on the pavement. What could he do? He couldn't be caught with Lana's car; that was intolerable. Not just for his sake—to thwart the humiliation and amusement she would vent on him—but for hers too. He knew she didn't want her father interfering with her affairs and he surely would when the cops in Pittsburgh contacted him.

Thomas took a deep breath, felt for his wallet in his leather jacket, and ran his hand over the cards. He'd learned from John to always keep an array of credit cards and drivers' licenses. None of them were his; he had no identification.

He watched the black cop closest to him move off after the tow truck, leaving behind the handsome ruddy Irish cop in blue, Pittsburgh blue. His gun was flat in its black leather holster. The gun was laughing at Thomas. It was blue-eyed.

He'd kept the cards for a day like today.

Thomas backed up against the side of an old house with a rotted porch and one red candle in a tinsel wreath showing in the broken glass door. A plastic Santa hung in the window too, grinning inside another tiny foil wreath. Could he bolt? Could he run and make it? It hadn't worked for his brothers. Thomas' back was streaked with pain. He rested his head against the Santa. His Afro was wet and kinky from the falling snow. Where to run? Quickly he scanned the porch, both sides of the house, the fence between the house and the next, the narrow dark walkway in between. A streetlight shone down on him. Nothing was easy. Nothing was sure. He zipped up his black leather jacket, putting his bleeding hand to his head as if to scratch it and very quietly slipped all the cards behind him into the back of the plastic Santa. All the cards except one. Slipping it back into his wallet, Thomas bowed his head, smearing blood over his hair, and waited.

"You the one driving the white Impala?"

Thomas jerked to attention. "That's correct, officer," he said to Irish.

"Let's see your ID."

Thomas offered up his wallet.

"Open it," said the cop. Irish got out his pad and pencil while the plastic Santa blinked over the opened wallet in Thomas' long thin dark hand.

"Give me that license," said Irish. "John Johnson, that's you?" he read.

"Yes, sir," answered Thomas humbly.

He hadn't used that license in a long time; it would be a while before they figured out he wasn't who he said he was.

"Address!" barked Irish.

"611 West 37th Street, Apartment 64A. New York."

They'd check out the plates soon enough though. He'd been in such a hurry to get away from New York he hadn't considered all the possibilities.

"Got an owner's card for that Impala, Johnson?"

"This isn't my car, officer."

"Yeah, don't I know it. That's what they all say."

"They?" said Thomas.

The cop stopped scribbling, stared at Thomas through the snowflakes, and then laughed.

"How do you like them apples, Joe?" he shouted to the black cop attempting to direct traffic out in the street. Joe Cop smiled back as if he understood, while he slowly raised and lowered his arms. Even from this distance, Joe's pink mouth shone with silvery fillings and broken teeth.

"If you give me a minute. If that tow truck driver will slow down and stop, I'll check the glove compartment," said Thomas.

"Hold it there—boy," Irish jabbed his notepad with the pencil. Thomas kept his back up against the wall. The crushed Santa scratched at his coat. When he moved back, plastic leaves from the wreath broke and fell to the snowy ground.

"Joe? Check the glove compartment," Irish shouted. He wrote some more in his little book as Joe left the intersection and hobbled through the slush after the slow-moving tow truck. Thomas watched him hail down the driver, walk around and open Lana's passenger door to look inside.

Finally Joe came back, "Nothing there," he said, sighing heavily. "Damn, I'm tired."

"Yeah," Irish glanced at him. "You don't look so good neither. Hey, what's the deal?" he addressed Thomas.

"I'm sorry," said Thomas. "It was there when I started out from New York this morning. It must be misplaced."

"Who you get this car from, boy?" asked Joe.

"His name was—Ed—Ed, uh, Meyers. I answered an ad in the Village Voice—he wanted someone to drive a car to Pittsburgh. I met him in a bar near Washington Square where he gave me all the papers and I showed him my ID. I thought everything was cool." Even as he spoke, Thomas was thinking faster and faster. Thank God he'd taken out his old suitcase from the trunk of the car last night and left it at Momma's.

"It has New York plates," hollered Irish.

"We gotta check on them when we get back to the office," said Joe.

"Okay, okay, if you say so. Johnson, you come with us."

Thomas wet his lips, "What for?"

"What's that? Hey, should I put you down for resisting arrest too?"

"What for," said Thomas again. He held his own wrists tight to keep from swinging out. Desperately he searched his mind for some angle, some scene he might have played before, to get him out of this. Would Lana cover for him? How? No, he couldn't count on her for anything.

He had forgotten what it was like here in Pittsburgh. Jail haunted him, as if it had been him and not his brother Richard who was locked up in Western Penitentiary or John on the lam from reform school or Lorn who joined the marines to kill or be killed in sunny Nam. It was hell enough in New York. He'd come home to get away from it and the theater scene where he felt like a failure too, not being able to land a paying part in months, any part would do, and to get away from Lana. And now look at him.

"Look here, boy." Panting for breath, Joe came up close beside Thomas.

"It's John," said Thomas.

Joe clutched his chest. Something was wrong with the cat, Thomas thought. He was slow, off-kilter. But Thomas couldn't smell any liquor. Was Joe on hard drugs? Impossible for Irish not to notice that.

"Boy, you don't have an owner's card," Joe said. "You don't even know whose car this is. At least that's what you tell us. How we know you didn't steal this Impala?"

"I didn't steal anything," said Thomas.

"Pretty fancy car for a…" Irish interrupted, coming up beside him.

"Nigger," Thomas finished the sentence.

"You said it, boy, not me." Irish glanced at his partner. "No offense, Joe."

"Naw, no offense," Joe haw-hawed back.

"What kind a car do you got, Joe?" bawled Irish.

"A '57 Ford," said Joe, wrenching his neck around like he was in pain. "Nine-year-old lemon."

"Don't you wish you had a brand new Impala? I bet you do. Like Johnson here. Ha ha. You been drinking, ain't you?" said Irish.

"A beer or two, that's all. That's no crime, is it? Look, that streetcar ran a red light. It plowed right into me. The light was green. Ask anybody. I had the light." Words began to rush out of Thomas' mouth in jumbled gasps. He heard his own slimy obeisance and felt grateful that Georgie G, Carlotta, and Christine-Marie were nowhere in sight.

"What the hell, let's go home," said Irish.

"No, no, we gotta check this out," said Joe, wincing and holding his shoulder.

"I don't know a damn thing about this town, officers. I'm just passing through this burg," said Thomas, concentrating on his delivery.

"Sure, sure, we hear that all the time. We just want to take you in for a little test," said Joe.

"What kind of test?" Thomas asked.

"Where you staying tonight, boy?" said Irish, ignoring the question.

"I've got business in Toledo. I'm leaving tonight, taking the Greyhound bus."

"Hell, it's almost Christmas. Let's drop him off at the bus station downtown," suggested Irish.

"No way, no way," Joe answered doggedly, sweat dripping down his brow. "We gotta check him out."

"Aw, look at the goddamn snow. We don't even have no line for him to walk," Irish demurred. Thomas saw that he was backing down. He was the weak one.

"We have to follow the rules," said Joe.

"Officers, I can assure you I am not inebriated," said Thomas in a mid-stage voice.

Irish opened his blue eyes wide, "Listen to him, will you. Hey, Joe, did you hear that?"

"He say what?" Joe perked up.

"Say that again, Johnson. Inn-Hee-Bree-Hay-TE," Irish laughed, his big mouth pink and shiny.

"So that's how you all talk in New York City," Joe said, frisking him.

"We all," mumbled Thomas, so soft only Joe could hear.

Twice Joe stumbled and nearly fell into him. "Is something wrong?" Thomas asked. When he saw Joe glaring back, he knew things were going to get worse.

Down the narrow wet brick street Joe slowly led him away from the old house with the red candle, acting as if he did not notice the blood trickling down the side of Thomas' face or his hands glimmering with slivers of glass.

Why hadn't they called an ambulance? He should have been taken to a hospital. To Emergency. But what was the point now of bringing it up? Just another road to prison.

Thomas could see Mellon's orange Gulf sign swinging above the gas station where Lana's Impala had been towed. The chassis, dangling from the tow truck, looked like a lamb set up for slaughter. He'd treated that car like a woman all that way from New York, traveling through one storm after another, checking the tires and replacing the oil in New Jersey, wiping off the slush from the chrome fenders at the Gulf stations where he bought Hi-Grade gas, cleaning the windows every ten miles on that treacherous Pennsylvania Turnpike through the Allegheny Mountains. When he'd hit Western Pennsylvania, he'd found a garage in Monroeville just past the turnpike exit and had the car waxed before he went home to Momma and the rest. And now—the bent hood, the battered front end, the glittering broken glass. Goddamn cops—it just didn't make sense.

It was as if somebody was out to get him.

Christmas

Thomas forced himself to grin at Joe. "Hey bro, it's Christmas," he said. "All I had was a beer. That ain't no crime, man."

"Come on, Johnson," Joe Cop said in a wheedling tone. "We don't want no more trouble tonight."

"Where's the girls was with you? Where's that kid?" asked Irish, all of a sudden.

That frightened Thomas more than the thought of the phone call he imagined Lana's father was going to receive soon. Offhandedly, nodding his head this way and that as he did on stage, Thomas jived, "Oh, they's just some chicks I met on the road. I don't even know their names. Lynette or Jacinth." Blindly, he looked around. His sisters were gone, thank god. And Georgie G? He might be still in the crowd. Thomas couldn't be sure. He felt angry, imagining that Georgie G was watching, seeing his father humiliated.

"Hey man, how's about letting me off this time. I ain't even seen this burg till today. Look I'll walk the line for you right here. See, you can't do that when you been in-he-bre-ated, what'ssss, right?"

Before they could stop him, Thomas leaped up onto the low brick porch railing, balanced himself, and effortlessly walked along the edge until Irish pulled him off.

"Johnson, it's the rules, I don't make them," Irish sighed in the blowing snow. "Come on, we'll let you go in time for a nightcap. I sure could use one. Why we'll even give you enough time to find them broads you had in the back seat." Irish looked at Joe and winked.

Thomas glanced back at the Santa decoration on the porch.

His heart jumped as he saw the rest of the cards slipping out from Santa's back onto the wet concrete. One of the IDs blew out onto the street past them.

"I'm cold as shit," said Irish. "Let's get this bozo to the station."

Run, run went his heart.

"Say, I don't think he believes us, Joe. Come on, boy, this way."

Run, run went his heart.

"Goddamn, I almost forgot these," said Joe. Before Thomas knew what was happening, Joe snapped a pair of cold handcuffs on his wrists. Thomas felt shocked. Joe's hands were wet and clammy.

"Wait a minute!" Thomas shouted out. "You can't do this."

"It's the rules," Joe said. Was he apologizing?

"I know my rights. What crime are you charging me with? Not having an owners' card? That's the fault of the idiot who hired me to drive the car to Toledo, Ohio. He must have forgotten to put it in the glove compartment like he said he would. I didn't cause this accident, officer. Ask the crowd. They'll tell you it was the goddamn Pittsburgh trolley conductor. Get your hands off me. I'm calling my lawyer right now."

Joe started, stumbled backward, and then righted himself. He grabbed for the large key ring on his belt and snapped it off. "You call your lawyer, son. I got the keys to the cuffs," he said, waving a small key rimmed in black at Thomas.

"Johnson," Irish said. "Who you think you are? Cassius Clay?"

"Mohammad Ali," corrected Joe, fastening the key chain back onto his belt.

"Yeah. Anyways, Johnson, we can do anything we want and don't you forget it."

Behind Joe, the Santa swung back and forth, grinning. Thomas saw his own hand driving through the cop and breaking the handcuffs on the wall.

Jesus, here come the voodoo Momma warned him to stay clear of.

Run, run went his heart as he was led to the police car.

Joe opened the back door and pushed him inside. Thomas sat down, hard and mean as stone. He watched Irish hop in the front. Joe tried to get into the police car from the passenger side but the front seat was filled with wrapped presents and boxes of ornaments.

"Shit, it's fucking crowded," said Joe. His gun stuck out from his side as he threw some of the packages in the back next to Thomas. The keys jangled from his belt.

Trapped as he was, Thomas tried to escape by closing his eyes. For a moment he dreamed he was sliding behind a snowdrift like the fake ID and falling into her arms, growing warm and pleasuring next to her light beautiful body. Rubbing against her, closing his eyes, never having to open them again. Loving her, he would be safe forever. But who was she? He couldn't see her face. It wasn't Lana. It was somebody he had never known. And in what country had all that happened? Thomas could no longer figure out how to get back there.

His wrists burned raw in the metal cuffs. He'd need a hacksaw and that for sure would break his bones. His brothers had been cuffed and had escaped. Lorn bragged how he used a paperclip to release the locking drive. If only he had a friend on the force with a common key.

Turning around, Joe poked Thomas with his finger. "No funny business, hear? This ain't Harlem."

Thomas' lip curled, but he didn't speak.

"Yeah, we don't have much traffic with you educated Negroes around these parts," continued Joe Cop. He made a swift icy sound gnashing his teeth, almost a dry laughing, as he pronounced 'nee-gros.'

The revolving red light on the police car swung like an irate ornament as the car began to move.

"Shit," said Irish, switching off the light.

People at intersections watched from the steamy windows of their cars. Smoky faces, heads covered with muffs and dark scarves and woolen hats, hats over noses and eyes like bandits, their mouths open with dumb curiosity.

Wedged in between the packages and boxes of decorations and Christmas tree balls, Thomas passed the Gulf station, orange icon dangling above the street. At every stoplight, Irish had to get out and wipe the windows with a rubber scraper.

Now the churn, the steady violent motor, the heartbeat drumming in Thomas' chest.

"Jesus," said Irish as Christmas music began to play from the police radio.

"Here we come a-wassailing among the leaves so green."

—wdzzz edzz zz zz went the radio.

"Here we come a-wand'ring so fair to be seen."

"Ever gone a wassailing, Joe?" asked Irish from the front.

"He he he," Joe laughed.

"How about you, Johnson? Ever wassailed? Man, if you haven't whizzled, I mean wassailed, what do I mean, Jesus, that truck's coming right at us. Did you see that? What a goddamn jerk. What a night. Well, if you haven't whizzled, you haven't done nothing."

"Yeah," said Thomas, lifting his handcuffed wrists and scratching at the dried blood on his hair.

Another truck skidded towards them. Irish swerved to the right causing Thomas to slam against the door, smashing the packages. A box of Christmas balls broke. Cops' balls. Thomas snorted at his own poor joke.

Irish swung around and glared. "Think something's funny, Johnson? He thinks it's funny, Joe."

"Yeah, funny," repeated Joe, attempting to take off his coat.

"Man, I'm hot," he said, unloosening his belt too. The keys fell on the carpeted floor. Thomas watched Joe pick them up and attempt to slide the ring back on his belt.

"You're nuts, it's freezing," said Irish. "I got an idea. Let's take a drive around Liberty Avenue, go to the morgue, show him a few stiffs. The dead drunks."

"Yeah, think it's funny, huh?" Joe leaned his arm back and poked Thomas in the gut. He was still fiddling with the key chain. Paying me back thought Thomas. It reminded him of Find, his stepfather. Thomas had never seen his birth father, could barely remember his name. Nobody knew if he were dead or alive.

"Here we come a-wassailing so fair to be seen."

"Some radio, uh, Joe? Goddamn broken record." Irish drummed the upbeat tempo of the carol on the steering wheel.

"Yeah." Joe rubbed his chest. "Man, I don't feel so good." He adjusted his cap.

"What's wrong now?" asked Irish.

"I think I got heartburn bad. That hamburger I ate."

"And may joy—joy joy joy zz z z z."

At the top of the hill, they slowed to a crawl. When the light changed, the car stalled. Irish turned the key once, twice, pushed in the clutch, his foot slamming down on the pedal.

"Jesus, I told you to get the automatic, Joe. This is the only stick in the whole department."

But the motor wouldn't turn over. Instead, there was only the sound of a twisted key in the ignition and the queer hard wrenching of fear in Thomas' gut.

"What do we do now, Joe?"

"Holy shit," said Joe.

"An hour and a half wasted over a lousy collision. I gotta take those presents home. My wife wants to me to decorate the tree, all that crap. That goddamn Port Authority. Those transit drivers don't know their ass from their elbow. Good thing Pittsburgh is getting rid of the trolleys. Shit, we should of been in Wilkinsburg by now to check out that burglary. This goddamn snow." Irish turned up the volume knob on the radio, but there was just silence.

"Battery's dead. What time you got?"

Joe sighed, jangled his keys, and looked at his watch, "Ten to eight."

"Put those goddamn keys away. Goddamn engine won't turn over. Look, we can't sit here all night. Why don't we just let this sucker go? You've learned your lesson, haven't you, boy? Hey! I'm talking to you!" hollered Irish.

Thomas swallowed. "Yes, officer."

"We need to make a report," said Joe.

"Aww, shit," said Irish, slamming his fist on the dashboard.

Groaning, Joe rubbed his chest. "I gotta get some air." He opened the passenger door and a cold wind blew in. Holding onto the door for support, Joe attempted to stand. In his fumbling, he dropped the key chain and all the keys fell off.

"Shit," groaned Joe, bending over in the snow.

A few of the keys had fallen inside the car and were wedged between the seat and the door. Thomas leaned forward.

"Got everything?" asked Irish when Joe finally fell back into his seat and slammed the door shut.

"Yep."

"Hey," Thomas spoke up, taking a chance. "Hey bro, what you say we just forget this, huh? Uh, it's cold as a hawk, like I'll come by tomorrow. Okay?"

"That's not a bad idea," said Irish.

Thomas took a deep breath. If he could win over the Man, he should be able to do the same for the flunky.

"Hey, whatever you guys want. Look, I just remembered. I know someone I can stay with, an actor. He owes me a favor."

There were three forgotten keys on the floor.

Hedging, it was hard, this cold, his voice grating like twisting gears, like the key in the starter, but he had no choice, he gotta bring off the jive now.

"I ain't joking. You'll see. You guys can check up on me tomorrow. Cause I don't want to cause no trouble. I just got out of Nam. I'm a little shook up about the goddamn trolley."

How did it go, the fast easy defenseless patter, he'd done it enough in the army, in Korea, knowing once he was out, he had his ticket to the world. He took all that money from the GI Bill and got himself an education at the University of Pittsburgh, a BS in political science. Momma was so proud and he was too, once.

"Hear that, Joe? He come from Nam, like you. Got any of that killer dope?" asked Irish.

He saw one small key with a black rim.

"No, sir! No sir! But look give me as many tests as you want. Hey, I can't go nowheres in this weather. You saw what the car looks like. Hey, where you all work? I'll come by the police station in the morning. Look, it was an accident; everybody has accidents. It's Christmas, let me go, will ya?"

"No way," said Joe Cop finally. "We gotta file the report."

Thomas wanted to slam his fists into him, but instead he kept his eye on the little key.

"You're right, Joe," Irish agreed. "Besides, we can't leave this hunk a junk in the middle of the street even if it is a goddamn blizzard." He rolled down his window. "Hey! Hey, yous! Give us a hand," Irish called out to the driver in the Coca Cola truck behind them.

He put the gear in neutral and took off the brake. "Joe, get out there and direct traffic. I know I can get this lemon to start sooner or later."

Slowly Joe got out, banging the door, only to have it swing open again. Thomas hunkered very close to the key. From his seat, gentle as snow, came the Christmas balls and boxes crashing to the floor. Joe slammed the door again. It swung open again. He turned, motioning the truck behind them. It bumped up against the police car. The door swung wide. Leaning over, very still, Thomas watched the key, a cat with a mouse.

The truck pushed from behind while Irish steered. There was a long line of cars behind them now on the narrow road and the streetlights blinked at crazy intervals at the intersection behind them.

The police car inched forward as Joe's door opened and closed. Some packages fell out on the wet stones. Wassail, whistle, Thomas, he got to. He ground his teeth to stay calm. His whole body hurt now with the effort. If only he had something up his sleeve, magic, voodoo like Momma feared. He pushed his foot into the gap between the front seat and the door. If only he could live up to his dreams. But he couldn't, not now, not in Pittsburgh. Why hadn't he just stayed away? Why did he have to come home? The Christmas carol from the dead radio tinkled in his head, taunting him.

"Here we come a-wassailing so fair to be seen."

They were over the crest of the hill, but the cop's car would not start, despite the many times Irish turned the key in the starter. Before them loomed a small bridge. Thomas could hear a train approaching. The red stop signal came on and the guardrails came down at the end of the bridge. He heard clanging and whistling. Whistle black. Whistle red. Snow softened the scream of the approaching train.

Outside, Joe vaguely waved at the truck to move on around. But the truck had stalled too. Traffic behind them began to move around the truck. Headlights from the slow moving cars beamed into the back seat blinding Thomas momentarily and then disappeared in the snow as each vehicle went around the cop car where Thomas and Irish were sitting.

Still the passenger door banged open and shut. Bags broke and then blew away. More tinkling in the snow. Cars driving by ran over the presents. The train whistle blew. Even the train whistle sounded heavy with snow.

Irish reached over and pulled the passenger door shut once again, glancing at the back seat.

"Give a fellow a break for Chrissake," said Thomas.

"Sure, bud. What's the matter, Johnson? Seen snow in New York City, ain't you? You seen snow in New York City. They say it's real cold in New York City."

"Real cold," repeated Thomas, licking his lips. He put his head down between his arms, inching his fingers in the heavy cuffs along the groove where the small key shone. He was going to be sick.

Suddenly the red and blue siren lights came on, revolving and whirling in the snow.

"Hold it! Wait!" screamed Irish, pressing the gas pedal, putting the car in gear. Still the motor did not turn over.

Thomas' fingers touched metal.

The truck behind the police car jerked forward, hitting them hard. Irish lost control of the wheel and swerved sideways. They flew toward the bridge and the oncoming train, hitting the lowered guardrails and bouncing back. Slamming the brakes, Irish turned the wheel madly as the train sped past them. The guardrails came back up and the police car slid by. Now they were edging over the icy tracks. The truck was still behind them as they cleared the railroad ties and began the steep descent.

Part way down the hill, the engine started up. Irish gave out a whoop as he steered around the piled-up ice through the blowing snow. "Joe! Get in here quick," he shouted, but Joe didn't move. He was slumped over against a bare tree, a bent shadow. At the moment they passed him by, Thomas threw himself against the door with the full weight of his body. In one handcuffed fist he clenched the small key. Leaping out of the cop car, he began running up the hill.

Lights revolving, siren screeching, the cop car slid further away as Thomas ran past Joe falling to the ground. Lurching up and away from the police car Thomas ran, but not fast enough to miss the sound of Joe's skull cracking on the stones and ice. Behind him the car skidded from right to left, down and down, way beyond the fallen cop.

Pittsburgh

Even after a five year absence, Thomas recognized all the narrow winding streets of the East End of Pittsburgh, even the narrow alleys of brick and cobblestone made in the late 1800s, the potholes filled with tar, the bends, the curves, the narrow driveways and dead ends. Surely there must be some place, some dark bar or all-night diner over here where he could slip in unnoticed. Thomas scanned the sidewalks, looking around frantically as he hustled between streets, zigzagging over curbs, walking in wet puddles in case his footprints were tracked.

He was afraid to race, to run as fast as he could, for fear that someone at the scene of the accident might recognize him. He walked with his head down, at a steady pace, keeping his hands under his coat, as if the handcuffs were a muff. Every so often he scooped up snow and rubbed it over his hands and face to wipe away the dirt and blood. His coat had blood spatters on it and one sleeve was torn. He'd have to get rid of it but not now, not with the handcuffs on.

Thomas turned into an alley near the train tracks approaching Wilkinsburg, following a concrete cavernous water runoff behind some abandoned warehouses. Leaning against a dumpster, he panted wildly, shaking away the voodoo fear, the panic. He knew he must calm down. He counted his breaths the way he did before a first entrance onstage. A train was approaching. Finally, finally, he unclenched his fist and with trembling fingers inserted the key into the lock. The handcuffs snapped open. Thomas gasped. He began to sob uncontrollably and nobody heard because the screaming train covered the cries. When the train was gone, he wiped his eyes and finally chanced moving and that's when he hit his head on the dumpster with a knife-sharp metal crack of pain.

Thomas held his head. As soon as his head stopped throbbing, he threw the key into the dumpster.

He ripped off his bloodied jacket and was about to throw it and the handcuffs into the dumpster too when he thought better of it. He didn't want to leave a trail; that was something he'd learned from his brothers, who had and were caught. Thomas put his jacket back on. The handcuffs he hid deep in his pockets.

Nothing like the Hawk, as Momma called cold weather, to clear the mind. Falling snow stuck to his eyelashes. Every few minutes he brushed it off and with it, for a second, the trolley accident and the thud of Joe Cop falling into the street. Instead he saw the other scene: the one he imagined where he was sitting in some grimy smoky station in East Liberty with Irish and his lackey, Joe Cop. Rage overtook him at that one too. Just another scene in another bad play he'd walk away from at the end of the night.

The prospect of jail had always terrified him. Lorn and Richard, his eldest brother, and John, his favorite brother, all were in and out for one thing or another, drugs, or burglary or armed robbery. It would never happen to him. He had promised this to Momma.

Thinking of Momma, he hurried faster. Now he backtracked, following the train tracks back into town. When he was sure he was in the colored section of East Liberty, he veered into the quiet snow-bound streets where Christmas lights sparkled under the web of snow-filled trees. For two miles he hurried along the streetcar tracks following the lights like mute sirens, making a scarlet path through the clogged streets of Pittsburgh.

Way down Third Avenue he could see the steel mills like fiery shadows of dinosaurs burning sulfur into the dark sky. When he heard church bells ring out, he flinched as if they were ringing for him. The same stark fear overtook him when he read the "Save Us Jesus" marquee rushing by a defunct movie theatre converted into a Negro Baptist church. Past Baum Boulevard the hills flattened out. To get out of the wind, he stopped in the doorway of an abandoned grocery story, its windows smashed in the race riots last summer. All the stores on this block were abandoned. It was there in the dark doorway that Thomas realized he was still free—the cops didn't know who he was, not yet anyway.

Relief flooded him like warmth from a fire he could not yet see. He turned the corner and there was Momma's house. She had come to Pittsburgh in the '40s when her family moved from North Carolina, looking for work during World War II. Momma and her two older sisters bought the house in 1950, an amazing feat for single black women. She managed to hold onto it even after her sisters went to California.

Hidden behind a large maple tree drooping with snow, Thomas spied Carlotta standing in the living room at the front window hanging colored lights. He hid behind a junked car and waited. Her thin ragged form taunted him as much as the cops' cruel bantering. After being away for five years, he had looked forward to reconnecting with her. After all they were only a few years apart and she had helped him when Georgina was strung out and Georgie G was still an infant. But on his first night back, Carlotta lashed out at him, wanting to know why he waited so long to come home. She was hard with her own kids too; she reminded him too much of Georgie G's mother the last time he saw her—resentful and accusatory. When Georgina died, that was the final cut disconnecting him from this cold mean place. When he left, he vowed never to come back.

He never should have.

Ever since he could remember, he had dreamt that he was adopted, and not really one of the Finds. He told himself that it was true so often that he believed it. Except for Momma and Georgie G, there was nothing here to come back to. Tears came to his eyes thinking of last night and how Momma had greeted him, holding him in her big strong arms. He had missed her too much and for too long. Thomas brushed away the tears.

It had all started with the laundry. He was just trying to help Momma out. Her washer was broken. It was always broken he remembered. If only they had stayed home tonight. But no, he offered to take the unwashed clothes to the laundromat. Naturally they all wanted to make a party out of it, and hang out with him. The worst thing was it had been fun hanging out with his son and sisters, laughing together in the heat and steam, watching the swishing driers and washers toss and turn.

Carlotta finished stringing the lights and left the window. Thomas approached the rundown red brick house, one of a row of identical houses that made up the block. He stepped high over the rickety fence onto the broken walk. A pyramid of six yellow candles blinked at him as he slipped past the porch and around the side to the backyard, 200 square feet of broken concrete covered with snow. He brushed past branches from the one snow-covered elm tree on his way to the shed out back where last night he'd left his suitcase containing the few presents he'd bought for the family.

Very quietly Thomas opened the shed door, entered, and pulled off his filthy coat, pants, and shirt. He kept the door slightly ajar so that light from the streetlight in the alley shone in. The alley was lined with tin garbage cans, junked cars, and broken appliances.

From the pile of folding chairs and old car parts, he pulled out his suitcase. He carefully unpacked his one good suit and changed into it, scraping the mud off his shoes and cleaning them in the snow outside the door. From his suitcase, he took out the black polish he always carried with him and wiped it on the shoes. He ran a long pronged comb through his thick Afro. Then he stuffed his ruined clothes and the handcuffs in his suitcase and hid it under some rusted bicycle wheels. Tonight he'd have to get rid of everything, but not now. No, now he had to rest. Thomas took a deep breath and quietly shut the shed door.

Stealthily he walked quickly over the snow through the broken down fence onto the back porch. Through the kitchen window he saw Georgie G and Carlotta at the table. His sister and son were bent together over a newspaper or something and he couldn't see their faces. Where were Christine-Marie and the twins? He heard their voices. They must be back too. Wet clothes were hung from rope strung up between the kitchen and the living room. They were safe, all of them at home. Thomas closed his eyes and breathed with relief.

He didn't see Momma—where was she? But then he remembered. Tonight was her church night she had said. He was going to surprise her with the clean laundry when she came back.

When he slid open the door to the tiny pantry, marijuana smoke drifted toward him. The radio blared so loud nobody heard him enter and that pleased him. Thomas ducked behind the ancient water heater.

Thomas stood quietly behind the white water heater sputtering and dripping. He watched as Christine-Marie appeared in the hallway dancing over the wet floor, a mop in her hand. Her feet were bare. From a line strung across the kitchen, Betty and Karlene were hanging sheets. He watched Carlotta pull out a washtub from under the metal sink, and begin filling it with wet clothes.

"Maybe Thomas'll get us a washer and drier," she said.

"He's coming back to take us to a movie downtown," said Christine-Marie.

Something kept Thomas from stepping out and revealing himself, as if this small unexpected respite was too precious to give up.

"He's taking us to his movie!" That was Georgie G's high crackling voice. A hint of something like peace overtook Thomas, an instant of light shining like one of those Christmas tree balls in the back of the cops' car that fell out when Thomas bolted.

"Ouch," cried one of the twins, he couldn't see who. Betty he guessed. Yep, he heard Betty's moan—he had forgotten how she always did that when something went wrong—and then she appeared in view holding her elbow, her long black arms like skinny branches. Karlene was right behind her. They each had on faded nightgowns and from behind he couldn't tell them apart.

"You better get this mess cleaned up before Thomas get home," said Georgie G.

"Momma be mad. Where he be, anyway? They better not mess with him, those cops," said Christine-Marie.

"Don't say nothing! You heard him. It's none of your business," Carlotta yelled. She was hanging her kids' stockings on a board in front of the sink.

"None of your damn business!" echoed Georgie G.

"Thomas got himself a gig with Diana Ross and the Supremes," said Christine-Marie.

"Ohh, you lie, girl," giggled Karlene.

"No, he said. He went out with Sandra Dee and Faye Dunaway too. He say she was BAAAD, even though she like girls."

"Thomas don't like white girls," said Betty, missing the point.

"How you know?"

"Cause he had a white girlfriend and he left the ho."

"He going to be a star someday," said Karlene.

"He going to make me a star," said Georgie G.

"Nobody can make YOU a star, boy. He bought me a fur coat," said Betty.

"Where is it? I don't see you wearing no fur coat."

"It's back in New York City. He's bringing it next time."

"Anybody want some ham sandwiches? Momma left food in the icebox," said Carlotta, opening the refrigerator.

Thinking of the dinner he had eaten last night, Thomas held his stomach to muffle the growling. They had had a big party for him. Pumpkin pie and cherry cheesecake, rib-eye steak, chicken and turkey, candied yams, sweet potato pie, greens. All the food he loved. Momma made it for him. Hiding in the pantry now, Thomas could still see Momma as she looked at him last night across her laden table.

"Momma, you been losing sleep cooking for me, haven't you?" Thomas had said, reached out to stroke her broad back covered in a bright red dress. A tall heavy woman with smooth skin, his mother looked like an ebony queen of indeterminate age and origin—she was part Cherokee she always told them proudly. Even Thomas wasn't sure how old she was.

"I stayed up as long as I needed to get this ready for you, son," she said. "Nothing's too good for my firstborn."

He had laughed and they all laughed too. Except for his purple brocade vest, a gift from Lana, he wore all black and he knew he had impressed them, though everyone was too tongue-tied to mention his fancy clothes.

Last night he told them everything they wanted to hear. Thinking of that now made him feel hopeless. He'd wanted to please so much. He didn't know how many lies he told.

"Tell us about all your shows," his son had cried.

"It's called Broadway," Carlotta snapped.

"Tell us about Broadway!" Georgie G corrected himself. "Tell us about Times Square."

"I seen the ball come down on TV on New Years in Times Square," said Betty.

Thomas' reverie was interrupted by Christine-Marie switching the radio dial to WAMO. He felt a little twinge of pleasure; he'd worked as an announcer at the station when he got out of college. He'd admired Big Daddy, the disc jockey broadcasting out of Buffalo, New York, and had done his best to emulate him.

Christine-Marie sashayed around dancing. "Ain't I mean," she said to no one in particular. Still hidden, Thomas smiled at her antics. She was still one fine girl. But Christine-Marie looked real thin—too thin—here in Momma's kitchen. How she blushed last night when he told her what a fine woman she'd become.

"Where he be? You think Thomas stopped by church to see Momma?" asked Karlene.

"Naw, Momma's just practicing with the choir."

"She's practicing the organ."

"Pastor Beemes' organ," snorted Georgie G. At that Thomas' eyes narrowed. That name was a ghost from the past. Pastor Leroy Beemes was Georgina's father, and Thomas could tell his son didn't like him either. Strange that old Pastor Beemes should still be alive when his daughter was dead.

"You hush, Momma kill you if she hear that shit," said Carlotta.

"Somebody's coming, I bet I know who," said Georgie G looking out the window.

"It's Thomas!" screamed the twins, rushing to the front door.

But no—it was just old Daddy Find. He'd come barging right in grinning thorough his broken teeth, big and mean in his overcoat and galoshes. At the sight of his stepfather holding a brown-bagged bottle of cheap wine, Thomas shivered.

"Where is Thomas? Ha ha. I heard he come home," Find shouted. "Where's my boy? I just had to drop by. Bring a little Christmas cheer for him."

"Momma told you not to come by ever again," said Georgie G backing away from the door.

"Ha ha, well, your momma always be talking too much. Where is he? I gotta come over for this I told myself, you bet I do, can't miss the chance to see the star."

"He ain't home now," glowered Georgie G.

"Oh, yes I am," Thomas cried, stepping into the kitchen light.

They all swung around, fear and excitement covering their faces. There was a moment of shock and confusion and then everyone began shouting and laughing.

"Ha Ha. How are you? Motherfucker!" sputtered Find, attempting to hug him. "You growed, boy! Hot damn, you growed, boy."

Backing out of Find's grasp, Thomas laughed and reached for Christine-Marie, swinging her round and round.

"You gonna sign your autograph for me, boy?" shouted Find. "It's been too long, boy. Heard you was making it big these days. Back from the Big Apple. Where's that fancy new Impala you come in? Oh man, oh man." Find slapped his hands on Thomas' back.

And before Thomas could pull away a second time from Find's big paws, Momma arrived in her red coat with the black fur collar, the hawk blowing wild behind her, holding Christmas bags and packages. Ignoring Find, Momma rushed up and hugged Thomas hard. He braced himself against her.

"Close the damn door!" shouted Georgie G. "Momma, Thomas here. Find ain't going to stay long, are you?"

"I brought us a little live tree!" Momma told them. "Merry Christmas!"

"Ain't it cute," said Carlotta taking the tiny pine tree in its silver pot from her.

"Anybody can come see me now that Thomas come home," Momma beamed. "I'm so glad you all here. Isn't he a sight?" she smiled at Find, forgetting that she had forbidden him to darken her door again.

"Ain't your daddy something!" Find said to Georgie G, swinging over the chair and grinning like a fool.

"What happened to the car?" asked Momma. "I don't see no Impala outside."

"Totaled," Thomas answered, his eyes sweeping the room as the others held their breath.

"What?" Momma shouted as Thomas helped her off with her coat.

Their faces frozen, Georgie G and Christine-Marie watched Thomas hang Momma's coat on a hook by the front door, turn around and give her a big smile. "We had a little traffic accident," he explained. "But don't worry none, the City of Pittsburgh's going to buy me a new car. That's right. Finally this burg is gonna do right by me. Hell, we all saw it was their Port Authority streetcar that slammed into me." He turned to Georgie G. "What color do you think I should get, boy?"

His son's eyes popped wide in his head. "Red," he said.

"Alright, it's red."

"The cops let you go just like that?" asked Carlotta.

"Yep, those white boys didn't want to mess with no big shot, no suh." Thomas rolled his eyes and his sisters laughed.

"Cops?" Momma's face tightened and her eyes narrowed. "Slow down, Thomas. What happened?"

"Like I said. A streetcar rammed into us as we were driving away from the laundromat. I'm sorry, Momma, but you got a mess of dirty clothes to clean again. I'm fine. I'm not complaining, am I? Now let's just have a good time."

As he grabbed his sisters and swung them around, Thomas felt Momma watching. He hugged them until they were dizzy with laughter. But she wouldn't let up; she kept looking at him throughout dinner. He knew what she wanted and that he wouldn't tell her. Not ever. After Thomas helped with the dishes, he strode across the room to the stairs. Momma was sitting in her rocking chair under the Christmas lights watching TV with the rest.

"Be right down. Just gotta make a phone call." His voice sounded strained to him, and he made a note to change it.

Momma waved at him, holding out her hand. He stopped himself from rushing over to take it. Instead he ducked under the laundry that hung, still wet, from ropes throughout the house.

"Is the phone still connected upstairs?" he asked. She nodded.

"Be right back, folks."

Before anyone could object, Thomas climbed the stairs two at a time, looking back to make sure no one was following him. As he dialed 212, the area code for New York City, his hands felt numb and cold. He picked at the dried blood beneath his nails while the phone rang. Pick up, pick up, he prayed. Finally Lana answered, screaming when she heard his voice.

"Thomas! I thought you'd fallen off the face of the earth. Are you finally home-sweet-home?"

Lana didn't allow him to answer, but rambled on about how she was sorry, so sorry, but now was a bad time to talk. She really wanted to talk, she assured him, but the cab was outside her apartment, meter ticking. "You know how that is, Tom Hon," she laughed.

"Daddy's expecting me," she told him. "I haven't taken the train in so long, I forget where to go at Penn Station. But I'm not complaining about being without a car. No, I'm glad you have it."

"Listen, Lana. This will only take a minute," Thomas said.

But her bags were at the bottom of the elevator she insisted and the doorman was holding open the door for her right now. It was just an accident she had come back to the apartment for her cigarettes or she'd never have gotten his call.

"Please, Lana, I'm afraid this won't wait," he said. "I gotta tell you something."

"Okay, Tommo, but hurry."

He'd been held up on the Pennsylvania Turnpike he told her, a pile-up due to the weather. All that snow. The Impala had no chains, remember? He'd had to leave the car on an off-ramp near Harrisburg and walk a half-mile in the storm to a Gulf at the exit. When he returned with the tow truck, he had a big surprise.

"The car was stolen while I was gone looking for help," Thomas finished up.

"Someone stole the Impala!" screamed Lana. "Daddy will kill you. Oh, my god, you're kidding me, aren't you, Tom?" she asked in a pleading tone.

"No, Lana, it's the truth."

He hadn't been able to reach her till now, he said. He'd tried calling earlier but the phones were out all over Western Pennsylvania. The phone here had been dead too—at first he thought it was just his Mom not able to pay the bill, but no, the problem was everywhere.

"I'm really sorry, Lana. I feel terrible. I haven't been able to enjoy myself thinking of the Impala."

"No problem, Tom. Don't sweat it. I just thought of something. Daddy's insurance covers stolen cars."

Slow down now, Thomas told himself. He forced himself to breathe. "Aww, Lana, I miss you," he said.

"So you're coming back to me?"

"Lana—now isn't the time, believe me. We'll talk about it later. Are you sure about the insurance? Your father won't like it when he learns about this."

"Oh, Hell, Daddy expects stuff like this. He wouldn't like it if I didn't fuck up, you know that."

"But it wasn't your fault," he checked himself from going further.

"Honey, let's pretend it was my fault, okay? Let's pretend, Thomas, love. You know how we both love to pretend."

"Come on, Lana. It was the weather."

"The weather! Of course, the weather. Oh, what a goddamn sexy voice you have over the phone, my Tom. "

"Lana, don't."

"Tom, I never liked white anyway."

"What?"

"The Impala is fucking white, Tom. And something else."

"What?" he toned down his panic.

"I'm thinking of you putting your black cock into my pussy. Hmm, let me check a minute. Oww, it's getting creamier and creamier. Tom, do you want me?"

"Lana, don't. Of course I want you," he forced himself to whisper in a breathy tone similar to hers and go on with the sex talk for a few more minutes.

"Tom, keep that hard-on all night while…"

"Lana, enough, what are you going to tell your father?"

"The truth! That some asshole stole my car!"

"Think, Lana, what would you be doing on the Pennsylvania Turnpike near Harrisburg?" Thomas asked in a disgusted, yet amused, tone.

"I went to an audition—do they have theatre in Harrisburg? Where the hell is Harrisburg anyway? Don't worry, Tom, I won't mention your name. I won't bring you into it. Why should I?"

"Okay, then, it's settled." He took a deep breath, but his anxiety remained.

Guilt and relief wormed their way through him after he hung up, leaving thin slimy tracks on his heart. Thomas stood by the window for a long time watching the snow fall on the shed out back.

I've always been lucky he told himself, but still he felt doomed. What can I do? But he wouldn't think about that now. No, he couldn't. Instead he'd go downstairs with Momma and the rest and sit in front of the TV. He could feel them hoping he'd come down and tell them more about his exciting life, make more promises about things he'd buy them.

But Thomas couldn't move. He just watched the snow fall. He felt very tired and alone. There was something still to do before he could rest, but what was it? Throughout the house he could hear the drone of the TV and the intermittent voices of his family, voices he once knew well. His sisters, his nephews, Carlotta's boys, Old Find, Momma and his son, Georgie G. The small house was filled with the pleasant odor of leftovers. He could smell the remains of the turkey he'd carved last night, the sweet potato pies, the stuffing. He could smell the scented candles, Momma's rose perfume and the tiny pine Christmas tree propped in the corner by the coat rack. It was all too much for him to deal with now. He'd deal with it later.

Finally Thomas could stand the silence no longer. "Hey!" he shouted, hurrying down the stairs. They all jumped up from the couch, offering candy and beer. Georgie G handed him the evening paper. Momma arranged her dress and offered him a hug. Carlotta's candles blinked behind him as he sat down on the sagging couch.

"Tell us again about being on *Secret Storm*, Thomas," said Christine-Marie.

"When you going to take us to New York?" asked Karlene.

"Can I come back with you to New York?" asked Georgie G.

"I want one of those colored TVs."

"How was church, Momma?" Thomas said, ignoring them, while he leafed through the Pittsburgh Press.

"Just fine, son. I just wish you was there to sing for them like you used to. Remember 'Amazing Grace'?"

"Aww, Momma, you can do it better." But when he saw the fallen look on her face, Thomas began to sing.

"Amazing Grace, how sweet it is."

His sisters chimed in with the harmony at the chorus and Georgie G clapped his hands in time.

But Momma's wide smile made Thomas feel sad. He stopped singing and went back to reading the paper again. Flipping the newsprint, he searched for the Theater section. "Experienced Shakespearean actors wanted," he read. "Black males between 20 and 30 only need apply. Auditions Tuesday at 4PM. Pittsburgh Playhouse." Thomas laughed.

"What?" asked Georgie G, looking over his shoulder.

"Nothing," Thomas said, shaking his head. How many black Shakespearean actors would be found in Pittsburgh? Or anywhere? He was thirty-two, black, and an actor. He'd been cast as a soldier in *Titus Andronicus* and as an aid in *Julius Caesar* in the Yonkers Shakespearean Festival last summer. No real lines to speak, though. Just a word or two. Still. Neatly he tore the notice out of the back page, leaving a small square even hole in the center of the paper.

"Gotta make one more call," he said, pulling himself off the couch. This time he didn't look back at them. Upstairs, he dialed the Playhouse and was surprised to actually reach someone and even more to set up an audition. It was that easy. He shook his head in amazement. Things just worked out for him in the theater. Ever since he was seven and Momma made him stand up and sing at the church events, he loved acting, loved being on stage in the spotlight. He loved being the focus of attention, center-stage. All those years of amateur productions in church and high school! He had never studied acting, never paid for a class. How could he, a black boy coming from a poor family, the oldest of eight, afford expensive training? When the GI Bill money came through, Thomas chose to major in social work, a field where a black, educated man could get a job in the early '60s.

Still Thomas took on every acting job he could find, even while he was getting his degree. It was easy. He'd been acting all his life, especially in front of white people. Momma had encouraged him from the first, "You lucky, Thomas. You a star. You gotta be up there in those lights. A star's gotta shine," she told him.

Besides, he loved theater people, and felt at home there, much more so than with his own family, except sometimes when he kidded around or played a part. Like when he was the Stinky Shoe Man for his little brothers and sisters all those years ago. "Here he comes! Here comes the Stinky Shoe Man!" they'd scream as he lumbered toward them clomping and flailing his arms in a big old pair of hobo shoes he found by the railroad tracks.

He felt happy on stage, truly himself, shining with a light from deep inside. Like when he was Porgy in *Porgy and Bess*, the senior class play. When he came home from rehearsals, Momma and the kids be hanging out around the dinner table or more likely sprawled in their beds asleep. He'd pace around the silent house until Momma finally got up. He'd wanna talk, wanna tell the story of

Gershwin's musical, go over his lines. He felt so safe and comfortable around actors he told Momma.

Come to think of it, he couldn't do anything else but act. Yeah, that was clearer than ever to Thomas now that he had finally returned home.

Later that night Thomas crouched on the edge of the double bed made up with Momma's best white chenille bedspread. Other than the small black and white TV, which he brought up into the bedroom, he was by himself. It was dark except for the TV and all that shone were Thomas' eyes. He sat very still, motionless, except for his bare feet which twitched now and then, as if flicking off flies that might have settled there, but it was too cold for flies. The hawk was flying tonight.

Thomas barely noticed the TV screen flickering across the room. When finally he did move, it was to brush his long thin hand in front of his eyes, but like the flies there was nothing there either.

The Avengers was on. Next was *Mission: Impossible.* He had wanted to see that, but now he could care less. He let himself go elsewhere in his mind. He was driving the Impala, steering over the slick trolley tracks, careful not to bang into the parked cars on either side of the street, watching, watching. But he didn't see the streetcar turn the corner. It came toward him way too fast, before he had time to swerve.

Was that the way it was? Or was he over too far? Had the Impala skidded on the tracks? Could he have swung by safely? Had he caused that accident? This question seemed very important to decipher here in the dark of his old room, now shared by the twins, where he had not been for many years. The outcome on this was still in the balance and for that reason much more compelling than whatever had happened later.

Because one thing he saw—he saw this clearly now—was that the instant he bolted from the cops' car was the first and only true moment in his whole life. He saw it clearly. He knew it better than anything he had ever known. The fear he had been avoiding when he left New York, which he had in him in some form or another since before he could remember, faced him head on and won. It was too big. It was bigger than he would ever be and truer and very very dark.

And now it was over. The chasm he jumped over leaping out of the police car was way behind him. Tonight he had made the leap into a new life. No, there was no point in going over it again.

But still he wondered if the Impala was hanging from the tow truck at the Gulf station. And whether Lana would be able to replace it. She'd be sure to get her daddy to buy her something brand new and outrageous. A red Mustang? A yellow T-Bird? Not white. Would she have it delivered to her pad on West Fourth Street?

And still he couldn't stop himself from replaying the rap he'd laid on Joe Cop and Irish. When they'd asked if he had an owner's card, what had his reply been? Whatever, it had worked. In the long run, it had all worked. Did he tell them the one about the cop's balls? Or had they told him? What had happened to Joe out there on the street? He had fallen. Probably drunk. Poor Joe, another Uncle Tom.

As scenes from *The Avengers* flickered by, Thomas replayed his phone conversation with Lana too. That story about the turnpike was okay alright. Yeah, he worked that one good. She didn't have a clue. She bought it all. Maybe her daddy would foot the bill like she was convinced of. He hoped so.

He felt like some big cat licking himself after a good meal. A big cat licking his chops after the kill. He had done good after all.

Christ, that was what he was, a big satisfied cat. Thomas felt a great sense of relief. But so shit-ass tired. He stretched his arms above his head and lay back on the bed thinking of the audition he'd arrange with the Negro Repertory Company for tomorrow night. All in all his luck had held out and would continue to do so.

Thomas smiled in the darkness—the stars were in good aspect he decided. All he had to have was hope. Where was Jupiter? He'd check the planets later, but he thought it was in Aquarius, a good sign. Where was Mars? In good aspect to his natal sun, he remembered. Like Momma said, he'd always been lucky.

Annie

When Annie finished playing the sonata, she laid her violin down on her twin bed. Throwing out her arms, she danced around her bedroom. Normally she practiced at the Carnegie Tech music rooms where there was more light, more space. But the college was closed for winter break, so she had to practice at home. Annie was rehearsing for the Western Pennsylvania Music Showcase her teacher, Leo Thurmond, had insisted she enter in preparation for her application to Julliard. And today, for the first time, she actually felt the confidence Leo insisted an accomplished violinist must have.

Downstairs four red felt stockings hung from the Ryan fireplace where wood never burned. Each year as winter approached, Annie hoped that this would be the year they'd make a fire in their fireplace. When she was younger, she'd offer to collect wood from the fallen branches on the undeveloped hillside around their house in the East Hills of Pittsburgh, but Mother didn't like the mess the ashes made. According to her, the chimney flue didn't work and the smoke wouldn't draw properly. The several times Dad attempted to build a fire in spite of Mother's objections, the living room had filled with smoke. But they had never had the chimney fixed though during the ten years they had lived in this house, and Annie didn't understand why. She heard her sister Melinda unpacking the Christmas boxes, busily putting up the tree.

Annie was ten when they had moved in the mid '50s to this house on Elmwood Street in Forestridge, a tree-filled Pittsburgh suburb. Annie couldn't recall much about herself from her childhood. Oh, a general feeling of anxiety, hope and fear that masqueraded as excitement at leaving her childhood friends, which she, taking notice of her parents' attitudes, disparaged as ridiculous even while feeling resentful. All she remembered was that her parents had moved them all too quickly out of their old triplex, high on a Wilkinsburg hill covered with elms and maples, before the house had even been sold or their new one completely built. The Ryans had fled eight miles east to the suburbs where all the neighbors were, like themselves, white.

Even though it was never spoken of, Annie knew why they had moved and felt ashamed for her parents and for herself. More than that, she felt sorrow and regret, as if she had lost something of value that could never be named. All the time she was growing up in the '50s, she'd see the black kids—they were called "colored"—peeking from behind their mothers' or their aunties' skirts while Annie waited at her school bus stop on Wood Avenue in Wilkinsburg. She'd see them get on the 76 Hamilton streetcar going downtown, or turning into the A&P supermarket when she accompanied her mother shopping, or went to her violin lessons in Shadyside.

The colored children looked past her with their beautiful opaque faces and brown eyes, so dark, so different from her own pale Irish face and blue eyes. There was no sign, no acknowledgement on the children's faces, which in itself was a kind of rebuke, as if they too knew why the Ryans moved to their new house. But Annie sometimes caught their expressions changing. Did they wait until they thought she wasn't looking to laugh and play among themselves? Because she saw them and envied them, wanting to play too, all the more because it was forbidden and would never happen.

But why was she thinking these depressing thoughts this late snowy afternoon? It was Christmas time and her first day free of college. Besides that was a long, long time ago. Her arms, shoulders and neck were taut with a nameless rigid excitement that often overtook her when she practiced for a long while. Everything in her room seemed opulent and mysterious and charged with a particular light for her alone. She felt pretty, hopeful and expectant in her new fishnet stockings and green vest decorated with tiny mirrors from India that she wore over her red turtleneck and black mini skirt. Melinda had bought the vest at a crafts fair and gave it to Annie just today, an early Christmas present.

Soft light suffused her desk and bureau, her metal music stand, and the rich copper wood of her violin. One lamp lit her desk where her college textbooks were stacked in two neat piles. The pile on the left indicated work done, the one on the right work to do. Another lamp stood on her maple dresser highlighting a neat arrangement of earrings, Ankh pendants from Egypt, God's eyes, bracelets, and love bead necklaces hanging out of the blue Japanese jars she had bought at the Three Rivers Art Festival. Her makeup was along the back of the dresser beneath the mirror; hairbrush, comb and hand mirror were centered on her lace doily. All in place —how this pleased her now.

Snow fell endlessly against her window. Annie stretched her arms over her head and swung around. Once, twice. She reached for her violin but stopped when she saw the snow, clapped her hands together and rushed to the window, pressing her face against the cold wet glass. I want, I want, I want she murmured to the snowflakes. What do I want? I want to be loved. The answer came too quickly, like a mantra she knew by heart and no longer even listened to. Annie turned back to her violin, plucking nervously at the strings. Was she finished? Should she stop practicing? She played a few exercises, a carol or two, then began her next week's assignment, the 1st movement of the Sibelius *Violin Concerto in D Minor* with lots of vibrato that Leo said she would probably never learn, a taunt he knew would make her feel compelled to refute.

"That was just beautiful, Annie."

Annie swirled around to face Dad in the doorway. "Oh, you scared me. Don't do that!"

Jim Ryan, a thin tall dignified man of 60 with appealing

watery blue eyes and a professorial air, was still in his overcoat, glistening with melting flicks of snow. Steam covered his glasses.

"Hi Dad, you're home early!" she amended, wishing she hadn't reacted so strongly, imagining he took her remark negatively. She could not see his pale blue eyes, so much like her own.

"The weather is a doozy," he grimaced, gesturing toward the snowy window. "I had to leave the car at the bottom of the hill," he added, rubbing his arm against his face while he took off his glasses. "Where's Mother?"

"Probably cooking or with Melinda unpacking the Christmas boxes," answered Annie.

"What?"

Annie stared at him, irritated he wanted her to repeat herself, refusing to believe he didn't hear her.

"Let's hear some more, go on," said Dad, taking off his heavy dark gray wool coat, seemingly forgetting his inquiry. "Don't let me interrupt you." He motioned her back to her music. But you already have interrupted me, Annie thought, feeling a sense of disappointment. Let's just keep on talking, she might have said, but she didn't. What was the point of that? She already felt mad at him.

Trying to ignore him, Annie began to play, but this time it was not the Sibelius but Mozart's *Violin Concerto Number 4*, Dad's favorite and she played it by heart. In her dresser mirror, she saw him in the hallway shaking out his coat and she saw herself, a slight pretty young woman in a spangled vest, pensively framed in long filmy light hair, playing a violin. Her figure consoled her. See, said the image in the mirror, you look fine. There is nothing wrong with you. Her fingers whizzed up and down from first to fifth to third position. Her bow moving rapidly across the strings made a droning unpleasant sound to her ears. She played a few more bars, and then stopped. Dad had been listening intently, his nearly bald head cocked to one side, lips pursed, and now he waited for her to pick up her bow again. But she didn't want to. She was struggling with a big hard NO of resistance, as if she were a toddler being told to do something she didn't want to do.

"Oh, Dad," she smiled faintly, "Don't look so serious. I'm not doing anything important. And anyway, I'm through." Provocatively, Annie threw her bow on the bed. When he didn't contradict her, she cried, "It's just a game!"

"You always win when you keep on with it," he said.

"No, Dad, there are losers."

"Winners, losers, what's the difference?" he shrugged. "If you're doing something worthwhile. Annie, don't forget that."

"Okay, okay."

Dad was screwing up his face when she took up her bow and began the Mozart Concerto again. He walked behind her, standing at attention as if this were the first time he had ever heard it.

"Who wrote that piece, Annie?" he asked over her shoulder. She raised her eyes, stopping her bow midair.

"Dad, you've only heard it a thousand times. You must know," she said.

He laughed, rubbing at the sparse hair on his smooth pink head, made pinker by the cold. "Hey?"

"It's Mozart, Dad, your favorite. You're just pretending you don't know!"

He laughed again, his mouth opening so wide that she could see his silver molars.

"Mozart's what?" asked Dad, blue eyes glittering.

"We have the Nathan Milstein record on the turntable downstairs. Look at the record!" Annie exclaimed indignantly. Why couldn't he just talk straight to her? "Let me alone. I thought you wanted me to practice."

Dad turned away, a frown on his face. Annie felt rebuffed, because the least he could do was object, or lecture her for being rude. Besides, now she wanted him to hear the Mozart. But instead he silently left her room, as she had demanded. Annie's euphoria of fifteen minutes ago vanished.

She sat down on her bed, cradling her instrument in her lap, feeling defeated, as if she were in battle with no enemy and the enemy had won. She remembered that there was going to be a party at Leo's home in Shadyside tonight, which she had promised herself she definitely wouldn't go to, but now her resolve felt less certain. She had to do something. She couldn't just stay home.

The room seemed smaller now, the light duller, and the smudges on the walls uglier. Her back began to hurt. She leaned against her dresser. Slowly Annie took off her shoulder rest, unwound the bow a bit, and put the violin away in its leather case.

When she walked downstairs, Dad was in the orange lounge chair reading the evening *Pittsburgh Press*. She could hear Mother in the kitchen banging pots. Melinda was wrapping presents under the tree with its shimmery blue, green, red and white lights. Framed with four red stockings, the fireplace was dark and cold as usual. Their old dog slept behind the sofa. Lucky was a neutered female, short and squat, part beagle and part husky with a brown beagle nose and a long bushy brown and white coat, perfect for winter. Her legs were short like a beagle but her body was wide and muscular as if intended for a much larger animal. Melinda had won her at a Fourth of July carnival in Scranton years ago, but she was Dad's dog now.

"Good session?" Dad greeted her as she came in, as if he hadn't just interrupted her, as if they hadn't even talked. "Nice to hear some music around here again. You're sounding very good, Annie."

How would you know? Annie thought sullenly. You don't know anything about me. She glanced at him to see if he could intuit her bad feelings, but Dad had his head back in the paper. The TV was on and the 5PM Evening News had just started, but no one was looking at it. She heard the phone ring upstairs.

"It's for me!" Melinda cried, dropping the tinsel. She sprang up the steps to answer before the phone stopped ringing. Melinda was a junior at Churchill High School.

Dad looked up from the paper. "Rubbish!" he announced. "What kind of an outfit is the Negro Repertory Company?" He held out the paper to her.

"What?" Annie approached, looking over his shoulder at the newsprint.

"It's about this outfit from New York putting on a Shakespeare play down at the Pittsburgh Playhouse. It sounds like a real fiasco." Dad shook his head in amused disgust.

"Thou shall not take the name of the Lord in vain," said Annie, scanning the fine print.

"What?" said Dad.

"I said thou shall not take the name of the Lord in vain. How could anything with Shakespeare in it be a fiasco, Dad?"

"Alright, alright, have it your way, but I've seen some lousy Shakespeare in my day." He shook the paper in front of his face and sank lower in the orange armchair. Dad was an aficionado of Renaissance literature and each year ordered season tickets to the Shakespeare in Schenley Park series.

"They say this is a colored outfit putting on *Midsummer's Night's Dream*. Sounds like a real dud."

Annie laughed. "Dud"—only her father would say something so lame and old-fashioned as that. "Shakespeare's been dead for almost 400 years. Isn't it time to move on?" She rearranged the pine boughs on the mantle.

Just then Mother walked into the living room. Still in her work clothes—a red wool sheath dress and black heels—she had put on an apron decorated with poinsettias and was holding out a highball. "In honor of the season. Can I offer you one, Dad?" she said in a loud trilling voice. Annie winced. Why did her mother call him by that title? He was her dad, not her mother's.

Elizabeth McArdle Ryan was a small plump woman of 62—

older than her husband—with a face still beautiful and skin barely wrinkled. Her flushed face was framed with curly gray hair. She set the full glass down on the coffee table.

"Dinner's almost ready," Mother said.

"Harrumph," said Dad from behind the paper, reaching out to take the icy glass. Annie watched Mother's eyes narrow.

"Don't worry, Mom. He's not upset with you," Annie said quickly. She could hear Melinda laughing into the phone upstairs.

"He better not be," Mother said, feigning anger. "I've been slaving in the kitchen while you three are relaxing."

While she was practicing, Annie had heard her mother arrive home from an office Christmas party and she felt glad she had cleaned the kitchen and peeled the potatoes, tasks Mother had instructed her to do this morning. If things weren't done as Mother wanted, it could be most unpleasant.

"Dad's the only one relaxing. I've been practicing and Melinda's put up the tree—or haven't you noticed that?"

Mother gave her a sharp look.

"I suppose being rude is the way young people act these days," Dad chimed in, shaking the paper. "We never acted that way with our parents."

"Our parents wouldn't tolerate it. I don't have time for this," said Mother, as she walked back out of the living room, wiping her small, capable, yet delicate hands on her apron. Dad looked after her.

"What else does the paper say about the play?" Annie asked to change the subject.

"Humph?" Leaning over, Dad took off his shoes, carefully placing them beneath the maple coffee table at the end of the sofa. Annie sat down across from him, feeling chastened as he picked up the paper again. She was almost twenty-one, but Dad still treated her like an ornery child. But she was an ornery brat at times. Like now. She knew that. Annie unlaced her black leather shoes and took them off too. The thick beige rug felt soft and luxurious on her stocking feet.

Sitting silently in her chair, Annie wondered what was so wrong with this scene and why she felt so powerless to change it. Was it the stockings over the unused fireplace? She felt dismissed but didn't know why or how. This—the first day of her college vacation—she should be happy. Upstairs she heard Melinda talking to her boyfriend, Gary, who had moved to Ohio. I wonder if they will get married, she thought enviously. She closed her eyes and imagined that the next phone call would be for her. But who would call her? She stared at the tree Melinda had just finished decorating. It was beautiful and the lights, the smell of the pine, the brilliant colored ornaments from years back, all called out to her in ways that used to please her. What was the matter with her? She was changing, growing up that was all. Annie closed her eyes and sighed.

"Awful," Dad pronounced a few minutes later. He looked over at her. "Listen to this, Annie."

She opened her eyes quickly, feeling suddenly better. "What?"

"*Midsummer's Night's Dream* by William Shakespeare," Dad read in his formal, sonorous voice. "Shining comic star of classical literature transformed into funky rock and roll by the outrageously in-your-face Negro Repertory Company from New York City. 'Funky', what kind of a word is that?" he looked over at Annie running her fingers through her net stockings.

"It's a word black people use—I'm not sure what it means. Maybe earthy or something like that."

Sexy is what she thought, but she knew not to say it aloud. That would really set off Dad.

"Still talking about Shakespeare?" Mother asked, coming back with another highball.

"What's in-your-face mean?" asked Dad, ignoring Mother's question.

"Oh, Dad. I don't know. Provocative? Shocking?" Annie said.

Mother looked from one to the other. "What a pretty tree!" she said, taking a drink.

Dad took up his full glass and held it in his long delicate hands. "Yes, it is. Annie and I were just discussing this Shakespearean production at the Playhouse." He took a sip, put down the glass and went back behind his paper.

"Humph, Shakespeare's been dead for 400 years, Jim," said Mother disgustedly. Dad laughed. She sat down on the sofa in front of the TV where Walter Cronkite was explaining why the war was expanding in Vietnam. Annie jumped up and began to rearrange the holly on the mantle.

She moved some ornaments, putting a few silver bells up higher and a few old chipped red balls on the lower boughs. The atmosphere had changed. It had become more dangerous, more problematical. Annie was about to leave when the timer rang on the kitchen stove and Mother left instead to tend the roast in the oven.

"We need some red candles," Annie said. "Go on, Dad, I'm listening."

"Here's that word again. 'Funky black comedy dragged out of a reluctant bard.' Is that the only word they know?" Dad harrumphed, shaking the paper back and forth. He read on in his deep, sonorous baritone. "Not to be believed. A once-in-a-lifetime experience. Drag yourself out from your cozy chair by the fireplace in this stormy weather and come down to the Pittsburgh Playhouse. *Midsummer Night's Dream* will be playing through January 27th."

Annie set an artificial wreath on a hook at the center of the mantle. "Let me see," she said, leaning over his shoulder, brushing his sparse white hair. She almost patted his head, but stopped herself.

"What drivel," said Dad. "Why do they put stuff like this in the paper? It's just plain bad, garbage, all of it."

"Why do you say that?" Annie said, taking the devil's advocate position. "It sounds exciting to me."

"Me too," said Melinda, coming down the stairs with another present to lay under the tree. Flushed from her phone conversation, her face looked soft and pink, like Mother's. Her color was accentuated by her deep blue eyes. Her dark hair was still in curlers.

"Huh? Oh, Hi Melinda, how was your phone call?" asked Dad.

"Fine," answered her sister, making a face at Annie. Were she and her boyfriend out of sorts since his family moved to Dayton? Maybe they were breaking up. Annie felt a perverse pleasure at that thought.

"Hey, that vest looks good on you, Annie. I'm glad I got it," Melinda volunteered.

Annie smiled, remembering the fishnet stockings she'd bought her sister. Fishnet stockings were the latest fashion from London. Twiggy always wore them.

"Annie and I were talking about this Shakespeare production, a lot of drivel if you ask me," explained Dad. "I see enough garbage, if you'll pardon the expression, just taking the trolley down Penn Avenue through Wilkinsburg."

"Dad, you don't take the streetcar, so how would you know?" Annie answered and then, seeing his pained look, bit her tongue. Maybe he did take the streetcar sometimes. But it was she, not Dad who most often went through Wilkinsburg, their old hometown, where she had been born. Before she got her '64 VW last year, she boarded the streetcar everyday on her way to Immaculate Heart High School and then to Carnegie Institute of Technology. Each day she rode the tracks beginning on Wood Street in the East End of Wilkinsburg, along Homewood Avenue and into Oakland.

Who was she to rebuke her father? Insolent, rude, that's what she was. She watched Dad put down the newspaper and shut his eyes. If only he would explain himself. He doesn't know any better, she thought, and then snickered because that was a phrase Dad often used to explain her actions. But indignation burned inside her anyway. She picked up the silver candlestick in the center of the mantle and began to shine it madly with the end of her sweater.

After shining the candlesticks, she set about putting red berries in a large glass decanter. With heavy scissors, she cut some of the branches off the bushy tree, and placed them on the mantle along with some gold and silver Christmas tree balls Melinda had left. It wasn't fair or right, she thought. The Ryans had lived in the Hill District in the beginning of the 20th century, before the 1st World War, when it had been an Irish neighborhood; Mother told her the Irish were called "white niggers" back then. They too might just as well be one of those poor colored families living on the edge of the slums. Annie felt humiliated at the unfairness, and angry with Dad because, no matter what, he should know better.

Black or white it makes no difference, she thought, feeling herself twist with pain she imagined a colored person feeling at such prejudice. How could Dad not see that we are all the same? Annie picked up the newspaper at his feet and began reading the theater review. When Mother called them to dinner, she was still reading.

"Dinner's ready, Dad. Come on, wake up!" Annie called.

He opened his eyes and smiled at her. Surprised, Annie smiled back. She helped him out of his chair and Melinda followed them into the dining room where the table was set with Mother's good silver, china and crystal, and covered with a poinsettia-patterned tablecloth.

"What's the occasion, Mother?" asked Dad, glancing into kitchen.

"I don't know," shrugged Mother, the gleam in her eye giving the lie to her words. "Just that we're all together for once."

"That's not so surprising. We all live together. Besides it's the beginning of our Christmas vacation," Annie hastened to add.

"Not for me," said Dad.

"Well, it is for everybody else!" said Mother indignantly, as if she had been insulted. "Annie, go get the gravy, will you?"

From the living room the TV blared with more news about the war. Annie went back to switch it off. She heard Dad turning on the radio station in the dining room. He always needed to have music. Tonight it was the usual Christmas music—Nat King Cole singing "Chestnuts Roasting on an Open Fire", Bing Crosby and Peggy Lee singing "Sliver Bells." Dad switched stations till he reached the classical music station where Handel's *Messiah* was on, as usual.

"Here, Lucky," he called, sitting down. Their old dog emerged from behind the sofa and padded in, pushing past Annie to her usual spot beneath Dad's chair, wagging her tail. "No, we aren't going for a walk. It's too cold tonight," said Dad to the dog. "No, it's dinnertime. Come on. Ouch, leave me some room."

Opening a Coke bottle from the sideboard, Melinda announced she would be babysitting at the Sawyers tonight.

"You have to curl your hair to babysit?" asked Annie.

Melinda made a face that said "Shut up." She's going to invite Gary over, thought Annie enviously. All her old friends were engaged or getting married.

"How nice. The Sawyers go every night to church during Advent," said Mother, bringing in the mashed potatoes and putting a bowl in front of her.

Annie surveyed the full table of roast beef, mashed potatoes, gravy, green beans, cranberries, and even, she saw on the countertop, fruitcake for desert.

"That's what we should do. Hey, let's all go to midnight mass on Christmas Eve," said Dad.

"Immaculate Heart still has the mass in Latin," said Mother.

Melinda made another face at Annie, who made one back.

"Just like the old days," Dad rubbed his hands before he picked up the plate with the roast beef. "The choirboys will be singing. What do you say, Maureen? What time does it start?"

"When it always starts—midnight." Now it was Mother who made the face. Both girls laughed and even Dad had a little smirk as he forked a piece of rare meat.

"Count me out," said Melinda.

"Me too," said Annie.

"Oh, don't say that," reproached Mother. "You liked Immaculate Heart when you went there, Annie."

"Yeah, I wanted to go to Immaculate Heart too, but they wouldn't let me," Melinda gestured across the table at Mother and Dad.

"It was too expensive," said Dad.

"You were happy at the public high school," said Mother. "Besides Annie couldn't get along there. She was too wild."

Annie put her finger down her throat and silently retched while Melinda rolled her eyes.

"Too bad you weren't wild enough, Melinda," Annie said, laughing as her sister picked up the bowl of steaming string beans.

"Annie, if you can't act nice..." warned Mother.

"It's the thing to do," interrupted Dad. "You go to college and suddenly you think you know everything."

"Please," said Mother in a hard tight voice indicating the conversation was over, "Pass the breadbasket."

"All kids are like that," Dad said unheedingly. "They don't know any better. Mother and I probably thought we knew everything when we were young."

"Oh, no, not you," said Annie, spearing a piece of beef with her fork. Even while she answered back, she felt foolish and guilty.

"Speak for yourself," Mother hissed.

Dad laughed and then so did Annie and Melinda.

"Okay, okay. Enough," he said.

Mother buttered her roll, her lips tight.

The phone began to ring upstairs.

"Don't answer it," said Mother sharply. "We're having dinner."

"But I have to," cried Melinda, leaving the table to run upstairs. Annie cut her meat, dabbing applesauce and mint on her plate. She took a few bites. In a minute, Melinda came back down.

"It's for you."

"Me? Who is it?"

"A man with a high voice."

"Leo? Oh, tell him I'm sick. Tell him we're eating."

"You tell him," Melinda retorted.

Annie hurried up the stairs, two steps at a time. She didn't want to talk to her violin teacher, especially not from home. Stopping at the upstairs landing, she took a few breaths, watching the snow fall outside the window, and then went in to pick up the phone in her parent's darkened bedroom.

"Hello? Hi Leo. No, I'm sorry. No, the weather's too bad. I'd like to come, of course. Thank you. Yes, I'm studying the Bach and the Sibelius. Yes, I'm working on them. Thank you. Oh, yes. I'll try, but don't count on me tonight. Goodbye and Merry Christmas."

She put the phone down and stood in the dark over her parents' double bed. She felt depressed by the conversation; why couldn't she have just told him the truth—she didn't want to go to his party. She was afraid of the loneliness she imagined she would feel there. She wasn't close to the other music students. Slowly she walked back downstairs.

Dad was talking about the time he'd taken Mother to Shakespeare's *All's Well That End's Well* on their honeymoon in New York.

"Now that was a production you didn't want to miss!" he said with enthusiasm.

"But that was in 1943!" said Annie. "I wasn't even born."

"True, true. But believe me, there was a lot going on then," Dad laughed. "Besides real art is timeless. You must have learned that at school."

"Somehow you make me feel so stupid, Dad," said Annie, sitting down again.

"Stupid?" Dad reflected. "We're all stupid when we are young, I suppose."

"Speak for yourself," said Melinda, but nobody laughed.

Annie dabbled at the food on her plate.

"So who's calling you in this terrible weather?" Dad asked.

"Leo Thurmond, nobody."

"Her teacher at Carnegie Tech," Mother explained, as if Dad hadn't heard the name before. "Have some rolls," she said, giving Annie the breadbasket.

"No, thanks." She didn't feel hungry at all.

"The least you could do is eat what I cook," said Mother sharply.

"I'm not hungry," Annie whined, pushing her food around on her plate. "Besides, I have somewhere I have to go." She jumped up from the table.

"Where are you going, Annie?" asked Dad.

"Don't even ask," said Mother. "Look at her, she's not going to even give a civil answer."

"My teacher, Leo, invited me to a party and I'm going. So don't try to stop me."

But Dad wouldn't forbid her to go. No, once he saw she was going anyway, he'd make peace, tell her to be careful driving, that the storm was a doozy, that the weatherman promised more of the same. Maybe he'd even suggest driving her himself or picking her up, something she often took him up on. But not tonight. No, not tonight. Hurriedly she changed her mini skirt for tight black slacks like the ones that actress Audrey Hepburn wore.

Midsummer Night's Dream

It was way below freezing when she drove west on the Parkway to Oakland from the East Hills. The narrow cobblestone and brick side streets glimmered with ice that had a smooth treacherous glaze. Annie was not paying much attention to the ice, though. She was remembering how Mother stopped her as she was about to go out the door, pulling on her black Chesterfield coat and twisting her wine-colored scarf around her neck. In a complete about-face, Mother had not been angry or objected to her leaving.

"You'll have fun with the other students, like yourself," she said. "But be careful. Take your time driving." Annie nodded, relieved at Mother's response.

She wants me to have fun at Leo's party and to be safe, Annie realized now with a sense of surprise, her hands, warm in her angora gloves, holding tight the steering wheel.

And then there was Dad who had brought up the play again. Annie was standing in front of the oval gold-framed wall mirror, combing and parting her hair in the middle so that it fell down on either side of her face, when he called out from the bottom of the stairs.

"If you weren't going to that party, we might go into Oakland and check out the play. It's on tonight I see," he said.

"You're kidding!" she stared down at him, shocked. "But you know you would hate it!"

Dad shrugged, "Miracles do happen."

"Dad!" Annie had laughed, coming down the steps wearing her new black dancer tights. He actually looked offended, as if she were rejecting him somehow, even though he was the one who called the play "garbage."

But now she almost wished he were here beside her to answer her troubling questions. Why do you want me to see something you expect will be awful? Why did you pretend not to know the Mozart? Why do you ask me questions you know the answers to? Why do you act like you don't know anything, while at the same time being a know-it-all?

Why didn't I tell you the truth? Why do I even care?

She was so used to driving with Dad. Dad took her to and from the Carnegie Library, to the movies, to her friends' houses. Always it was Dad at the wheel of some late model Chevrolet, either blue or green. The car she had liked the best was a two-tone '57 Chevrolet, turquoise with white fins.

There were all those Thursday violin lessons he used to drive her to, the Wilkinsburg Junior Orchestra on Tuesday night, the art lessons at the Carnegie Museum on Saturday, the trips to Buhl Planetarium on the South City, recitals she had at Syria Mosque when she was in Leo's Advanced Violin Workshop, even the operettas at Carnegie Tech's little theatre they went to in the summertime. Melinda never wanted to go. As for Mother, prior to any planned event, she would often get angry and begin yelling about something, sending herself into a frenzy, screaming insults at Dad for some innocuous comment he made or job he hadn't done. Dad, in turn, would ignore her. So often he and Annie went together.

Then there were all the times he took her to and picked her up from Immaculate Heart High School in Shadyside. And all that driving to and from dances at Schenley Catholic, the boy's high school where she and her girlfriends went each Saturday night for dances. Annie spent all her earnings from her part-time salesgirl work at the Horne's department store buying the latest fashions to wear to those dances—blouses with wide ruffles at the neck, sweaters with little lace collars.

In a strange way, even with all his disapproval, Annie felt

safest with Dad. He never intruded on her thoughts. Whereas at school she experienced envy and often rejection from her friends, and at home there was always the possibility of criticism and betrayal, arguments and disputes, driving anywhere with Dad was peaceful. Even adventurous.

These moments of traveling, this space between one destination and another where she was now—in flight as it were, moving yet sitting still in silence—this calmed Annie and made her whole. An amazing thought occurred to her—she really did love her Dad. Thank you for taking care of me, Dad, she thought and for good measure, said again aloud. "Thank you, Dad."

"I love you," she added, feeling an immediate pang of guilt.

She had lied. Annie had no intention of going to Leo's party. No, she was going to the play by herself. She was ashamed she had not told her parents the truth. Was that such a humiliating thing—to do what she wanted? Then why couldn't she tell them the truth? Annie felt humiliated at her pretense, then resentful.

She got off the parkway at the Greenfield exit, driving carefully through Schenley Park past the glass-domed Phipps Conservatory, past Carnegie Tech and over the bridge into downtown Oakland. At the corner of Fifth Avenue where the Carnegie Museum loomed, she stopped for a red light. There was a crowd of colored boys on the curb. "Westinghouse High" she read on their bulky football jackets. Some held beer bottles and all of them seemed to be yelling and laughing. Annie reached over to check that her car doors were locked.

After parking her car on a narrow hill close by, she hurried to the theater. The Pittsburgh Playhouse was half full, a good crowd for the middle of the week and the bad weather she realized as she sat down in her seat. Annie smoothed out her tights around her legs, scratched at a wrinkle in her sweater, shined the tiny mirrors on her vest, and looked down, admiring her new boots. She imagined herself posing for an old fashioned daguerreotype like the picture of her grandmother on Mother's bureau. That treasured photo was replaced with another image—herself as a self-conscious schoolgirl playing at a pompous grown-up game, a primping unctuous caricature in a theater seat. "You creep!" Annie giggled at herself, and then blushed when the person in front of her turned around.

She tried to remember what *Midsummer Night's Dream* was about. She had read it in her college sophomore English class. Something about mistaken identities, love of course, losing it and finding it again. There was a play within a play too, a least one queen, a king, fairies, and bumbling actor jokesters. Annie didn't like what she remembered about the ridiculous plot—and it was full of that archaic Elizabethan English, so hard to understand.

The Negro Repertory Company couldn't do any worse than the play itself. Why was Dad so judgmental? Annie just wouldn't think about it any more.

She watched the other people arriving in their heavy winter gear, single nearly bald men, a few women in hats, groups, maybe classes of students, some professional types, probably teachers from Pitt or Tech. Two teenage girls were dressed as beatniks. A few Asian couples and a woman from India with a red spot on her forehead. No colored people. She was not at all surprised at that.

Then the lights went out abruptly. Darkness and the violins of Mendelssohn's *Midsummer Night's Dream Overture* took her up in their soft stringed hands. The curtain rose then and she saw on the stage an island out of the South Seas. It was an outrageously splendid stage set, a hodgepodge of Africa, Elizabethan England, and Athens. The actors, all male and nearly naked, had highly oiled dark bodies decorated with rainbow-colored silk loincloths, brilliant feathers, and gold jewelry. Annie smiled with delight. The black actors flitted across the stage in a parody of classical drama like birds of paradise, while symphonic music played. Not as good Mendelssohn as the *Scottish Symphony* maybe, but still haunting.

These actors from the Negro Repertory Company spoke a mixture of impeccable Elizabethan English and Negro drawl, jiving about like those groups of kids she'd seen at the corner earlier. After awhile Annie got used to the diction and could follow the bantering. Maybe this was what taking drugs was like. Like taking LSD. She'd read about Dr. Timothy Leary of Harvard saying he'd learned more on his acid trips than in his fifteen years in academia.

That colored gang in front of the museum had frightened, even repelled her, but now she felt only excitement mixed with comfort and safety too, as if she were driving with Dad on an even more exotic journey.

Lysander and Oberon's leotards bulged beneath their gauze tunics. Oberon, so handsome, oozed sensuality and lust; Annie felt all his caresses. Imagine being alone with him in the spotlight. She shivered, unconsciously touching the tip of each of her ten nails, counting her fingers.

Titania was so authentic a queen that no one would suspect she was played by a male impersonating a woman. Annie blushed to think of what was beneath "her" rose-colored robes. Were those breasts made of silicon like that go-go dancer in San Francisco, Carol Doda, she heard about? Titania flirted outrageously with Oberon, laying her hand over his pink silk codpiece.

The entire ensemble lured the audience on with their exaggerated, provocative gestures. Everybody howled as the fairies flitted like the gays, the homosexuals Annie often saw on campus, especially in the Fine Arts Department. Even Bottom and Company radiated with erotic seductiveness. Everyone had sexual secrets and Annie pretended she did too.

At intermission a few couples that had come in late filed by, talking animatedly as they searched for their seats, while Annie sat alone reading the program. She felt impatient for the play to continue and irritated by the latecomers who seemed too satisfied being spectators, whereas she could not rest. She was stunned, driven to a place that she used to see from a distance and only recognized by her own longing and envy. She felt like a kid watching a game of kickball who desperately wants to be asked to play. If only they would choose her. She was Bottom braying at the moon for the fairy queen! Replayed in her mind, it seemed so childish and innocent, so silly, even funny! The thought made her giggle behind her hand.

She could barely believe that the second half of Shakespeare's comedy was even more shocking. Not a moment of rest from the double-entendres and sexual parody that crescendoed to an ever-rising climax. Annie laughed so hard tears streamed from her eyes. She too fell in love, found her beloved after trials and tribulations, and got married forever after. Her hands ached from clapping so hard. If only it would last!

The lights came up all too soon and the crowd put back on their heavy coats and scarves and began shuffling up the aisles. But Annie didn't want to leave. She buttoned her Chesterfield slowly, smoothed her hair around her face and under her scarf, and watched the stagehands beginning to dismantle the set and lights.

Mendelssohn's Overture was long over when she stood, having no longer any excuse to stay. Stepping carefully between the piles of blowing snow, she walked down the cement steps of the playhouse, a small, strange building of yellow brick, octagonal shaped, wedged between two gray skyscrapers like an irregularly cut piece of cheddar cheese. When she got to the corner of Baum Boulevard, the light turned red. She nibbled on her glove to keep her fingers from freezing as she waited for the light to turn to green again. Cars were filing out of the parking lot to her right. The snow was falling again, but heavier. Where had she put her keys? Before the streetlight could change again, Annie found them in her pocket. Reluctantly she stepped off the curb and hurried across the cobblestones to the other side and then up the hill past Fifth Avenue where she'd parked her VW.

When she considered it later, she decided that the glow she felt rising inside her as she walked up that hill shone like actual bright light, that her light met his light and that she must have known he was coming. It was a miracle that, instead of keeping her head down and averting her eyes as she normally would have done, Annie looked straight up at the dark figure approaching from the top of the hill as if, from the beginning, her intent was to be there in the light for him, and to see everything there was to see.

This powerful light took the place of the usual self-recrimination and self-ridicule Annie visited on herself, having perfected since adolescence. She felt free, supported by a halo like those Christmas angels had around their heads. There were silent harps playing too, singular and finely tuned, made of something rare, more rare than diamonds, harps with strings of spun gold. Alive with luminous intensity, the moment was in fact the miracle Dad had spoken of.

She could see that this man—he was a black man—intended to pass her. But he didn't because her eyes held his—she saw his eyes even before she saw his handsome dark face—and because her eyes kept holding his, and because she stopped right in front of him.

"Hello," he said, nodding his head so that Annie only glimpsed one side of his face.

"Hello," she replied gaily, as if it were a line from a play that she had rehearsed often. Annie started to giggle.

"What's so funny? Do I know you from somewhere?" he asked.

"I was in the audience," she gasped in the cold air, making little clouds in the night. "I saw you!" she exclaimed in a whispery voice. "You must be Oberon."

His face opened up like a passionate dark flower and he laughed. Annie laughed too.

"Oberon! His flunky you mean," he said.

Annie felt amazement at her great good fortune to be talking to the star of the play she had just seen. "Funky! Oh, yes, you were funky, alright," she answered.

They both laughed again.

They stood there in the middle of the block exchanging inanities, which Annie forgot immediately. Much older, a head taller, the man was meticulously dressed and very black. Only the collar of his starched white shirt shone in the streetlight. His face was finely modeled with high cheekbones and a broad chiseled nose. His lips were curved and pink and wet, his chin dimpled. He wore his hair long and kinky, an Afro, she remembered it was called. She had seen the style on models in the *New York Times*.

His eyes, large and deep-set, a velvet brown, were separate from his laughter and his deep resonating voice with its perfect diction. Large and fathomless, those eyes seemed even then like small animals peering intently, dumbly, covertly from a place far away, and throughout their conversation they shone past her down the hill, in the direction of the emptying playhouse.

"You were so powerful and mysterious," Annie remembered saying at one point. He laughed again, just like Oberon had.

A few cars passed by, windshield wipers scraping back and forth. A few more. Bare trees and telephone poles hovered over them like wasted angels. What else did they say to each other in those first minutes? His name was Thomas—Thomas what? He hadn't said, or had he? He'd been acting in New York for the last five years, off Broadway mostly. He was back in Pittsburgh after a long absence to see his Momma and the rest of his family. Listening closely, so closely, Annie forgot the wind, the snow, the time, the darkness, and her freezing hands still holding her keys.

"You'll get cold out here," he said, noticing her jumping around, up and down, to keep warm.

She blushed, pleased at his concern. "Oh, I almost forgot. I have my gloves." Annie pulled them out of her pockets to show him.

"And see, brand new boots." She held out her booted foot. "They're an early present from my Dad for my twenty-first birthday. It's in January." And she blushed again to have in one breath mentioned Dad and revealed her age. How young she felt.

How long did they stand there in all? Maybe ten minutes, maybe twenty. Finally Thomas said he had to go, he really did, he was already late, there was a man he had to meet, and, not being able to just say goodbye (forever? Forever!), Annie just stared at him as he backed down the hill.

"What?" he called out.

"Nothing," she lied.

"You look woebegone," he said, coming back up the hill a little.

"I am. I don't want it to end." Annie flung her arms out in dismay. "I don't want our play to be over."

"Our play?" asked Thomas.

"Did I really say that?" Annie said, laughing.

Then something happened between them. A light passed from her eyes to his that he understood, because he said if she wanted, though she didn't have to, she could meet—"wait" was his actual word—Annie could wait for him at the Howard Johnson's coffee shop several blocks away.

"Oh, I know where that is!" she cried.

His meeting would only take a short time, he said. These things always did. Annie nodded as if she knew what he meant. And nodded again to tell him she would go to the coffee shop and wait for him.

She couldn't believe how easy it was!

The coffee shop in the lobby of the Howard Johnson's motel was decorated with Styrofoam wreathes and plastic Santas, fake decorations Annie had disliked until just this minute. How nice they looked! How colorful and quaint! She sat down in the back booth and ordered coffee with cream from a stone-faced waitress sporting a red Santa cap. There was a lit candle in a red glass on the table. Delicately she sucked at her cold, pink fingertips, and then held them high over the candle, feeling the heat, shivering with excitement and fear.

Waiting for Thomas to arrive, Annie listened to the Christmas music from the jukebox in the corner. It was playing "Have Yourself A Merry Little Christmas." She knew the hackneyed words by heart. But tonight they seemed unbidden and sweet. How she had yearned for romance. Oh, yes, she had prayed for love and even had a boyfriend in high school. But like the play she just saw tonight—free, wild, and funny, colorful, exotic—for her, love had been temporal and rarely experienced, almost never repeated, mostly forbidden. Never—she thought soberly—unless you paid for another ticket to the next performance.

"Thank you," Annie said when the waitress brought her coffee and a little metal pitcher of milk.

There had been that crush she'd had on her instructor in Music Theory her freshman year at Tech. A tiny, intense, dark Jewish intellectual, he would discuss Nietzsche and Wagner with her in the hallways. Then one day he announced he was eighteen years older than she, as if she didn't know that already, and twice married which she also knew too well. "So what?" Annie had answered, but after that he avoided her in the halls and she felt too humiliated to search him out.

Before that there was Steven from Israel, her college friend, Cynthia's, boyfriend. Steven was a silent, tall young man who seemed to perk up whenever Annie joined him and Cynthia in the Skibo Student Union for coffee. Once while Cynthia was home in Philadelphia, he and Annie kissed. They kissed more and longer over the next weeks in the front seat of her VW. Simon and Garfunkel's "Sounds of Silence" played on Annie's car radio as Steven probed her mouth and felt her breasts. But Annie felt guilty and just as she was about to confess to her friend, Cynthia let her know she was breaking up with Steven, intimating he was a homosexual. Annie felt confused. How could he be when they were making out? What did it mean? She never found out. Nothing was resolved and Steven dropped out of school and went back to his home on Long Island.

And before that there was Bob, her high school steady. After months of weekend dates and heavy petting in the back seat of his father's Rambler, Bob drove off without any explanation with a group of friends from Schenley Catholic. She heard they took Route 66 to LA, leaving Annie guilt-ridden and mystified, wondering if she should have done something more to make him stay.

Would Thomas come? Why would he come? Did she dare sit here and for how long? Slowly Annie poured milk into her cup and sipped the lukewarm coffee as the Christmas music ebbed and flowed like warm waves.

When Thomas finally appeared through the swinging glass doors, her heart started like a racehorse rushing out of the gate. As he walked toward her, she smiled, imagining the waitress's shock at seeing a white woman greeting a black man, not at all common in Pittsburgh in respectable places. For some people, the Civil Rights movement just wasn't happening, Annie thought disgustedly.

The first thing Thomas did when he reached the booth was bow to her. "Excuse the décor; you know Howard Johnson's and the fine arts don't go together," he apologized.

She laughed, enchanted at his bow and that he included her in whatever he meant by "fine arts." Whatever it was, she wanted to be part of it.

He sat down across from her and blew into his hands. She stared at them with amazement. Annie blushed, realizing she had taken for granted that everyone had hands like her own, the color of which seemed pale and distasteful in comparison to his. Feeling suddenly hot, she took off her coat while he watched her. She felt exquisitely confused by his attention.

"It's nice they let you go so soon after the performance," she said, sipping her coffee. "The play was wonderful. But then, you know that already." By now she was certain he was Oberon.

"The Negro Rep's a good company to get into," he answered seriously.

"I'm sure," she agreed.

Across the Formica tabletop, his face was still and dark like the night, in contrast to his eyes. She wondered if her eyes reflected the single flame of the candle decoration the way his eyes did.

Thomas continued to study her while she fidgeted, barely noticing the waitress's disapproving glance as she walked by to clear the dirty dishes from the booth behind them. Through the Howard Johnson windows lined with colored lights, Annie saw more snow falling. This silence between Thomas and her was beginning to wear on her. How late it was. Dad would be up waiting for her. Even the unspoken word "Dad" seemed ominous—like a silent plea or whine, a signal of fear. If Dad had come, none of this would have happened. She was so glad he hadn't, and yet, she was afraid.

Suddenly he reached out his long elegant hand on the table and asked, "So are you going to tell me your name? And why you wanted to meet me?"

She felt her excitement rise at his direct questions, as seductive as his appearance and speech.

"My name is Annie Ryan. I'm a senior in college at Carnegie-Tech, a music major. My music is everything to me."

"Everything?" he asked, smiling, showing his perfect white teeth.

"Really, it's saved me. I'm not kidding. I've read a bunch of psychology books—Freud, Jung, Fritz Perls—and I really think I've been suffering from serious depression since I went to college. It wasn't easy for me to grow up I guess." She stopped to consider. "What else did you ask? Oh, I don't know why I wanted to meet you, except—except that I am attracted to you." Annie gasped. She couldn't believe she was saying these things to a perfect stranger.

"Where's your family, Annie?" he asked in a professional manner.

"Here in Pittsburgh. I live with them." She made a face. "I'm just a commuter," Annie added self-deprecatingly, wondering if he knew what that meant. She started to explain she didn't board at college, but Thomas interrupted. "Ah, and here I thought you were a little lost girl."

"Oh, I am that too. Right now I feel like Wendy about to step off the gangplank."

"Wendy?" He looked confused for a second.

"*Peter Pan.* You know, the musical?"

He nodded then. She saw his eyes dart by her toward the counter. Two policemen had just sat down and their surly waitress was taking their order, though now she was laughing.

"The book of Peter Pan is much better than the musical. I saw it last summer at the Civic Auditorium. Isn't that what you meant when you said that about the lost girl?" Annie asked anxiously, looking across at him. He hadn't taken his eyes off the cops with the waitress. Had she made a mistake?

"I feel like Wendy," she said. "I'd love to be able to act the part of Wendy in the play and fly to Neverland."

"I acted in that once in White Plains, New York," he said, slouching in the booth. Picking up a knife, he walked his long dark fingers down it.

"What does Wendy say?" he asked while Annie stared at his fingers, thinking how beautiful they were.

"Help! Help! I'm falling," she laughed.

He let his fingers drop off the edge of the knife. "On my side of the tracks, we don't know too much about Peter Pan. That's a white folks' tale."

"Do you think me shallow and spoiled?" Annie asked.

His lips parted, as if surprised by the question. "You're putting me on the spot."

"I am?" She asked, pouting. "I must be spoiled."

He nodded. "No, just of a certain disposition."

"You mean I'm white," Annie said, thrilled at her outspokenness.

"Hey," he said, "No little lost girl talks like that."

"Oh," she replied, unable to think of an answer, feeling worried that she'd made another mistake. Thinking to change the subject, she gazed at his hands, noticing the recent cuts on his wrists.

"I didn't realize those gold bracelets you wore tonight were so heavy and sharp," she said.

"What do you mean?" Thomas asked.

"Your wrists are cut," she said, pointing.

Pulling his white shirt cuffs down, he sat up in the booth and stared across at her with fierce eyes. Frightened, Annie looked away, realizing she had said the wrong thing. But what?

"Do you want some coffee?" Annie asked, flinging back her long light hair. When he nodded, she put up her hand to signal the waitress at the counter smoking with the cops. The waitress stared pointedly down the aisle and then slowly put her cigarette on the ashtray, but didn't get up.

"What kind of music do you play?" Thomas asked.

"Classical. You might have known, right?"

"Well, I thought so." He looked off into the distance.

"Do you like classical?" Annie asked, drinking the last of her coffee. She could have said more but was afraid of offending him. She followed his eyes toward the counter where the cops were putting on their heavy storm coats.

"I'm not that familiar with it like I am with rock and roll, rhythm and blues, gospel like my momma's church choir." He smiled at that last reference, his eyes lingering on the cops waving at the waitress as they went out the door.

When Thomas looked back, Annie added, "Then we're even, because I'm not familiar with your music either."

Thomas didn't reply, leaving her more anxious.

"Maybe we're just imagining this," Annie said. "Maybe we're not really sitting here."

"Yeah, well the waitress must think so too."

"What do we care!" Annie said. "Her prejudice is her problem."

"I'd sure like a cup of coffee."

"I'm sorry. Of course. Waitress!" she called out. "Don't you love Christmas?" she asked as the waitress came down the aisle and stood expressionless at their booth. Quietly, Thomas gave his order.

Annie listened to the jukebox playing "I saw Mommy Kissing Santa Claus" while Thomas drummed his fingers on the table. Finally the waitress reappeared with two full cups. Was she scowling? Annie wondered. Thomas thanked her with the same intimate deep resonating voice he had used with Annie. He's so considerate, she thought, holding that idea in her mind like chocolate in her mouth. The waitress tore off the bill from her pad and threw it on the table.

They sipped their coffee in silence. Annie noted he drank his black.

"So you're a girl about to fall into the sea."

"Not really," she said. "I'm a violinist actually. Or I want to be."

"Maybe I'm not an actor with the Negro Repertory Company," he said. "Maybe I want to be."

"Oh, you're tricking me!" she laughed. "Just like in the play!"

"What play?"

"THE play. *Midsummer Night's Dream.*" How could he not remember? She rushed to explain, "Tonight. Everybody was tricked. All the humans I mean. They were all stupid and foolish because they were in love. I know this from my own experience. My own attempts at love have been so stupid and childish, far more ridiculous than Bottom's, the ass. I was a far bigger ass. And from that moment—and tonight I realized this—it's as if I were in a play too; as if on cue, I concentrated upon loss.

"I'm sorry. Am I talking too much? But really, only my music has saved me from despair. Really." She took a deep breath. "I'm just talking about myself. I loved your performance, Thomas. I really did."

"From your side of the stage it looks easy," he answered somberly. "But I don't see the glitter, the great set. I see hard times. No pay. It's a long stormy road that actors take—those guys on the stage. You starve a lot. Oh, yeah, you get a few big breaks, a few fancy dinners, a few good women, but it all leaves you sick afterward because you aren't used to it and it don't last."

"But it's worth it?" she asked anxiously.

"Only if you win, Annie."

"No, anyway," she said. "Even if you don't win. Because winning doesn't count. I mean, you're doing something worthwhile, something you love, aren't you? Doesn't that count the most? You were Oberon, weren't you?" she pressed him.

His eyes glittered across the table. "Who are you anyway, girl?"

Girl. He called her "girl." That word had never seemed so full of wonder and meaning. With each word they spoke, Annie was diving deeper. She noticed a tiny scar above his eye.

She closed her eyes, whispering, "I'm a blind girl who strings beads all day for a living." When she didn't hear any response, Annie opened her eyes to explain, "It's from *A Patch of Blue*. Did you see that movie? With Sidney Poitier and Elizabeth Hartmann."

"No," said Thomas.

"She was blind, and white. She had a horrible life but he saved her."

"Ahh, an interracial farce," he said.

"No, a fated connection," she said.

"You're something else, Annie."

She blushed in pleased confusion. They both stood at the same time, as if together sensing the same unease. Annie fiddled with her coat. Thomas had never taken his off. The bill was still on the table and she picked it up. Looking around, she noticed only a few out-of-town stragglers remained in the booths, at the counter. Everyone was watching her and Thomas. Annie took a deep breath, leading the way toward the cashier.

"Could we meet again? After the performance, of course," she added emphatically.

"You're some adventurer, aren't you, Annie."

"What about Thursday after the show?" asked Annie, opening her purse.

"Maybe."

After she paid their bill, Thomas held the door open for her and they walked out into the blowing snow. She watched him moving away as she headed toward the large parking lot.

"I'll buy next time," he called out.

"You mean there's going to be a next time?" Annie asked.

"I have to pay you back."

"Next Thursday then?" Annie asked. "After the show. Like tonight?"

He nodded. At least that's what she thought, trying to remember it later, when the experience of meeting Thomas was a precious stone to be saved in her jewelry box.

"Good night, little lost girl," he said, walking away into the darkness.

Despite the stormy weather, Annie drove beyond the speed limit on the parkway. She was relieved there were so few cars on the road. The windshield wipers swished back and forth and the motor sputtered steadily. Perched high on the seat, Annie struggled to see through the clear circle the defroster made in the center of the window glass.

Once she lost control of the VW coming out of the Squirrel Hill tunnel toward Regent Square and Swissvale. Her heart jumped, but thankfully there was no one on either side of her when she swerved out of her lane. The weather is too bad for anybody else but me to be out now, she thought, feeling pleased with herself. Leaving the parkway at the Greensburg Pike exit close to her house, she slowly pumped her brakes to the stop sign.

Happy and content, she felt like the only person in Pittsburgh, which now with the snow on the trees and streets and the Christmas lights blinking, seemed like Neverland. "Good night, little lost girl," went the refrain in her head like a precious, singsong nursery rhyme.

Dad

Dad was already eating his corn flakes at the kitchen table when Annie walked in early the morning after the play. Normally she was the first one up, leaving for classes before either Mother or Dad went off to work and Melinda went to school. But this was vacation.

"So how was the party?" Dad asked, pushing himself closer to the small Formica table with the thick aluminum legs.

"Good," she answered, looking at Mother frying eggs at the stove.

"Do you want any?" Mother looked at her pointedly, as if she knew what had happened last night.

"No, thanks." Annie got a bowl from the cupboard over the sink and sat down across from Dad. He stirred a teaspoon of sugar into his full coffee cup.

"But you wouldn't have liked it," she told him, looking into his blue eyes.

"That's enough," said Mother putting a plate of over-easy eggs in front of Dad. "Why can't you just be civil for once, Annie? Say 'Good morning' or something nice."

"I'm sorry," said Annie, looking chastened. "But Dad understands. He knows I didn't mean to be rude, don't you, Dad?"

He laughed as he reached for his fork to tackle the eggs.

* * *

"You should see *Midsummer Night's Dream.*" Annie and Melinda were sitting side by side on the top step of the landing talking, a habit the sisters had, though neither of them could tell why.

"Why?" asked Melinda with a sideways glance.

Her sister looked cute, Annie thought.

Melinda was wearing blue corduroy bell-bottoms and a pink angora turtleneck with go-go boots with tassels. Her long dark brown hair shone like the buckeyes Annie used to pick up off the sidewalk walking home from school.

"I want to see the play again," Annie said. "I'll go with you. C'mon."

Melinda looked bemused. She had just broken off with Gary for the third time that week. It was all over, she assured Annie.

"You'll really like it." Annie coaxed her.

"Oh, I don't know. I don't want to spend the money." Melinda was babysitting for two families, saving money for a graduation trip to the shore.

"I met an actor there."

"You did?"

"Yeah. We had coffee at Howard Johnson's after the show," Annie confided.

"Cool. Can he get us free tickets?"

"I don't know."

"What's he like?" asked Melinda.

"He's handsome and really smart. He's older and he's black," answered Annie.

"Wow!" said Melinda. "That's cool."

Annie's eyes sparkled at her sister's positive response. "I can never tell Mother or Dad," she said.

"No," Melinda agreed.

"But at least I can talk to you. I'm glad of that. I'm seeing him this Thursday," Annie confided.

"But that's Christmas Eve," Melinda reminded her.

"Oh, shit, you're right," Annie groaned.

* * *

Now that she had met Thomas, Annie could savor the warmth and sweetness of her home like she remembered she had done as a child. The smells of the pine and juniper greens, the furniture newly polished, the shine of the porcelain figurines on the end tables, everything radiated with sweet, familiar comfort. She began to appreciate the Venetian reproductions of Tintoretto paintings that Dad framed so lovingly above the orange couch, the well-matched gold recliner set Mother chose at Kaufmann's years ago, the brass lamps on the end tables; everything impressed her now with its understated good taste. Fortified by her dreams and a sense of righteousness, she reveled in her secret life. She was being selfish, she knew—and she felt sorry for lying to her parents, but then she could do no differently she told herself.

From her desire, everything became illuminated. The Christmas tree glowed. Fairies hid behind the furniture, beckoning like twinkling tree lights. Titania masqueraded as the Christmas angel. The presents beneath the tree turned into gay daisies and cowslips. Her living room became the outrageous woods outside Athens. She imagined herself as a female Puck, disguised, jumping in and out of mossy doorways. She was Titania too. Most exciting was jealous Oberon who beckoned her to his magic forest. "And am I not thy lord?" he commanded her. That afternoon Annie reread Shakespeare's entire play, laughing to herself.

* * *

By Christmas Eve the trees in the front and beneath Annie's bedroom window were covered with hard snow that caked and hid their bare twisted branches and the shrubbery around the house.

"Annie, Annie, when can we expect you? Tomorrow? It's 10 o'clock. Your mother wants to be sure to get a seat for Midnight Mass. The church will be overflowing."

"Just a minute, Dad."

Annie closed her rose tapestry drapes and folded over her bedspread where she had been daydreaming. Poised with concentration at the prospect of her magical future, she examined the fresh red nail polish she'd spread on her long fingernails. She turned her thin hands this way and that, admiring them.

"Annie!" Dad called again. He sounded happy which, set against his sure disapproval of her plans tonight, soured her wonderful secret instantly, turning it into shallow dregs of guilt. But she couldn't let him stop her! Hadn't he been the one who led her to the play in the first place? She couldn't live her own life by her Dad's prejudices, she told herself.

When Annie walked down the stairs, her father was putting on his dark wool overcoat by the closet. "I'll take my own car tonight," she announced as Dad held out her Chesterfield coat. She put her hand into the silk coat sleeve.

"But why?" said Dad, looking shocked. "The Buick will hold all of us."

"Oh, I don't know. I just want to be alone," she said, fastening the black buttons all the way to the top.

How strong was the pull to give up and go with them, just to make them happy! But the thought of all four of them crowded into the car was unbearable to Annie at this minute. And she'd miss Thomas after his play. If—if he came. The uncertainty tortured her. No, she had to find out if he would really come.

"We're all going to Midnight Mass together," pronounced Mother from the open doorway. She wore her best cashmere coat with the fur collar and a black hat. Her Irish cheeks were pink from the cold.

"I promise I'll be at church, Dad. I'll meet you in the vestibule before Mass if you like. Please understand."

Dad set his jaw, "No, I don't understand. It will be too hard to find you in the crowd. You come with us. Your place is with us."

Annie looked down at the floor so as not to see his face twisted with disappointment, but still she felt sick suddenly and dirtied.

"Let her alone," said Mother, from outside on the porch. "Can't you see she doesn't want to, Jim. Let her go."

Dad turned away from her and rushed out the door. Melinda

followed behind him in her pale blue parka and dark maxi-skirt.

"It's Thursday. Lucky you," she murmured to Annie.

"Oh, shut up," said Annie.

"Shut up yourself!" Melinda called back, taking Dad's arm.

Feeling worse for having been so harsh to her sister, Annie shut the door behind them and hurried down the icy front steps. In the driveway, Dad was brushing the snow from the front windows of his Chevy, his back toward her, his sparse hair flying in the wind. She saw he had cleared the snow from the windshield of her car and started the motor.

"Thanks!" Annie called out as she picked her way over the ice and jumped into the warm car. "I'll meet you in the church," she yelled, rolling down the window. Nobody answered, but she didn't expect them to. Annie backed the VW out of the driveway as fast as she could.

* * *

The red Vacancy signed blinked on and off as Annie drove into Howard Johnson's parking lot. Normally the motel would be full at Christmas but since the riots last spring, most visitors would not stay outside of downtown Pittsburgh so close to the black ghettos of the Hill District, East Liberty and Oakland.

The play would be about over now. She parked right in front of the coffee shop window where she had sat with Thomas before, the frosted windowpanes framed by the same blinking Christmas lights. Dad had grown up nearby on a high shady hill in one of a row of brick houses built by her grandfather, Michael Ryan, a master bricklayer. Then the neighborhood was all Irish. Her Dad's family had emigrated from Sligo after the first potato famine, before the American Civil War. After moving up and down the Ohio River following the bricklaying jobs, the Ryans and their eight kids settled in Pittsburgh. Dad's side of the family was nice, if boring, distant like pictures of Swiss hamlets or pastoral scenes from children's classics, and, according to Mother, befuddled with balmy, artistic pretensions. In contrast, Annie's mother's family, the McArdles, came from Cork, Ireland in the early 1900s. They seemed mean, brilliant and sloppy in comparison. Both Annie and Melinda avoided the McArdles as much as possible, which wasn't hard since they never visited or celebrated holidays, even Christmas.

When she opened the door to the coffee shop, she saw a few people, all white, at the counter bundled up in dark coats, but nobody further down in the booths. Now that she was here, her own excitement sickened her and made her fearful. She should have gone with Dad and her family to Midnight Mass instead. But she had to make an attempt to see Thomas! Besides she didn't believe in Catholicism any longer—or did she? She felt confused, anxious. Throughout high school, Annie had heard too many sermons on guilt and shame. Nothing she got from the priests and nuns supported her dream to be free and self-expressed, but rather taught her to hate herself and her body. A religion based on fear and punishment was just another grandiose, entrenched bureaucracy to control her, she had decided.

But still she should have explained meeting Thomas to Dad, told him the whole story no matter what his response. She should have...should have. Annie sat down at the counter and ordered a chocolate ice cream soda, willing herself to feel better.

Then out of the corner of her eye, she saw Thomas sitting with his head bowed in a booth in the very back, nearly hidden by the phone booth. As she took her soda from the counter and walked with it in front of her down the narrow aisle, her heart was beating so loudly she was sure everyone else heard it. Grinning foolishly, she stood next to him.

Thomas looked up at her. With his mane of frizzy hair and bleak, distant eyes, he seemed a different person than the man she had met a week ago. "You're back," he said, as if it were an everyday occurrence.

"So are you," she answered.

The same starched white shirt. No suit coat tonight though—instead a dark sweater of indeterminate color. "Sit down," he said, and she saw a quick gleam of white teeth suggesting a smile that made her feel welcome.

She slipped into the booth across from him. As she sat down, Annie was conscious of the other people at the counter staring. She thought she saw a heavy-set man in a wool hat watch her take off her coat. An old woman in a black all-weather coat walking toward them turned around and lumbered back. In the mirror behind Thomas, she saw the waitress from the other night looking pointedly in their direction as she smoked a cigarette.

"It's hard just to talk here, isn't it?" Annie looked pleadingly at Thomas. He raised his eyebrows, but didn't answer.

"I can't talk to my own family. Every time I try..." she stopped. She saw his coffee cup was full and there was an untouched piece of cherry pie in front of him.

"The pie's pretty good here, isn't it?" she asked apologetically. "My Dad and I used to come here all the time after the symphony. Did everything go well tonight?"

For an instant he looked confused, perplexed, as if he didn't know what she meant. Something passed over his face, a shadow of sadness and fear. His eyes were like two deep pools daring her to make them happy.

"Fine," he said. He put his hand out flat on the table and pulled the pie closer to him. Such beautiful long dark fingers. She wanted to touch them, but didn't dare.

"I'm glad," she said, watching him slowly take up his fork.

"Tell me about yourself, Annie."

"But I already have. Oh, dear, what should I say? You don't really want to know, do you? My life isn't very exciting. I live with my sister, my parents. But something's missing. Something's wrong."

He nodded as if he understood.

"Take tonight for example," she said. "I couldn't tell Dad I was going to meet you. Or Mother. We're supposed to all go together to Midnight Mass at Immaculate Heart Church. I was supposed to go with them."

"So how did you end up here?" asked Thomas.

"I lied. That's the truth," she giggled. "Do I sound pitiful and heartless?" she asked.

"No," he said, without a hint of a smile.

"That's the way it is with me. It's the same with my friends. My best friend Phyllis just got married to some really dumb guy."

She told him about Phyllis' huge wedding at the Pittsburgh Cathedral. Too bad she and her husband had been fighting ever since. But now Don was about to be sent to Vietnam and Phyllis was spending Christmas with him in Fort Bragg before he was shipped out. Annie was taking care of their rented house.

The conversation moved to the war. Thomas said he was too old for the draft and besides he had "served his country", as he put it sarcastically, when he had been stationed in Korea for eleven months. They talked about where they were when President Kennedy was assassinated, the proliferating race riots, the Watts incident and President Johnson's warmongering. He mentioned the hope and fear he felt hearing Reverend Martin Luther King, Jr. who had led the marchers in Selma, Alabama. He even recited a few lines of the speeches for her. Thomas had read Malcolm X and had even met Alex Haley once in New York, he told her.

"You have? WOW! I loved the autobiography." Annie took a deep breath, as if resurfacing for air. She could feel the bond between them growing and looked at him gratefully as she sipped her chocolate soda, savoring the sweetness on her tongue. Across from her, he carefully cut his pie slice into little pieces.

"I'll bet you are really good at your music," he said when he had finished eating.

Annie blushed. "Sometimes I do think I am good. Sometimes I think I'll be a real master violinist like my teacher, Leo, insists I can be. But tell me more about you. You're an actor with the Negro Repertory Company."

"I've always loved the theater," Thomas said. "I'm a full-time actor now though I graduated with a B.S. in Sociology from the University of Pittsburgh."

Annie wanted to ask him how old he was, but she felt too shy.

"See that glitter," Thomas said, pointing to the tinsel around the cash register on the counter. "Looks like little stars, don't it? My Momma always told me, 'Boy, I want you up there in lights too, where everyone can see you, where nobody else is.'" He pounded his fist on the table. "Momma is counting on me. My whole family is counting on me." He pounded again.

Annie looked at him, eyes full of admiration. She had never felt so good, so understood in her whole life, she thought. She wanted to stay here forever.

Thomas folded his hands together. The cuff of his shirt shone whiter against the dark skin of his wrists, the amber of his light-skinned palms. Opening his palm, Thomas held it out to her as if it had something precious in it. Annie stared at his hands, the changing colors of his skin, brown on the edges fading to pink. She laughed with delight.

"Yes! Yes! Anything's possible," she said. "For you and me I mean. Don't you think?" And she blushed.

"You know, you are fascinating, girl."

Annie smiled, and then glanced at the clock—it was almost 11:30, a half an hour until midnight. She'd promised Dad she'd be at Midnight Mass.

"I have to leave." Standing up to put her coat on, Annie stammered on until Thomas waved her away.

"Go!" he smiled.

"When will I see you again?" she asked plaintively.

"Give me your phone number."

After writing it down on a paper napkin, Annie left Thomas in the booth. She handed a five-dollar bill to the cashier hurriedly and rushed out into the dark. Would she ever see him again? Annie wrapped her coat around herself tightly. The wind had come up.

* * *

Immaculate Heart Church was an immense gothic cathedral between the ghetto of East Liberty and the upscale college area around Shadyside where the professors, intellectuals and beatniks lived. Annie arrived in time for the Te Deum. The vestibule was full of people, but Dad was not among them. She would never find her family now.

Even the aisles were crowded. Men, women, and more than a few children, stood in heavy winter coats and scarves against the gray stone walls beneath the arched blue and red stained-glass windows depicting the Stations of the Cross. Some sat in folding chairs on either side of the pews. Annie stood at the back, close to the heavy oak doors swinging open and shut. Finally someone offered her a metal chair. Unfolding it, she sat down, shivering, beneath a large, lit beeswax candle in a brass holder in the shape of the cross.

Far away diminutive, red and white silk-clothed figures of three priests and four altar boys passed back and forth on the raised white-spiraled altar, performing the ritual of the Catholic High Mass accompanied by a Dresden organ. Tonight the Mass was said in the old way—in Latin, which Mother and Dad loved so much, even though the edict had come down from the Pope that English could now be spoken.

How bittersweet, though, to be here, especially after seeing Thomas. Every Friday for four years she had sat in this church for noon mass with all the other girls at Immaculate Heart High School. She felt suspicious of the girl that once was her, the girl in her blue and green-checked uniform, Annie Ryan, age fourteen, who was long gone. And yet how close that girl had come to being reborn tonight with Thomas. The funny one who loved to laugh, the girl Annie had buried when she went to college. How she missed her tonight! Annie held her hands tight to her heart.

She felt estranged from all the beauty and pomp, as if Catholicism was just an old doll she held onto from habit and fear of offending her family, especially Dad. And yet tonight, right now and here, from far away in the very back of the church, she loved the doll and wanted to hold it.

The music lifted her spirits higher. The crescendo of the majestic organ and the girls' choir singing Mozart's Kyrie filled the church during Communion. She didn't take Communion of course. Tears filled her eyes as she realized this part of her life was over. Yet hearing Handel's *Messiah Oratorio* at the final procession, she no longer felt alone. No, there was the music, the beauty of tonight, and the Christmas story. She herself was an important part of this long and powerful tradition—the yearly ritual reenacting the birth of Christ. How spectacular! She and the crowd pulsated with reverence and significance.

Her heart rose with the triumphant organ music. She would play like this! She would love like this! Her life would be this magnificent!

When Annie spotted Dad in his black overcoat and hat filing out of his pew behind the priests and altar boys afterward, she waved excitedly. Behind him came Mother in her fake fur and Melinda in her pale blue parka.

"Isn't this wonderful?" Dad greeted her.

"I've been here all along," Annie said in reply. Dad hugged her and gave her a little kiss.

Desire

All that Christmas it was as if she lay on a cloud, dreaming above the snowy landscape of the Western Pennsylvania hills and valleys. During the day while she practiced, she held her desire close like she did her violin, making music from both. How desperate she was to see Thomas again.

The night after New Year's, Annie drove to Phyllis' rented tract home to feed the two scrawny cats and water the spider plants. Already Annie had received several postcards from her high school friend. "Hey, Annie, Wish you were here—Not really! Don and me are acting like two rabbits—you get what I mean! S-E-X!" Phyllis had written. Funny, Annie thought, but disgusting too. Who wants to be a rabbit?

After leaving Phyllis', Annie drove back toward town along Allegheny River Boulevard toward Oakland and Howard Johnson's coffee shop. Thomas had finally called her and they had agreed to meet at 8PM. As she pulled into a parking spot, she saw him walking across the nearly empty lot with a large book under his arm. She rolled down her window and called out, waving from her car. He stopped, looking around.

"Thomas! I'm over here."

There was no snow tonight, just bitter cold. The temperature was near zero. In his heavy black coat, Thomas approached warily as Annie had seen German Shepherd dogs do sniffing for dope at the Greyhound bus terminal. And that's when it occurred to her she didn't know this man at all. What was she thinking?

But then he was there at her car door, looking in on her, and she forgot her fear.

"Hi! What book do you have?" asked Annie.

"*The Complete Shakespeare*," he said, looking at the title.

Bending toward her, Thomas smiled. "Let me in, girl."

It pleased her that he had called her "girl" again. Was she his girl? She leaned across the clutch and opened the passenger door while Thomas walked around to the other side of the VW.

"Sorry about the torn seat," she apologized as he got in. "Did the play get out early tonight?"

Thomas shut his door. "You're late," he said.

"Sorry," she said, turning the key in the starter back and forth.

They both faced out in the same direction, looking into the lighted parking lot. Thomas had to hunch over. He was far too big for the VW, filling up the car. He didn't ask her where she had been and she didn't expect him to. Already she understood they wouldn't talk about things like that.

"Let's drive somewhere," Annie exclaimed. "Let's not go into the coffee shop." Something told her Thomas would never have suggested that by himself, but when he laughed in reply, she knew she'd suggested the right thing.

Annie extended her right hand to disengage the brake and accidentally touched the sleeve of his black wool coat.

"Sorry," she gasped.

"Sorry again? For what?"

"I don't know!" she laughed.

"You are something else, girl," he said. "Where'd you get to be so bold and yet so shy at the same time."

"I'm not the only one. You want to run away too," she said.

"How do you know that?" he asked in a soft wary tone.

"I just do." But she felt reprimanded, uncertain. Driving out of the parking lot, she headed west, stopping at a four-way red light. They both watched the traffic cross the intersection. Annie turned the heater on.

She drove out Fifth Avenue past the better parts of Oakland and Shadyside where the private girls' schools were. Taking a detour, she pointed out the gothic façade of the Roman Catholic

Church on Shady Avenue.

"That's where I went to high school," she said. "Immaculate Heart."

"Immaculate Heart," he repeated. "Did you get yours there, Annie?"

"What?" At first she didn't understand. "Oh, I get it." Flattered, she giggled, turning on the radio to a popular rock and roll station. They were approaching the outskirts of Homewood. Slowing down for the traffic light, Annie stared out the window, vaguely aware of the crowd crossing the street. Nearly all the faces were black. Women large and harried with small children tagging along, men faceless and slow on their feet wandering aimlessly, menacing-looking teenagers. How rundown the buildings around here were, how small, tacky and distasteful. Dad had told her all about the history of Homewood. Wealthy industrialists built expensive mansions here, but later secreted themselves and their families away to Sewickley and Mt. Lebanon when the Irish, Scotch and Germans arrived. These Northern European immigrants set up their neighborhoods among the abandoned Victorians. After that came the Italians, Poles and Lithuanians. Their enclaves had been threatened too, this time by the colored workers who had moved up from the South during WWII in search of jobs waiting to be filled. The white communities, including her family, had moved further away. Dad had never spelled out the reason for their exodus; he took the taboo of racism for granted and assumed she did too.

Now they were on Penn Avenue going through Wilkinsburg and up Braddock Road towards Penn Hills. The sky was clear, with stars like diamonds in the black velvet night. They wound through streets of identical small, neatly landscaped, two-story red brick houses. When they were close to Forestridge, her own neighborhood, she abruptly turned east and headed onto Greensburg Pike toward Phyllis' place.

Annie stopped the VW in front of one of the many new single-story homes laid out in rows on the rocky hillside. Nearly every house was outlined in multi-colored blinking Christmas lights dotted with packed snow. Some of the barren yards had full-blown manger scenes, reindeer and Santa Claus, stars and candy canes.

"What will your parents say?" Thomas asked.

"Oh, this isn't my house," she answered blithely. "This is Phyllis'. Donald and she moved into it right after they got married, but she's the only one who really lives here."

Annie jumped out, slamming the door, and he did too, following her up the icy steps to the small bare porch, still holding his books.

"So nobody's home?" Thomas looked over the wrought iron railing at the crusty white lawn and the sloping driveway splotched with icy drifts of old snow.

"No." Annie said, fumbling with her keys, jiggling them in the door. "Phyllis is seeing her husband off to war. We have the house to ourselves."

Thomas laughed shortly, "Should we thank Phyllis or the Defense Department?"

Annie looked at him uncertainly as he closed the door behind them.

Switching on a light in the hall, Annie turned up the thermostat and went into the living room. There she lit a ceramic lamp decorated with protruding plaster flowers while Thomas stood motionless, tall and dark, on the other side of the room, his eyes darting back and forth. She could feel those eyes on her as if they were strobe lights.

A bowl of unshelled walnuts sat on the coffee table. A 13-inch TV console, the largest and best piece of furniture, loomed in the corner like an empty fireplace. Boxes of Christmas presents waiting for Phyllis and Don were piled on the buffet.

"I'm sort of a caretaker," she laughed nervously, taking off her coat and throwing it on the chair by the door. As she walked around, she glimpsed herself in the entryway mirror. She was glad she had chosen to wear the tight blue jeans and the black turtleneck sweater under her spangled vest.

Thomas put the book on the coffee table and took off his coat, carefully folding it and laying it on top of a chair. "Some pad," he said, going into a bedroom. Annie followed. The two bedrooms each had double beds covered with white chenille, a chest of painted drawers, a nightstand painted the same white and a lamp. The windows were hidden behind Venetian blinds and identical red and blue paisley drapes. Each room was as impersonal as a motel room Annie thought. She wondered if he noticed that too.

Annie walked back into the living room and sat down as Thomas paced the house. Her eyes followed him as he checked out the kitchen, the hallway, and the small den. Finally he sat down across from her in an oversize armchair and leaned his arm on the back, stretching his long legs out in front of him. His other arm lay on the chair rest, long dark fingers half-curling down the sides.

She had never been alone with Thomas before.

"It feels so small and cheap and doomed here, don't you think?" she said.

"Doomed? That's a pretty strong word." She noticed his leg jiggling.

"Oh, I always think in strong terms," Annie laughed, looking at him for approval. But Thomas didn't reply.

"I don't come here much—just to water the plants and pick up the mail and…" she winced, "To get away from home."

Thomas jiggled his legs.

"Do you want something to drink? There's lots in the refrigerator. Beer. Wine. Bourbon."

"I don't drink," he answered.

"That's good. I mean it just fogs up your brain, doesn't it—

drugs and alcohol?" she asked, anxious in case he did not agree.

"It's not good for my stomach." Thomas reached for the bowl of unshelled nuts on the maple table.

"Help yourself!" Annie encouraged him.

"So why do you have to get away from home?" he asked.

"Doesn't everybody want to get away from home?"

She watched him crack a walnut in his bare hand. He had really strong hands she realized.

"Some people want to stay where they are," he said. "I'm not one of them though." She was conscious that he'd leaned back in his chair again and his leg had stopped moving.

"Me either." Warm air was beginning to circulate through the air vents along the floor. Annie jumped up and went to the window.

"Better pull the drapes if you're going to stand there," he said. Before she realized, he was beside her, much taller and reaching for the cords.

"Why? I love to see the Christmas lights." She grabbed the cords back.

"Not a good idea," he said.

"But I don't care what they think!" she said excitedly, even as she recalled the suspicious eyes of the waitress at the coffee shop

"You don't want to cut off your nose to spite your face," he answered, taking the cord away from her and pulling the curtains together.

"Did Shakespeare say that?" she asked flirtatiously, pointing to the book.

"You tell me," he answered, reaching over to the coffee table and handing her the Riverside edition of *The Compleat Shakespeare.*

Feeling like this was some kind of test, Annie sat down and began to flip through the pages. The plays were arranged in order from early to late and comedy to tragedy.

"You know them all I bet," Thomas said, sitting down across from her.

"Not all of them. Just the ones they teach in college English courses. *Macbeth, Othello, The Tempest.* Here is your play. "Oh methinks how slow this old moon wanes," she read aloud from *Midsummer Night's Dream.*

After a few more lines, Annie stopped reading and held out the heavy book to him. "You read it, Thomas, you're so much better than me."

He looked at her, but didn't move to take it. Just when she was about to say something, anything, he took the book and set it on his lap. She watched as he turned the pages, one after another, without speaking. Something was wrong, Annie realized. She didn't know what, but she felt afraid suddenly, of what she didn't know, except the obvious—that they were alone and she both wanted him and was scared to death. But there was something else. Something deep and still and recognizable—and much more frightening. Fighting off the impulse to laugh or cry, she put her hand over her mouth. Still she could not take her eyes off him.

"You really want me to do this?" Thomas asked, watching her.

"Of course! Please. Why not?"

He turned some more pages. She heard the heater blowing hot air from the hall vent. She remembered about the wine in the refrigerator. Phyllis had said to drink whatever she wanted. She wanted a glass now. Annie stood up timidly. Should she say something? Thomas didn't drink alcohol he said. But that didn't mean she couldn't, did it? She wanted to do the right thing. But what was it? She stood there paralyzed by her confusion, her mind a dark and cloudy sky. It was only when Thomas threw the book on the floor that she heard the deep silence of the room.

"This is a joke, right?" she asked anxiously.

"What do you think?"

"I don't know," she lied.

"Yes, you do."

"No!"

"You're lying, Annie."

"No, you are the one lying. You weren't in the play, were you, Thomas? You never were in it. You've been lying all along. You never were Oberon." Again Annie rushed to the window, opening the drapes defiantly. The street outside was bare and desolate under the naked streetlight. She felt abandoned and alone. When she turned around, she saw him staring at her. "Nobody's watching but you," she taunted, her voice rising. "Who are you? Is your name Thomas? Are you really an actor? Is your home in Pittsburgh? Did you just come from New York or are you lying about that too?" She wanted to get out of here, she realized. She wanted to go home.

Thomas laid his head back in the chair and looked up at the ceiling. He sighed, "Yes, Annie, I'm an actor. I do live in New York. I came home for Christmas like I told you."

He bowed his head. Annie began to doodle on the steamy windows, watching the thick lines her fingers were making on the fogging glass.

"I was a fool to pretend with you. I should have known better. You're too smart for that. But I didn't expect to ever see you again. That's the truth. Why should I burst your bubble? Come on, even you know how these things go. I mean, look at us."

"Oh, sure," she mumbled, biting her lip to hold back the tears. She stopped doodling and looked at him. "Why did you bring that Shakespeare book tonight?"

"Because I wanted you to find out the truth. That night we met I was going to an audition at the Negro Rep to try out for another part in another play. I was too late and I never got that audition. The director, Mel, couldn't wait around for me. He put me off till next week. Maybe he'll see me, maybe not. I have to call to confirm. But you don't believe me, do you? I can see why."

"So you weren't ever in *Midsummer Night's Dream*?" she asked, as if pleading with him to deny it. Her face felt raw as she dried her tears with her sleeve. She could no longer see the barren lawns outside the window. She might as well be on the moon.

Annie closed the curtains and sat back down on the couch, putting her head in her hands. She felt Thomas get out of the chair and move over next to her. Her body began to soften and grow warm with desire.

"Listen," he said finally. "You want the truth. Here's the truth. I didn't lie to you. I just let you believe your own stories. If I'd wanted to, I could have conned you tonight. If I hadn't brought this Shakespeare book, you'd never have known. If I told you I didn't want to read this shit, you'd have believed me. C'mon now, tell the truth. If I said I was too tired, you'd have turned those big blue eyes up at me and flirted just like you do so well and ate up every word."

When she didn't answer, Thomas leaned over and touched her knee. "You like me a little, don't you, Annie?"

"Yes," she mumbled.

"More than a little?" he asked, bending close, softly rubbing her knee.

"Yes," she whispered. She put her head on his chest, feeling the unfamiliar black kinky chest hair beneath his white shirt.

"I want to ask you something. Annie, hey, look at me." He raised her head. "Tell me, why did you bring me here tonight?"

She snuggled deep into his shoulder.

"You smell so good," she said, kissing his neck. "I think I'm falling in love with you."

"Don't," he answered, putting his arms around her and pulling her close.

Audition

They had sex for the first time a week or so later. When Thomas pulled out of her at the last moment, groaning into the sofa pillow, Annie cried. He held her while she sobbed. Thomas asked her, "What do you want from me?"

"To be close like this," she said, her body tingling all over.

"How close?" He leaned over her. "This close?" He pulled her to him. "Or this close," he murmured in her ear, holding her tight. A veil of ice and fire dropped over her, leaving her singed, yet freezing too. Annie straightened her back, struggling to hold herself upright in his arms. Her fingers around his neck burned hot and cold. She wanted to be there and at the same time push away.

It didn't matter now that Thomas had lied to her about being in the Negro Repertory Company. Lied was surely too strong a word. She had lied too. Anyway, she should have known he wasn't Oberon. She had never actually seen him on that stage. She must have been kidding herself from the beginning. Isn't that why she had never gone back a second time to see the show? Just because her sister didn't want to go was no reason for her not to. Thomas had merely given her what she wanted.

Oh, he was so gentle! Stroking her, giving her all the time she needed. "I've never done it before—never had sex, " she admitted.

"You mean you were a virgin?" Startled, he moved off her.

"Yes," she mumbled, lowering her head.

"Goddamn," he said, sighing.

Was being a virgin a shameful thing? More than anything she wanted to get rid of shame. Annie hid her face as Thomas raised himself up off the couch, picking up his shirt and pants from the rug.

She felt as if she had committed a crime. She was a prisoner of shame, locked up with longing.

"Come here, babe," said Thomas, seeing her face. "I didn't mean that. Hey, give me a kiss."

She leaned up to him and he kissed her, pushing his tongue into her mouth.

"I take it you aren't on the Pill," he said, slipping back down next to her, his naked body warm and muscular.

Annie shook her head. "But I can make an appointment at Planned Parenthood tomorrow. Phyllis told me how."

"The last thing I need is to get you pregnant."

Annie burrowed deep in his shoulder.

"I can't feel anything with condoms," he said. "But I sure do feel you. And you feel so good." He kissed her again and this time he didn't stop.

Later he said, "You need somebody to respect you, to love you as you deserve. I'm not that person."

"Who are you?" she asked.

"Just a dreamer."

Wiping her eyes, Annie laughed and then he did too.

Their laughter spoke more than any words they might have said, telling Annie what she wanted to hear. She felt wildly elated at the mystery unraveling for her alone. They were allies, together against an unjust world. They would have a mysterious adventure together. There was a future if she wanted to make one. She would get those birth control pills so he wouldn't need to use a condom.

* * *

Annie felt intensely happy. Whereas a part of herself had always remained alien, unalterably different and isolated from her friends and family, now she felt connected. Now she had no past to wrestle with, no future to fear or hope for, no one's expectations to disappoint, to justify or condemn. She was no more and no less than invisible light radiating from their connected bodies.

She could barely stand to practice her violin—music had become a diversion from her lust. Much closer to her ears was Thomas' voice. At night in her bed she felt her body rising and contracting with desire. Every day of vacation break and even after when she was taking mid-year exams, she drove into Oakland looking for Thomas at Howard Johnson's. Some days he didn't show up and some days he did. She never asked him where he'd been or what he had been doing. This unknowing fueled her desire.

Mystery and intrigue weren't new to Annie. Backed by the traditions of the Catholic religion and Irish culture laced with famine and immigration, her own family had thrived on mystery and unremitting silence. One or another of her aunts, uncles or cousins had acted like amnesia victims with lapses in communication for whole blocks of time, years even. On Dad's side, they had merely stopped talking to each other, retreating to their houses in North Side or Rankin, whereas her mother's family had been angry and judgmental, in particular about small, irrelevant issues. Who sent whom a Christmas card or what ridiculous name a distant cousin had been given caused years of shunning and gossip. No, mystery wasn't new. What was new to Annie was the feeling that now she was in on the secret. That she made all the difference.

Alone each night she saw it all as if in a crystal ball. There was Thomas in his immaculate dark clothes with his vibrant eyes and still face. And there she was, light hair and pounding heart, reaching out to him, her arms tight from disuse and from wrenching in, poisoned from longing. There was their rendezvous, her friend's one-story house in a cheap new development outside Pittsburgh. There was the past, for her a bubble of loneliness and painful dreams now breaking apart. There was their future together, impossible of course, as if that mattered. But it didn't matter. All that mattered was seeing him again.

"How can you hold onto everything and at the same time let it all go?" she asked him. Thomas looked at her as if she were a very young child or a small animal that had surprised him. Then something in his face changed, giving it that mysterious and sad expression he sometimes wore.

"You can't do both," he said.

* * *

Phyllis had written she'd be back in another week or two. Now Annie drove Thomas to the rented house with an ever-growing sense of anxiety mixed with anticipation. Where would they go once Phyllis returned? Could she tell her friend?

Sometimes she brought records from the Carnegie-Tech library; together they listened to Laurence Olivier and Ralph Richardson reciting Shakespeare. Thomas often had bags of nuts and dried fruits with him.

"Try them, Annie. They're good for you. It's all I eat on performance days. Try some, go ahead."

Eagerly she reached for the nuts he cracked in his hand. He pressed more on her, and sometimes oranges or dried apricots, once purple grapes with seeds.

One day Thomas brought along a curled paperback of *Plays of the '60s* and read a few scenes from a one-act called *Whitewash* he said he'd acted in on Long Island.

"This is what the world is really about," he told her. "Ed Bullins, Leroi Jones, these playwrights say it like it is. Not that I'm knocking ol' Will."

Annie shivered with the danger and excitement, delighted to be his only audience, curling and uncurling her legs on the couch.

"Goddamn white cunt, I don't need you or your money," Thomas read in his soft deep riveting voice. "Take back dat fancy car. You and I come from different worlds."

The story was about a white prostitute who seduces a colored pimp after a race riot in a neighborhood ghetto in East LA. Surprised by the police, the prostitute unwittingly exposes the pimp as the murderer they've been looking for. Thomas read all the parts, playing the woman as well as the pimp and the police.

"Bravo!" Annie clapped when he had finished.

"I know this pimp, Annie," Thomas said. "He could be me ten years ago. Or my brothers. He's dying. He can't help himself. He thinks he knows what he's doing, but he's blind. Blind to everything but cold hard cash. And his color. That's all that counts in the good old U-S-of-A."

"But it shouldn't happen that way," she cried, looking up at him with desperation.

He shook his head. "You crazy little fool."

"Maybe I am, but you make me happy," she answered, biting her lip.

Thomas flopped down on the rug beside the sofa. "You remind me of Momma. All my life, I've wanted to show her that I loved her."

Annie blushed, pleased to hear that. From the floor, Thomas extended a hand. Taking it, she looked down and saw tears in his eyes.

"Why are you crying?"

"It hurts to remember," he answered.

Annie reached out and touched his wet cheek. "My Dad tells stories of me when I was little," she said. "But I don't remember them."

"You probably made your Dad tear his hair out," he grinned, and she felt glad to have made him smile. What would Dad think if he could see her now? Mother and Dad both thought she was practicing in the music rooms at Carnegie Tech every evening. That reminded Annie her parents were expecting her for dinner tonight.

"I need to call home," she said, slipping off the sofa, looking for the phone. Surprisingly Dad was back from work already and answered. Annie told him she was at Phyllis', cleaning up the place and getting it ready for her friend's homecoming.

"Don't wait on me for dinner," she said. Besides, she might

even go to a movie. Dad and she discussed several movies that were up for Oscars, one he particularly recommended, *A Man for All Seasons*. As they chatted, she saw Thomas step over to the window and peer through the Venetian blinds at the decaying winter afternoon. The last orange line of the sun was fading from view. When she hung up, she rubbed her lips as if to blot out the conversation the way she might old lipstick.

"Dad told me not to stay out too late," Annie said, joining Thomas at the window.

"That sounds like something a Dad would say," Thomas said, stepping back to pull shut the blinds. He went back to the couch.

"Do you have any children?" she asked suddenly.

"Yes, one son. He lives with my mother and my sisters."

"Are you married?"

"No, I'm not married. His mother died young. What else do you want to know?"

"Nothing," said Annie, sitting down next to him, hugging her knees together. 'Do you love me?' she wanted to ask.

* * *

"Phyllis is coming back on Monday," she told him one day after sex. "We won't be able to come here anymore."

"I've been expecting this. And truthfully, I can't hide here all winter waiting for a phone call from the Negro Repertory Company, can I? I gotta go back to New York and deal with my life."

"So you're leaving," she said.

"Things happen. I don't need a young pretty white girl like you, Annie. Not in Pittsburgh, I don't. I already have a white girl in New York, though she's not half so nice as you."

"You already have a girlfriend?" she cried. Frantically Annie put on her coat, grabbing her purse, hat and gloves.

"Don't be mad at me, Annie. Anyway, she's an ex-girlfriend. C'mon, you have boyfriends, don't you? Shit, look at us. We don't stand a chance."

She threw open the door, nearly falling on the icy path in her rush to the car. Slipping on his shoes, Thomas followed her, carrying his coat. They didn't speak all the way back to Oakland. Annie felt furious. She refused to look at him. How dare he give up so quickly—how dare he give up on her! And them! Even if he left Pittsburgh—why, she could always come to New York. The angrier she became, the better she felt. Righteous and indignant, she felt even more vindicated by his silence. For once she was unafraid. When she stopped the car in the Howard Johnson's lot, Thomas tried to take her hand.

"Don't!" Annie cried, pulling back, willing him to leave.

"So this is it?" he asked.

She shrugged. Thomas flicked his hand over his eyes. "You are one hard nut to crack, Annie." Then he began to stroke her cheek.

"You should know," she answered, but now she was smiling. He kissed her. Annie closed her eyes, breathing deep.

* * *

She was in the kitchen making herself a sandwich when Dad came in for lunch.

"I haven't heard you practicing your violin lately, Annie," he said.

"I always practice in the music rooms at Tech. You know that, Dad," she said. "But I'll play for you soon. I promise. Do you want me to make you a ham sandwich?"

He nodded, looking over her shoulder while she put the ham, mayonnaise, and lettuce on the white sandwich bread. Setting a teapot of water on the stove, he asked her about her plans for the coming year and if she was still interested in auditioning for Julliard.

"Of course I am!" she answered.

Pursing his lips as he did whenever he said something

important, he told her he'd pay for her travel costs if she needed to go to New York.

"Oh, Dad! You're wonderful," Annie said, giving him a quick hug. "I am going to work with Leo every morning next semester. He's giving me extra sessions to prepare for the audition. It's in March. I'll let you know how it goes, I promise you. Thank you!"

"Good, good," he nodded, looking pleased as he searched the cupboard for tea bags. "Did you get that message I left you? Someone called when you were out."

"No," she answered. "Was it Phyllis?" She looked in the refrigerator for a Coca-Cola.

"Thomas I think he said his name was. Nice sounding chap. Is he in the Music Department?"

Her heart stopped. "Uh—yes. What did he say? Did he leave a number?"

"No. Let me think. He said something about an audition at the Playhouse. Next Wednesday at 3PM I think he said. Look on the phone stand for the message."

Leaving the Coke on the counter, she rushed up the stairs where she found Dad's message on the phone stand written in his small tight ornate script. "Thomas—audition—pgh playhouse—Wed 3PM." He must have gotten an audition with the Negro Repertory Company after all! And he wanted her to come!

That third Wednesday in January was a bleak cold afternoon even for Pittsburgh. The weather report on the radio said the wind from Ohio and the Midwest was approaching gale warnings. By 2PM the sky was dark and snow threatened. Annie parked her VW in the Carnegie Tech lot where she had a free parking pass and started out through the campus towards the Playhouse, exhilarated with her adventure. But as she walked along the Campus Green, a crowd of angry protesters stopped her. Over a hundred young people, nearly all white, were gathered near Skibo Student Union, named after the town in Scotland where Andrew Carnegie, the college benefactor, bought a castle after making his fortune. Carnegie family names permeated the entire campus. Unofficial rumor had it the college was going to merge with Mellon Institute and be renamed Carnegie-Mellon University.

The crowd was protesting the escalation of the war and the draft policies of the Johnson administration. Some had signs and banners. One said "5,000 American boys will die this year in Vietnam." Other signs showed monstrous clenched fists. A few demonstrators were dressed in body bags. Cops ringed the crowd, holding heavy sticks, belts sagging with holsters and guns. Annie began to walk faster as the menacing crowd chanted, "Yankee Go Home" and "No Draft, No War." Rushing down the path as fast as she could, she saw a pair of cops push over a black man with an Afro holding a sign that said, "If War is Good Business, Invest Your Son."

Ignoring the hopelessness she felt about the anti-war demonstration, Annie ran across the asphalt parking lot into Schenley Park, and hurried down the path and over the bridge toward Forbes and the Pittsburgh Playhouse. Her stomach was empty; she had forgotten the lunch she had packed this morning. Yesterday was her birthday and she was looking forward to eating those two pieces of chocolate cake she wrapped up.

Garbage cans bordered the Pittsburgh Playhouse parking lot. Annie tried the closest door, but it was locked. She went down an alley and around to a back door at the bottom of a fire escape facing another parking lot, empty too except for an old Chevrolet from the '50s like a car they used to have. Under its rusted, bent, maroon fenders, a stray cat meowed. The cat meowed again. Where was it? She looked under the car but didn't see the cat.

Where was Thomas? Nothing seemed real or certain as she stood outside on this bleak afternoon, knocking on the door of an empty building. It was like her birthday. Being twenty-one, legally an adult, meant nothing. "How close? This close? Or this close?"

he had asked. She would tell him today. I want to be as close as we can get, Thomas. I want to be that close to you.

Annie heard the cat meow again and called back, "Meow? Meow?" It answered her, but still Annie couldn't find it. She walked back along the narrow alley to the front of the playhouse. There was Thomas, his back to her, staring up at the Greek terra cotta masks of comedy and tragedy above the front doors. He stood on the steps in his black suit, the same one he wore the night she met him. When he turned and saw her, a look of wariness and something else passed over his face. She came up to him.

"Annie."

"Are you nervous?" she asked.

"What are you doing here?"

"I got your message," she said.

"So your Dad really gave you my message. I'm surprised."

He didn't seem to want her here. She felt afraid. "Maybe I shouldn't have come."

"Never mind," he told her. "Come. This way."

She followed him around to the back and watched as Thomas banged the door. Finally a man with a pale face and blond hair, wearing a stained sweater and baggy dark pants, opened it. He had a scruffy beard.

"What do you want?" he said in an irritated voice, flicking back the strands of yellowish hair falling on his face. "We've closed the auditions for *Great White Hope*."

"I'm looking for Mel Manning," said Thomas.

"He's busy."

"I have an appointment."

"Hold on." Closing the door part way, he shouted over his shoulder, "Mel? Do you have anyone scheduled for today?"

Two steps below Thomas, Annie clasped her hands in her lined leather gloves.

"I have an appointment," repeated Thomas. He put his shiny

black shoe in the doorway. The man called out frantically, "Mel?" A voice answered. "What?" When Thomas heard that, he pushed by and hurried down the hallway, leaving Annie to face the man.

"I'm with him," she whispered.

"I couldn't have guessed," he said sarcastically, but he stood aside, motioning her forward with a flourish. He's gay, she thought, and felt relief as if, being different, he might understand her position better.

Annie followed Thomas down the dark hall into a lighted room where the director of the Negro Repertory Company greeted him loudly and enthusiastically. "Hey, wha's happening—" Mel Manning said, shaking Thomas' hand up and down. Mel was huge and black with a face so puffy you could barely see his eyes. He was smoking Camels and the kinky Afro he wore gave him another six inches of height.

"Let's go down to the stage," said Mel, pumping Thomas' hand and leading him into the hallway. "And who's this pretty young thing?" he said, glancing at Annie.

"I won't be any trouble. I'll sit in the back," Annie replied meekly when Thomas didn't respond.

"Suit yourself," Mel answered.

She followed them down the hall, painted institutional yellow, into the theatre where she'd seen *Midsummer Night's Dream* a month before. The set was still up.

Annie sat in the back row and soon the man with the pale hair joined her. Down in front, Mel was laughing. Sitting down, he said something to Thomas who leaped onto the stage. Thomas stood motionless with his back toward them. Annie felt her heart rushing toward the spot where he stood on the stage, empty and dark except for him. His arms were bent, head bowed, his fingers cupped as if preparing to lunge or dive. How close? This close or this close.

The pale man next to her rose and skittered down the aisle,

whispering in Mel's ear. Mel put his fists into his voluminous black leather jacket and pulled out the Camels, sticking one in his mouth. The man lit it for him, then walked back up the aisle. Mel stood, flicked his cigarette out against the chair, and shouted, "How about a monologue from *Othello*?" he boomed.

Thomas stood there, unmoving, silent.

"*Othello*," Mel shouted again. "The opening scene on the parapet."

The pale man snorted from where he sat in the aisle close to Annie. From the back seat, she slipped her legs one over the other, tightening them. She thought of mice waiting for the cat to spring. Thomas was the cat. What would he do? She thought of the cat outside. She should look for it afterward. Oh, God, why doesn't he do something!

"I've not prepared any Shakespeare for today," Thomas said, turning around to face them. "I was told to have a scene ready from *Electronic Nigger*." Stage front, he leaned on one foot in a relaxed manner.

"Shit," Mel growled, flicking his cigarette. He stood.

The pale man stood too, as if preparing to leave.

"I've prepared a monologue from *Whitewash* I performed at the Long Island Summer Festival last year," said Thomas in a strong, resonant voice.

Mel sat back down. "Okay, let's see what you can do."

The coy devious white prostitute, the blustering cowardly black pimp, the good ol' boy cop—Thomas played them with such conviction and power that Annie was enthralled. She felt she was watching a full production even though there was no one on stage but him. She watched Mel lean forward as if listening hard, then recline back in his seat. He lit a cigarette and then let it burn down in his fingers.

'Bravo!' Annie wanted to shout when the scene was over. She wished she had the nerve. The pale man came back down the aisle and whispered something in Mel's ear. He and Thomas walked back up the aisle, Mel between them holding onto both their shoulders.

Afterwards Annie waited in the hallway while Thomas went into Mel's office. She sat by the door, hugging her purse to her chest. When she could stand it no longer, she buttoned up her coat and walked back outside the way she had come.

It was very cold now, too cold for snow, and she had to bounce up and down in her leather boots to keep from shivering in the fierce wind. The cat was no longer meowing and in any case she didn't bother looking for it. Raw with anticipation and excitement, Annie went around to the front. Finally Thomas came out. His face was impassive.

"What happened? You were great!" she cried, hurrying up to him.

He looked past her with a blank stare as if he she wasn't there.

"Are you okay?"

He mumbled something, and then began to walk away, leaving her on the sidewalk. "Wait! Wait!" she called out. "Thomas! What's the matter with you? There will be other chances," she said in desperation. "I just know it."

He whipped around like a sapling in the wind. His face was frozen, his eyes empty.

"Annie, you got it all wrong. I got a job. There's an opening in New York, Mel says. The Negro Rep is leasing a theatre over on the lower East Side. In a church. It's near Union Square. I've been there a few times. They're going to mount a new play soon. I don't know what kind of part they'll offer me, but it will be something. At least that's what Mel told me."

"Then what's wrong?" she asked. "You didn't want me to be here, is that it? Why did you phone me and tell me about the audition if you didn't want me to come?"

"I just called to say goodbye. Your dad forgot that part. I

never thought he would take the message."

"So you're saying it's Dad's fault?" Her voice rose with indignation.

She stood closer, close enough to hear him say, "It's my fault." He stepped toward her, bowing his head, holding his coat tight around his neck. "I have to leave," he said.

"I don't understand," she answered.

"I have to leave Pittsburgh."

"So? Thomas, you got me wrong. I'm no child. I can say goodbye. I know we don't have a future. I know you don't want a goddamn virgin," she heard her voice rise in panic. She felt like a mechanical doll with a wind-up voice box whose string had been pulled too hard.

Out here in the street he appeared sinister, impenetrable, unreachable. A sense of privation permeated her. Annie turned around and began to walk toward campus. She knew Thomas was following her, but she didn't look back. They passed the University of Pittsburgh and the Carnegie Museum with the two lions guarding the heavy doors. They went over the bridge and through Schenley Park. When she reached the Carnegie-Tech Green, she headed for her car in the Skibo parking lot. The protesters were all gone, though a few torn signs remained on the frozen ground.

"Are you coming with me?" she said finally, turning to face him.

"Looks like it," he smiled sheepishly.

The VW started up right away. Turning on the defroster and the wipers, she put her cold hands in her pockets to wait for the windows to clear.

"New York's cold but this is cold, cold as the hawk, Momma would say," he said, glancing at her, rubbing his hands. She stared at them, marveling. She had forgotten about those beautiful hands, the color of mahogany.

When the windshield wipers began to move over the

encrusted ice, Annie let the brake out and gingerly drove out of the lot. She drove down Penn near the outskirts of East Liberty, past gutted buildings in the redevelopment area, empty spaces where only garbage collected and blew into random patterns constantly shifted by the unobstructed wind.

Annie felt panic, then exhilaration, jerking to a stop at a red light. With Thomas next to her, she looked out her window for what seemed like forever across the blocks and blocks of concrete and brick rubble to the Nabisco factory. The light changed from red to green. She took her foot off the brake and started up again.

A streetcar passed, jangling and cranking on the rails, people standing in the aisle. Her eyes followed the green streetcar on its wire leash across the intersection past the abandoned lots and darkening sky. Another streetcar went by in the opposite direction and then another. Why didn't he say something? Surely she deserved that.

"Where do you want to go, Thomas?"

"Just drive," he said.

Turning on her AM radio, she headed down Washington Boulevard towards the railroad tracks and the river. Bob Dylan's "The Times They Are A Changing" was playing. Thomas turned up the volume.

"Go that way," Thomas said, pointing to a dirt road leading off to the left of a stone wall. Annie maneuvered the car around the potholes and protruding bushes to the river's edge. Beyond them the river was still, pale and sleek as the flat gray sky, seemingly without depth, and the trees on both sides threw their bare branches over the water with offerings. It was getting late. She could see a few brown birds flying by into the trees.

"Look, a robin," she said. "But it's too early for them."

Thomas glanced out the window.

"Is it? I don't see a lot of birds from my penthouse in New York," he said. "I've been thinking, Annie, you don't know anything about me."

"I know some things."

"Suppose I'm a criminal. Suppose I'm a dope dealer, a liar and a cheat. Suppose I'm running from the pigs."

"Suppose, suppose, suppose," she said. "What do you want me to say?"

He stretched his arm and put his hand on the back of her neck, sighing deeply.

The river was streaked in darkness now, the light fading along the rolling hills behind it. Thomas leaned over and whispered in her ear. "You're too much for me, girl."

She flushed with pleasure. He lifted her chin and kissed her.

"Feels good, doesn't it," he said sighing. "I might as well go back to New York. We can't go to your friend's no more."

He said more words between kissing her, strange, seductive, confusing words, like poetry. But what did words matter when he was touching her. When he was leaving.

* * *

Thomas sat in the car while she went into the Howard Johnson's motel office and paid for the room. Room 214 was on the second floor of a long row of rooms and they had to climb steep, narrow steps slippery with ice to reach it.

From the window above the parking lot, Annie looked out as Thomas lit the lamps over the bed. She tried to find her VW below among the cars, but the cars all looked the same, like toys dusted with icy glitter. She sat down in a chair by the window.

He turned on the TV and lay back on the bed. They watched a replay of an old football game between the Steelers and the Raiders, interrupted by a Ford commercial where a big animal leaped over some trees.

"Is that a lion?" asked Annie.

"A cougar."

"Oh."

Finally he looked at her. Was he smiling just a little?

"We can have drinks or some food brought up," he said.

"You said you don't drink," she answered brightly.

Now he did smile. "I've missed you," he said, looking at the TV where the cougar was running side by side with the Ford truck.

"I missed you too," she answered, feeling oblivious to any danger. His hands were at his sides and he made no movement toward her. He's waiting for me, Annie thought, coming over to him.

Mozart's Birthday

Her house was dark by the time Annie arrived home after midnight. Mother and Dad were in bed long ago and even Melinda's light was out. Even though she came in without making a sound, Lucky began to bark.

"Annie?" Mother called out from the upstairs bedroom.

Annie felt a pang of guilt at the worry she heard in her mother's voice. "Yes?" she murmured, bending down to rub Lucky's hindquarters. The old dog wagged her tail and went back to her bed behind the sofa.

Dad came to the stairs in his bathrobe. He stared down at her. "Whatever you've been doing, Annie. I want you to know I don't approve."

"I don't know what you mean," she mumbled.

"You're not the same girl you used to be," he harrumphed, pulling the sash of his worn-out flannel bathrobe.

"I'm not a girl, Dad," she sighed, hanging her coat in the hall closet and throwing her scarf and gloves on a dining room chair.

"Okay, okay, so you think you can argue with me now that you've turned twenty-one. But there's more to being an adult than that."

"Please, Dad. I'm tired. Please let me alone. Can we talk another time?"

She heard him padding back into the bedroom and closing the door. Annie slowly walked up the stairs and into her dark warm room. Dropping onto her bed, she fell into a dead sleep, still in her clothes.

When she registered for her last semester at Carnegie Tech, she felt like an alien from a distant planet. As usual the lines were long, the rooms cold, and the atmosphere unwelcoming. She looked just as stylish and "mod" as the other students in her Chesterfield coat, boots, jeans and black turtleneck. Yet why were they all doing this? Annie didn't trust the value of college any longer. "Get an education first; then you can do what you want," her father always said. And so here she was signing up for her last semester—but was it only to please him and Mother? She just felt depressed.

A young woman with a red dot on her forehead, wearing a pea coat from Army Surplus over her long orange sari, pushed in front her in a hurry to reach another table. It made Annie wonder if the exchange students who arrived from foreign countries felt as confused and uncertain as she did, or were they committed to their education in a way she had never been? Following the woman's example, Annie too pushed her way forward in the Senior Admissions line. Sucking in her breath, she handed her class roster to the clerk at the table.

She retraced the very steps she had walked to meet Thomas for his audition at the Pittsburgh Playhouse, passing the spot where the campus cops battered the black man with the Afro. All that remained were a few painted-out signs in the wet earth saying, "No War in Vietnam." How discouraged she felt reading them. She had no faith in the government, especially not President Johnson. Just look how he had escalated the fighting.

The snow had left the ground wet and the air clean and even the sun was shining. She had just enough time before her music lesson to stop off at the just-completed Mellon Library. Holding her violin case with one hand, she shaded her eyes from the brilliant reflection of the sun off the brand new glass and steel-framed building.

She told the librarian she was looking for Chopin's *Sonata Number 2 in B-Flat Minor*, one of Dad's favorite piano sonatas. Today was Dad's birthday and she planned to take out the record. As his present, she was going to buy him the score. She just knew

Dad would love following along while listening to the music. She'd do it with him.

Annie found the Chopin record easily and checked it out for the next two weeks. It was a full half an hour before she was to meet Leo at five o'clock. Soon she was pacing the gothic halls of the Fine Arts Building. She was looking forward to her lesson today.

While she waited, her eyes skimmed the "Wanted" and "For Sale" bulletin boards by the large glass doors of the gray stone entryway. Were there any rides to New York? She searched the index cards. "Rides wanted to California." "Rides to Boston and Cape Cod." There were also notices like "Apartment to sublet in Regent Square", "Skis for sale" and "Tickets to the Bob Dylan concert" at Syria Mosque.

Her eyes passed over another flyer, printed in large black print.

> Teachers Desperately Needed
> —Music Students
> —Teach at the Hill House.
> Give all the children of Pittsburgh a chance.
> If you are an advanced music student,
> YOU are needed now!
> Give music to the community!
> Small stipend.

She had a vague idea of where The Hill was located, a few blocks east of the new downtown skyscrapers she thought. Thanks to President Lyndon Johnson's programs, it was being redeveloped. The old two-story brick and wooden row houses were being demolished to put in a spectacular circular steel-domed Civic Auditorium. Thomas had mentioned the Hill once or twice—did members of his family live there? She couldn't be sure. He had never told her where he lived. A hundred years ago her grandmother, Mary McArdle, had been born on one of those narrow winding streets. Then it was all Irish living in the dilapidated run-down rentals. Her grandmother learned to read by spelling out the "Help Wanted" signs hanging in the windows of shops owned by absentee landlords that said, "Irish Need Not Apply."

Annie jotted down the phone number of the Hill House on the edge of her violin score. How much, she wondered, was the small stipend? She was living free at home, and her parents paid for her college expenses, even giving her a monthly stipend for gas and car tune ups, but she always needed more money. Her savings from last year's summer job at Sun Drug Store in Wilkinsburg was almost gone. A part-time job would make all the difference. She could save for the New York audition, if she made it that far. She could save to go and see Thomas.

The hour started off awkwardly with Leo acting impatient when her bow kept sticking to the strings and she had to stop to put rosin on it. He hated interrupting the lesson to deal with details, and she apologized for taking up his time this way.

"Let's go, let's go," he admonished her, beginning to play a few bars of the duet they were about to work on. In his forties, Leo Thurmond was built like a short football player, chunky, and balding. He had a clubfoot that sometimes dragged when he walked fast. She'd heard he had come to the Pittsburgh Symphony from the Cleveland Orchestra, where he had been concertmaster of the first violin section. Leo was renowned for his virtuosity and bad temper in the Music Department. Teaching was a waste of time, he told all his students, and they were all to understand they were only superficial extras in his life. But Annie didn't mind his sarcasm and irritability, his brutal asides. With Leo she felt impersonal, like a well-regulated machine set at a certain calibrated frequency and effortlessly carrying out instructions. Sometimes she even thought he did respect her playing and that gave her a feeling of satisfaction.

"I'll get you in shape yet, Annie Ryan," he said at the end of the hour, brushing back the few long black stringy hairs from his shining head with one hand. His violin was wedged under his chin in its usual position. "You might end up being just good enough when I'm through with you."

"And when will that be?" Annie said, bending over to put her instrument away in its red felt-lined case. She was surprised, smiling a little. In the six months he had taught Advanced Strings, Leo had never once praised her.

He seemed taken aback by her question, as if he didn't expect to be called on his statements.

"You'll know—just like you know this," he answered. adjusting the violin under his chin, hurling himself into the Bach *G Minor Sonata.*

Nodding as if she understood, Annie stopped to listen. Though Leo had the most unpleasant speaking voice, shrill as an out-of-tune A string on the violin, his playing was superb. She was sorry when he stopped, not wanting the music to end. She sensed he too seemed lost. For a moment they both stood side by side in the small bare room looking out through the window at the early evening sky. Over the tops of the naked trees, flames from the Jones and Laughlin steel mill across the Schenley Homewood ravine spewed out orange flames into the dusky sky.

Picking up her violin case, Annie headed toward the door with her belongings.

"Today's Mozart's birthday," Leo said, clumping behind her.

"Yes, it's my Dad's birthday too."

"Is that so? Is he a musical genius too? I'm having my usual monthly get-together at my apartment in Shadyside tonight. Think of it as a birthday party. You know where it is. Come on by—if you dare," he smirked knowingly.

"Maybe. But I think I'll be busy."

He laughed, as if she'd made a joke, but it was a joke she didn't get. If he had been Thomas, she would have asked why. With

Leo, she didn't care.

On her way home, Annie stopped at a shopping mall in East Hills near her house, parking her car in the large windswept snowy lot. She headed down the cement walkway toward the Record Factory, her scarf blowing over her face. Looking for the tiny classical musical score section took some time. Happily for her, she found one copy of the *Sonata No 2 in B-Flat Minor* displayed next to copies of the same album she'd taken out of the music library. Annie picked up the record. Dad would love to have it!

But then, on her way to the checkout counter, she saw a Beatles display featuring their new album, *Revolver.* This was the kind of music Thomas listened to on her car radio as they drove around Pittsburgh together. He knew all the lyrics. She loved listening to his baritone voice and now, because of him, she liked this popular music. She could recognize the names of the superstar recording artists—the Beatles naturally, Neil Diamond, Judy Collins, Joan Baez, Dylan, and lots more.

But she was about to spend all her cash on Dad's present and didn't have enough to purchase it, the Chopin record and the score. Dad wouldn't care she rationalized. She didn't need to buy him the record; he could listen to the album from the library like she already planned. Annie put aside the Chopin record and stepped to the checkout area with the music score and the Beatles album. Giving her dollars to the clerk made her feel happy. It didn't make sense—because Thomas was gone. She no longer had reason to go to Howard Johnson's in search of him. She was in love with a man she would never see again. But in her heart she didn't believe that. Even now in the record store, she felt their love-making shielding her like the trees of summer, soothing her like sweet dreams half-remembered before she came fully awake. She felt full of love and promise. And now she had *Revolver* to listen to when she got home. And she had a present for Dad.

Annie was upstairs in her warm, well-lit bedroom practicing

when she heard Dad come in the front door. Feeling full of purpose, she continued playing the pieces Leo and she had gone over earlier. She was a little disappointed Dad didn't come up to see her.

After she put her violin away, Annie wrapped the Chopin score in silvery paper and purple ribbon, and carried it downstairs along with the library record. Dad was relaxing in his orange chair with tonight's *Pittsburgh Press* in front of him, his eyes closed. Annie leaned over his shoulder and dropped the present in his lap.

"What?" Dad mumbled, rubbing his eyes, and putting his paper down.

"Open it, Dad. It's your birthday, remember?"

Dad pulled at the purple ribbon.

"What? For me? Nobody gets anything for me around here," he chuckled.

"Watch out. You'll have to eat your words, Dad." Eagerly Annie watched as he unwrapped the sheet music.

"Hmmm," Dad said, holding up the score.

"Chopin! The sonata you love—And look—I even got the record. I borrowed it from the music library. I'll put it on and we can follow along with the score." She slipped the record out of its case and put it on the turntable.

"Why, thank you, Annie. Now I have something to enjoy in my spare time—if I ever get any, that is, what with working late and trying to pay all your bills."

She felt a pang of confused anxiousness, as if it was she who made him work so much, she who never gave anything back. Was that so?

"Now, Dad, I know you give me too much," she said, as she turned on the stereo console. "But I want to change that. Listen, I found out about a job—a music job—instructing kids at the Hill House. I want to apply for it to help pay for my Julliard audition." Actually she hadn't decided that until right this minute, but suddenly it seemed to make a lot of sense.

"The Hill House? Near downtown? That's in a bad section of Pittsburgh."

"It will be in the daytime," she said.

"But you don't want to jeopardize your schoolwork at this late stage," Dad said quickly. His eyes drifted back to the score.

"I won't!" Annie said defensively, and then lowered her voice. "It's only part-time in the afternoons."

They both listened as the record began to play. A few long slow opening bars of *Sonata No. 2 in B-flat Minor* rippled into fast trilling cadences as the 'Grave', or doppio movimento, began.

"Here is where we are," she said, pointing out the same measure on the music sheet.

Laying his long thin index finger on the paper, Dad hummed along, following the notes while Chopin tinkled in the air like icicles in the wind. Annie relaxed, letting the music soothe her as she stood above Dad in his chair, looking down over his shoulder. Once she rubbed his shiny white bald head with affection. He seemed to nod off and Annie slid to the side of his chair, kneeling by the armrest.

"Now where are we?" he asked after a while, rising up.

"Here, Dad, here."

She helped him find the place, putting her hand over his while the piano played. Again his eyes closed.

"Don't you like it?" Annie asked.

"I've always liked Chopin," said Dad, opening his eyes. "I like Mozart better, naturally."

"Of course," she said quickly, feeling a little hurt. "Mozart and you—I was talking to my teacher, Leo, today about how you have the same birthdays."

"Oh, ha ha. Is that so? Two geniuses, me and Mozart." Dad shook the music score with emphasis.

"So, Dad, what do you think about that job?"

"Huh? You know what I always say. Get your education first. I had my doubts about your majoring in music, but you've stuck with it no matter what I thought. Yes, I said I'd help you out with the audition fee, Annie, and I will. What have you done about the Julliard application, if anything?"

"I haven't finished it yet, Dad, but I will. I promise. The auditions are coming up, but first I have to be accepted for the Masters Program on my academic record. But, Dad?" Annie took a deep breath, while the piano music danced into the second movement, the "Scherzo." "I have something I want to tell you. Are you listening?"

Dad looked up at her. "Is something wrong?" he asked.

"No, yes. That man you talked to, Thomas, who called. Do you remember?"

"Yes, I believe I do."

"I'm in love with him," she pronounced, laughing with surprise at her own courage.

Dad laughed too, showing the silver fillings in the back of his mouth. "Are you now?" he said, rustling the music score in his hands. "So when are Mother and I going to meet this young man?"

Should she tell him the truth? But how could she? Did she dare?

"You can't meet him, I'm afraid. He's gone back to New York."

"Oh, is he going to Julliard too?" asked Dad absent-mindedly, his eyes traveling over the bars of music.

"No."

"Humph," said Dad.

Her heart thumping, Annie continued following along with the music. But Dad's eyes were closing. He didn't say anything more, just nodded in his chair. She felt as if she and Dad were walking along a precipice, at any moment in danger of falling. "Don't you care at all?" she finally asked.

"Huh?" Dad said, opening his eyes. "You have lots of time to fall in love, Annie."

"Oh, don't say that!" She heard the click of Mother's high heels in the dining room. Annie froze, but Mother went into the kitchen instead. Annie heard the oven door bang.

When the phone rang, Annie jumped up, running out of the living room and up the stairs to Melinda's bedroom where the phone extension usually was. Her sister was stretched out on her twin bed, her hair in big pink rollers under the electric hair dryer.

"Hello?" Annie's heart was leaping as she put the heavy black receiver to her ear.

"Hi, Annie! Guess who?"

"Oh, it's you, Phyllis," Annie said, hiding her disappointment.

"Yes, it's Phyllis Donovan, I mean Pilkowski! I keep forgetting I'm married. Isn't that a scream? I got back a little early. Donny had to go out on the next ship to Saigon or wherever the hell they send the troops. I had to call you right away. When can we talk, I mean really talk?"

As usual, Phyllis didn't wait for her to answer, but talked on, something that always bothered Annie.

"Florida was great. It's so much fun being married. All that S-E-X. I have to tell you all the gory details. Can you come on over tonight? It's weird, being alone in this house."

"I can't. It's my Dad's birthday." She didn't want to talk, but Annie couldn't tell Phyllis this.

"Gosh, say 'Happy Birthday' to your Dad from me, will you! But Annie, you can't let me down. You know how I hate to be alone. Did I tell you we went snorkeling?"

Phyllis talked on and on in her loud frenetic joking way, while Annie sat at the foot of Melinda's bed staring at the posters of Joni Mitchell and Leonard Cohen. Every so often her sister nudged her with her foot to let her know she should leave her alone.

Holding the phone tightly to her ear, Annie felt like a robot, numbed by all that had happened at her friend's house, which Phyllis would never know about unless Annie told her. But how could she? Annie might as well have been a deaf mute. Would Phyllis understand or would she be shocked that she was in love with a black actor? That she had had sex with him. No, she didn't dare tell her—she didn't dare face Phyllis' shocked response.

All through high school Phyllis was her best friend, but now Annie felt only a nostalgic connection with her. In high school, Phyllis had seemed funny and wild and carefree, all that Annie loved in a friend. But once she began college, everything changed. All her friends disappeared to nearby, mostly Catholic, colleges like Phyllis had, an option Annie didn't allow herself, thinking those institutions parochial and without prestige, though her parents were willing to let her go and even pay for her room and board there. Instead she chose the one local university with a recognized reputation—even if it was in the field of technology more than music, and even though she ended up being a "commuter," who lived at home.

Phyllis was saying something. "Hey, Annie, I have a present for you. I had to bring you a little something to thank you for the great work you did taking care of my house. Don suggested it. And you better like it. I made him buy me one for myself."

"Okay, okay." Annie said, looking at the little balls of ice hit the window. The snow had turned to rain. Soon it would be February, with those few brief brilliant days lighting the gloomy chasm between late winter and early spring in Western Pennsylvania. It was her last semester in college. What, if anything, of importance could happen to her now? She could not wait to finish school and leave home. She could not wait to begin her new life!

When she hung up, the light patter-patter of hail punctuated the silence in Melinda's small disheveled room. Her sister groaned as she pulled herself up from the bed and switched off the hair dryer. Annie threw her arms around Melinda as she stood up.

"What's that for?" Melinda looked at her. "You're weird."

"I'm in love, I'm in love, I'm in love, I'm in love—" Annie sang from the *South Pacific* refrain.

"You're nuts." Melinda said, bounding out of her bedroom.

Mother called them to dinner and Annie skipped down the stairs two at a time. They all sat down at the table, Lucky burrowing under Dad's chair as he said grace.

"Bless us O Lord and these thy gifts, which we are about to receive, through thy bounty, through Christ, Our Lord, Amen."

"Amen," added Mother.

Annie ate rapidly, taking two helpings of the steaming macaroni and beef casserole Mother had made the night before and even a few forkfuls of the green salad. Afterwards, Mother put away the leftovers while Melinda cleared off the table and Annie ran the water in the sink. Tonight she didn't even mind doing the dishes. When she was finished, she rushed upstairs to get *Revolver*. By the time she returned with it to the living room, Dad was asleep in his chair again, the newspaper over his face, and the Chopin score on the rug.

Annie switched the library album on the record changer with the Beatles. She lay down on the soft warm rug and began humming along to "Here, There and Everywhere." Annie buried her head in her arms, letting the refrain lull her into a wordless longing.

Next came the loud, fast beat of "Got to Get You Into My Life."

"Goddamn it! Turn that off," Dad shouted suddenly.

"Dad!"

"I can't stand that nigger music."

Dad shook the paper for emphasis.

"The Beatles are from England," Annie said. Angrily she picked up the cover of the record on the floor and held it out so that he could see the photograph of the four very white boys from Liverpool.

"I'm talking about taste, Annie, and beauty," he said.

"What do you know!"

"Huh? What did you say? Look, if you want to say something to me, turn that down. I can't hear you with that garbage playing."

"Just look at them!" she shouted.

"Well, they sound just like the scum from the Hill to me."

"Dad, how can you say things like that!"

"I'm just saying how I feel, Annie."

"But Dad. Is it their fault they never had the opportunities we —I—had."

Mother, hearing the loud voices, came into the room. Her hands were shaking. "What's this all about?" she asked. "What is this, Jim—a birthday record? Is this something new?" She turned to Annie, a forced smile on her face.

"It's just the Beatles. I've felt angry and ashamed of our family ever since I was little," Annie said. "I remember when we left Wilkinsburg just to get away from the Negroes moving in."

"Oh, don't mention that," Mother interjected. "That was a terrible time. We lost so much money. Our house would have been worth so much more. Don't mention that, not on Dad's birthday."

"You act as if they are animals and inferior to us," Annie went on, her voice rising.

Dad put down his paper. "When you hear Chopin, what do you hear? You hear taste and culture. Good music. Like great literature, not drivel. Why that stuff you are playing is just garbage and it hurts my ears. It's like that piece of junk at the playhouse a few weeks ago. You remember. That so-called Shakespeare by the Negro Ensemble Group. You can't just muck up fine literature and music and get away with it."

"It's 'Negro Repertory Company'. But nobody's getting away with anything!" shouted Annie. "Dad, face it, it's prejudice." Her voice broke, but she forced herself to go on. "Black people are the same as we are. They have families and hopes and dreams. They can love and be loved in return. They're the same as we are!"

"I'm not saying that," Dad's voice took on a mollifying tone as Mother sat down on the edge of the chair across from him. "Your mother and I trained you to be tolerant."

"Don't kid me!" Mother laughed sarcastically "How dare you bring me into this? None of you listen to me. You're ungrateful slobs, all of you!"

"I'm talking culture, Maureen, I'm talking Chopin," Dad addressed Mother, attempting to calm her.

"Listen to him! Culture! What do you know about culture? Why your whole family comes from the pigsty. Irish immigrants!"

"I'm not intolerant of them or anyone," Dad went on, ignoring Mother's tirade.

"Oh you!" Mother shouted. "Listen to him. You're not intolerant! How could you be so stupid! I suppose you aren't intolerant of me. I work my fingers to the bone, unlike other wives."

"Annie and I were having a discussion and you just barged in, lashing out willy-nilly," said Dad to Mother.

"I wouldn't have to lash out if I didn't have such an ungrateful family! If I didn't have to work so hard!"

Dad shrugged his shoulders.

"Oh, dear God, when will it ever end? When do I get any peace and quiet?" Mother screamed. Tears came to her eyes.

"What's wrong now?" asked Melinda, appearing from the stairwell.

Annie came over and patted Mother's hand. "I'm sorry," she said. "I didn't mean it that way."

Mother wiped her cheeks. Dad had turned back to his paper, his face wrinkled in a mixed expression of hurt and disgust. The Beatles were still singing.

"Turn it off, Annie. Now!" Mother ordered.

Annie went over to the console and changed the record back. Now the Chopin tinkled brightly in the background.

"Listen to me," Annie said, facing them. "That man I told you about—the one I'm in love with—Thomas—he's black, a Negro. Yes, you heard me."

"Oh, my God! How could you?" Mother gasped and began to cry in earnest.

Annie opened her mouth to say more, but stopped herself at the sight of her mother's tears. Tears were flowing down her cheeks too when she left her parents in the living room. As she climbed the steps to her bedroom, she was thinking that she had nowhere to go. She felt hopeless. Then she remembered Leo's party.

* * *

They didn't stop her from leaving although Mother warned her about the roads. Dad hadn't said a word. How awkward she had been standing at Leo's door, intent on obliterating all that had gone before with her parents. She had worn her best pink wool sheath over black tights, her high boots. Immediately after taking her coat, Leo had complimented her on her taste. Everything they said felt phony, his compliments, her responses.

The hallway was full of African art—Bambara masks, Dogon statues, headdresses from the Congo and Kenya. Painstakingly Leo pointed out each one, instructing her on how to identify the marks of an authentic objet d'art, as he led her into the living room where the party was in full swing.

He introduced her to the seven other music majors, mostly women, predominantly Jewish from New York, whom she knew a little. They sat around a circular glass coffee table on some big Indian pillows. There was a fire in the open brick fireplace, which Leo tended off and on. He offered Annie glass after glass of white and then red wine. In the midst of the animated conversation about who would be chosen for Julliard, Annie found herself staring into the flames.

Several African statues of naked women squatted on the coffee table as if giving birth. Annie imagined herself as one of them, peaceful and emotionless, solidified and made sacred by time. One of Thomas' ancestors, she thought, and put her hand out to touch the woodcarving.

Leo fiddled with his stereo. Short, wearing an ill-fitting jacket, his broad shoulders out of proportion to his small torso, still he radiated power, charisma. When he leaned over and whispered in her ear about a recommendation he intended to send off to Julliard for her, she felt a thrill of pleasure.

Annie could tell the other guests were impressed with the special attention he paid her. The wine was taking effect. Leo's energy, authority, and above all his contempt for everyone but himself—and seemingly her—gave him great stature. Even his habit of pulling up his socks over his pale white calves no longer bothered her. Half-lying on a pillow, Annie kicked off her too tight boots, stretching her feet in their black stockings as Leo refilled her plate with different kinds of cheese, small crackers, and grapes. He offered her more wine. He himself had switched to vodka. He pressed a bitter olive into her mouth, laughing at the face she made. Annie's vision was blurred when she tried to stand and she laughed as she fell back down onto the couch.

Now he began whispering in her ear in earnest, "If you're as good in bed as you are on the violin, Annie Ryan." She had forced a giggle, letting her hair fall over her face.

In the end it was all a blur. The departing guests, the Mozart sonata he played over and over, the glowing coals in the fireplace, her panties on the floor besides the Japanese style bed—a futon he called it—spread out on a bamboo mat in a tiny cold room behind the kitchen. "Oh, my dearest darling," Leo whispered as Annie watched the rice paper swinging above their heads. A small puddle of semen sat on her bare stomach; she wiped it off quickly with his sheet.

Even before she was completely sober, she felt isolated with regret. She drove home after 3AM. There were a few cars on the parkway, but nobody on the side streets leading to her home. No sounds when she got out of her parked car in the driveway. Even Lucky didn't bark as she opened the door. Her parents didn't call out from the stairs.

That night Annie ended up curled in a little ball under the covers. In the dark, she touched her arms and legs, her stomach and breasts. Some part of her was gone. She hugged herself, rolling over one way and then the other, over and over again, as if trying to obliterate what was already lost.

Lana

Now that Annie had gone, Thomas reveled in the thought that the Howard Johnson's motel room was his—for the night anyway. She had prepaid for the room and he had it to himself. It still glowed with her breathless sweet warmth and the smell of good sex. Thomas indulged himself in remembering how he had held himself above her, entering her, watching her excitement rise, and her body writhe, her soft moans. He had wanted to lose himself, come all over her, and never stop.

Annie cried in his arms for a long time but she wasn't sad she told him as she straightened her clothes later. She said her tears were tears of joy and relief.

Thomas couldn't deny her eyes were bright and her face transformed by happiness. "I'm glad, because I hate to make a woman cry," he said, stroking her cheeks.

"No more holding back, no more lies, no more denial, no more games, I promise," she said, which puzzled him because he was leaving and promises were the last thing on his mind. Promises were another language, one they couldn't speak. "I feel so free, so wonderful. And all because of you," she cried, throwing her arms out in abandonment.

"Nothing like sex. You are great in bed, girl," he had answered. "You like that, don't you?" he added, seeing her blush.

And yet, he acknowledged to himself now, he couldn't wait until she left. He admitted that he was afraid of their leave taking. Thankfully Annie hadn't said goodbye, just waved as she walked out the door, and that was fine with him. He had no use for goodbyes.

As the hail hit the roof of the motel, Thomas watched old reruns of the *Avengers* and *Mission Impossible* on the black and white

TV. He was mesmerized, seeing himself in the shadowy white heroes running from danger, dodging pitfalls, hunting out the criminal elements. Exhausted by the drama and his own feelings for each anonymous fugitive, he finally fell into a deep blind sleep.

* * *

On the bus to New York, words from Martin Luther King, Jr.'s "I Have A Dream" speech kept going through Thomas' mind. Yet he didn't feel free. No, he felt haunted by Pittsburgh—by Momma, Georgie G, and Carlotta. The twins. Pappy Find. Even Annie. Each one called to him, repeating the same refrain, "Take care of me. I need you." He could not bear to say goodbye to any of them, especially to Georgie G. At the station, Thomas kept telling his son to get on home, but the boy wouldn't go, not even after Thomas jumped up on the bus with his new suitcase and a brown paper package containing an old photo album Momma insisted he take back with him. Georgie G just stood there waiting for the bus to pull out of the terminal. Thomas could swear he had tears in his eyes.

"You don't want to go with me," he had scolded Georgie G a few hours earlier. "New York is mean. Meaner than the hawk Momma talks about. There's lots of shit going down in New York. Demonstrations. Vets fighting anti-war protestors."

"I don't care," mumbled Georgie G. "I ain't scared."

He was wearing an old flannel shirt and jeans, castoffs from Thomas or one of his other, absent uncles. Sprawled on the bed, Georgie G flipped through an old photo album, watching Thomas fold his clothes neatly into a new leather suitcase.

"I ain't afraid of no hawk," he said.

"Besides you can't come. You have school," continued Thomas. "How you doing in school anyway?"

"All right," said Georgie G, hanging his head. Thomas knew by his face—so downcast, punched in like a soft rag doll, like his mother's face—that it wasn't all right.

"Just all right?" Thomas prodded. He felt uncomfortable asking questions that he knew his son didn't want to answer. He himself hated answering questions and avoided them as much as he could. He felt like a stranger—that thought made him feel worse. How bad is it when your own son is a stranger to you? But he wouldn't think of that now. He had gotten to the point where he just wanted to pack and be done with it all, just leave as quickly as he could.

"I passed English this time," Georgie G said glumly, thrusting the album aside. From under the bed he pulled out an old, dirty basketball Thomas recognized as his.

"That's not good enough," Thomas growled, taking a freshly-washed shirt out of the closet. "Move over, will you."

Georgie G threw his legs over the edge of the bed so that Thomas could lay out his blue and black striped button-down shirt on the bedspread. The twins had washed and ironed all his clothes, each shirt carefully pressed and buttoned, and he wanted to keep them that way. He folded the shirt carefully along its seams to prevent it from wrinkling. It bothered him that he didn't even own an iron in New York.

Georgie G rolled over and jumped off the bed. "I want to come with you," he said again. He threw the ball into the air and caught it.

"Another time," said Thomas, not looking at his son. Georgie G slunk away into the next room and Thomas heard him begin to strum the broken guitar Carlotta brought home a few days ago. She found it on the corner with a box of other discards left for the Salvation Army.

Here on the Greyhound bus, he realized what he had missed by not continuing the conversation and what he wanted to say. He wanted to tell his son to be happy, to be safe, to stay away from from the rioting, the street gangs, the out-of-town looters, dope dealers, LSD, and most of all, from the police. Oh, shit, the police.

* * *

He was still raw with loneliness when he called Lana at five in the morning from a freezing phone booth at a rest stop on the Pennsylvania Turnpike. He hadn't meant to call her, but he couldn't stop himself, and even as he heard her pick up the phone he considered hanging up. He could see Lana in her sleeveless pale silk nightgown, sprawled on her new queen Posterpedic mattress with the gold and red embossed coverlet kicked onto the hardwood floor. Her black curly hair would be falling over her soft bare shoulders. She'd hold the cream-colored phone in those manicured hands with the chipped nails of brilliant barnyard red. She was beautiful yes, but yet he couldn't imagine her face—or maybe he just didn't want to. In any case, it would be swollen and indistinct, dulled from the previous night's festivities, which always included large doses of alcohol and drugs, drugs she counted on Thomas to provide.

"Hello, Lana, it's Thomas. Sorry to call so early." When she didn't reply, he said it again, this time in a more measured voice.

"Tom, is that you?"

"I'm sorry to call you so early. I have a favor to ask."

Hearing himself, he felt like a fool. How quickly he had abandoned the jive talking of down-home Pittsburgh and put on his other face. It was second nature with him now; aping Walter Cronkite he called it. It reminded him of when he'd spoken with Annie's father on the phone a few weeks before. Trying to please the Man. He'd had to sound white for Mr. Ryan. And, he admitted, it was the same with Lana. But it made him ashamed. Left him with a poisonous taste in his mouth. With the exception of Georgie G and Annie, that's how all of Pittsburgh tasted. And now, nearly four hundred miles away, Thomas had the same sour taste in his mouth.

Lana, who had dropped the phone twice, was mumbling something unintelligible, but he felt no desire to know what.

Talking to her didn't give him the satisfaction talking with Annie had. No, Lana was a poor substitute for Annie. Poor Lana. His gut tightened thinking of her sarcastic, coy replies to his queries about the Impala. Shit, she had him now but good.

After he hung up, Thomas bought a barbequed chicken at the deli of the Eat and Park restaurant. Before boarding the bus again, he devoured it to the bones. But still he felt fierce and hungry inside. Cool it, he told himself, forget it. He hunkered down in his seat, careful not to wrinkle his clothes. Folding his arms over his package, he closed his eyes. For a while he forgot about Lana and that he'd just asked her to pick him up at the bus station.

It was a rare sunny morning in New York and the air was cold and clean when the Greyhound bus finally pulled into the Port Authority. Thomas felt skittish as he dragged his suitcase off the rack and stepped down to the curb with it and the package. Where was Lana? What car would she be driving? His eyes darted around the busy garage full of monster buses spewing fumes, irate taxi drivers in shiny cabs, and frustrated drivers in late model cars yelling and blaring horns. Thomas forced himself to look around though he was dying to bolt. When he was just about to head off to the subway, there she was honking at him—this time the Impala was baby blue.

"Tom! Tom Find! I found you at last! Get in quick!" Lana shouted from the driver's seat, throwing her pale plump arms out, flicking away her mane of dark shining hair. A small woman, she seemed bigger because of her heavy shoulders and big breasts.

"Uh, thanks for coming," Thomas said, stuffing his suitcase in the back seat and jumping into the car.

"No problem," she answered, blowing him a kiss as she twisted the steering wheel covered in blue leather.

Thomas laid his package in his lap and readjusted the crease in his pants.

"Wha's up, bro?" Lana laughed, affecting po' nigger talk, a

habit that always irritated him. Without waiting for an answer, she spun out of the parking zone as if it were the fast lane of a highway. He watched her push the shiny chrome radio dials, searching the rock and roll stations for Wolfman Jack.

"Nice color, huh? Oh, that's a sour face. Did I say the wrong word? I should learn to shut my goddamn mouth. Why don't you just shut it for me, Tommy boy?"

"C'mon, Lana."

"C'mon, what, lover boy?" In and out she pushed the dials, jackknifing between stations. He forced himself not to show his irritation.

"I didn't get much sleep last night," he mumbled.

"Oh, poor baby," she said, reaching over and stroking his thigh. The collar of her wrinkled silk blouse with the Saks label was bundled up beneath a slightly soiled purple angora sweater. Lana relished dressing sloppily in expensive clothes, and loved getting them torn and soiled. Her careless extravagance used to amuse him, but not today. Now he was disgusted. What he wished most was that he'd never taken her Impala.

She skidded to a stop sign. They waited, the motor humming. Thomas reached over and straightened her collar. Quickly she put her ringed hand over his and held it tight.

"It's green," he said, pulling his hand away and pointing to the traffic light.

"I know how to drive," she shot back. Behind them drivers were honking loudly, repeatedly. Finally Lana pulled out and made a quick turn right, driving uptown.

"Isn't this a great car?" she called out.

"Yeah." Thomas ran his fingers over the new navy upholstery, the shiny customized dashboard, and the 8-track tape deck.

"I'm real sorry about the other car," he said.

"I'm glad it was stolen. Really. I never liked white anyway."

"Be serious for once, Lana, please."

She rummaged for her cigarettes in the clutter on the seat and, when she found the pack of Marlboroughs, pulled one out for him to light. He took out his BIC lighter and lit the cigarette.

"Thanks!" she puffed, giggling behind the smoke. "You're sexy as ever, Tom, even when you're tired. Oh, Tom, Tom's a killer with his black pants on—or off. I like them better off."

"What's been happening?" he asked nonchalantly, ignoring her teasing.

"Same old same old. Daddy was his usual difficult self over Xmas. Did I tell you he's moved out—or is it in—with his sixteen-year-old girlfriend from Sweden? Her name is Kala or Mala. I'm lousy at names. She's an exchange student, ten years younger than me! Mom's having a fit. She says his old girl friend was at least presentable. That's the one she caught him cheating with, you know, the secretary from Hartford World Headquarters, the insurance office where Daddy works. Oh, Tom, don't shake your nappy head. I know I told you this on the phone. Can you believe he actually made us all eat Christmas dinner with her!"

"Those things happen," he mumbled.

"Are you bummed, Tom? You ARE! What happened back there? I didn't think anything happened in Pittsburgh," she laughed, waving a ringed hand in the air.

"It wasn't easy, Lana. My family is poor. I told you already."

"Don't worry, hon. Things will pick up and you'll be rolling in cash. Everybody I know says you're going to be discovered some day."

"I can't wait till some day."

"Honey, you won't have to," she crooned. "You'll be able to send hundred dollar bills to Pittsburgh or wherever by the trunk-full before you know it. Even Walt Disney will be calling you—hey, did you hear he died around Christmas? Listen, why even I got a callback yesterday from the Riverside Theatre—they want me to play Violetta in an Off-Off-Broadway production of *Camille*!"

Thomas took a big breath and plunged in, "Lana, pull over. I need to talk to you."

"I'm so glad you called this morning," she continued as if she hadn't heard. But she moved to the right lane and slowed down a little. "I did have a visitor, Tom, if you could call the creep that." She looked over at him pointedly. "He wasn't a trick either. You know I don't do tricks, except for you, of course."

"Why would you?" he said, ignoring her empty provocation.

"Oh, Tom, my stash is all gone. My cupboard's empty."

"Get a life, Lana. You don't need that shit, you know that."

"Yeah, yeah. Well, my source has dried up, as you well know. Anyhow, this guy said he had the best shit and I invited him over to try it. I was afraid he'd never leave, but then you called! How opportune. I told him you were a wrestler and coming by in a half hour. You should have seen how fast he split."

They were passing brownstones on the narrow streets of the upper West Side, approaching Central Park. He watched for open spaces where they could park.

"I was afraid, you know, afraid we'd drift apart," she said.

"Awww, I told you I'd get in touch."

"Are we drifting, Tom? We are drifting, aren't we? Drifting, drifting, always drifting." Lana belted in her Broadway voice.

She screeched to a stop by a fire hydrant at the end of West 74th Street.

"Okay, what do you want to talk about?" she said, grinning.

Thomas unrolled the window and took a deep breath of the cool damp air. "I called you from the turnpike rest stop because I wanted to clear things up about the car."

Lana leaned over to caress him, but he stopped her hand.

"Oh, Tom, we've been over that already. I miss you. Why did you move out?"

"We've been over that too, Lana. But about the car . . ."

"Wait, hon," she stopped him. "I need a cigarette."

He helped her light another. She took a long, slow puff.

"What were we talking about? Oh, the car. Hey, no problem. Daddy didn't even squirm. He made a few phone calls and we drove down to the Impala dealership the next day. It's run by a friend of his. This baby here was in the showroom. How do you like it? I picked it myself. Baby blue. I like the color so much, better than that sickly white."

She flicked the burning cigarette out the window onto a patch of brown grass and looked at him provocatively, combing her fingers through her thick black curls with quick repetitive movements.

"Did anyone from the insurance company talk to your father? Any official?" he asked.

"Of course not. Daddy *is* the insurance company, remember."

"Yeah, right." Thomas' gut contracted.

"I did exactly as you told me. I parked my body next to the phone in our hallway all Christmas vacation and answered every call that came in. There's nothing to worry about."

Thomas drummed his fingers on the shiny dashboard.

"What phone calls?" he asked. "I thought there weren't any."

"Let's see, it was one of those nights I was waiting for a Gentleman Caller."

She looked at him with that particular mixture of sexual exuberance and coyness that used to fascinate him and make him want her. But now sex was the furthest thing from his mind.

"Tennessee Williams would approve of me. I made a good Rose, didn't I?" Lana held her head in mock reflection, affecting her disjointed performance as the young crippled sister in *The Glass Menagerie*, which ran a few seasons ago in Hoboken.

Thomas took a deep breath. "When was this?"

"Did I tell you I got an answering machine? They're the latest thing. You should get one, Thomas. I did it just so I didn't have to talk to that sicko inspector from someplace—let's see, can I remember?—oh, yes, Allegheny County."

"What inspector? You didn't tell me about an inspector."

"Some asshole. He asked the usual bullshit."

"What did he want?" Thomas asked quietly.

"Who was I? Who owned the car? Did I know a —John—a John Johnson? He's the guy who stole it, I guess. I don't know. How should I know? I don't care. Like I said, I don't even like white. Tom, don't look like that. I told him just what you told me to. Chill out, will you? Hey, fuckhead, I'm joking. But there's nothing to worry about, believe me."

"What did you say exactly, Lana? Try to remember."

"I left my car in the lot near the train station as I always do, and when I came back to pick it up, it was gone. GONE!" she answered in a singsong voice.

"I told you to say you parked it in the street," he said carefully.

"What's the difference if it was stolen in the street or in the lot or in Harrisburg?" her voice got higher, angry.

"They'll question the attendants," said Thomas.

"Who cares? They're Puerto-Ricans. Besides, the lot is coin-operated. Remember when I got my typewriter stolen and I only left the Impala—the other one!—overnight. Listen, I know what I'm doing! You should have heard me talking to the cops. You would have been proud of me."

"Cops? I thought you were talking to an inspector. What cops?"

"A cop called once—maybe twice. Was I ragged! 'Get the motherfucker who stole my daddy's car', I screamed—SCREAMED, Tom—into the phone. How many times do I have to tell you? Daddy doesn't care. He's loaded with insurance. He fuckin OWNs an insurance company! Don't be paranoid. That's your only failing. You're paranoid."

"I want to pay you back," he said.

"Are you kidding? Well, suit yourself. Pay Hartford Life

Insurance! Their address is in the phone book."

"Lana, think, that inspector—did you get his name?"

"Why?"

Thomas shrugged, "Maybe I want to call him. Give it to him straight."

"Oh, Tom, believe me, you don't want to deal with that asshole. And speaking of that, why am I all alone in Sutton Place while you're living in that rat hole on East Fourth Street? Admit it, Tom. You're too proud to take anything from a honky. If I'm not too proud to take this brand new car from Daddy, why should you begrudge me paying the rent?"

"I don't begrudge you. That's not the only reason, Lana, you know that," he growled.

"I love you too much," she crooned, affecting Ava Gardner in an old movie retrospective they saw once at a Union Square theater.

He was too tired to think up a clever reply. Lana snuggled against him, her voice turning soft and silky. "We do have good sex together, don't we, Tom?"

"We sure did, babe." He forced himself to be still, show nothing.

"C'mon, your place or mine?" she asked, nudging him. When he didn't respond, her voice got louder. "Okay, twist my arm. We'll go to mine. I don't have cockroaches, or as many."

Still he said nothing.

"Did I open my big mouth and say something stupid like I usually do? I'm just kidding, Tom. You aren't mad at me, are you?" Lana said, her voice shrinking small and mouse-like.

"No, I'm just tired." How much had she made up? As much as he had? What did she really know about the accident? It occurred to him that lying came easy now to both of them. She might know about his fake ID. Lana often went through his wallet after sex when he feigned sleep. How could he not have realized the cops would interrogate her? What about Joe? Irish? Thomas' head throbbed. She had to know something more than she let on.

Once Lana had disappeared for a week. When finally he brought himself to ask where she'd been, she said she'd gone somewhere "to-remain-nameless" to have an abortion. "It was yours," she cried. She couldn't bear to have it, not because she didn't want his baby, but because she did. It would just remind her of him, now and forever.

"We both know we'll never stay together, isn't that right, Tom?" She hadn't waited for his reply but went on about how she'd have to bring up the kid alone.

He'd argued with her, angry that she'd had an abortion without telling him. She was on the pill, wasn't she? "Of course," she insisted. It took him back to the time Georgina told him she was pregnant with Georgie G. Thomas made her promise not to have an abortion. They were illegal and too dangerous, he said, too easy to botch. He knew that from his momma and his sisters. Women died from them he told Georgina, and she believed him. But Lana had responded with ridicule to Thomas' objections. Even as they were arguing though, he admitted to himself he felt relieved she'd taken care of the problem herself.

But then, a few weeks later, he heard Lana talking with her mother on the phone about a vacation in the Bahamas that they had just returned from.

"When did you go to the Bahamas?" he asked her when she finally hung up.

"Oh, a few weeks ago. Before St. Patrick's Day. There was a parade on the islands—in honor of the Irish! Can you believe it?"

Thomas calculated. That was the week she said she'd had the abortion. Did she go to the Bahamas to have an abortion? People did go to the Caribbean for things that were illegal in the US. Or had that story been just another twisted path to lead him down and bind him tighter to her? He never knew, but he never let on, of course, never said a word. That was the best way to handle Lana.

"So things are looking up?" Thomas asked now, taking his arm away on the pretext of closing the window. Christ, he was getting rummy from lack of sleep. Plus he was hungry again.

"For everybody but me. I can't stand just sitting in this car and bull-shitting. Let's get stoned." Lana pulled a newly rolled jumbo joint out of her purse and put it to her lips, waiting for him to light it.

He clicked the lighter, holding it in front of her face even after the joint was lit. Lana took a big drag, sucking the smoke into her mouth and lungs.

"Oh, Tom Find!" she breathed out.

Several minutes passed while she took a few more tokes.

"Don't call me that," he said finally, taking the joint from her hand.

"What do you want me to call you?" Lana asked.

"Call me Dreamer," he said, staring at the bare trees in Central Park. He had hoped that the dope would relax him but he was not any more relaxed. Instead he felt trapped and confused. Ghosts were following him, he realized, and had been ever since he left Pittsburgh. I've got to think this out, he thought. I've got to get away and think this through.

"Okay, Thomas Dreamer. What's that?" she smirked, grabbing for the package on his lap.

"A photo album," said Thomas ignoring her hand on his genitals.

"Oh! What of?"

"Me."

"Pictures of you! Let me see," she cried, pulling at the brown paper.

"I'll show you." He stopped her hand even while pulling her closer. Hazel eyes sparkling with excitement, Lana opened her mouth wide and laughed. He could see her picture-perfect teeth gleaming between her red lips.

Thomas turned the plastic-covered pages while Lana snuggled in his arms. There were newspaper clippings, photographs, old letters, his high school diploma and birth certificate, even his honorable discharge from the Army. They were all marked with his given name, remnants of a life he'd left behind in that old beat-up suitcase in the shack behind Momma's house.

Most of the snapshots were from newspapers Momma had clipped and underlined. Thomas at ten, Chamber of Commerce winner, at twelve, Pittsburgh Eagle Scout, at fourteen, Homewood Junior High Varsity and Forensic Winner. At eighteen, he was runner-up Valedictorian, Quarterback, and King of the Prom at the predominantly all-black Schenley High. Carefully he folded and refolded the yellow moth-eaten, pencil-marked pages of the *East Liberty Gazette, Pittsburgh Press, Brushton Star,* and *Pittsburgh Courier.* Lana was delighted with the photos. She pointed out how he had the same smile then as now and he began to feel better.

He showed her all the programs from the shows he'd been in. Mostly he was just a little boy in the crowd, but the parts got bigger over the years. *Meet Me In Saint Louis. Our Town. Showboat. Raison in the Sun.* The lines he said, if any, the pauses, the costumes, the backstage politics, all this he could remember and now, sitting in her brand-new blue Impala getting more and more stoned, he repeated them for her as if he were auditioning. Thomas smiling. Thomas bowing. He could call up each roll, even the walk-on parts.

"Thomas, you're a scream. This is the most fun I've had in ages," Lana cried, wiping her eyes.

It amazed him that she found fascinating and loveable the child that used to be him, while to Thomas the boy was haunted and lost, covered in fear that swarmed like locusts.

When they had smoked the whole joint, Lana bought them two foot-long hot dogs with sauerkraut and relish and large Cokes from a vendor at the corner. After they finished eating, Lana took out the horse. When she showed him the drug paraphernalia, Thomas was dozing, eyes closed, drifting in a soft gray safe space.

"How about it?" she asked.

"Too dangerous to mind and body," he answered, shaking his head.

"Hey, I bought this from you," she reminded him.

"Lana, I quit that," he said quickly. "I don't do that shit no more."

"What! When did this happen?" she screeched, her hazel eyes narrowing, turning dark, the yellow glint in them disappearing.

"You've known that for a while," he growled.

"Maybe I should go into the business," she said. "Seeing as I can't count on you anymore."

He felt as if he were being blamed, but for what he couldn't figure out. He just knew he felt guilty for everything between them, and, far worse, he wanted her to understand.

"I saw what this shit did to my family—my People." Even as he was speaking, he was shocked at his words. Why was he telling her this? She'd only ridicule him. But he went on. "I had a kid when I was just a teenager—I know I told you this—well, his mother died right in front of his eyes. I thought it was her heart—I thought she died of a heart attack. That's what her daddy said, what everyone said. But no, it was an overdose. Believe me, Lana, you don't want to get involved in this line of business."

"It's just a little plaything. Another toy," she whined. But then she turned morose and put it all away, eager to leave.

They drove down West Side Drive, weaving in and out of the crowded lanes, sometimes driving slow, sometimes fast, while taxis and trucks darted out crazily around them. Thomas closed his eyes after Lana just missed a passing truck.

He jumped out of the car as soon as Lana pulled up to his building on East Fourth Street. Not wanting to see her face, or have her see his, Thomas reached in the back seat for his suitcase.

"I'll be in touch," he said.

"Do, Tom. You know how I love your touch. Next time we'll talk, really talk, I mean. None of this bullshit."

He lurched, feeling sick to his stomach. What did she mean? Lana had this uncanny way of reading his thoughts.

"I gotta go, Lana. I don't feel so hot." Holding the album and the suitcase, he scanned the street up and down from habit.

"On second thought, don't bother," she laughed.

"Don't bother—about what?"

In reply, she gunned the engine and drove away. Thomas watched her go. It surprised him how hurt he felt at her leave-taking. He shouldn't have shown her the album, he thought. He shouldn't have done that. Next time he called home, Thomas vowed to himself he'd make sure Momma burned that suitcase. He must get rid of everything.

New York

But it was even harder here than in Pittsburgh. The winter seemed to stay on and on. Wind blew the garbage falling out of the overstuffed cans on the Lower East Side, moving it from side to side of the narrow streets. Old snow lay crusted on top of abandoned cars and dumpsters. When Thomas wasn't out hustling up work or going to an occasional acting class, he sat inside his apartment listening hard for the phone to ring downstairs. His own phone had been disconnected while he was still in Pittsburgh, and now he had to use the pay phone in the run-down lobby one flight down smelling of urine, cigarette smoke, and mildew. He called Mel from the Negro Repertory Company and left a message—many messages—but neither Mel nor anyone else in the Company called back. He consoled himself that even if Mel didn't call, come spring, new shows would begin casting.

Thomas pasted pictures from his photo album to purple velveteen that hung from the wall to cover the dry rot from the leaking pipes running across his ceiling. Lana had filched the material from a *Richard II* production where she'd been on the crew. But the old photos weighed on him, looking flat and stale, so after a few weeks he took the pictures all down and put them in a stack on the radiator where they curled up from the heat and then fell behind it.

He wore the same shirt and pants for a week, leaving his good clothes hanging in the closet for the interview that never came. Maybe he should have joined Actors' Equity while he had the chance? Mel had asked him if he was in Equity when Thomas auditioned in Pittsburgh. He figured that was why Mel had offered him a gig at all—cause he wouldn't need to be paid as much as the other actors. But Thomas didn't want to spend the dough on dues when he had only the little spare change he kept in the pocket of his army jacket.

One night he called home from the pay phone. Georgie G answered. "Momma is out at the church," he said. "Carlotta is . . ."

"Listen, boy," Thomas stopped him. "It's you I want to talk to. How you been doing anyhow?"

"Fine," Georgie G said.

"Everything okay?"

"Yeah."

"Did you ever hear anything more about the trolley accident?"

"Naw."

"Yeah? Momma got all those damned clothes cleaned?"

"Naw, I did it," said Georgie G. "When you gonna send for me?"

"Send for you?" Thomas grinned. He could just see his son's sour expression. "What for would I do that?"

"To come to New York," Georgie G's voice broke with indignation.

Thomas laughed. "You crazy, boy. I don't want you here. There are firebomb attacks and snipers, gunfire every day. It ain't no place for a black boy. You stay with Momma where you safe. I want you to be alive, boy, when I finally make it here. Then I'll call for you. Not till then. For now, you stay away from trouble, know what I mean?"

"Sure I know what you mean, Dad."

Thomas' heart swelled with pride. Georgie G had called him "Dad."

"I'm sorry I haven't been much of a Dad to you."

"That's alright," Georgie G answered. "I know you're going to be a star someday."

"Yeah," Thomas sighed. "One of these days."

"Hey, Dad? Listen to this."

Over the crackling phone line, Thomas heard several bangs and then some guitar notes, halting, but on key, and even a few chords.

"I'm taking lessons at the Hill House now," said Georgie G.

"With that old broken down guitar Carlotta found?" asked Thomas.

"Yeah."

"I'm gonna buy you a new one, don't you worry none," said Thomas. And his heart felt lighter when he hung up.

* * *

One very long, very cold day in March just before another big assault of the Vietnam War started, he put in a call to the Pittsburgh Police Department. Affecting a southern accent, Thomas said he was a friend of Joe's.

"Joe who?" asked the dispatcher with a thick Pittsburgh accent.

"Joe, the cop."

"There are a lot of Joes," said the dispatcher.

"The one involved in the trolley accident over Christmas."

"Hey, what did you say your name was?"

But Thomas had already hung up.

* * *

His mailbox filled up with bills. Thomas marked everything "Address Unknown" and "Return to Sender" and put the mail back in the box. He felt a tiny sense of satisfaction when he saw the mailman take them away. He rarely ate out, settling for a steady diet of Campbell's soup, pasta and pancakes, the cheapest meals he could make. His stomach gnawed continually. He hadn't eaten well since he left Pittsburgh when Momma had cooked baked ham, pot roast, barbeque chicken, and even tomato pork chops just for him. How he missed her cooking! He even missed those Howard Johnson Specials he ate waiting for Annie to arrive.

He started writing a letter to her, though he didn't know her address. With his purple magic marker, his "signature" pen he called it jokingly, he began:

> Dearest Annie,
> I'm thinking of you in this hellhole of NYC. Something big's gonna happen to me here—I can feel it. But when? When? When! I can hear you telling me to be patient. I'm trying, love. But my rent's due. I don't want to talk about that. I want to talk about you, your tight little pussy. How I loved making love to you. I wanted you to be a virgin. Maybe I'm a romantic after all. When's your birthday? I want to do your astrology chart.

He wondered what Annie's father looked like. You could learn a lot about a person from her family. "Dad" she called him, just like Georgie G. Thomas remembered Annie's father's voice—a cultured voice, deep, but not heavy. He spoke in an uptight, formal, genteel way, drawing Thomas out to say more than he intended. It scared him how much he had wanted to impress the Man for those few seconds. But fear was only one way through life and he wouldn't let it stop him. Not ever. He would write Annie's father a letter.

> Dear Mr. Ryan,
> I apologize for not addressing you by your full name, but unfortunately I don't know it. I am a friend of Annie. She's a wonderful girl. You must be very proud of her. I hear you are a fan of Shakespeare. I am too.

Rereading it, he crossed out "girl" and wrote "woman." But that's all the further he got. Later he threw both letters out with the trash.

At night the wind howled above the sounds of his radio and the drone of the TV, shaking the high loft windows. The wind blew hardest through the cracks in the one large window facing the street. Garbage cans banged or rolled over against the iron railings of the fence around the abandoned lot below his window. Streetlights flickered here and there, and cars sped around the corner, shining their headlights at him.

From his second floor window, all the buildings were dirty, dark and heavy, like dungeons or ruins. Shit, and he owed the landlord four hundred in back rent.

Long emaciated cats slipped beneath the old cars that sat abandoned, slinking in and out between the garbage and the dirty slush. Small squat figures walked by on the pavement below, hurrying fast. Most were going to the Cuban church on the corner. He met a prostitute one day who took him out for coffee and told him she got twenty dollars for a blow job she gave the priest. Thomas didn't believe her, but the coffee was good and hot and sometimes when he was feeling lonely he thought about her. He wondered if the priest had worn his black cassock.

All the while he waited—for the wind to stop, for Mel to call. He heard the Actors Stage needed black male actors for a Civil War musical, a black *Gone with the Wind.* He'd seen the script a few drafts back at one of the actor's workshops he'd dropped in on. Remembering that poor-ass script, Thomas laughed with derision. There was talk of putting on *Great White Hope.* Yeah, Jack Johnson, now there was a part for him. He could go into training today. He'd done it before—wrestling, boxing. What was it the Harlem Theatre offered him once? It wasn't really an offer, but some woman, a producer—was it Dory or Rory?—was real interested in him. A real mover, and her husband too.

He was dead broke. Some days he felt like calling up his contact. But like he told Lana, he didn't deal any more.

Some days he just waited for spring. Finally the sun came out and Thomas opened the window to sit on the patch of sunlight on the fire escape. A thin orange cat slunk up the metal stairway toward him and crawled into his lap. It began to purr even before he touched it.

Today it was even sunnier and the cat was there when he opened the window, an orange fur ball asleep in the one patch of sun. He stroked it absentmindedly, and then fed it crackers and milk. When he went inside, the cat came too. It was so soft.

Whenever Thomas petted the cat, it arched its back and moved out of his reach. But if he waited, it came back. He started calling the cat, "Annie."

"Annie, I love your pussy."

One afternoon Thomas went shopping on 14th Street and made himself a rare meal of chuck roast and potatoes. How he savored the smell of the meat roasting in the tiny old oven while the cat played with the bits of brown, black and red paint that rubbed off the floor and sometimes stuck between Thomas' toes. Half-stoned from a toke or two of fine grass, he watched the animal grabbing for the chips of paint as if they were mice. Together they shared the roast.

He recalled the name of the casting agency that gave him the lead about *Great White Hope,* but held back calling them. He felt too low, lacking confidence he confided to the cat. It just purred louder. When his mood had changed for the better, he bounded down the rickety stairs to the lobby and called Westside Casting. The receptionist seemed to have forgotten his name but Thomas charmed her and she gave him the boss' direct number. He left a message.

He kept the radio on all the time. The Turtles. Bob Dylan. Elvis singing "In the Ghetto." Damn white boys stealing James Brown and the other black R&B music. Nevertheless, his feet danced on the floorboards to their tunes. Johnny Cash sang "Folsom Prison." Connie Stevens sang, "Who's Sorry Now." More Oldies but Goodies. Thomas shivered with something, not nostalgia, more like dread. The songs reminded him of the Army. He'd listened to these same songs over and over when he was stationed in Korea, desperate with boredom, looking for a way to pursue his acting dream. At least he'd gotten his time over with. He didn't need to worry about being drafted, sent to the killing fields of Vietnam. He knew what was going down over there. He'd heard way too much at the VA where he went periodically to get tested for VD. It was there he used to score his sweetest dope deals too. But no more. He was done with that.

At night, he perused astrology manuals. He made charts for every audition he went to, potentially important dates that he compared to his own birth chart, hoping for a sign of his luck changing, even though he didn't get called back. One lonely night he made a chart of December 21st, 1966, the night of the trolley accident, using red and blue and yellow pencils. He made another for the night he went to audition for the Negro Repertory Company and met Annie instead. Carefully and with great concentration, he matched aspects and analyzed the relationships of the planets.

His own astrological chart fascinated him and he looked at it for hours. He walked to the second-hand occult bookstore on Lower Broadway, holing up in the Astrology section on a small stool, consulting the experts. Feet folded under him, dark long hands sticking out of his heavy army sweater, Thomas pondered the circular charts and symbols calling to him, especially when he was stoned. What did it mean that he was born with Leo ascending on the horizon, a Sagittarian sun, and the moon in the sign of Cancer? He had a prominent Pluto rising too; this, he decided, was the key to his whole personality. He belonged in the underworld, the world of illusion between life and death, the world of the theater. Thinking of himself that way, it all made sense—even the drugs he'd dealt in the past. Maybe he was destined to rise out of the ashes of addiction into stardom? One thing he was thankful for —he hadn't seen Lana since she'd picked him up at the bus station.

He felt too antsy to stick around the bookstore very long. Back at home, he couldn't stand being still either. He had to move, had to leave. Something was just around the corner and he had to be there. Somebody was waiting for him, somebody he must see.

Thomas pulled on his boots, bunching his green cotton pants over the tops. Damn, there was a hole in the knee. He didn't have time to sew it now. Why hadn't he given those pants to Momma when she asked for them? In the little bathroom mirror he looked dark and forbidding to himself, humped like an owl or a vulture. But he liked the look and accentuated it with a scarf around his neck to better hide his face so that only his eyes and nose were visible. Next he rubbed hand lotion over his long hands. It depressed him that they looked like the hands of an old nigger. Shit, he could pass for Pappy Find. Taking a box of Saltines out of the kitchen cupboard, he stuffed some crackers in his mouth and put the rest in the pocket of his army jacket. Before he left, he poured some milk in a dish for the cat.

As Thomas ran down the crowded steps to the subway, he brushed against a Puerto Rican girl with her boyfriend. The girl cried out.

"Sorry," he mumbled.

"Fucker!" yelled the boyfriend, shoving Thomas against the wall.

The train to Brooklyn was full and he nearly fell over an old white lady reading the *New York Times*. "Sorry," he said again. Standing above her in the aisle, he scanned the headlines. Ten thousand hippies had rallied at a Be-In in San Francisco. Bras were burned along with banana skins. He wished the old lady would get to the theater section. His mind jumped from one thing to the next. He needed a job. Hell, if he left acting, he could get a job anywhere with his degree in Social Work. Nowadays there was a chance for a black man with a degree. That's what he had told Georgie G, trying to convince him to take his education seriously and stay in school. He hoped his son had listened, but now that he really considered it, why should Georgie G listen to him? He'd abandoned his own kid. Thomas felt a sharp stab of pain remembering Georgie G plucking that old guitar.

He had to get a job. He had to find Mel. In a frenzy, he got out of the subway at the next stop, running through the turnstile and up the steps into a narrow deserted street. The smell of rotten fish hung over the air. Pulling his coat tighter to keep out the cold, Thomas stood on the corner to check out the action, looking left and right down dark alleys. Where was he? Where was he going? He didn't know. The street was full of ancient crumbling warehouses, each one forbidding, boarded up. This wasn't where he wanted to be.

Thomas turned back, heading into the subway again.

East Village

His head buzzing from lack of sleep, Thomas hurried toward the all-night diner in the East Village. It was about ten in the morning. He had barely eaten or slept, having spent yesterday unsuccessfully hustling down a promoter for an all-black production of *Hello Dolly* he'd heard about. He'd stayed out most of last night with a Jamaican actress whose name he'd already forgotten.

Thomas pushed open the chrome door and sat down at the end of the counter. On impulse he ordered steak and eggs. Even as he relaxed, he felt panic arise. He shouldn't stop now or here, it warned him. He shouldn't rest. He had something important to do, but what was it? He was so damn tired.

If he half-shut his eyes, he could suspend himself and become anything. Imagine himself as a director. The camera pans from the eye of the waitress to show a whole sorry lot of customers like himself. A young black kid in white Levis rushes to the empty seat behind the pie display rack. The camera follows. Zoom in; pan to the right and to the left. Pause. A teenager like the one over there nervously swinging her foot in the booth eyes the kid. She's chewing her gum just like now. Maybe she'll hide me thinks the kid, sliding his hurt wrist deeper under his jacket. Cut to the bank teller's window three blocks away. A man in a brown suit lies crumpled behind the safe. No surprise, the kid gets caught. No, he couldn't get caught. There had to be a different ending. The kid had to survive. How? Thomas was deep in thought when the waitress brought his order.

"Tom Find! Ho! What do you say, Tom. Hey, brother, how's it going?"

Thomas put down his fork and turned to face Vern Law.

"Where yo been, Tom. Somebody say you headed for LA to try the movies."

"Naw, man, the movies ain't ready for me yet," Thomas said. He forked at the steak, cut a piece off with his knife and put it into his mouth, chewing mindfully.

"Tried to call you, man, but the cord been cut," said Vern.

"Uh-huh," chewed Thomas.

"I'll have the same thing he has," Vern told the waitress pointing to Thomas' plate.

He didn't trust Vern. He didn't trust most men, especially black men, because they rarely came through for him. They were all variations on Pappy Find. Vern and he had attended the same acting classes at the NYU Theatre Project. Several years ago they'd had a gig together, a dance and darky act Thomas wrote. A contemporary minstrel show, "A gut-wrenching, color-driven parody of white liberals in the Civil Rights Movement," the *Village Voice* had called it. He and Vern played the white guys. They'd had some success and had taken the show to Ocean Grove Playhouse, New Jersey that summer. Thomas had been working on bringing it to the Brooklyn schools, getting approval from the Board of Education, when Vern disappeared. Thomas had heard Vern was back on the hard stuff, then off and on methadone, and hadn't even tried to find him.

Now he struggled to pay attention. Vern was going on about a new show he'd been cast in, a remake of *Guys and Dolls* set in Harlem. The biggest bank on Wall Street was funding it, Vern said.

"What bank's that?" asked Thomas vacantly. He didn't believe a word of it.

"Uh, I forget. Chase, yeah. Chase."

"Now ain't that something," Thomas jived, slapping Vern on the back. He said he'd been very busy too. "Can you believe it, the Negro Rep is interested in signing me on!"

Now Vern slapped him on the back. "I thought that Mel was

too whip-assed to hire his own brothers anymore," he said.

"Shit, that ain't what he said to me," answered Thomas.

"Yeah, well, don't believe everything you hear. Hey, I heard they're casting Randall in *Slow Dance on the Killing Ground* uptown," said Vern. "Didn't you play that before? Maybe you should check it out—just in case that other part don't come through," he grinned.

Thomas nodded.

When the waitress came around again, Thomas ordered a piece of cherry pie and a refill of coffee. Then he had the last cut of the custard pie. Vern seemed to want to hang there all morning bullshitting, but Thomas had had enough. He got up and walked to the cash register. Vern's eyes widened when Thomas held out a hundred dollar bill and asked for change. It was the last, the very last of his cash, but he felt suddenly lucky. He just knew he was gonna score an acting job soon. Thomas took a toothpick from the plastic dispenser on the counter and stuck it in the side of his mouth.

"You in the money, ain't you?" said Vern when they were both out on the curb. He had a toothpick in the corner of his mouth too. "Lana's been keeping you in the green, I guess."

"I haven't seen her in weeks," Thomas said.

"That girl's something. All that dough. I hear she's been looking for me. I know you two been…" Vern's voice dwindled to a mumble.

"I moved out months ago. She's free to look you up or do anything else she wants," said Thomas. Hell, he didn't care and he wanted Vern to know it.

"Why's that?"

"She sucked me dry. I didn't feel like a man no more," Thomas answered, moving the toothpick from side to side in his mouth. He didn't know if that were true or not but hell, Vern could identify with it.

"Yeah, but you can't sneeze at her bread."

"Her money ain't mine," said Thomas.

"Know where I can get me some shit cheap?"

"You're talking to the wrong person," said Thomas stiffly.

"No offense, man. No crime in dreaming, huh? They don't lock up dreamers last I heard. Hey!" Vern interrupted himself, hailing a thin black woman in red pants and a fur jacket heading into the diner. "Hey, brown sugar!" She looked uncertainly across the street and then waved back.

"Hey, I remember you. You sure look good. What's your name, brown sugar?" Vern headed toward her. "You remember to check out Slow Dance," he called back to Thomas. "And hold onto them hundred dollar bills."

Thomas walked away fast, unseeing, toward the subway as a rush of panic overtook him. He quickly put it down, but he felt blind and confused and couldn't think why or what it meant. Strange that Vern should mention Randall in *Slow Dance on the Killing Ground.* That was one of his better roles. With these rumpled clothes and his bristling chin, he looked like the fugitive, Randall. Was it '64 or '65 when he was in that play? He remembered taking a bus to New Jersey all one winter and spring to rehearse. Busting his butt for two weekend shows at a church in West Orange. He could get his teeth into Randall though. Thomas swayed to and fro with the moving subway car remembering the part. He didn't even notice the girl with blond hair and beads across from him who smiled and gave him the peace sign. He wouldn't wait for Mel. He'd seek him out instead.

The building housing the Negro Repertory Company, formerly an old factory, covered an entire block of the Bowery. White blinds hung from the large square display windows in front. The word TEXTILES was painted above the big warehouse doors. The doors were opened when he arrived and he rushed right in. The lobby was empty. He went into the theater itself where there was a rehearsal going on. A short breathless girl with curly red hair came up to him whispering in a very soft voice that they were in the middle of a rehearsal of a brand new play, *No Place to Be Somebody*. "The author", she gasped, "is right down there in the front row."

"Where?" Thomas asked as they stood at the back. He looked around for Charles Gordone, who he had met when they both were waiters in midtown Manhattan, looking for acting jobs.

"There! Who are you here to see?" she whispered.

"Mel. He knows who I am. Tell him Thomas Dreamer is here."

Mel was not here today, the girl apologized. He was up on the Cape recuperating. "You know how he gets," she said confidentially.

"Yeah," Thomas said. He looked around for that other gay guy with the light hair, but couldn't find him.

"You're welcome to watch. I'd stay but I have to make some calls," she said. Was she coming on to him? He'd check that out later, but for now he just wanted to stay where he was. The girl left. Thomas edged forward, hunkering down in a second row aisle seat where he stayed until the rehearsal was over, almost six hours later. Never had he felt so good in his life. Luck was calling. This was the play for him. He'd leave Mel a message with the girl but, when he looked for her, she had disappeared. As he left the building, Thomas looked down and saw a twenty-dollar bill at the curb. Was this his lucky day or not?

He went to an A&P and bought wine, bread, rice and ground meat. At a corner produce stand, he picked up some onions, tomatoes, green bell peppers and oranges. The cat was waiting for him at the landing.

Setting down the groceries on the wooden table, he turned on his small radio to the FM progressive rock station. Carefully he hung up his blue-striped shirt and blue corduroy pants, putting on his jeans and white T-shirt. He browned the meat and onions in the pan. Steam filled up the tiny kitchen, clouding the dirty window above the stove. Thomas peeled an orange and ate it while the rice cooked, adding tomatoes to the ground meat and onions. He spooned the cooked mixture of meat and rice into the peppers and put them in the heated oven.

Waiting for his dinner to cook, he sat down at his small painted table studying the label on the wine bottle. "Napa Valley, California," he read. He'd always wanted to go to California. The label showed green hills and vineyards, white clouds, blue sky under a bright yellow sun. He imagined women wearing next to nothing, silk panties and no bras, laughing their beautiful smiles and driving the latest cars. He could imagine making love to them all day, working a paid acting gig at night, and smoking weed in between.

Visitors

He was staring at the TV screen, eating his dinner, when he heard noises. Putting down his plate, Thomas tiptoed down the hallway and peeked through the peephole in the door. He saw vague figures, dark faces. Puerto Ricans probably. Junkies? Were they here to see him, thinking he had some shit to sell? Best be still, he told himself, slinking back down the hall. He turned off the TV and got under the covers. Thomas put the blankets over his head but the noise didn't go away. It just became louder.

When he walked back down the hall, he recognized the voices. The door burst open before he could unlock the chain.

"Hey! What's happening?"

"Let us in!" Lana screeched, tottering on spike heels. She was wearing a black fur coat, black dress and black felt hat. A sparkling necklace glimmered between her pale full breasts.

"How'd you get the key?" he asked as he unbolted the chain.

"Honey, I didn't get the key. I have the key. I always have the key!"

"How's it going?" Thomas said, stepping aside to let Vern in. He had one arm around Lana and the other around the woman from the diner. Vern wore a black leather jacket over a white silk shirt, and tight black pants. He had on Italian boots with cleats on the pointed toes that made a brittle click click sound when he walked.

"I happen to meet up with this here lady and she insisted we drop by," Vern said.

Lana lurched by them. "I couldn't stay away," she gushed. She reached forward, pressing her bright red mouth against Thomas' cheek.

"And this here's Ruth," Vern said, nodding to the black woman behind him. Thomas stepped back to look at the tall, thin, dark rail of a woman in a red dress.

"You remind me of somebody," he said, locking the door.

Ruth gave him a cold stare. "Who might that be?" she said, as if it were the last thing she wanted to know.

"We're home! I'll just lay me down and go to sleep," giggled Lana, stumbling ahead into the room. Thomas watched her list from side to side.

"No, you don't!" Vern shouted, grabbing for Lana. But before he could stop her fall, she slid down to the floor.

"Aww, girl, pull yourself together," Vern said as Ruth stomped past them.

"Shit," he said, looking to Thomas for help. "She's wasted."

"He pushed me," Lana whined, holding out her arms to Thomas.

Her arms around his neck, he got hold of her to pull her up, but then she let go. Her head swung backwards and hit the wall, making a loud thump. She gave a cry.

Thomas and Vern picked her up again and carried her into the room, laying her on his unmade bed. Ruth sat in his one good chair, swinging her crossed legs.

"Oooo," Lana whispered, staring up at Thomas through the plastic beads of his curtain. Flinging out her arm, she ran her fingers through the strands of swinging beads. Her necklace gleamed like diamonds around her pale neck.

"What are you on?" he asked, leaning over to check her arms for needle marks.

"You're hurting me," she whimpered.

"Sorry. Pretty rhinestones," he said, reaching for her necklace.

"Not rhinestones, diamonds," she corrected him.

"Oh, yeah? Nice." But he didn't believe her.

"Tom, will you get me a cigarette?" she said in a whispery

voice. He stood up, looking for her purse. He handed her the red and white pack of Marlboroughs.

"Light it for me." From under her black hat, Lana gave him a look both provocative and blank. Thomas lit her cigarette.

"Hey!" Ruth said from across the room, stretching out her long dark legs in the silky hose. "I thought you told me this was going to be a swanky place in the East Village. This is just a dump."

"Shut up!" said Vern, staring at the TV. He turned up the volume.

Lana reached up from the bed and caressed Thomas' arm with the hand that held the burning cigarette. "Vern said you might have some, Tom. I said I didn't think so, but then what do I know."

"Vern's crazy. Is that why you came? "

"Hey, man, no offense, see?" Vern turned toward them. "We were just cruising. I thought maybe you could help us out. If you get what I mean."

"You are talking to the wrong person. I am outta that line of work, I told you that before," Thomas said angrily, looking hard at Lana. But she didn't notice because she was pulling herself up from his mattress. She stumbled to the window. "Oh, look, a kitten!" she cried, pointing to the fire escape where the cat lay curled up in the pale sunlight. At the sound of her voice, it raised its head and meowed.

"Oh, how cute," Lana exclaimed.

The cat came to the window and meowed frantically to get in. But Lana appeared to have forgotten about it and was bending down to fix her stockings. Her nylons caught in her nails and two runs appeared, one on each leg. When she noticed Thomas looking, she wet her fingers, tracing the rips slowly all the way up to her fleshy ripe thighs, one at a time. He saw her black lace panties underneath her dress. Smiling innocently, Lana stood up.

"Tom, the least you could do is offer us a joint," she said.

He took out his tray of papers and grass in a neat plastic bag.

"I only got enough for one or two joints," he said. The cat was still meowing.

"How do you shut it up?" Ruth asked.

"Cat food," he grinned at her. "I keep Annie's cat food in the kitchen."

"Annie?" Ruth said, rolling her eyes.

"Yeah, Annie the pussy." He gave Vern the tray.

"I'll get it," Ruth snapped, jumping up.

"Next to the stove," Thomas told her.

Lana took Ruth's chair and motioned to Vern to give her the tray. Reluctantly he handed it over, watching as she rolled a large doobie.

When Ruth came back with a dish of cat food, Thomas opened the window and put it on the fire escape. Ruth and he watched the cat devour it.

"So you from Pittsburgh?" she asked.

"What about Pittsburgh?"

"I heard you was from Pittsburgh."

"Who told you that?" Thomas mumbled.

"Who do you think?" Lana interjected behind them. "Or were all those photos you showed me from somewhere else?"

"Did you go to Larimer School in Homewood?" asked Ruth.

Shaking his head no, Thomas sat down heavily on the mattress. He knew who Ruth reminded him of now. Down to the red dress, she was Georgina all over again. The same childlike bravura, the hard pose of anger and indignation. The same resignation in her pinched face, mouth shut tight with resentment. Her eyes out of kilter, her too thin body. Everything shouting she was a victim, though she'd be damned if she was going to take it lying down. Thomas shivered.

"I had the pick of anyone at Larimer," Ruth said. "I would have had at Fifth Avenue High too, if I hadn't got knocked up. Hey!" Ruth pointed to a tiny scar over Thomas' eye.

"Where'd you get that?" she asked.

Thomas looked away, out the window.

"What?" Lana looked up from licking the paper around the fat joint she had made. He watched her light it.

"Hey, I'm talking to you, nigger!" said Ruth.

"Didn't I tell you to behave, girl?" Vern said. He did a half-dance in Lana's direction, tapping his feet. When she ignored him, he stepped over to Ruth, making an attempt to slide his hands over her breasts, but she pushed him away.

"All I asked is where he got that there scar!" said Ruth.

"A preacher pushed me out a window," said Thomas.

"Damn," commented Vern. Lana barked a laugh.

"Did you know a girl called Georgina?" Thomas asked.

"Georgina don't sound familiar. What's her last name?"

Taking a puff of the joint, Lana asked, "Is she one of your little chickies?"

"She been under ground for a long time," Thomas growled. "Georgina Beemes' long dead. Her father was pastor of the First Time Evangelical Church, Pastor Leroy Beemes."

"That the pastor pushed you out the window?" Ruth asked.

Thomas stood. He had had enough. "Anybody want coffee or tea?" he asked. Ruth followed him into the kitchen, where he put on some water to boil.

"I'd like to ditch them both," she said. "Vern's crazy if he expects me to hang with her."

"Uh-huh." Thomas busied himself cleaning the stovetop.

"I remember who you remind me of now," he said. "Georgina. She was the mother of my son."

"That so?"

"Yeah."

"You still in love with her, a dead woman?"

"Nah," he answered.

He remembered how he took Georgina in the back seat of an

abandoned car perched on the Hill. It was fall or maybe spring. He was twenty, back on leave, and she was fourteen. They met in the car every afternoon after her school was out. Thomas was sitting next to her in the broken-down seat holding her hand when she told him she was pregnant. She was proud, tall and beautiful, with small breasts and large hips. She didn't care who knew. She had plans. Even when the Pastor threw her out, she didn't seem to care. She was going back to high school after their baby was born she said. She wanted to be a hairdresser or a nurse.

"I love you," he had whispered in her ear.

"You're the only one, Tom," Georgina had answered in her tiny little girl's voice. "I fool around with the others, but you are the only one."

The Pastor came after him, running through Momma's house, up the steps. Attempting to duck the steel-hard hand, Thomas fell hard against a bedroom window. The Pastor pushed him and he fell through, falling two floors, puncturing his left eye. When Momma got him to Emergency at Pittsburgh Hospital, they told her not to expect Thomas to be able to see again out of that eye. But it had healed, and he could see, though even now he favored the right.

"What's the matter with you, girl?" Vern appeared in the kitchen with the remains of the joint that he offered to them.

"No, thanks," said Thomas.

"I got the curse," Ruth said, refusing the dope too. "Let me be."

From the other room, Lana was belting her own version of a pop song. "Bad girl, you're outta your mind," she sang along with the radio.

When the song was over, she joined them in the crowded kitchen.

"I'm horny," she said.

Ruth gave Thomas a dispirited look. "They're all the same, know what I mean?"

"What's that supposed to mean, bitch?" Lana replied.

"Lana doesn't know any better," said Thomas, and wondered why he was defending her.

"Like hell she don't," Ruth answered.

"Like hell I don't," said Lana, stomping out. Vern followed her, banging his cleats on the bare floor.

Ruth was right. Lana did know better. He was the one who didn't know any better. Like when Georgina told him she was too young to marry, even though he begged her to. Momma hadn't wanted him to either. They were too young, she said, and she didn't like Georgina much, even if she were the pastor's daughter. Later on, after he got out of the Army, Georgina changed her mind. But he couldn't marry a drug addict and she went off to Cincinnati, leaving Georgie G still in diapers. Momma said she'd take him. When Georgina tried to get her son back, Momma threatened to have the social worker from the county testify. All this Thomas learned from letters Carlotta wrote him. Anyone could see Georgina was killing herself, she wrote. The Pastor insisted Georgina was consumed by the devil. He never did change his mind, even at her funeral.

There was something going on in the other room. He heard Lana shouting angrily, Vern yelling back. Thomas began to wash the cups and noticed Ruth watching him. She laughed, more a bark than a laugh.

"What's the matter?" he asked.

"None of the dudes I knew did the dishes. And you from Pittsburgh too. Isn't that a scream? Oww." She leaned against the counter. "My insides are all fucked up from when I had the baby. How'd you like to get your insides fucked up for good?" She looked at him accusingly the way Georgina had.

"I wouldn't," he answered.

Thomas would come home on leave and before he could put down his suitcase, Georgina would be nagging and crying at him.

He told Momma not to let her know when he was coming home. But sooner or later there'd be Georgina strolling on down Homewood Avenue with her red dress on. "Redbreast," he called her. "Ain't you noticed the color of my skin?" she asked him once. Sometimes he stayed with her. He remembered the last time—she was living in a room in the abandoned Strip District then, facing out on a dirty dilapidated wharf on the Monongahela River. He'd held her out of pity. She was so wasted. When he got the telegram that she died, he was on R&R in Honolulu. There was nothing to go back to. He didn't even come home for the funeral.

Ruth was talking about how she was planning a new life once she got a job with the postal department. She'd already taken the test. It was just a matter of time.

Lana appeared in the kitchen doorway, wobbling in her high heels. "It's no damn use," she said to no one in particular. The left side of her face was red, smarting.

"Shut up," Vern called from the other room.

"Did Vern do that?" Thomas said, pointing to her face.

Lana sidled up to him. "You wouldn't hit me, would you, Thomas? You feel sorry for me, don't you?"

"Ain't nobody can help you until you help yourself," said Ruth.

"Who's asking you?" snapped Lana taking out her pocket mirror from her purse and peering at her bruised face. "I'll make him pay," she said. She glanced at Ruth. "You have nice skin. I hate the way my white skin shows every little blotch and wrinkle. If I had your color skin, nobody would know anything happened."

"When I was twelve, the boys called me brown sugar. Still do," said Ruth.

"Brown sugar," Lana repeated. She pulled out a cigarette from her purse and held it out for Thomas to light. "Don't misunderstand me. I take care of my skin. I take care of everything. Which reminds me, Tom, the insurance problem is all fixed. You know, that accident. I cleared things up. Well, almost.

There's one itty bitty little problem." Looking at Thomas holding out the BIC with its tiny flame, Lana stopped herself. "Oh, sorry, I'm not supposed to talk about it. I forgot."

She put down her coffee cup, still full, and took a long puff.

"Hey, I need me some white sugar, no offense," Lana said, nodding in Ruth's direction. Turning, she tripped on her heel. "We gotta go find some."

Thomas grabbed her hand to steady her. "Don't do this," he said, looking into her unfocused eyes.

She stamped her foot and marched into the hallway. Thomas followed.

"What's up?" asked Vern, coming toward them.

"Listen to me!" said Thomas. "I don't deal and I don't sell. Lana, I told you that before and now I'm telling anyone else who cares to listen."

"Hey, we're cool. We're splitting," said Vern. "Could you lend us a bill or two—till Lana here gets her allowance?"

Thomas reached into his pocket and brought out the twenty.

Vern took it. Lana dusted off her purse.

"I think I'll buy gold shoes to go with this purse," she said in a faint voice. "Do you like gold shoes?" she asked Ruth. Ruth didn't bother to answer.

"Come on, girls. Don't bother the man," Vern growled. "He's into bigger things these days. Got no time for his friends no more."

"I think I'll stay here," said Ruth, looking into the kitchen cabinets.

"You come on, girl!" ordered Vern.

"Let her stay!" said Lana. "Who the hell cares what she does?" Unchaining the lock, she opened the door and pulled Vern out into the hall, slamming the door loudly behind them.

Thomas watched Ruth opening and closing the kitchen cabinets.

"Don't look at me," she said.

Thomas went back to the living room. From the window, he watched Lana and Vern step over the broken walkway into the street below. They turned the corner and disappeared. What did Lana mean she had cleared things up except for one little problem? His head hurt.

He turned to see Ruth watching him. "Thanks for letting me stay. I just want to wait here awhile till I know they are good and gone," she said.

Thomas nodded.

"How'd you get messed up with that sorry girl anyway?" she asked.

"It's a long story I don't wanna think about now," he told her.

Ruth sat down heavily in the chair. "I know what you mean."

"So you have a child?" he asked.

"I didn't get to raise him."

"Your mother take him?" he asked.

"Yeah, for awhile. He died in a fire at six months. They were burning candles, cause the electricity been turned off. One candle caught the house on fire." Ruth spoke quietly.

"I'm sorry," he said.

"You have any pictures?" she asked.

Thomas took out the snapshot of Georgie G in his wallet and showed it to her.

"Hey, he's something," said Ruth.

"He gave me this picture at Christmas," he told her.

"He looks like a real good kid." Ruth smiled. "I like you," she said. "But I'm not hitting on you, understand?"

"Yeah, I understand. I'm not hitting on you either."

He took her phone number, though he doubted he'd call.

After she left, Thomas lay down on his bed and stared at the ceiling. Flat on his back, his head didn't hurt so much. What did Lana mean about an "itty bitty little problem"? He had to get away from her, find a place where she didn't have a key. But how? He needed money for a deposit, money for rent. Sighing, Thomas put his hands behind his head, willing himself to relax. He felt something small and sharp. Turning over, he pulled out Lana's necklace hidden in the folds of his bedspread. He held it to the light. The stones sparkled like rainbows. It must have fallen off her neck. They spoke to him. "Take me," they said.

He took the necklace to a pawnshop in Greenwich Village. The owner was an Iranian with a black mustache who Thomas had dealt with before. The Iranian offered him $50 but Thomas held out. The man offered $200, then $500 and $700. Thomas realized Lana had been right; it wasn't rhinestones, but diamonds. "You won't get a better deal," the pawnshop owner told him. "If you take it anywhere else, they'll do a search and arrest you for stealing it." Thomas left the shop with a thousand in cash.

With the money from Lana's necklace, he rented another place —a one-room flat—on Houston Street. It had movie star posters all over the walls. Thomas moved his belongings furtively out of his old place at night. When it was totally empty, he walked through it one last time, the cat meowing at his feet. "I can't take you with me," he said, but he felt bad leaving it behind. He made sure to leave the window open, so it could go in and out and down the fire escape.

Even though he liked his new pad, he was hit by an attack of loneliness. Still it was quiet here and full of light. He unpacked, pulling out the old photo album full of empty pages. He realized his photos were missing and remembered he'd thrown them somewhere. So one night he went back to his old place. He was able to use his key to get in. The place was empty, dark, but he found his photos behind the heater where they'd curled up. The window was closed now but the cat was still there on the fire escape.

"Meow, meow," it cried, scratching frantically at the window. Thomas opened it a crack. "Hush, stop, your crying. Hush, Annie," he whispered as it rubbed against his leg. "I don't have nothing for you." The cat wouldn't stop purring and finally he swooped it up and put it beneath his coat. Holding the photos, he left with the cat through the front door.

* * *

Finally Mel Manning agreed to meet with him. The night before Thomas stayed up studying the plays the Negro Repertory Company had slated for production this coming season.

The spring morning was warm and gray and misty from a soft rain. He pressed his corduroy pants and long-sleeved blue-striped shirt with his new iron, put on his leather vest, and rode crosstown on the IRT.

Just as he remembered, Mel was impressive, deep-voiced and huge. "This is a new one for me," Thomas said, taking the director's huge hand.

"What is?" Mel looked at him suspiciously.

"Getting a job from a Negro," said Thomas, straight-faced.

Mel laughed. "Hey brother, we're seated at the table now." Thomas saw he had made an impression, but what pleased him even more was that Mel had let the part about getting the job go by. Did that mean he was going to get an offer?

"Refresh my memory, Tom—is it?"

"Thomas Dreamer."

Mel nodded as if he recalled the name, but Thomas hadn't been Dreamer in Pittsburgh, hadn't been anybody.

They stood alone in the dark anteroom. Mel puffed away on what Thomas would come to learn was one of his innumerable cigarettes. Much heavier and taller than Thomas, he was bearded now and wore a long black coat.

"Where did we meet? Was it Detroit? Some pissass theater in the Midwest?" asked Mel laconically.

"Pittsburgh," Thomas told him, ignoring the bad feeling that came up as he realized he had made no impression on the man.

But Mel was nodding his head. Now it came back to him, he said, mentioning a certain pale white girl Thomas had trailing him the day of the audition.

"Oh, you must mean Annie," Thomas said, hiding his surprise. "She's just…someone I met."

"Ah, a groupie," Mel grinned. "A white groupie."

Thomas grinned back, though it made him a little sick to consider Annie that way.

Mel flicked his ashes into the ancient brass spittoon in the hallway. "Come," he said, leading Thomas into the theater itself. They stood at the back for fifteen minutes or so watching a rehearsal of a play Thomas didn't recognize. His hands in his pockets, Thomas made and remade a fist over and over again. Finally Mel motioned him into a tiny office hidden beneath some stairs.

"So what's next?" Thomas asked.

"Next?"

"For me? What do you have for me?" Thomas said.

Mel mumbled something about not having anymore Shakespeare in the works for the season.

"What about that play by Charles Gordone?" Thomas pressed.

"That's a work in progress, but yes," Mel admitted, adding they were doing a read-through of it tonight. He seemed surprised when Thomas pulled the script out of his pocket and said he'd been studying several of the parts.

"Let's hear you then," said Mel, sitting down in one of two cheap folding chairs with "Director" painted on the back.

Thomas opened to a random page.

"You read Johnny," said Mel. "I'll play the brother."

Thomas stuttered a little, which infuriated him, and broke the rhythm they fell into naturally once or twice, but overall he was in control, moving all over that tiny office as if it were a large stage.

The bad-assed nigger jive, the barroom bantering, the violence, the distorted family, Momma overseeing too many children old beyond their years with her bitter loving eye, all he took for granted growing up—the lies, the humor, the raucous parody of meanness, the loud in-your-face bravado and the tenderness beneath the constant threat of violence. It was all here. He played it just like he was back home.

When he finished, Thomas threw himself down on the other Director's chair. He was shivering and sweating at the same time, but he felt exhilarated.

"So when do I start?" he asked, breaking the silence.

Mel slowly lit a cigarette. "Who said anything about starting?"

"You did," answered Thomas. "Back in Pittsburgh. You offered me a job. I'm here to collect. C'mon man, you know I'm good."

"Maybe. But how about the white ladies in the front row? Will they know you're so damn good?"

"They will," said Thomas with assurance.

Mel took a long puff and flicked the ash against the desk in front of him covered with papers and books.

"It's just a bit part," Mel said, pointing to the scene from the script. "You don't even come on until the second act."

"When do I start?" asked Thomas, looking away to hide his excitement.

"I got all my regulars to take of," Mel said, putting his hands in the pockets of his voluminous trench coat. "We aren't union either. I can't touch you if you belong to Equity."

"I'm not Equity, not no more," said Thomas.

"Well, go on out and tell Mandy to sign you up," boomed Mel.

"Have I met Mandy?" asked Thomas.

"My assistant. The one with the frizzy red hair. You'll find her down the hall," Mel smiled, motioning. Standing up, Thomas put his hand out, but Mel didn't take it.

"Tuesday at 4PM sharp. Rehearsals run to 11, " he called out as Thomas hurried down the hall without looking back.

* * *

Rubbing his hands and flinging his arms up in the air as if he were master chef at the Ritz-Carlton, he poured oil in a frying pan and then dusted off the chicken wings with flour and garlic salt. He felt like dancing and now and then he did a little, a two-step shuffle back and forth on his kitchen floor. He hadn't even taken off his good clothes to keep them clean for the next audition. Switching on the radio to the R&B station, he sang along with Sam Cooke in a deep tuneful baritone as he set the chicken pieces in the pan. The aroma of chicken frying filled the kitchen. He thought of Momma shuttling between the table and the stove, turning the chicken backs as they talked. The two of them, mother and son, her firstborn. How she went on about one thing or the other, alternately praising and scolding him till he'd give up trying to defend himself and just settle down to eat. He thought of Georgie G too and promised himself he'd send him money for a new guitar when he got his first paycheck. He wanted his boy to have everything.

Thomas spooned the cut up tomatoes and onions over the chicken, added a few handfuls of rice, and put the lid on the skillet. His place felt different now, better. When he was finished eating, he cleaned up the dishes, happy and satisfied with himself. If he hadn't been so tired, he might have gone out to that party Mandy, Mel's assistant, had invited him to at her pad. He could meet a lot of the actors she said. But once he turned on the TV and lay down, Thomas felt too tired and contented to consider going anywhere tonight.

He was dozing off when he heard what sounded like a tentative knock. There it was again. Someone was right outside. He froze. But nobody knew he lived here! He pulled himself up off the bed, eyes darting around. Whoever it was would realize someone was home. The light gave him away. The smells. The TV.

Damn. He held his breath.

Now there was silence. Now there was another knock. It wasn't Lana. She would be yelling his name by now. Vern too would be swearing and ranting. A junkie would make more noise, or have passed out already. The cops, hell, they would just barge right in, knocking down the door.

He'd better check. Thomas stood up, straightened his clothes, and tiptoed toward the door. He peered through the peephole, then slowly unlocked the deadbolts and slipped off the chain.

"My god, girl, what are you doing here?"

A scarf hiding her long blond hair, Annie looked like a refugee, a small cornered animal. Wrapped in a beige trench coat, she held her purse. Her face was peaked and drawn and at her feet a suitcase and a violin.

Then her eyes met his and moved beyond them to the room within. "Can I come inside?" she asked.

Thomas opened the door wide.

Flight Ticket

After Dad bought her flight ticket, Annie made a list of everything she might need, following it assiduously and with such deliberation, as if her life depended on it. Her clothes had to be just right. She packed her new gray angora mini skirt and matching vest to wear to the audition with a white silk blouse, one good black sheath dress, a black turtleneck, her pink straw hat, bell bottom jeans, a pink T-shirt, three pairs of underpants—rayon, so they could be washed and dried quickly, a black bra and a white one, pajamas and her trench coat. Her music for the audition, the Bach *G Minor Sonata*, along with the Sibelius and the Bartok, in case they wanted to hear more. Her violin of course.

Annie was as meticulous in her deceit as in her packing. She told Mother and Dad she was going to stay at the 92nd Street YMCA for a few nights to see New York before coming back home, but of course she had other plans.

"I don't want you going to that horrible place," Mother had cried the night before she left. "You're too young. You don't know what you are doing. Anything could happen. Tell her, Jim. I can't tell her anything. Maybe she'll listen to you." Mother sat in the dining room chair and held her shaking hands while Dad paced back and forth.

"What's the world coming to? What children do this to their parents willy-nilly without so much as the slightest consideration," he said. As he spoke, he took his hands out of his waistband, making wide motions with his arms in his white long-sleeved shirt, snapping his fingers and grimacing. Sensing excitement, Lucky came out from behind the chair and wagged her tail at him.

Early next morning, Annie went into Melinda's room. Her

sister stood in front of her mirror, styling her hair with hair gel.

"I'm going to New York for my audition today."

"Yeah?" Melinda flipped her bangs back with her brush.

"Remember Thomas?"

"Who?" She flipped them forward, a frown on her face.

"Thomas! I told you, Melinda," Annie said, a little offended that her sister hadn't remembered.

"Oh, yeah, the black actor. What about him?"

"I know where he lives. I'm going to look him up."

"You are!" Melinda looked at her with a mixture of shock, disapproval, and admiration. "Are you going to tell that in Confession?" she added.

"Never!"

Melinda giggled. Annie's eyes shone with excitement as she locked arms with her sister and together they ran down the stairs.

* * *

"I hope you're not planning to see that Negro actor while you're in New York," said Dad beside her. He had taken off work to drive her to the airport.

"Dad!" Annie said, horrified to have her father bring up Thomas.

"Good. That's not the way to go, Annie, you know that."

Annie held her breath but he didn't ask any more questions. She began to relax as he relayed newspaper reports of the New York weather in great and boring detail. She listened from far away, nodding and blowing a kiss goodbye as she got out of the car with her suitcase and violin.

"Have a good trip!" said Dad. "Good luck!" She waved as he drove off.

Yet standing at the boarding gate, Annie wished Dad had parked and seen her off like the other well-wishers around her. But once the plane took off, she forgot everything in her enchantment of the flight itself. Her first plane trip, she was mesmerized by the clouds, the view, and the ease of flying. After landing at La Guardia, she took the airport bus to Penn Station. Lights from nudie shows blinked on and off as she stepped off the bus. Cardboard breasts hung from buildings on the opposite side of Seventh Avenue, looking like monsters in a fairy tale she wouldn't ever read. Now her mind flew anywhere it wanted, as when she went whipping around on the red blinking Tilt-a-Whirl at Kennywood Park overlooking the Monongahela River. Her family had come to New York City once when she was twelve. Dad and she had walked from the Empire State Building to Times Square. Then they went on the subway, joining Mother and Melinda on the Staten Island Ferry to the Statue of Liberty.

She felt so brave to have come alone! Oh, she was bursting with longing and expectation! Yes, she felt sorry for the lies she had told her parents, and guilty about accepting the plane ticket Dad bought her, but still she was here.

Annie found her way to the subway heading for Columbus Circle where the Julliard School of Music was located. Back up on the street, she assessed her reflection in the huge shining windows of Lincoln Center, adjusting her pink felt hat. Slap slap went her high-heeled shoes against the broken slats of the concrete. Annie, you invincible doll, said her shoes.

With more than enough time to spare, she made it to her 3PM audition. She had been too excited by the trip to feel nervous and knew she was going to do well today.

* * *

Afterwards Annie quickly forgot about the audition, her real attention elsewhere. Dragging her blue suitcase, she went down into the IRT, paid for several tokens, and put them in the slot. The metal turnstiles clicked open and then shut behind her as she walked over to the subway map on the filthy wall to search for the subways going Downtown to the Lower East Side.

Once on the platform, she swung her long legs, walking back

and forth, smiling at herself in the small dirty mirror on top of a Dentine gum vending machine. Deebee deebee do do do. Deebee Deebee do do do. A short man leaned against the dirty tile reading the *Daily News*. The headlines said, "Girl Murdered in Bank Line." Behind him, two teenage boys sat sullenly on a bench, acne curling over their cheeks in waves. They tried to catch her eye, but she looked into the Dentine mirror instead.

All of her life growing up in Pittsburgh had receded into a gray horizon, like the fluffy indistinct clouds she saw from the plane today. She was not about to let her parents break her down—not in Pittsburgh, and not in New York. Yet things were precarious she realized, as if she were balancing on a tightrope above the center ring of the Ringling Brothers Barnum and Bailey Circus. How to concentrate on staying aloft and still applaud from the ringside seat—if only she had an audience to believe in her! Silly. Clutching her purse, suitcase and violin, Annie made a face in the chewing gum mirror and then giggled at her reflection. The boys, mistaking her look, hissed, "How much you got in that tight little purse, miss?"

Suddenly her face looked neither fey nor appealing. Instead she saw someone sad and broken, a face similar to her mother's.

"Mother, don't grieve over me. I'm doing fine. I'm learning about life. I have to, don't I?" she thought.

In the lull of waiting, while the crowd streamed through the turnstile, Annie promised herself that from now on she would never be so attached that the leaving would hurt. Nobody would ever cry when she said goodbye. She would make it easy for them the way it had not been easy for her. Everyone else was so locked in, frozen in such commonplace unhappiness. But she would live her life differently. She would be free. Why, look how different she felt right now. Like Alice in Wonderland, she had descended underground. But Alice was merely dreaming in the pages of a book while she was already underneath the streets of New York!

Clutching her purse, Annie dragged her belongings to the other side of the platform to avoid the boys. Peering anxiously at the oncoming trains, she searched for the Downtown Express. A rancid man in a baseball cap pushed in front of her. Above her the light bulbs shone greasy and brown in wire cages.

The subway train approached, a dark and dirty metal snake with one lighted eye that screeched to a halt just beyond her. Annie entered a door farthest away from the two boys. It was hot and crowded inside. She held onto the bar, lulled by the jerking twist of the cars, and closed her eyes. The image of the rancid man in the baseball cap to encourage her, she pushed her way out of the train a few stops later.

It was drizzling when Annie came out from underground. Her hair stuck to her neck as she walked, high heels clicking. Hundreds of pigeons pecking beneath benches for litter and garbage flew up overhead when she passed by.

Everywhere there were crowds. Stylish women in mini or maxi skirts and white boots, their long hair straight, parted in the middle and hanging over their eyes. Men in floral shirts and skinny low-slung bellbottoms with long hair too. They pushed against her with stiff and vacant faces, carrying their bursting bags and expensive purses and attaché cases. Just walking along with them made Annie feel envious. The Times lay in a patch of grass bordering the curb. A candy wrapper flapped under her shoe. She shook her foot up and down to get it off while the rain pitter-pattered on her legs.

She paused in front of a window of a tiny jewelry store to look at a coral necklace with a small sign reading, "Was $400, reduced to $250." Oh, how she wanted it! She had to have it. A minute ago she hadn't known it was there, but now she yearned for it desperately.

"Move along, girlie," said an emaciated woman in furs all splotched and faded. Her lips were smeared orange. "Get out of my way," she added indignantly when Annie didn't move off the curb quickly enough.

I'm really a woman now, she thought, humming the chorus from "Baby Love," the popular Diana Ross song. She felt just like she had back in Pittsburgh those few weeks around Christmas, after *Midsummer's Night's Dream.* Dragging her suitcase and her violin, Annie hurried down East Forth Street.

* * *

"Would you like something to drink?" Thomas asked politely in those first moments after closing his door.

Nodding, Annie followed him into the kitchen. She was in shock, not believing that they were finally together. She had imagined this moment for months and yet here was a stranger with dark bare feet in a blue-striped shirt and black corduroy bell-bottoms. His face was different, more gaunt, his Afro longer than she remembered.

Together they peered into the cupboard as if this were a normal everyday occurrence. There were racks of spices above the stove and some Saltines in the cupboard. She noticed the cheese, a bottle of Sauterne cooking wine, some oranges and tomatoes.

"I have tea and coffee," said Thomas, tipping over boxes of rice and cereal as he reached for a canister.

"Tea, please," she said, though she didn't drink tea.

He put a pot of water on the stove and turned on the burner while she sat down at his small table and watched him put the tea bags into two cups. He took out a jar of honey.

"Did I tell you I only use honey?" he asked conversationally.

"No," she said, looking around.

"It's getting hot in here," he said. "I was cooking earlier." He took off his shirt and carefully hung it on the back of the chair. "Don't look so serious," he said. "I'm not going to bite you."

Annie laughed nervously, noticing how his muscles bulged on his smooth hairless shoulders beneath his white T-shirt.

While they waited for the water to boil, Thomas disentangled a pipe from the debris of cigarette papers, matchboxes, rubber bands and bits of purple velvet on the top of the refrigerator, dumping out the old ashes in a tin wastebasket. From a plastic bag he took out some tobacco and put it into the pipe.

"Where is your bathroom?" Annie asked.

He pointed down the hall.

When she returned, the teapot was whistling and steam from the boiling water had fogged up the window. Annie sat down on the chair again, unbuttoning her beige trench coat and patting her short skirt ceremoniously. He placed a napkin and a full teacup on the table in front of her and sat down on the opposite side. Annie sipped the hot tea while Thomas lit his pipe.

"So you came all this way to see me?" he asked.

"I came for an audition. I've applied to the Masters Program at Julliard. Do you remember me talking about it? Well, I had the audition this afternoon."

He puffed slowly on his pipe.

"How did it go?"

"The audition? Good, I think."

Slowly Thomas inhaled and exhaled, sending the burning smell of cherry tobacco throughout the kitchen. She could hear dogs barking in the street below them. Now there was the sound of sirens. An ambulance, she wondered, or was it a police car?

Annie pulled her fishnet stockings up on her calves and fingered the pleat in her skirt. She bit the nail of her smallest finger, delicately running her tongue over the pink tip, sucking.

"I don't know what to say," she said. "I feel as if I am in somebody's movie."

"You could start by letting me in on how you found me," he answered.

"Well, I started teaching music lessons at the Hill House."

"That old abandoned firehouse on Wylie Avenue?"

"Yes, that's the one!"

"So you met Georgie G there," Thomas said, nodding.

"Yes. I didn't know, of course. I had no idea. Then one day he was showing the other kids a letter with your address on it. He couldn't stop talking about his dad, the famous actor. He was so proud."

Thomas gave a little smile, letting out a big puff of smoke.

"I thought of writing to you," Annie said. "But then I got this audition and there wasn't time. Besides it seemed kind of useless." She took a deep breath and continued, "I was afraid if I wrote, you might say no. I had to come here and see for myself."

Thomas exhaled rings of pungent smoke.

"I won't bother you. Just a few days."

Thomas inhaled and then grinned. "Just a few days?"

"Why, yes, I'm just here for the weekend," she said, thinking the weekend could last forever.

He leaned back in his chair, legs spread apart, and stretched out his muscled arms while Annie put her legs underneath her and sat smoothing her skirt.

"I don't have to stay here, of course. Really. I can go to the YWCA. I can leave now," she said abjectly. Then she noticed a little orange cat uncurl itself from a shelf.

"Oh, how cute," she said, holding out her hand.

"That's Annie," he said.

"Annie!" She laughed as the cat jumped off and sniffed her boots. It began to investigate a bug skittering underneath the counter.

"New York is cockroach heaven," said Thomas. "You get used to them."

Annie made a face as the cat bolted away.

He relit his pipe. The odor of the tobacco was heavy. Smoke curled over his fingers.

"It's pretty cold out there tonight to be walking around," he said.

She watched his eyes darting back and forth.

"Why not take off your coat and stay awhile?" he asked.

Annie stood up, holding her coat tight. "The time we spent together, Thomas? It changed my life." When he didn't answer, she looked anxiously around for the cat.

"Come with me," he said, standing too.

Annie followed him to the main room. Thomas sat down while she walked over to a bookshelf, her eyes glazing over the books.

"You read a lot," she said, peering at the titles in the dim light. "Franz Fanon, Marx, Margaret Mead, Ayn Rand, James Baldwin."

"Some of us darkies did get an education once Lincoln set us free."

She blushed. "I didn't mean it like that."

"I'm teasing, girl. A lot of these are from college. But I always liked those big bad words. When I was little, I used to read to my little brothers and sisters. They'd bring me books, magazines, newspapers, even the Bible."

Thomas swept his hands in front of his face as if to get rid of the memory. Slowly taking off her trench coat, Annie looked away, then back, flicking her hair over her shoulder. The phone rang in the kitchen and Thomas answered it, saying something she couldn't hear.

"Your eyes are fantastic," he said, coming back. "They remind me of my youngest sister, Christine-Marie's eyes, right after she was born, though hers were brown. When I am onstage I play to the women in the audience—only the women—they all have eyes like yours. 'I want you,' they say. Is that what yours say, Annie?"

"I don't know." Annie looked away, embarrassed. She felt like a newborn, like his little sister. Her eyes flitted anxiously, settling on the movie stars posters tacked on the walls. She looked at them more closely: Lauren Bacall, Harry Belafonte, Sidney Poitier, Faye Dunaway, Jason Robards, and Marilyn Monroe.

"Some day I'll walk down Broadway and see your name," she said.

"You're sure, eh?" But he smiled, and by that she knew she had said the right thing. When she sat down, the cat appeared and jumped into her lap.

"You are welcome to sleep there," Thomas said, pointing to a bed behind a beaded curtain.

"But where will you be?" she asked, blushing. She had stopped herself from adding "sleeping."

"I was just getting ready to leave. The phone call? A prior engagement—a professional meeting. So you'll have the place to yourself. But I'll be back in the morning. We can have breakfast together."

"Okay," Annie mumbled though shame overwhelmed her. She had never thought beyond the moment of her arrival. Here she was throwing herself at him. Her heart was here for the asking and he didn't seem to want it. The strobe beam pulsating in the corner mirrored her broken thoughts, her shattered hopes, as if she were not real but merely an eerie, electronic flicker. She felt so uninteresting and worthless.

"You ever have Eggs Benedict?" he asked disarmingly.

Annie shook her head, attempting to feel as upbeat as he sounded. The cat meowed in her lap.

"You must try my Eggs Benedict. You're in for a treat." Laying down his pipe, Thomas stood tall. "Did I tell you about my job as a chef at the Pittsburgh Sheraton?"

She shook her head.

"I'll tell you all about it tomorrow," he said, grabbing a dark jacket from the closet. "You will still be here, won't you?"

Annie nodded, bending over the cat.

"You better be!"

She watched him disappear down the hallway. "Lock the bolts after I leave!" he called out, slamming the door.

Annie lay on Thomas' bed in her coat and put a pillow over her head, falling asleep immediately. She was sweating profusely when she woke. Where was she? She had been dreaming she was at a party at her teacher, Leo's, apartment. The place was full of heavyset men with dead white faces and black bodies. She was alone.

Annie sat up in the dark, confused. For a minute or two she thought she was back at Leo's in Shadyside. But no, she was here in New York, at Thomas' place, and he was somewhere else. Where had he gone? A meeting? In the middle of the night? It just didn't make sense.

Sight-Seeing

Annie clittered from block to block in midtown Manhattan, lost in a lunging, pushing crowd. Ahead, she spotted Macy's, the famous department store that hosted the Thanksgiving Parade her family always watched on television. Should she go in and buy herself a dress? Something to show to Thomas? He hadn't returned this morning like he said. He hadn't made her Eggs Benedict. But she wasn't bothered, Annie told herself. She was on an adventure and however it turned out, well, that was just fine. At a corner newsstand she bought the *New York Times* and then hurried inside Macy's on the heels of the other eager shoppers.

On a counter surrounded by mirrors by the big front doors was a display of gaudy, cheap, pierced earrings. Annie fingered the jewelry.

"I'm just looking," she said hurriedly to a saleslady who approached her, bracelets covering her arms. Seeing herself in the mirror, Annie tilted her pink hat over one eye, wishing she had pierced ears. She felt happy. If only Thomas could see her now!

She got off the escalator at the third floor and began slowly walking down the aisles through a bathing suit display in the Juniors Department. "California Dreaming", "Bahama Girl", and "Bermuda Mermaid" advertised the bright green and pink signs highlighting the mannequins. She yearned to buy a yellow, green, and blue bikini and checked the tops for wired padded cups to make her look more bosomy. Where was the glass slipper for her delicate foot? And where was that prince waiting with the shoe? Was it Thomas? Oh, she wanted it to be him!

"Can't Buy Me Love," by the Beatles blared from the

sound system hidden behind the pastel pantsuits.

Annie fingered the dresses, eyeing a sleeveless sheath made of silvery cloth. Racks of dreams, just pay your money and have love. Why, it was all around her. She could have it too! Look at the grinning mannequins taunting her with their smooth eyeless faces.

And then she found the very dress—the one she had to have —with a scooped neckline, a red and white dress to weave around her heart, oh sweet girl on a valentine hanger, oh shiny aluminum doll. Annie picked both a size 5 and a size 7 off the rack.

"Where is the fitting room?" Annie asked the ancient sales lady, a tiny dark woman in a blue wool suit who motioned her to the corner. In the dressing room, she carefully undressed before the wall-length mirror.

"Does it fit? Do you need anything?" breathed the sales lady outside the curtain.

"No, not quite. No, I'm fine," said Annie. She hoped the woman would not pull back the curtain. Feeling she was being watched, she quickly put her clothes on and gave the dresses back to the sales lady.

Leaving Macy's behind, she went on to Orbachs and Gimbels, checking out the pierced earrings while Neil Diamond sang "Song Sung Blue" over the store loudspeakers. Oh, she hoped Thomas would be back by the time she got to his place. She hadn't locked his door when she left, in case he wasn't home and she had to get back inside herself.

The wind blew her hat backwards. Hundreds of purple shoes twinkled in the department store windows below a cloud of glitter and glass. She imagined herself walking in purple shoes. Look what I bought, Thomas. Look at my pretty legs. In the gutter she saw turds of decomposing dog shit. She hurried on.

Now she was a schoolgirl running in her blue and green plaid uniform skirt, a cross dangling around her neck, to meet Phyllis and her other friends. How they all laughed to see Sister Mary Paul standing by the cafeteria door, ready to pinch their waists with her tiny fat thumbs to make sure their skirts weren't rolled up. The nuns didn't want their legs to show, oh no, Catholic girls had to be modest! Annie laughed. If they could see her now. Oh, she had fooled them for sure.

Clutching her newspaper, Annie hurried across 34th Street and bought a chocolate-mint ice cream cone. Licking the ice cream, tasting the sweetness, kept her daydreams alive. Do you want to share it with me? Here, take a lick.

How lovely you are, Annie. Oh, thank you, Thomas. You're the prettiest girl in the whole world. I'm so proud to have you by my side.

She walked uptown to Times Square where she bought a sandwich and a soft drink at the Automat on 42nd Street. She remembered the old eatery from her visit as a girl, a cavernous room with wall-high, glass vending machines. At a much-used, scuffed table, Annie sat down and ate while pouring over the Times. Free concerts in Central Park, avant-garde theater on Off-Off Broadway, boat rides up the Hudson—there were so many exciting, wonderful things she could do.

She didn't buy anything that day and Thomas had not returned when she got back. "To hell with you," she said, faking a cute rakish grin in front of his bathroom mirror, affecting a pose like the mannequins in Macy's. Toasting her image, she threw an imaginary champagne glass into an imaginary crowd of old ladies in ratty furs and black chignons.

Annie ran hot water in the tub and when it was full, she peeled off her clothes, dropping them on the black and white octagonal-tiled floor. Just before she stepped into the tub, she locked the bathroom door. Then she slipped into the steaming water, gasping from the heat.

Her shopping excursion into Midtown Manhattan had given her a sense of well-being. She realized she didn't need Thomas to be here, not really. Seeing him was enough. They had had a nice conversation, hadn't they? She had had her audition and it went well. It was kind of him to give her a free place to stay. This meant she could use her money to see all the traditional sights. She wanted to go on the Staten Island Ferry and see the Statue of Liberty again like she had with her father. She wanted to go to the Metropolitan Museum of Art. She wanted to see Greenwich Village. There wasn't time to do all that she wanted!

No, it didn't matter now that Thomas wasn't here. In fact, she felt safer by herself. Annie dozed in the steeping bath water, looking forward to her next adventure.

Her eyes were closed, her hair trailing in the water, when she heard someone come in.

"Thomas, is that you?"

"Yes," said a deep voice from the other side of the bathroom door. She saw the doorknob jiggle, but it didn't open. She giggled at the thought he wanted to come in and she'd prevented him.

"What's so funny?" asked Thomas from the other side of the door.

"Oh, I've been imagining a conversation with you and it's weird to actually have you here answering."

"Well, open this door and we can continue it."

Annie splashed her legs in the bathtub.

"I'm sorry about the Eggs Benedict," he said. "There was a rehearsal this morning I forgot about."

"That's okay," she said, slipping deeper into the water. All that mattered was that he was here now. What did she care why he was away? The silence beyond the door made her impatient. Sex loomed between them. The water had turned tepid. Annie pulled herself upright. Wrapping a towel around herself, she stepped out onto the floor.

"Thomas?"

"Come on out when you're ready," she heard him say. "I'm

anxious to see you."

Annie unlocked the bathroom door, dropped the towel and jumped back into the tub. She turned the hot water tap on, letting the water run. Was Thomas still outside? Annie roused herself, leaned out of the tub and picked up her shoe. She threw it with a crash and the door banged open.

Over her shoulder, she saw him standing in the doorway, smoking a joint. Annie hunkered down in the water, her back to him, her hair lying on her shoulders in pale straight strings. Thomas came in and sat across from her on the toilet seat.

"Why did you do that?" he asked.

"I couldn't stand the closed door," she said. "It reminded me of home. It felt provocative. Do you understand?"

"No. This is provocative," he smiled, perfect white teeth gleaming.

Annie folded her arms over her chest, a serious expression on her face.

"Don't do that," he said. "Your breasts are pretty."

Looking down at herself, she placed the washcloth over them. Thomas leaned over and ran his fingers through the water, pulling the washcloth away. Annie sank down further.

"What's that?" he asked, touching the thin white scar on her wrist.

"Nothing. A scratch. Actually I got it climbing over a fence at Lake Erie. My cousins and I were running away from some boys we had been teasing."

"So you aren't suicidal, just a tease," he laughed, taking a toke.

"Did you think I slit my wrist?" she asked.

"Something like that," said Thomas. "Want some?" he asked, offering her a drag. Annie took it, coughing from the smoke. "Aren't you cold?" he asked.

"A little."

"Time to get out." He held out a blue towel. "Here."

Standing, she let him wrap it around her and followed him into the main room where she fell onto the couch. Throwing her a blanket from his bed, Thomas sat across from her.

"So tell me about Georgie G and how you got here," he said.

Annie curled up under the blanket. "Well, I went to the Hill House every Thursday to teach a group of kids music. We had this orchestra, well, kind of one."

She could see herself parking in front of the converted firehouse at the end of Wylie Avenue, a wide blustery street. "Serving the Needs of the People" said the homemade billboard above the door. A closed fist had been drawn in white chalk on each of the windows, and faded flyers of Malcolm X and Martin Luther King, Jr. flapped from the graffiti-covered fence. Inside was a children's playground with a seesaw, some broken swings and a toddler slide.

Her own grandma had been born around the corner from the Hill House. In the early nineteen hundreds, the neighborhood was well-kept, with two-story brick houses of Scottish and English settlers lining the elm and maple–shaded streets. But the neighborhood was deteriorating even then. The Episcopalians and Presbyterians had moved out and the Irish Catholics were already moving in.

"And then what?" Thomas prodded her.

"I remember Georgie G came late to my first class. Of course I didn't know who he was. He had a broken guitar with him that needed new strings."

"Damn! I know the one," said Thomas. He left the room and came back in a few minutes with a plate of cheese and fruit. Annie took a wedge of apple. She was thinking of how Grandma's whole family had died of the influenza there on Wylie Street: mother, father, sister, sister's husband and their two babies. Grandma was twelve when she was orphaned and went to work as a maid in the fine mansions overlooking the Allegheny River on the North Side, packing all she owned in a green wood trunk that Mother still kept in the cellar.

"What else?" Thomas asked.

"He asked me to teach him how to play chords."

She remembered how shyly Georgie G approached her. About eleven or twelve, he was wearing a too-large flannel shirt and jeans. All eyes, he was tall and thin, very dark, with long delicate hands. Something about those hands looked familiar to Annie.

"I told him I didn't know much about the guitar, but that there was another instructor down the hall who did. So he left. But later I was locking up the instruments in the cabinet when I saw him standing in the doorway. He said he wanted to learn to play the violin too. He was going to be a musician." She laughed. "He talked about you but I didn't really pay attention."

"What did he say?"

"Oh, something like he wanted to be a star just like his daddy. Things like that."

"What did you teach the kids?" Thomas asked, sitting closer to her on the couch.

Annie thought for a moment. "They really got into 'Baby Love' by the Supremes."

"Yeah?"

"Well, they already knew the melody and the harmonics by ear," she said. "I wanted to skip the usual childish pieces from the Thompson *Beginner Book for Strings*. Like 'Twinkle Twinkle Little Star' and 'Home on the Range'. So I found some easy versions of popular music at the library."

Annie smiled thinking of the kids first taking up their instruments, the ear-splitting screech of bows scraping against wood, hitting and scratching the strings. But after awhile it settled down. They learned how to handle the instruments and the sound got better.

"It was very difficult for them to sight read, so I would play first. I taught them to listen to me and then play by ear. It was easy for them. I was surprised."

He looked at her quizzically. "So you just asked Georgie G about me?"

"Oh, no, it wasn't like that." She watched Thomas take down the tray of dope paraphernalia from the shelf and begin to roll another joint.

"One day Georgie G showed me—all of us—the letter you wrote. I just read your address off the envelope. I remember it was just before the end of the class. He hadn't been there that day, but then he came barging in while we were finishing 'Please Please Me', you know, the early Beatles song. 'My daddy gave me hundred dollars for a new guitar!' he said—shouted actually. That was the end of the practicing! The kids went crazy."

Annie smiled, thinking of Georgie G holding out the hundred-dollar bill and the kids gathering around, jabbering excitedly.

"My daddy lives right here," Georgie G had said, pointing to the envelope in his fist. She hadn't intended to look at the envelope, but through the smudged fingerprints she read Thomas' name and address. A wave of astonishment overtook her. It was unbelievable to think Georgie G was Thomas' son. Even more amazing, she realized that now she could reach Thomas. It was a sign, a bright omen! She felt the excitement of a challenge and the promise of fulfillment—pointing her to a place she desperately wanted to go.

"That's wonderful, Georgie G. Don't lose that money now, okay?" she had said.

And here she was. After sharing the joint with her, Thomas left her on the couch. Time passed. Annie felt dazed, happy and stoned. Now she could hear him running water in the bathtub. She sighed, curling up under the blanket.

"Hey, Annie?"

She opened her eyes to see Thomas standing over her in a

long white bathrobe. "Do you have any plans for tomorrow?" he asked.

"Oh, go sight-seeing," she said, struggling to rise. "Maybe, see the Statue of Liberty. I'd love to see Empire State Building again before I go back."

He sat down beside her and took her hand. Water dripped off his frizzy ringlets.

"Do you have to go?"

Her heart stopped. He bent closer.

"I like you being here. I really do." Gently he massaged her fingers, moving over her hands and wrists, touching the faded scar.

"My parents expect me back," she murmured. "But maybe, maybe I could stay a few more days."

"Yeah," he said.

"You know, I could say I was waiting to hear from Julliard. That's true, I am! I could check out jobs, apartments—I mean, if I get in I'll need...."

"Why don't you do that? Stay here while you look for a place. I'd like that." Carefully he took the blanket off her. His robe fell open as he kissed her long and gently.

Pop Music

Janis Joplin was blasting from the radio when Annie finally called home. Her parents weren't there.

"They're really mad you skipped your own graduation. I'm not doing your dirty work for you," Melinda said. "You tell Mother and Dad. They're over at Aunt Lou's and Uncle George's. You know their number, don't you?"

"Please, please. I'm broke. I can't afford to make any more long distance calls. Please, Melinda, I'm just staying for another week."

Her sister had finally relented, promising to tell their parents Annie would be in New York a little longer, but only after Annie vowed Melinda could use the VW as soon as she passed her driving test.

That week had turned into two, and now three and four. She hadn't heard anything from Mother and Dad and she didn't expect to. Still, Annie was homesick. But whenever Thomas was with her, everything was fine. After all, it was 1967, the Summer of Love. Sex fueled the flame of her love for Thomas. His words, his look, his touch, the feel of him inside her filled her with passion and intensity. And when Thomas was gone, Annie busied herself discovering New York City. She visited Harlem and Brooklyn, the Bronx and Queens, Coney Island too. Even the slums intrigued her. Tomorrow, she told herself, she'd take the train to Long Island. Oh, she couldn't go home! She had graduated, hadn't she? If only she could find a job while she was waiting to find out the results of her audition. Then she wouldn't ever have to go back to Pittsburgh.

After a few weeks, Annie landed an interview with the New York Outreach Program way up on Amsterdam Avenue and 115th. She hoped to get a job teaching music like the one she'd had at the

Hill House, but the only opening was for a Girl Friday. After waiting around for two hours, she had been referred to another department three blocks away in Harlem. The interview had gone okay; they said they'd let her know.

On the subway downtown she read The Times, checking for studio apartments. She would have to leave Thomas'—she felt insecure there, unsafe. He was rarely home, leaving her alone for days at a time. He had a whole other life that she could never mention lest everything between them evaporate. She had no right to an accounting. There were no commitments between them. Why should there be? They were free, weren't they?

Yet how happy she was when she got back to find him sitting at the kitchen table reading a play in his underwear. He followed her down the hall to the closet where she hung up her black dress, changing into a T-shirt and jeans.

"I'm glad you're here," he said. "I need somebody to listen to me. This shit is too close to home." He tapped on the script.

"Where did you go?" he asked.

"I had an interview," she said proudly. "They said they'd call in a few days."

"Cool." Thomas put on a Jefferson Airplane album and they ate peaches from a can sitting on the mattress while she listened to him recite a scene or two.

He took out a long tooth comb and began pulling at his mat of black frizzy hair. "Shit. What time is it? Mel wants me there early."

He took her arm to look at her watch. It was delicate, made of 14-karat gold.

"Nice," he commented.

"It's a present from Dad—a graduation present. It keeps perfect time even when I forget and put my hand in water."

"He understands you better than you think."

"What do you mean?" Annie said, leaning on his shoulder.

"He's a smart man. I could tell that on the phone."

"That's right. You talked to him," Annie said, feeling pleased about this one small connection Thomas had made with her father. A stream of warmth went up and down her spine as he fiddled with her watchband.

"I guess he loves me," she said. "But I feel Dad's failures more than his good qualities, the things he doesn't give me. When Mother yells at him for stupid things—and it's always a stupid thing, like why he hasn't vacuumed the rug or remembered something—I blame him, even though I know she's the one who's wrong. Why is that?"

Thomas chucked her under her chin. "You're just human like the rest of us. I wish my old man gave me a gold watch. The only way I'll get one is to steal it," he laughed bitterly.

"You can have my watch," she said, taking it off her arm.

He sighed, patting her hair. "No. But thanks. Why do I feel so good with you, girl?"

She wrapped her arms around him, listening to his heartbeat. But too soon he broke away.

Annie was rinsing off some dirty plates when the phone rang. She busied herself running the water. The hot water slid down the plates scalding her fingers, but she didn't notice. As long as the water ran, she couldn't hear what he was saying or think about to whom he was talking. What she wanted, she told herself, was to be uninvolved. Free.

* * *

The organ recital had already begun when she arrived at St. John the Divine Church on 118th Street. Sitting in a pew, Annie felt safe, as if she were soaking in a warm bath, or drinking the glass of milk Dad used to bring her in at bedtime when she was a little girl. The majestic music uplifted her with its beautiful harmonics and grand contrapuntal. She was so glad she'd come to this free concert —glad she'd gotten herself out of Thomas' place. Away from him, perhaps she could see what was wrong.

The fun she had anticipated coming to New York, at first pell-mell, falling, tousled and grinning like a witch bounding through a fairy tale, had now turned sour. Too much was unknown and strange and distorted; too much was beyond her. What was wrong? What had she done? Maybe she didn't want this. But her thoughts dissolved with the beautiful music making her heart feel lighter. As soon as she got back today, she would get out her violin and practice.

Afterwards, she stood outside watching the crowds disperse. She didn't want it to be over. Finally she headed down Broadway, across 117th Street, passing open construction sites and the beginnings of a high rise. She was shocked to see large gray rats slinking in and out of the foundation.

Annie rushed down Upper Broadway past small stores. In each glass windowpane she saw herself, but her image didn't hold her, didn't please her the way it used to. She was all the way to 93rd Street when a drunk with a stocking cap caught her eye. Quickly she put her head down and walked across Broadway to the other side of the street, dodging a taxicab and a truck.

At a newsstand, Annie bought the Sunday Times. She went into a coffee shop, ordered coffee and a chocolate donut, and began rifling through the newspaper for the Want Ads under Women. She circled a few possibilities and then began reading the comics.

* * *

Adjusting the headphones over his ears carefully so as not to mess up his Afro, Thomas sang from "*Sgt. Pepper's Lonely Hearts Club Band*." His feet, the brown skin turning pinkish at the soles, skipped back and forth to the loud buzz of Indian instruments.

"Annie? What's wrong?" he called out in a loud voice, the cord to the stereo trailing behind him. She waited till he took off the headphone before she answered. "I have spotty underpants," she said. "I'm itchy and everything burns down there."

He didn't answer. She panicked. She was so uncomfortable and moreover felt betrayed. After all, she had been responsible, religiously taking her birth control pills. Why wasn't he? He must have given her a disease.

"Hey, kid, don't look so down. Dope will stop the itching. Believe me, I know," he laughed. "There's a health clinic on East Twelfth. Make an appointment and get that itch taken are of. You don't want it to cramp our sex life, know what I mean?" Beneath his robe, she could see the bulge beneath his white jockey shorts as he danced away from her. He would leave soon, and she would be alone again.

"I've got to get going," he said a few songs later while getting dressed. "I tell you, Annie. Things are finally happening for me. Hey, what happened with that job interview anyway?"

"I didn't get it. But I have another interview on Monday with the Metro Knife Company in Queens. They want an Administrative Assistant."

"Good for you." Thomas stopped in front of the mirror to comb his sideburns. "Where did I put my coat?"

Annie brought him his coat. Slinging it over his shoulder, he blew her a kiss goodbye.

After Thomas left, she took a small amount of grass and rolled herself a joint, something she had just learned to do. Lighting it, she lay back on the mattress. She should practice. Julliard gnawed at her. That uncertainty throbbed like an open wound. For all the hours she forced herself to practice, something was wrong. Though her tempo was good, fast-paced, her bow strokes were labored and the sound uneven, as if she were playing on a small weaving sailboat.

Annie took another puff, holding the smoke in her lungs a long time. I'll never be Phyllis in that tract home in suburbia she thought inside her hazy tent of marijuana. I'll never be that sexless student in music school again. Nor even that playful, easily frightened girl from Immaculate Heart High School.

In the heavy fog of the dope, the room no longer appeared shabby and ugly. Every bit of junk looked valuable. The glass beads shimmered in the afternoon light and the purple cloth glowed on the wall. Even Lauren Bacall and Marilyn Monroe looked happy. Annie pulled herself upright to load the turntable, choosing her favorite singles: Neil Diamond, the Moody Blues, and Buffalo Springfield.

With pop music filling her ears, she flopped down in front of the flickering TV buzzing in the background. Thomas' favorite show, "Dialing for Dollars," was just over. A movie was about to begin. The *TV Guide* that Thomas followed religiously lay open face down on the dusty console. He had doodled in purple pen in the margins, making circles inside of squares and dots inside of oval eggs.

Following Thomas' example, Annie too kept the TV on all day even when he wasn't there. Sometimes she felt like she was doing it to spite Dad who considered television to be junk. "Garbage," he called most of the shows she watched. He and Mother hadn't permitted one in the house until she was twelve.

The captions changed every half hour with the soap operas, but the message was the same. How the TV taunted her with her longing for Thomas—the crude monster of love dolled up with advertising. The camera screen captured the crass, superficial, hollow lonesomeness of her life and longing. It mirrored her own mind, voyeuristic and secretive, like the TV at a checkout counter showing footage from a camera installed to prevent shoplifting. Annie herself felt like a hidden camera, searching for telltale signs of theft.

But what of value did she have that could be stolen? The truth was that the TV was her only sure undemanding, loyal companion besides the cat. Annie couldn't get used to calling the cat by her own name, so she renamed her Figaro after Mozart's opera.

Thomas didn't come back that night and her itching got worse, so the next day Annie went to the Lower East Side Public Health Clinic in her little gray miniskirt and sweater vest. She whispered her symptoms to a receptionist and then slid into a seat at the back of a large waiting room.

"Wednesday's a drag. County Jail day," said somebody on her left.

In front of were her three men in orange jumpsuits who turned around and looked her over. The biggest one asked Annie for a cigarette, but she pretended not to hear.

Then a heavy-set nurse with a mustache came in, eyes flashing, and the men all stood up together.

"You! Follow me," she ordered. Annie was shocked to see they were handcuffed to each other.

Her turn came finally.

"I always faint from blood tests. Can I lie down?" asked Annie.

"Look the other way," she was told by a brisk nurse wearing white stacked heels who inserted the needle.

The nurse had her take off her clothes and put on a paper gown with a slit down the back. Annie lay back on the gurney with her feet in the stirrups, clenching her teeth as the cold instrument was inserted. She wouldn't blame Thomas, no, she wouldn't stoop to that. She concentrated instead on feeling proud of herself to have come. She thought of other courageous tasks she had done, promising herself that this week she would look harder for a job. After she dressed, the nurse gave her a slip of paper and told her to wait outside.

While she waited, a group of young women wearing lots of makeup with teased dyed hair in the bouffant style of Jacqueline Kennedy emerged from a white van escorted by two broad-faced policemen who prodded them forward as if in line for tickets at a baseball game. Annie wondered what the girls had done.

Finally she was summoned to a small office. "Sit down," the nurse said, examining her clipboard. "Pregnancy—Negative. Syphilis—Negative. Gonorrhea—Positive," she read and then offered Annie a small packet. "Take these as directed. Douche with vinegar twice a day for three days. And tell your partners to come in and be checked."

"There's only one," Annie said faintly.

"He needs to be tested. And don't have sex until he is. Otherwise, the penicillin is useless."

Back at the apartment, she looked up "gonorrhea" in the dictionary. "A venereal disease characterized by inflammation of the mucous membrane of the genitourinary tract and the discharge of mucus and pus." Annie felt relieved. There was nothing judgmental about the dictionary.

She took the pills and within a few hours she felt better, but she couldn't get rid of her humiliation or the realization that Thomas had infected her. Then why hadn't he come to the clinic? Maybe he had. Maybe he was waiting to see if she had it too. In any case, he must be tested. She knew she shouldn't make excuses for him, for after all, it was she who showed up uninvited on his doorstep.

Sitting in front of the TV that night, she wrote a letter to her sister.

> Dear Melinda,
> I am so glad you are my sister and that I have somebody to talk to. This is strange to say but I think you are the only one who might understand. I am not sure where I am going. I've been searching for answers, for the truth. All my dreams have crumbled here in New York City. I feel like a selfish whiney little girl. Thomas is not who I imagined him to be. Of course I should have known better! I feel like I'm staring at myself starving in the mirror. What I miss most is not

> being in touch—with you, with Mother and Dad, even
> Lucky. If only I would hear from Julliard.
> XXXX, Annie
> p.s. Thank you for telling Mother and Dad. I'm sure it
> wasn't easy. I hope they weren't too mad.

After writing to Melinda, she began another letter to herself. On and on she wrote, page after page of self-conscious truths, half-truths and just plain old wishful lies scripted in her tiny, meticulous, ornate hand.

A late night movie with Betty Davis was just starting. Carefully she addressed the envelope to Melinda. The letter to herself she threw away. Turning up the TV, she flopped onto the mattress and fell asleep.

Trust

Annie arrived early to Thomas' opening night performance clutching the ticket he had given her. The subway had been empty when she got on. Each time it turned in the cavernous tunnel at breakneck speed, her head jerked around. She was excited as she hurried up the subway steps to the street. It had sprinkled earlier, but now the sky had cleared and the air smelled uncommonly clean.

For all that Thomas had described the theater to her, it was smaller than she expected, shoddy and conspicuously rundown. The seats were uncomfortable and cramped, narrow, no doubt picked up from some old movie theatre uptown. Behind the pit rose several levels of tattered rows. She sat down in one of the ancient velvet-covered seats in the front. An ornate silver and red jukebox dominated the center stage, diamond-shaped, with a barebones design. The scene was a barroom with several round tables covered with red and white oilcloth. Green and yellow fluorescent signs spelled BEER and WINE. There were a few scuffed wood chairs that could have come from Thomas' flat.

Her mind wandered during the play. It wasn't what she expected. Thomas' role was very small. He only came on twice. Once he loitered around a jukebox saying nothing and another time he was part of a gang and spoke about ten lines. She felt disappointed, but she didn't allow herself to think of it, as even this small criticism would amount to a betrayal. And not of him but of herself. She couldn't afford to think badly of him. Otherwise, all her actions would be called into question—she couldn't be so wrong.

Afterwards, Annie wandered about in the lobby with the rest of the enthusiastic, mostly white, bohemian audience.

As she waited for the cast to appear, she looked at large mounted photos of the entire troupe on a wall covered with black velveteen. Thomas looked so handsome framed in white. The air was thick with cigarette smoke, accentuating the sense of illusion in the crowded, noisy foyer.

"Isn't it amazing what they can do with nothing?" asked a loud crackling-voiced female behind her. Annie turned around, but the woman, youngish with puffed hair, draped in gold lame, wasn't speaking to her.

"Negroes have so much—I don't know—energy, joie de vivre," said the woman with her who was wearing blue denim Levis, high heels, and a white satin blouse.

"Watch what you're saying, honey," said a man with a deep resonant voice Annie vaguely remembered. "That French shit scares us."

"Oh, and I was just about to apologize for acting like a racist pig," laughed the woman in gold lame, hugging him. "Mel, how are you? The show was just marvelous. Denise, I want you to meet Mel Manning, the man behind it all."

"Glad to meet you, Denise. Glad you came. You and…"

"It's Honey! Honey Graham. I wouldn't have missed it."

"Honey! Great name!" Dark, looming, Mel towered over them. Amused and sardonic, he played the admiring crowd. "Bring your brothers, sisters, aunts and uncles, Honey and Denise. Your lovers. Everybody. All you honkies, we need you. We need your money!"

The women laughed uproariously. Mel's darting eyes found Annie's and he winked.

"Haven't I seen you here before?" he asked, waving away Honey and her friend.

"Once, but it wasn't here," Annie mumbled.

"Wherever it was, I'm glad you're here now," said Mel, staring at her hard.

Annie felt herself grow warm but Mel didn't notice as his gaze was now fixed on a plump girl in a see-through blouse and mini-skirt. At that moment the cast came through the doors—eight actors looking smaller and more commonplace than their stage counterparts, the men homely with bald, dark heads, the women without makeup, with flat hair and blotched faces. But Thomas was not among them.

Anne went over by the water fountain, letting the spray trickle down her mouth as she watched the lobby empty. Even Mel had gone off now with his retinue of fans. Still Thomas didn't appear. Finally she approached the swinging doors where the actors had emerged. A light was shining from a small room at the very end of the hall. She tiptoed towards it.

Inside Thomas was slumped in a chair, his head in his hands. Across from him a short, plump, untidy attractive woman was shouting.

"Where is my diamond necklace anyway? What did you do with it! Why did you make me find you!" she screamed. She had long black hair, wore a low-cut black dress and carried a red purse.

"I can explain. Don't worry, Lana. I intended to look you up as soon as I had the time. You're all wrong about this. Annie!" Startled, Thomas stood. His dark chest hair curled beneath his white undershirt. Makeup smeared his brow.

Lana jerked around, swinging her curly mane, "Annie? And when have I had the pleasure?" Her face was white with powder, and her mouth bright red. "Annie! How are you?" She pulled Annie into the small windowless room.

"Annie's from out of town," Thomas explained. "She's been staying at my place just until she gets settled."

"Just until she gets settled." Lana mimicked. "A temporary roommate."

"Yeah, you could say that."

"Where are you from?" Lana asked Annie. "I'm from

Hartford, Connecticut."

"Pittsburgh, Pennsylvania," Annie said.

"And did you know Tomboy here in Pittsburgh?"

"I met Thomas there. Yes."

"A friend of Tom's is a friend of mine. Hey, I can show you the town. I know a lot of places, believe me. I know some pretty cool musicians."

"I'd like that," Annie said. She smiled at Lana.

"Do you sing, Anna? Dance?"

"I'm a violinist," Annie said. "I came here for an audition at Julliard. I'm hoping I'll be moving here soon."

"I'm impressed! Sit," Lana ordered, pointing Annie to a jute hammock strung in the corner of the dressing room. "Don't be shy. My, a violinist! I act myself. I love the theater. That's how I met Tom here." Lana laughed, a loud bark. "Tom, put on a shirt, I'll have an orgasm if I have to look at your bare chest another moment," she cried. "He just dropped out of my life," she addressed Annie. "What you think of that?"

"You don't have to answer that," Thomas said. He was looking into the mirror, wiping off his makeup.

"Let's celebrate. I just happen to have something." Lana took a half-full bottle of French champagne out of her large red purse, took a swig, and passed it around. She began a rambling story about how she and Thomas ran out of a theater dressing room naked one opening night somewhere in upstate New York. Attempting to follow the story, Annie held the champagne bottle awkwardly, trying not to notice herself in the mirror and yet desperate to see if she looked all right, if she looked good. But it got easier with the liquor and she began to relax.

Thomas was silent, cracking his knuckles once in awhile. "Let's go!" he said when Lana finally took a breath.

"Where we going?" Lana asked, draining the dregs of the champagne from the bottle.

He jumped up and straightened out his tight bellbottoms.

"Don't forget this, hon," she said, handing Thomas his black leather belt.

He threaded the belt through his pants, picked up his shirt and slid his arms into it. Annie watched him fold a clean handkerchief in his side pocket.

"It's late." Thomas said, holding out his hand to her.

"What about me?" Lana cried.

"I'll see you later."

"Like hell you will." Lana said and threw the empty bottle onto the floor where it smashed to pieces.

Annie stared at the broken glass in dismay.

"Lana," said Thomas.

"Asshole," said Lana.

"Lana."

"Asshole. Now don't forget, Annie. Let's you and I do something sometime. We need to talk."

Lana stomped out the dressing room door.

"Not very appealing, is she?" Thomas said as he and Annie walked along the pavement outside the theater a few minutes later.

"Lana seems nice, but you don't treat her very well."

"I hate it when she's loaded."

"But I don't understand," Annie said. "I feel like I was intruding. But you asked me to come tonight. You gave me a ticket. Why didn't you come out and meet me?"

"I wanted to. But then Lana showed up. I just got distracted. Lana and I—well, it's a long boring story. She owes me. Someday I'll tell you, but now isn't the right time."

"Oh, Thomas, when is the right time? I'm not some wilting flower in a hothouse, you know."

"Hey, babe, I know."

"I went to the clinic. I have gonorrhea."

"Damn!"

"I'm taking the pills. But they said you should be tested."

"I will, I promise. Anything else that's bothering you?"

"Oh, no, it's just, we can't make love until you do. I'm wondering why you didn't tell me before. I mean, you had it first."

"I didn't feel anything. I'm sorry. You don't believe me?"

"Yes, no, that's not it," she lied. She felt awkward. One false move and she might topple. "Thomas, I need to know. Is that all I am to you—a girl from out of town hanging round your apartment? A temporary roommate as you called me?"

"I didn't mean it like that," said Thomas. "Hey!" There on the corner, waiting for the red light to change, he reached out and touched her hair. Annie stood beside him, motionless, a warm rush filling her.

"Feels good, doesn't it?" he said his hands circling her neck. "Goddamn it, girl."

"I've got to get some sleep," he said. "I have rehearsal all day tomorrow. You know what will happen if I go back home with you now. We'll end up fucking like rabbits all night. And we can't—you said so yourself."

She could feel him waiting to hear what she would say. If she could just understand, she'd know what to say. Was Thomas manipulating her? Because if he was, who could she trust? They kissed goodbye too quickly. As Annie took the subway back to his place alone, she had a sense that there was life all around her that she didn't see, people whom she couldn't hear. Like a Gregorian chant, a refrain kept repeating in her head along with the screech and roll of the train. Liar, liar. How many lies before it all catches up with you, it went over and over again.

It was all there for her to see, if she would. Something in her was reaching out, but at the wrong time and in the wrong direction. Why did she keep herself in a prison of swarming confusion? Why did she delude herself? Or was he deluding her and much better at it than she?

She recognized the confusion, the disgust, and the desire to flee. She couldn't use the excuse anymore that she was too young and naïve. She had been here before. She should know better. But she felt lost, the same way she felt a few months ago, right after she started working at the Hill House. She had had another argument with her parents that night and rushed to her car, spinning out of the driveway in the rain to get away from it. The streetcar tracks were slippery as Annie steered to the right and left to avoid them. But several times she miscalculated and the VW skidded anyway.

That night she drove into Pittsburgh she passed a boarded up school, a gutted gas station, a burnt-down supermarket, and a corner where she had dropped Thomas off once. The wet narrow streets sloped down to the steel mills along the Monongahela River. One street twisted easily into the next.

She forgot the way she had come. The narrow streets were full of potholes and the car bumped along as the drizzle continued. She missed a few stop signs but there was so little traffic it made no difference. Finally she admitted she was lost. Turning off into one of the dark alleys, she glimpsed a few figures darting by, their faces dark and hidden. At the end of a long solid row of attached brick houses was a small grocery lit with blinking red and green Iron City beer signs. Two black men stood in the doorway. She needed directions. She needed help.

Annie parked and got out, stepping gingerly over the stream of water in the gutter. The men, perhaps forty, perhaps sixty years old, reeked of liquor. Their faces were inscrutable.

"What's that you say?" said one, blocking her way.

"What's your name, sugar?"

Ignoring them, she pushed by into the store. At the counter, a short bald man of Middle Eastern descent was watching TV. Perhaps she should buy something. Annie pulled a small bag of potato chips from a rack and set it on the counter.

"Twenty-nine cents," said the clerk. Awkwardly Annie pulled

her wallet out. She threw a dollar on the counter as one of the men appeared at her left. The other lounged by the candy rack.

"You don't look like you come from this neighborhood, hon," said the man on her left.

"I don't," she whispered, watching the clerk count out her change.

Clutching her bag of chips, she took a step backward and stumbled. Just then the front door swung opened and in came a boy of eight or nine carrying a soggy brown bag of empty bottles. He had no coat and was panting. For a second she thought the boy was one of her students and would help her! But no, this boy was younger than they.

"Pack of Camels and a Three Musketeers," said the boy, lifting the bag of bottles onto the countertop. One of the men put his arm on her shoulder. Annie froze.

The clerk turned to get the cigarettes. The boy leaned onto the counter and the bag of bottles slid, slamming onto the floor. "Damn!" the men shouted, jumping away. The boy gave a cry. Kicking away the broken glass, Annie ran out the door.

"Hey! You forgot your change."

Annie rushed to her car. She pulled out, tires screeching, and drove away. What was she thinking of coming into this dangerous neighborhood? How could she imagine a boy would save her? A few turns later and she was back on Wood Street heading home.

And now? She knew better now she told herself as the subway raced along the tracks. But where was her home? Wherever it was, she wasn't going there.

The next day, a Sunday, Annie didn't wake up until after nine. The first thing she noticed was Thomas' message machine blinking red on the telephone stand. She ignored it. An hour later Thomas surprised her by coming back with donuts and coffee.

"I left you a message," he said.

"Did you really?"

"Yeah, if you don't believe me, listen to it."

Annie listened to the messages, including his long rambling one. There was another from the woman who'd interviewed her at the Metro Knife Company offering Annie a job.

"Now I'll be able to get my own place," she told Thomas.

"I won't make you stay if that's what you're thinking," he said.

"It's not that—it's that... All I really want is to understand you," she said, knowing that was a lie. What she wanted was for him to beg her to stay, to want her the way she wanted him. In any case, he wasn't making her stay, so what he said was a lie too.

"I think you do understand me, babe," said Thomas. "That's why we get along so well."

Annie brushed away her tears before they fell.

Studio

Three weeks later, she rented a studio on the upper West Side. She had just signed the rental agreement and was walking down West 96th Street toward Amsterdam when she saw Lana coming out of a dingy unmarked storefront. She held the arm of an attractive dapper black man in black leather and boots. Annie had only seen Lana that one time, but had no trouble recognizing her. She was wearing tight blue jeans, a tiny white sleeveless T-shirt, love beads and open-toed heels. Her dark curly hair swung back and forth in a ponytail.

"Lana? Is that you?" Annie stepped out across the narrow street.

"Hi! Do I know you?"

"It's Annie—I met you at Thomas' play a few weeks ago."

"Of course, the violinist from Pittsburgh!" Lana said, putting out her arms as if to give her a big hug. "Annie, meet Vern. Vern, this is Tom's friend from Pittsburgh! You know!"

Annie put out her hand as Vern looked her up and down, his eyes darting past hers like ferrets.

"Hey, we're going for coffee. Come and talk," said Lana.

Annie sat down across from Lana at Deepa's Donuts on Amsterdam, a dark little hole in the wall smelling of stale cigarettes, hot grease and fried dough. Vern had begged off, saying he had some business to take care of and now Lana and she were talking like the best of friends.

"Sorry about that shitty night we met," Lana said, waving a lit cigarette in Annie's face.

"I was a little worried," Annie said. "You throwing the glass and all. Honestly, I didn't understand what was going on."

"Yeah," said Lana. "So what's up?"

"I guess I told you. I'm hoping to get into Julliard in the fall, but I haven't heard anything yet."

"Oh, you'll get in. Don't worry," said Lana.

"Oh, I don't know. You never even heard me play," Annie said, giving her a doubting look.

"But I will! Hey, I'm in a new show." She told Annie that the building she and Vern were coming out of was the brand new home of the Sixties Expressions Theater Project. Lana had put up the first six months rent herself and was going to produce their first show. "It's *Endgame,* by Samuel Becket. Do you know that one?"

"I think I've heard of it," said Annie.

"I'll get you two tickets. You can bring anyone you want."

Annie laughed. "You are the only person I know in New York —except for Thomas."

"And how well do you know him?" Lana asked, biting into a chocolate-covered donut.

Annie shrugged. "I met him last Christmas."

"Jesus, of course. Pittsburgh. Here, take this." She offered Annie the donut. "My stomach doesn't feel so good. Too much partying last night. So, how did you and Thomas meet?"

"At a play. Well, not exactly, outside the Pittsburgh Playhouse."

"He was in a play? He never told me, the jerk."

"Well, not exactly. I thought he was in the play. It was *Midsummer's Night's Dream* with the Negro Repertory Company."

"Oh, Mel and his outfit. I heard he took the show on the road."

"I made a mistake. I thought Thomas was Oberon, but he had just come for an audition. Honestly, he looked just like the actor who played Oberon." Annie took a big bite of the donut.

"Want one?" Lana said, lighting a cigarette.

"I don't smoke. We ended up having coffee at Howard Johnson's."

Why was she telling Lana all this? She didn't trust her, but she liked her.

"So you two literally ran into each other outside the theater and then you got real tight?" Lana asked.

"I don't know about that."

"Oh, I'm sorry. Do I sound mean and sarcastic? I suppose I do. That's just the way I am," said Lana.

"It's okay."

"The hell it is. I can tell by your face. Go ahead, tell the truth. You can trust old Lana."

"Alright," said Annie. "I wish I was tight with him, but I'm not. When I met Thomas, I fell in love for the first time."

"Hell, I had a real deep thing for that man too, but it's gone now. He's dirt in my book. As Billie Holliday says, 'He done me wrong'."

"Thomas didn't treat you very well at his opening," Annie admitted.

"You saw it too? Hell, let's not talk about that creep anymore. Let's talk about you."

Annie told her that she'd gotten a job a few weeks ago and that she was still waiting to hear from Julliard.

"I know somebody who teaches at Julliard, an old family friend. What's his name? I'll remember. I could call him."

"Oh, you don't need to."

"Hell, he could put in a good word for you," said Lana.

They were still talking as Annie walked Lana to her car, a brand new blue Impala Annie couldn't help admiring. When Annie pointed out a five-story apartment building around the corner and said she'd just signed a month-to-month lease for it, Lana insisted on checking it out. They walked up the five flights to the studio and Annie proudly used her new key to let them in.

It was a small dark rectangular room with a toilet and mirror in the closet. There was a kitchen area with a two-burner stove, a mini-refrigerator, and a sink that also served as a bathtub and smelled of mildew. Two high windows over a radiator heater faced the street. Through the dirty windows a few bedraggled trees blew in the sultry afternoon breeze in front of a red brick school surrounded by a fenced concrete playground. The furniture consisted of a small Formica table with wobbly legs, two chairs with torn plastic seats, a blue serge sofa that converted to a single bed, one overstuffed chair, and coffee table made from a large wooden telephone spool.

"I've got some purple batik curtains that will look good here. And a red rug to put there," Lana added, pointing to the wooden floor in front of the sagging couch.

"Thank you," Annie said, surprised at her generosity.

"Let's see if these work," said Lana, flushing the toilet in the tiny closet and then turning on the spigots in the small grayish sink. "So what did Tom-Tom say when you told him you were moving out?" She flopped onto the overstuffed chair.

"He doesn't know yet. But I thought you didn't want to talk about him."

"Touché." Lana took out her cigarettes from her oversized leopard purse.

"He's never there," Annie admitted. "I spent nearly all my time alone. He sees other women. I know that."

"No shit."

"I just want to go forward. Do you know what I mean?" Annie said.

"Hell, yes. Can I ask you something?" Annie waited while Lana lit a cigarette. "When you were hanging out in Pittsburgh, how did you two get around?"

"Get around?" Annie was puzzled.

"You know, when you did things together. When you and Tom-Tom went out on the town." Lana took a drag.

"Oh, I drove my VW bug."

"He didn't take you around in a white Impala?"

"No, Thomas didn't have a car. Why?'

"Honest to God?" Lana said, flicking ash into her palm. The look on her face told Annie she didn't believe her.

"Honest to God," Annie repeated. "He's poor—and his family is too. He told me."

"Yeah, yeah, his family," Lana brushed the comment aside.

When they went back outside, the hot street was simmering in hazy light. Lana cajoled her to come and check out a dollar thrift store on upper Broadway. Annie picked out some light bulbs and toilet paper. Lana bought her an aluminum teapot. "A house gift," she said.

"You don't need to," said Annie, making a face. She felt embarrassed and pleased.

Lana pointed out a display of deadbolt locks that she insisted Annie get immediately.

"But there's already a lock. I have the key."

"Every single girl in New York needs this. I mean it," said Lana.

But Annie had no idea how to install a lock and no tools to attach it.

"You have to get it now!" Lana cried. "You are moving in today, aren't you?"

"I don't know. I have to get my things up here somehow," Annie said, shrugging her shoulders.

"It's a good thing you ran into me then." Lana grabbed the deadbolt, dragging Annie down the aisle to the checkout counter.

"Tom won't know what hit him," she said, pulling out of the narrow parking space on Amsterdam Avenue. "I can't wait to see his face. C'mon. Don't worry. He won't dare say anything with me there."

As Lana sped down the Westside Highway, Annie asked, "Are you doing this to see Thomas? Because he won't be there."

"Hell, no, I'm doing this for you. Don't look a gift horse in the mouth, my daddy always says."

"So you're the gift horse?" Annie said, smiling a little.

"Yeah, something like that."

Annie had to give her directions to his flat. She thought Lana knew where Thomas lived.

"Oh, he moves around alright. He's full of secrets, that boy," Lana said. "That's not the only one."

Annie brought up how she'd had to be treated at the clinic for gonorrhea.

"You don't want to hear this, but you are one of many, girl. And I'm one of them too, the fucker."

As Annie predicted, Thomas was not there. Quickly they collected her things.

"I'll write him a note," Annie said, looking around before they left. She saw the cat sleeping on the bed.

"Oh, let him figure it out. Don't humble yourself for him."

"I have to leave him my new address," Annie said, taking out her pen.

"Oh, no, you don't," said Lana, stopping her.

"I have to say goodbye to the cat at least."

Annie forced herself not to look back as she locked Thomas' door.

"I don't know how I could have done this without you," she said when Lana pulled up to her place. "Thank you. I mean it."

"Sure, sure," said Lana. Together they carried the bags and boxes up the five flights of steps. Lana said she'd bring Vern over in a day or two and install the lock. When she finally left, Annie was exhausted.

Just as Lana said they would, a few days later Vern and she came over and Vern drilled the holes for the deadbolt.

"Lock that door after we leave," Lana told her, hugging Annie on their way out.

Julliard

Each day Annie took two subways, transferring at Times' Square and walking the blocks of cavernous underground passageways to the crosstown trains. Each night after making herself dinner, she practiced. Though tired, she felt happier when she put her violin away an hour or so later. Then she set out her clothes on the chair for the next workday. Then she lay down on her small lumpy bed, opened the window wider to catch the breeze, and fell asleep.

The switchboard was always lit up during lunch hour. Annie never stopped answering calls from where she sat half-hidden behind the office fern in the Metro warehouse entryway. But by late afternoon, the phone calls had dwindled. When she discovered how to make free long-distance calls, she dialed home right away and Melinda picked up the phone.

"I was praying you'd answer! Did you get my letter? What's happening?" Realizing that was something Thomas would say, she felt embarrassed. "I finally got a job," Annie went on when Melinda didn't reply. "It's just a receptionist type job. I'm calling from work now. I have my own place too," she added proudly.

"I did get your letter," said Melinda finally.

"Okay. Well—?"

"I am worried about you," said Melinda.

Annie laughed, though it wasn't funny. It was as if her laughing were an unconscious tic, like a twitching eye or a stutter.

"I'm serious," Melinda said. "Your letter frightened me."

"It just didn't work out, me staying with Thomas, waiting to hear from Julliard—don't ask, I still haven't heard whether or not I'm accepted. With Thomas, I often felt like one of Dad's relatives. You know, how Mother makes them feel. Unwanted."

"Yeah," said Melinda. "I thought you were only staying with him a few days."

"Yeah, so did I," Annie admitted. She told her sister about the gonorrhea. "I had to go to the Lower East Side clinic and get tested and all."

"Now I really am worried. Are you alright?" Melinda sounded disgusted.

"Oh, sure. It's not serious, but still—"

"He sounds like a creep."

"I wish he was, but he's not. I love him! Especially now that I left. I miss him so."

"What are you going to do?"

"I have a favor to ask. Would you send my music to me? It's piled on my desk. There are a few scores on my music stand too. Bach and Schubert. Oh, send all the rest, please?"

"Well, just for you, though I barely have time to wash my hair these days. I got a job at Sears in the mall," said Melinda. "And I finally got my driver's license. I've been driving the VW—but, don't worry; it's just over to Don's house and work."

"You could drive to New York," said Annie hopefully.

"Yeah, right. Dad's even worried about me driving the parkway. He's still keeping up with your car insurance."

"Keeping up? Oh, you mean paying it. I owe him so much. He paid for my plane ticket too. How is he?"

"Like always."

"What about Mother?"

"We don't talk about you if that's what you mean," Melinda said.

"That's not what I meant. How is she doing?" Annie felt irritated, and, if she admitted it, a little hurt.

"She got transferred to a new district. She works out of the Regent Square social work office now, so it takes her a long time to get home at night. Of course, she's a real you–know-what when she does finally come home."

"Yeah."

"We've been going out to dinner a lot. I'm out late working so I can't cook and Mother's too tired. And you know Dad can't boil an egg."

"I wish I could do something for them—you know, make them happy," said Annie wistfully.

"You could come home. I'd like that."

"I can't come home, Melinda." Annie's voice broke. She shut her eyes, refusing to cry. When she opened them, the switchboard was lit up with incoming calls.

"I gotta go now," she said. "I'll call back soon. Let me know if you get a letter for me."

"Wait! The mailman's here right now. Hold on," said Melinda, dropping the phone. Waiting for her sister, Annie watched the switchboard for incoming calls. A production supervisor walked by.

"Oh, Annie! There's something for you. It's from Julliard," Melinda said.

"Oh, my God!" Annie cried.

"I'll forward it to you. What's your address again?"

"No. Open it now," Annie said, lowering her voice.

She heard the envelope tear and held her breath. "You got in!" Melinda gasped. "They've accepted you for the fall." Melinda began reading the acceptance letter aloud.

"Oh, my God!" Annie held her hand over her mouth.

"Good news?" asked the supervisor from the other side of the fern.

"Yes!" she mouthed, hanging up quickly.

* * *

A few weeks later, on a Saturday, Annie was leaving her apartment when she saw Lana getting out of her car in front of the storefront theater across the street.

"Lana!" she called out, waving.

"Hey, I was just thinking of you," said Lana. "Being as I'm in the neighborhood and all. I'm getting ready for a party and you're not invited. Seriously, it's for the Sixties Expression Theater patrons. A benefit for the filthy wealthy. A musical extravaganza. Will you come to my place and help me with the posters and stuff? Tomorrow?"

"Sure," said Annie.

Following Lana's directions, she took the Downtown local to West 12th Street and walked two blocks to Greenwich Village. A doorman let her into Lana's building and pointed her to the elevator and the penthouse.

"What a beautiful place you have," Annie exclaimed. From Lana's king size bed where she was perched, her eyes flitted over the wall-to-wall brick fireplace to the blond bedroom furniture, Indian rugs, brass lamps, rattan shutters, silk pillows and modern artwork. On a large table in one corner were stacked boxes of art supplies: chalk, pastels, and jars of murky water holding different sized brushes, squeezed tubes of oil paints, easels and half-finished canvases. Annie also noticed the full ashtrays, dirty wine glasses, and empty beer bottles.

"Is the deadbolt working?" Lana called out from the bathroom. She had stripped down to her pink bra, black bikini pants and magenta heels.

"Of course."

"Now that you have a job, you can get some new furniture."

"Yeah, when I make some money," said Annie. "What's this?" she stepped back to admire the large rectangular canvas of a tree in bloom behind the bed.

"An apricot tree," Lana said, appearing naked in the bathroom doorway. "It's just something I did when I was twelve."

"I didn't know you were an artist," Annie said, studying the oil painting. Flowery splotches of pink and red, some thick and spotty, some faint like drizzle, dribbled down the canvas. Splashes of sunny yellow merged into white and blue. On the bottom clumps of yellow dandelions grew in wild grass.

"Aunt Kathleen's the real artist in the family," said Lana. "The tree is in her front yard in Sunnyvale, California. My dad and mom shipped me there for the summer so they could have their raging battles in peace. But I got used to it. Then Daddy found himself a girlfriend, and another, and another. His latest is ten years younger than me."

"Yuk," said Annie.

"Oh, I don't care."

She watched Lana go into the shower stall and heard the water go on. Lana began singing loudly from *Fiddler on the Roof.* When she came out, she was wrapped in a fluffy white towel. "I can help you buy furniture," she said, continuing the conversation.

"No, no. I have to get used to making do if I'm going to be a musician," said Annie.

"I want to hear you play. I really do." Drying herself off with a towel, Lana slipped on her underwear and slid into her heels. "I love music, classical, reggae, everything. My daddy made me take piano for eight years. That's honest work, Annie. Theater's just a pimp. You slave and work your butt off, sell yourself body and soul, and get nothing. All your earnings end up in the closed fist of some crappy producer. Which reminds me, I'm so glad you aren't keeping house for that whore, Tom. How he used me I won't even get into. Why would you want a two-bit criminal?" Lana asked, wrapping her hair in the towel. "I know the answer to that one. He's so good in bed, is that it?" She did a two-step in front of the wall-length mirror, admiring her smooth legs and thighs.

"Why do you call him a criminal?" Annie asked.

Lana leaned confidentially over the bed to her. "He took my new Impala to Pittsburgh without telling me," she mock-whispered. "And 'somehow' it got stolen. The Assistant District Attorney called me, person to person. He had such a peculiar accent. Is that how they really talk?"

"Yeah," Annie said, recalling the distinctive Western Pennsylvania twang. "And he thinks Thomas stole it?"

"No, that's what Daddy thinks," said Lana "The DA was just asking question about an accident. But I'm not telling. My lips are sealed." From her dressing table, she took out a bottle of body cream and squeezed a long thin line of it on her stomach and arms.

"Could you rub some on my back?" she asked.

As Annie spread the cream on Lana's smooth wide powerful shoulders, she noticed blue bruise marks on her neck.

"How did you get these?"

"Three guesses."

"I don't know," said Annie. "What are they? Are they painful?"

"Love marks."

"From who?"

"Oh, I don't remember. Vern? Tom? Hey, it's just pretend strangling—very sexy. You haven't tried it? Don't worry. It was ages ago."

"They look new," said Annie feeling confused and uncomfortable. Skirting the area where the bruises were, she rubbed a few more dabs of cream into Lana's skin and then got up, smoothing out the satiny floral bedspread.

"What about those posters you wanted me to help you with?" Annie's gaze flitted over the canvas on the wall. "Your painting reminds me of one Van Gogh painted in Saint Remy, a big painting of white blossoms and pink on a very gnarled tree. I really like it."

"Well, then you're really going to like this too."

Annie watched dumbstruck as Lana skipped over to her worktable in her high heels, dipped a brush into black paint, and began to spread great smears over her body.

"What are you doing!"

"Making an impression no one will forget," Lana said. She

painted “Nigger” on her abdomen in black paint, “Whore” in red between her breasts, “Cunt” and “Bitch” in blue on her arms. On her forehead, she painted “Lana” in purple.

“What do you think?” she struck a pose, spread-eagled.

“You’re crazy,” Annie said.

“Hell, I’m the goddamn poster. Will I make an impression or what?”

“Can you get it off?”

“Look! It’s almost dry.”

Lana twirled around in front of her floor length mirror, admiring herself while the paint dripped down into her panties and black public hair. “I guess I’ll find out later, won’t I! Now, Annie darling, help me find something to wear.”

When Annie left, Lana was busy putting on her makeup.

Annie sat on the subway holding a sequined purse Lana gave her. She felt bereft when she got home. In a confused and disappointed state of mind, she forced herself to get out her violin. After a half-hour of warm-up exercises, she felt a little better.

** *

Annie was surprised to see the notice in her usually empty mailbox. There was a package waiting for her at Fed Ex. Quickly she changed into her blue jeans and T-shirt, rushing out of her apartment. On the subway platform, she was careful not to lean back against the wall where “Suppose They Gave a War and Nobody Came” was splattered in fresh black paint.

Annie walked away from the Federal Express desk carrying the heavy package tightly wrapped with brown paper and twine addressed to her in Dad’s handwriting. She could imagine Dad’s thin arms around the box like hers were now, could see him taking it to the Post Office in Wilkinsburg. She thought she could even smell Dad’s gray-striped wool suit on the box. She remembered burying her head in those sleeves when she was small.

Seeing a phone booth, Annie stopped to rifle through her new purse for her address book. Nobody answered when she called home. Where was Mother? Where were Melinda and Dad? She dialed Dad's office, picturing his desk in front of the window overlooking the Monongahela River on Second Street in downtown Pittsburgh. Maybe he would be working overtime. He often did on Saturday just to catch up.

She felt her mouth go dry as the phone rang.

"Hello, Schmidt Insurance, Jim Ryan speaking."

"Dad? Dad?"

"Why, Annie! Is that you?" At the sound of his voice—pleasant, well modulated and distant—Annie suddenly felt light-hearted.

"Dad! I got the package."

"So it did get there," he said, sounding pleased. "Let's see, I mailed it Thursday. It made good time."

"You're wonderful to take the trouble. What happened with Melinda? I asked her to send it."

"She was too busy, so I took on the job. I thought you'd appreciate your music."

"I missed you so much."

There was silence. She had said the wrong thing.

"So what do you know?" he said finally.

"Dad, I didn't mean to make you angry at me."

"You made your Mother and me very unhappy. We have had a lot of sleepless nights wondering if you are safe," he said. He cleared his throat in a way that made her throat hurt too.

"You know I got into Julliard? Did Melinda show you the letter?"

"Yes, she did."

Sweat ran down her bare arms. Wasn't he happy for her?

"I suppose you're upset that I was staying with Thomas. Well, I left him. I have my own place now. And a job too. I want to invite you to visit me. You and Mother."

"Mother and I don't know any Thomas," he said, ignoring her invitation.

"But I'm not living with him now!" She could hear the panic in her own voice.

"Please, Annie, I have a lot of work to do here."

"Could you just listen to me for once?" she cried.

"I have to get out the payroll. It's the end of the month. And frankly, I don't want to hear about you shacking up with some black actor," said Dad, his voice twisting round her like a heavy rope.

"Dad, please, it's not like that."

But what was it like? The words she dare not say choked her. She felt angry with her father for making this conversation impossible.

"Annie, it's time to grow up."

"You aren't listening! Oh, you'll never understand," she moaned, leaning against the glass inside the phone booth. Outside it had begun to drizzle.

"Well, enjoy the music," said Dad from very far away. "And congratulations on Julliard." It took a second or two before Annie realized he had hung up.

Back in her studio, she unpacked the box. Along with the music scores, there was an envelope with a letter. She stared in amazement at the check for $500, a huge sum, tucked inside.

> Dear Annie,
> This is to tide you over until you get on your feet.
> Mother and I hope you are happy, though we don't see how given the choices you have made.
> The weather is nice here. We've had a few thunderstorms and Lucky has been hiding under the dining room table a lot. You know she's afraid of the lightning. Remember how you used to get under the table with her to keep her company?
> Love, Dad

Carefully Annie took out each music score and set it neatly in chronological order: Brahms, Bruch, Handel, Mozart, Schubert and Vivaldi. All the music she knew and loved.

"Thank you, Dad." Tears trickled down her cheeks.

Painstakingly she folded the check and put it into her purse. She would tell Lana. Maybe they could go out together to the cut-rate furniture stores and get a used sofa. Maybe she'd invite Thomas over.

Gone

Thomas knew that Annie was gone as soon as he opened his door, even before he checked the closet where she hung her dresses, the drawers where her sweaters and underwear had been carefully folded and the bare shelf in the bathroom where she kept her shampoo and deodorant. She even took her favorite cereal. "A good thing. A short sweet relationship," he said aloud in his best actor's voice, magnifying the emptiness. But it didn't make him feel better.

Still he supposed it was a good thing that she was gone. It made things much simpler. Plus he was tired of crashing at Mandy's, Mel's assistant. They were just friends, but he had to sleep somewhere those nights he was out hunting after one woman or another. He couldn't expect Annie to understand, but Mandy was cool. Sometimes though he felt ashamed. Plus he had had enough of Mandy going on and on about Mel, over whom she had a hopeless crush.

That night he played *Sgt Pepper's Lonely Hearts Club Band* nonstop and smoked some pretty good dope. That chilled him out a little. But it really bothered him that Annie did not leave even a note. No goodbye. Did she know about the other women? It must be Lana gossiping, interfering. Then there was the gonorrhea thing. He could have used a condom, but, shit, he couldn't feel a thing with that rubber. Shit. Yes, he supposed Annie had the right to be upset at that. She never even asked how he got it. He didn't know himself. It wasn't a fair game and he was sorry he hadn't been straight with her.

Still the space that Annie left seemed alive with promise he couldn't turn his back on. Everywhere he turned there remained a strange yet familiar sense of her. Annie was like one of those old photographs of his Georgia relatives that Momma kept on her dresser top. Her absence echoed like the wind through the open window on warm summer evenings after a rain. She glowed in the morning light like the shadow of a rainbow or a floating scarf in the stage lights. It amazed him that he didn't feel the usual sense of loss and loneliness. He felt high thinking of her and took on a bravado he remembered as a boy of twelve getting ready for the Eighth Grade Achievement Award ceremony, Momma helping him with his first tie. Or like that young man just out of the Army, a bright and promising career ahead of him as a college student living on the GI Bill.

Annie had touched him in a way different from other white women he'd had. It started when he was stationed in Korea and some little guy from the army relay office sent for his new wife back in Tennessee. Her name was Shirley. Shirley was a pretty white girl who soon was working in the same office where Thomas was a medic. They used to walk down the unpaved road to the barracks together when he got off duty. One night he led her into the thicket. Even while he maneuvered Shirley's panties off, he kept his eyes on the road for her husband.

They met each other several more times out there on the dirt roads of Seoul. Just as Thomas began to relish the excitement of that secret, furtive sex, Shirley's husband took her to Hawaii on R&R and she never came back. White women left sooner or later, no matter what they said. Until Annie, Thomas had made sure he was the one to leave.

He began dreaming about his family. Once he dreamt about his sister being born. There she was behind the glass window of the hospital's colored ward, tiny ebony Christine-Marie, the prettiest thing he had ever seen. After so much trouble and pain for Momma, she had appeared in their life. How could that be? Yet here she was. It was a miracle, his baby sister with her small soft face and limbs, her fingers reaching out, her tiny toes. Momma said, you name her, Thomas Henry.

He was doing his stinky shoe routine for his brothers and sisters. He dangled one of Old Find's old shoes with its frayed ties, torn rubber soles, splotches of dried white paint and putrid smell of unwashed feet over her tiny head.

"Whew! Damn stinky shoe!" Thomas shouted. "Who's gonna help me get rid of this nasty old shoe?" he yelled, swinging it round and round. His brothers and sisters fell laughing and hollering in the dirt, especially Lorn, the little brother who adored him and was now in the Western Penitentiary for armed robbery.

Thomas woke up thinking of Lorn. Shit, he should have gone to see him while he was in Pittsburgh. Why hadn't he? He was chicken-shit and that was the sorry truth.

But new and wonderful things appeared. A single yellow crocus bloomed in the patch of dirt between his apartment building and the sidewalk. Thomas' neighbor spontaneously gave him a brand new color Sylvania TV when he moved back to Trinidad. Mel offered him the part of Johnny's understudy in the upcoming Fire Island Black Arts Festival production and paid him double to learn the part. Vowing to outshine him, Thomas studied every move of Carlo, the actor who played Johnny, hoping he wouldn't show up so Thomas could have a chance at the role.

Then there was Stan whom he had met a few weeks before. When he heard a producer from LA was going to be at the theater, Thomas had come in early. Several actors were on the bare stage arguing over their entrances when he arrived. A group of white men sat in the front row with Mel who had the familiar overbearing pose of someone about to con a mark that Thomas recognized so well. Waiting in the back, he overheard talk of a West Coast production, a musical, maybe even a movie. He felt his mouth go dry. Slipping his sunglasses in his vest pocket, Thomas sauntered over to Mel and a small man in a black suit sporting round wire glasses and a clipped goatee.

"What's happening?" he asked, putting down his briefcase, extending his hand.

"This here is Tom, one of my actors. Tom, meet Stan Marvelous, of Marvelous West Productions," Mel interjected.

"So you're marvelous," Thomas said, grinning.

"You got it right," said Stan, putting out a soft hand small as a child's. He said he'd changed his name from Mahoney when he came to the West Coast. "Sounded like baloney and there's too much of that in LA. Ha ha. And who the hell did you say you are?"

"I didn't. It's Thomas Dreamer."

"Good. I like it," Stan said.

The actors on stage had stopped bickering and were listening to their conversation. So was Mel, while feigning indifference.

"I've done my share of directing too," Thomas said.

"Where was that?" Wringing his hands, Stan took off his glasses, wiping them with a linen handkerchief.

"West Orange, Upstate New York, Pittsburgh, Harlem," said Thomas. "What's up with you all?"

"I'm producing a movie you might be interested in," said Stan.

"He's still under contract with the Rep," Mel reminded him.

"I'm listening," said Thomas. He noticed Stan wasn't paying any attention to Mel either.

"It's set in New York—a gangsta flick—Othello as the leader," Stan told him. "Shakespeare, get it? Like *West Side Story,* but grittier. Nastier, more violent. Lots of con men, pimps and drugs. The usual. Then there's the race-sex thing with what's her name being snuffed out and all."

"Desdemona," Mel said too quickly.

"That's it. Bernstein's thinking about doing the music."

"I'd have to hear more, but yes, I'm interested," said Thomas. He picked up his briefcase. "Okay then." He turned to leave. "I'll be back. And Stan?"

"Yeah?"

"When should I pack my bags for LA?"

Stan laughed, though Mel did not.

* * *

Back stage he stopped studying Johnny's scenes and wrote out a check and a letter.

> Dear Georgie G,
> I want you to use this for guitar lessons. Now that I'm working steady in the theater, I'll be able to send you more money. How are you doing at school?
> Sorry you weren't home the last time I called. Momma said you were delivering papers. Did you know I was a paperboy too? Well, gotta get going. See you soon!
> XXXXX, Dad

He felt happy writing those Xs for love, signing it "Dad." When would he see his son next? Soon? He didn't know, but he liked writing it.

Within a week, Thomas got a letter back from Georgie G and one from Carlotta too. Everyone was doing fine. Georgie G was still taking lessons at the Hill House.

For the first time, Thomas spent more time at home and even began to enjoy his place. At night he saw from his bed through the front window the streetlights glowing like ripened fruit. He thought of Annie falling asleep after they made love. The motions she made under the blankets called up old unnamed soothing feelings. It reminded him of a bird he had once. At night it used to twitter and ruffle its feathers. For hours he'd hear it hopping and messing at the birdseed that fell on the floor below the cage. It prevented him from sleeping and he intended to cover the cage, though he never got around to it. Was it hoping to fly? One day he opened the cage and the bird flew out the window, disappearing into the New York haze. It never came back. Maybe he shouldn't have opened the cage? He fell asleep considering the question.

Gala

Hello stranger," Thomas said when he finally called Annie. "You sneaked out," he added.

"You weren't even there," she answered.

"But you knew where I was," he said.

"Did I?" She didn't wait for an answer. Instead she gave him her new address.

"So you finally went uptown," he said. "Be careful."

"Why?"

"Uptown is where the white folks live—but go too far and you get to Harlem."

"Oh."

"I'll have to come by sometime. I've been so busy."

There were so many more distractions these days, more acting opportunities, he told her. He even got the chance to play Johnny in a Saturday matinee at the Fire Island run. Though his performance wasn't reviewed, everybody said he was a better Johnny than Carlo.

"Wow," she said, laughing.

"The Fire Island show was extended two weeks," he said, laughing too. "And there's talk of taking it on the road. I'd play the lead role, naturally."

"Wow! I have some good news too."

"You still want me, is that it?"

Annie didn't answer.

"I'm glad you called," Thomas went on. "There's a Gala Celebration on Saturday. A big party. Some hotshots from Hollywood will be there. Do you want to come with me?"

"Yes, of course!"

"I'll pick you up."

They'd take a taxi to the mansion on the Upper East Side he told her. She was to be sure to be ready. He'd be on a tight schedule.

"Okay."

Before she could tell him about Julliard, he said he was sorry but he had to go.

She would tell him Saturday night, she thought. That would be a better night anyway.

* * *

All afternoon Annie had been feverishly preparing. She had washed her long hair in the sink and rinsed out her stockings, hanging them up to dry over the chair. While taking a sponge bath, she was overcome with fear and then lethargy, as if the party meant nothing to her. A feeling of worthlessness, heavy, drab and indistinct took over like some of those interminable summer afternoons in Pittsburgh, gray and muggy, that threatened to storm but didn't.

How could he find her desirable measured against all the other women—actresses—he knew? Annie frowned in the mirror, all her expectations shriveling like fruit left to rot. Even Lana and he had so much more in common, while she could only watch from the sidelines. She lay down between her new sheets. She had fallen asleep and when she woke, there he was knocking at her door.

"Why, it's nice outside tonight after all," Annie said, walking ahead of Thomas out into the soft air. She stood balanced precariously on the curb in her new high heels. The night was very warm. While Thomas stepped into the street to hail a taxi, she loosened the knit shawl she had wrapped around her shoulders.

"Ready for the party tonight?" he asked.

"Uh-huh."

Annie shivered with expectation, doubt. Would she have fun tonight? She slipped into the torn back seat, glancing at the taxi driver, an elderly man with buckteeth wearing an orange baseball cap.

Looking out the dirty windows of the taxi, she fingered the patterns on the sequined purse Lana had given her.

Even though it was the middle of summer, Thomas wore a white turtleneck with a huge collar rolled over twice and tightly fitting black velvet pants. On his finger was a wide gold ring with crisscrossed chevron designs.

"Miss me?" he asked, grinning.

She nodded. He seemed distant and preoccupied. She wondered who gave him the ring.

"Is something the matter?" she asked.

"No. Why?"

"You seem worried, I guess."

Thomas squeezed her knee. "It's you who look worried. Hmm, sweet, you sure are pretty. Why should you be worried?"

She shrugged.

"You know, you're right. I admit I am a little worried."

His admission made her feel better. Or was it his warm hand on her knee?

"Things are moving so fast. There's somebody I really want to talk to tonight, a producer who might be able to help me."

"Oh."

Thomas moved his hand higher to her lap.

"Who gave you that ring?" she asked finally, rolling her thumb over the sequined pattern on her purse.

"A present from a rich old lady from the Bronx. She came backstage three nights in a row and wanted me to go out with her and her daughter. She gave me this ring to remember her by," he said. "What's the matter? You don't have to be jealous of rich old ladies. How's your new place? My place is still free, still waiting." He grinned.

"Thomas, I got into Julliard."

"You what?" His eyes widened with surprise.

"I've been wanting to tell you."

"I knew you could do it." He hugged her.

Despite herself, Annie laughed. "You never even heard me play."

"I will now."

They sat in silence. Annie gazed out the window as the taxi zigzagged from street to street, passing theaters and movie houses with blinking marquees of *Bonnie and Clyde* and *The Dirty Dozen.*

When they got to Fifth and East 64th, Thomas yelled to the taxi driver. "You can stop here!" He jumped out. "Keep the change," he called, tossing a twenty.

She smiled at the doorman who opened the carved red-lacquer door of the East '60s mansion and at the bony middle-aged woman with short gray hair wearing a red satin pantsuit and at her yapping miniature poodle. She smiled at the squat black actor in a clown outfit who flew at Thomas, kneeling at his feet, gushing, "Here he is. My dark hero!"

"Cool it, Randy," Thomas said, pulling him upright. Thomas was grinning as Randy draped his multi-colored arms around him.

She smiled as Thomas introduced her to Carlo who, Annie knew, Thomas hoped to replace. She smiled in response to the pale starlets her own age tittering at Thomas, their low-cut dresses revealing full silk-smooth breasts. She smiled when Lana appeared in angora and lace—minus her body paint—and tipped her full glass in a toast. Over her black curls, Lana wore a red silk turban pinned with a gold six-pointed Jewish star. The tassels hung down over her bare shoulders accentuating the angora trim of her dress and her peachy skin. Annie smiled at Vern on whose arm Lana hung. Did anyone else notice Annie's smile obliterating her face like a large wet bite?

It was different than Leo's party—bigger, louder, more exciting, hinting at danger, wild and crazy, swarming with glittering people in taffeta, feathers, silk, polyester, nylon and lace. She felt overwhelmed, reeling in a carnival of color and light. The guests wore far-out styles and shocking costumes while loud rock music boomed, drowning their laughter. There were many beautiful dark and light-skinned men and women, so young and elegant, with long shining hair or frizzled Afros, and the sense of wealth and privilege everywhere.

Thomas disappeared into the throng and someone in a leopard caftan put a full glass of wine in her hand. Annie drank it, tiptoeing from one opulent room to the next. A strange assortment of couples, many interracial, stood in high doorways talking about the recent riot in Newark where twenty-seven people had been killed. Annie heard mention of other disturbances in Roxbury, Boston's black district, a welfare sit-in around Tampa, riots in Cincinnati and Buffalo, Atlanta and Milwaukee.

There were men in black suits and white shirts. Twirling indolently on spiked heels and smoking cigarettes or dope, the women exhibited smooth flesh in scant dresses beneath pounds of glittering jewelry. Their cold chiseled stone faces reminded her of the models in the department stores or rich girls at Ellis School, catty and supercilious. Or was she the one who felt that way? It was painful the way every judgment Annie made she had to try on herself first.

Couples were snorting cocaine in the corners. One heavy man in horned-rimmed glasses held out a mirror sprinkled with white powder to her.

"No, thank you," she said.

She saw no black women. Was it that they didn't find white men attractive? Or maybe they thought them insubstantial and disappointing the way Annie thought of Leo or even her Dad? Or had they not been invited? Were they just not welcome? Maybe they refused to come. She could understand why.

Just then Thomas appeared, flanked by Lana and Vern. "Hey,

girl! There's the Hollywood producer I was telling you about, Stan Marvelous." He squeezed Annie's shoulder.

"Vern! Get your black ass over here!" Lana called out, but Vern was following a tall Swedish girl in a Playboy bunny outfit into a hallway.

"Asshole. Let's split. Let's go to my place, Tom," she added under her breath.

"Annie's here. Do you want me to ignore her?" Thomas took Annie's arm.

Lana spit out her imported champagne, spraying the tablecloth. "Someone else is looking for you too."

"Who?" he asked, as if mollifying a demanding child.

"I have secrets too."

"I'll bet." Thomas turned his head, scrutinizing the crowd.

"Let's go find that famous producer!" Lana squealed, grabbing his arm.

"There he is! Hello, Stan!" Thomas called out across the room. "C'mon!"

With Lana and Annie following, he dodged through the crowd to grab the producer's hand. "Remember me?"

"Uh, have we met?" asked Stan, glassy-eyed. He was a small man in black with round wire glasses and a gray goatee. He wore a white blousy shirt, open to reveal a mat of black chest hair.

"Thomas Dreamer. We met at the Negro Rep."

"Nice to see you, Tom."

"I've been thinking about your offer. Can we go somewhere and talk privately?" Thomas asked, holding onto Stan's hand. "How long are you going to be in New York? Just name the time and place!" Thomas shouted louder over the crowd.

"It's up to Mel." Stan shouted back, pulling his hand away.

"Are you taking the play to LA?" Thomas asked.

Stan brushed the question aside, leaning closer. "We'll talk later. Introduce me to your date," he said, his mouth twisting into a grin. He put out his hand and stroked Lana's silky thigh.

"Stan, meet Lana."

Lana pursed her lips toward Stan and winked.

Thomas put his arm around Annie, pulling her to him. "And this is Annie."

"Yeah, yeah," Stan said, surveying her with tiny yellow eyes. He mumbled something and then ducked, his head sinking into his neck.

"When can we talk?" Thomas called out as Stan disappeared into the throng. Lana rushed after him with Thomas behind.

Annie asked a woman where the bathroom was. The woman pointed with her cigarette holder, dropping ashes onto the parquet floor. Annie tottered down the hall past an oversized reproduction of a Greek statue, a headless torso of a woman with wings done in paper mache. She remembered it from a course on European Art History. It was called the Winged Victory. Through opened doorways, she spied half-naked couples, men with women and men with men, lounging on mattresses in smoke-filled bedrooms. Reaching the white and purple gold embossed bathroom, she pulled down her underpants. She sat down with relief on the toilet sprinkled with glitter and gazed blankly above her at an open skylight. Jets with red flashing lights crisscrossed beneath a mat of twinkling stars.

When she came out, there was a big commotion in the hallway. She recognized Mel's deep voice. He was arguing loudly with someone else. Stan? Someone was laughing hysterically. Where was Lana? Where was Thomas? The arguing got louder. Somebody got hit. A woman wept, then shrieked. A crowd formed, egging on the fight. It looked like Mel slammed Stan into the wall. The crowd loved it.

Annie rushed past the Winged Victory, past the magnificent dining room with its tables piled with seafood and pasta, crab and oysters, past chilled bottles of French champagne in silver ice buckets and past the open bar framed by jewel-colored bottles reflected in a wall-length mirror.

Finally, she stumbled down the steps into a large sunken living room furnished in black and white leather. There was Thomas leaning against a grand piano singing Negro spirituals for an admiring crowd.

"Nobody knows the trouble I've seen," he crooned in a deep melodic baritone.

Wending her way through the clamoring crowd, she applauded with the others when he finished.

"Thomas!"

He turned around and grabbed her shoulders, "Annie! Here you are. Where have you been? I thought somebody had taken you off." Smiling, he led her away through French doors to the porch.

"Oh, Thomas. I haven't seen you all night. I want to talk to you."

"You have your chance now, baby." He closed the doors and took her in his arms. They looked out on the twinkling lights of the New York skyline.

"What's up?" he asked.

"Did you see Mel fighting in the hallway?" she asked.

"I heard it was ugly."

He hugged her, smoothing back her hair. "Oh baby, you are so nice, you really are. I've been around too many actors I guess. Speak of the devil . . ."

As if listening for her cue, Lana banged on the other side of the French doors. Thomas stepped aside and she came barging in, holding out a lit joint.

"Talking about me?" Lana slid her arm in his, kissing him.

"Good news," Thomas said, taking a hit. "Tell her," he said to Annie, encouragingly, offering her the joint. "Julliard," he prompted.

"I got accepted to Julliard for the fall semester," said Annie, taking a toke and then another.

"Didn't I tell you!" shouted Lana.

Annie laughed, remembering.

"Congratulations. Let's go dance!" Lana cried, pulling Thomas toward her.

He looked back through the beveled glass. "You really want to get out there in that crowd?"

"Come on!" Lana said, yanking open the door. "Don't be a party pooper. Annie, come!"

Following them, Annie gazed dumbly at the scene before her. On the stage were two electric guitarists with long hair in their eyes, a fat boy in a baseball cap pounding an electric organ, and a man on the drums. Below, the dancers' heads bobbed up and down to the beat as their feet pounded the floor. Jumping up and down in front were two very large men with black beards in wrinkled suits, one on either side of a tiny frizzled blond with a baby doll face in a purple halter, black short shorts and sparkly heels.

"Assholes," Thomas said in her ear, noticing where she was looking. "They're brothers. Filmmakers, identical twins. They just asked me to be in a porno flick. I was to fly to LA and work two months for nothing. I suppose they think just because I'm black, I'm dumb."

"Really?" She was finding it hard to concentrate.

The men took turns rubbing their bulging crotches against the blond.

"What are you whispering about?" Lana came between them.

"We're talking about those bozos out on the floor." Thomas pointed at the girl and the men gyrating under the lights. Behind them, the band accelerated to a frenzy.

"She seems to be having a good time," said Lana. "And that's what I'm going to have. No way am I going to hang around you two dumbos any more." She stomped off, knocking over an orchid on a marble table.

Behind a mask of doped indifference, Annie held onto Thomas' arm. Her ears were ringing with the loud, metallic sound, like the pounding of huge welding rigs or cement drills used to demolish buildings.

"Let's go home, Thomas. I really want to go," Annie said, pulling his arm. "Thomas? Did you hear me?"

"I'll call you a cab," he said.

"But I don't want to go alone."

"Tom, Tom!" Annie heard a woman shouting. Looking around, she saw Lana standing on the stage with the microphone. "Tom, Tom the piper's son, stole a pig and away he run."

From the dance floor, some very drunk men waved their arms at her, bleary-eyed with alcoholic lust. Lana's red turban wobbled and fell to the ground. Sweat stained the armpits of her dress, torn and dragging.

"Tom, Tom, the preacher's son, stole a car and away he run," Lana sang in a gravelly voice. She leaned over the microphone to the drummer, pulling his drumsticks away and beating his drum wildly.

"Tom, Tom the piper's son. Stole a car and away he run!" she shrieked from the stage.

"What is she saying?" Annie cried.

"I've got to stop her. She's making a fool of herself," Thomas said through his teeth. "Wait for me here."

The smoke was heavy and the noise deafening as Thomas leaped through the crowd toward the blazing stage. Annie closed her eyes. She felt the floor shake and told herself not to pass out. Her eyes were still closed when one of the brothers from LA grabbed her, pulling her onto the dance floor. She opened her eyes to see Thomas drag Lana off the stage. She was slumped against his chest, a rag doll.

Annie ran, forcing herself up the steps of the sunken living room through the dining room to the bar. There she sat down, stunned, on a red leather stool, staring at the full colored bottles lining the mirrored wall. When the bartender asked her what she wanted to drink, she said, "Nothing." Where was her shawl? Where was her sequined purse? She didn't belong here. She should go. A sad-faced man in a suit offered to buy her a drink, but she shook her head. Time and space collapsed in a shower of boozy cloudiness. Finally she stood up and began to retrace her steps, going from room to room, looking for her purse and her shawl. On the way she thought she saw Thomas and Lana, or maybe Thomas by himself, or maybe Lana. Were they fighting? She wouldn't look. She wouldn't intrude. She just wanted to get away. Finally she found her belongings. Now she had to find her way out. Which way was the door? She saw Thomas approaching her as if he'd been there all along.

"C'mon, I'll see that you get home," he said. Numbly, Annie followed him through the elegant candle-lit anteroom past the doorman and out the red lacquered door into the street. Lana was there too, smoking a cigarette as she leaned against a telephone booth on the corner next to a boarded up newsstand. When Annie said, "Hi", Lana blew smoke at her.

"I'll call you a cab," Thomas said, walking out into the empty street while Annie tottered on the curb.

"What about me? Asshole! God, can't you forget that skinny nervous ding-a-ling? Look at her," Lana yelled, pointing to Annie. "She's scared of her own shadow." Abandoning her languorous pose, Lana did a masterful imitation of Annie tremulously perched on her high heels.

"Lana, stop that shit now," Thomas said, hailing a cab.

"Can you see that Lana gets home?" Thomas whispered to Annie as he opened the cab door for her.

"I suppose."

"I'm not going with that ding-a-ling. Tomboy, I'm coming with you."

"I told you I have to meet someone. By myself," he said.

"Someone I know?" Lana leered, falling into the back seat beside Annie.

Thomas slammed the door shut, telling the cab driver where to go. "Si, si," said the man.

"Tom wants me to die," Lana told Annie as they drove past Thomas hurrying away. "It would be so much easier for everybody if I were dead."

"How can you say something like that?"

"I've thought of how to do it. All I need is some pure stuff—I'm out of it now unfortunately—to mix with that sweet Italian baby laxative everybody uses and stick into one of those filthy needles sitting in my sink." Lana sighed deeply. "You don't know what I'm talking about, you stupid kid."

"You're drunk."

"Am I? Am I? Oh, Annie, I'm sorry I bad-mouthed you. I'm a no-good girl. Don't listen to me. You know I'm just kidding about Tom. He's a real good man and I love him to death."

"Sure, sure."

When they reached Lana's building, she pulled out a hundred dollar bill and gave it to the cab driver, telling him to keep the change.

"That's too much," Annie said, but Lana insisted. "Take her home too," she told the cabbie.

"No, wait here, please," Annie told him. She would help Lana get inside and then she would be back.

"I don't think he understands," she said.

"Who cares?" Lana said, looking for her keys under the streetlight.

Finally they got up to the penthouse. "Your place looks different now," Annie said, surveying the darkened room. Litter was everywhere, on chairs, the sofa, bed, dressers and all the available tabletops. In the sink, there were dirty dishes in a basin half filled with water. Scum floated on the top along with bits of ash and what looked like dead flies.

"What happened?" asked Annie, shocked.

"Life," Lana said. She told Annie she'd sold her expensive furniture for drugs or they were stolen.

"I'm sorry," Annie said. She felt very tired. "Will you be alright?"

"Hell, yes."

"I'll come by and help you clean up tomorrow."

"Don't bother. I have a maid who comes on Mondays. Go home!" Lana kicked off her shoes. "Don't come, hear me? I won't be here."

"Alright. Goodbye," Annie called out as she left.

As she feared, the taxi was gone. But at least the evening was behind her now and she was glad. Annie vowed not to drink like that ever again. She walked toward the 7th Street subway, measuring every step that took her further away from Lana's. Thomas was behind her too in a strange, but irrefutable way. She felt sad, but determined. The cool night air had sobered her up fast.

Night

How relieved Thomas was when the cab driver drove away with Lana and Annie in the back seat. The night was his again.

Now he could admit to himself that he'd felt happy seeing Annie in her tiny studio apartment. She was softer, sexier, than before. Sweet, so vulnerable. He had forgotten how much he enjoyed confiding in her, talking about petty theater politics. When they stepped out of the taxi and were greeted by a uniformed doorman who recognized him, he felt on top of the world!

He had acted cool even though Lana was there and more wired than usual. He was glad he'd stuck to grass and seltzer water when Vern tried to get him loaded.

It seemed like things were going fine, especially after he set up the meeting with Stan. But when Lana climbed onto the stage and begin her threatening rhyme, he knew things were going to get bad. They could have been worse though.

But he had been wrong to think he could shake her off his back, wrong to expect her to leave him alone. He had to force her hand. Thomas relived the events of the last half hour as if replaying the rushes from a B-movie. He had pulled Lana through the crowd, past the doorman in his red and gold uniform, and out the front door.

"This way," he had said, holding her arm tight, leading her toward the phone booth on the corner.

"Oh, you're hurting me, but don't stop!" she had cried.

"What's the number?" He put a dime in the coin slot.

"What the hell are you talking about?"

"The Assistant DA. What's his number?" Thomas asked.

"How the hell do I know? It's three o-clock in the morning, asshole."

"Assistant DAs are always up in Pittsburgh."

"I forgot it."

"Look in your little black book," he said.

He made her empty her purse and look through each page of her address book until she found it.

"Go ahead," he said, dialing the number for her. "The DA will appreciate it. I promise you."

Then the phone began to ring and Lana reached for her cigarettes, clutching the receiver. "What do I tell him?" There was that same high girlish voice. It was one of the things that had attracted Thomas when they first met at the Actor's Workshop. He had thought she was acting then, mocking herself. But no, that was her natural voice, stripped of sophistication and glamour, like her plump dimply body without the expensive clothes.

"Tell him you found the guy who stole your car. Do it now. I'm serious, Lana. I'm the one they want."

"You didn't steal the Impala from me, asshole. I made you take it. How could you forget? I begged you, remember? Nobody steals from Lana. Besides, I got better things to do than snitch on you."

"So you snitched on me, did you?"

"Why should I want you in jail? I might need you someday, honey."

"I asked you a question," he said. The phone was still ringing.

"Nobody's there. Didn't I tell you?" Lana threw the phone receiver against the booth wall where it buzzed like a hornet against the glass. "So what are you staring at, Tomboy? Go on, leave. That's what you do best, isn't it?"

She lit a cigarette, puffing madly as if in the middle of some madcap routine.

"Don't worry," she puffed. "The cops don't know a fucking thing. Joe Johnson alias Thomas Find alias Dreamer alias who the hell knows what else. That's a secret between you and me—and maybe her, you know, your date."

"What did you tell Annie?"

"Don't be upset with me. She's in love with you and didn't hear a thing I said." Throwing her cigarette butt away, Lana leaned toward him, attempting to hug him. "The truth is you don't need me any more."

Thomas stared at the phone hanging from its cord but he didn't see it. He didn't see anything. He was drowning in pale cold fear. Immersed, paralyzed, he slipped deeper beneath the surface, holding his breath in terror.

Lana tried lighting another cigarette. "Oh, damn it," she cried as it slipped out of her fingers.

"Be careful!" Thomas brushed off the burning ashes from her dress. She stumbled on the curb. He got her just before she fell.

"What do you want from me?" he asked, holding her in his arms.

"Just don't leave me here."

"I'm meeting Stan. I can't take you, you know that."

"So drop me off at the outpatient clinic at Bellevue where the crazed druggies go. That's where Daddy thinks I belong. He had me committed once, remember? They know me there."

"You need some sleep," he said, propping her up.

"You know the only thing that makes me sleep, Tom. And you got it in your tight black pants."

Those bitter joking confidences he once considered a form of intimacy disgusted him now. Sex was the last thing he wanted. But it wouldn't be that hard said the voice of experience in his head. It was just another performance with his cock as the star. He was used to that.

"Don't leave me, Tom," wept Lana.

"Okay. I'll come by after my meeting. But now I have to find Annie. Wait here."

Lana was still propped up against the telephone pole, cigarette in her hand, when he returned from the Gala with Annie. Thankfully, they had both gotten into that taxi.

* * *

Stan didn't pick up when he called the Plaza from the corner phone booth, nor did he pick up when Thomas called again from the hotel lobby. He hung around there for an hour despite the suspicious looks from the staff, but Stan still didn't show.

When he turned the corner toward home at around dawn in a depressed state of mind, he saw a figure slumped over on his steps. For an instant he mistook it for Annie and ran toward her, shivering with cold. But no, he was mistaken. It was Lana. That mistake he took as a sign of bad luck, a foreboding that he struggled to shake as he might Momma's warnings about voodoo.

Lana's face was bruised and puffy. Thomas' gaze moved down to her torn party dress and the trickle of blood oozing down her legs.

"Lana, what happened? Talk to me, talk to me. Where's Annie?"

"Who knows? Don't worry. She took me back to my place like the good little girl she is." She mumbled something else he could not understand.

"But how could this happen? Who did this?"

"No one you know, hot shot. Don't worry your nappy little head about me."

Shock and pity overwhelmed him. He helped her inside to his apartment and then called the paramedics. "Don't argue," he said. "You need help."

Now he was sitting next to her as she lay on the gurney in the ambulance on their way to Belleview. Even in the early morning, the street approaching the Emergency entrance was clogged with cars, delivery trucks, and ambulances with flashing lights.

"You didn't come," she mumbled. "You said you would."

"Aww, shit, Lana. I'm sorry. Things didn't go so well for me after you left."

He started to tell her about Stan not showing up, but stopped when he saw she was about to pass out.

"Hurry! Hurry!" he shouted to the ambulance driver.

Thomas was ashamed at how relieved he felt when Lana insisted on admitting herself. When he got back home from the hospital, he lay down in his dress clothes and bunched a pillow under his head.

He dreamt he was on his way to the theater when he just happened to look in the window of a coffee shop. Recognizing the cook at the grill flipping hamburgers, Thomas waved. That was when he saw Joe sitting at the far counter staring at him. Joe wore his Pittsburgh blue, his uniform pressed neat and clean, the shiny badge on his chest pocket, the black holster and gun at his right hip. His police cap was perched on the countertop. He was holding a full cup of black coffee, thick as sludge. Thomas halted and pulled open the door.

"Hi ya," said Joe.

"You still looking for me?"

"Naw, it's riot time."

"I heard you were looking for me. Making phone calls. Asking questions."

"I got too many more important things to do. Can I have my bill?" Joe summoned the counter girl.

"You gotta tell them to close the case," said Thomas.

"Yeah, sure I will," Joe said, putting a dollar tip under his plate.

"Tell them I didn't do it. I didn't steal that car."

"Yeah, yeah," Joe said.

"I'm sorry about running away."

"Yeah." Taking his hat, Joe pushed himself away, adjusting his gun on his belt.

Joe was down the aisle at the door when Thomas called out, "Hey! Aren't you going to say goodbye?"

"I done that the moment I hit the ground. What you want with me, boy?" said Joe.

"Are you dead or alive I want to know?"

When Thomas woke up, anxious and sweating, the question was repeating in his mind like a throbbing headache. He wanted to run.

Palm Reader

Annie was willing herself to feel adventurous. Thomas had called to ask if she could visit Lana in the hospital, but she couldn't seem to get the courage to do that. At least she could go see the palm reader who lived right around the corner from her. Lana had pointed out the address when they were walking out of Deepa's Donuts that day.

"You should go visit her," Lana had said. "I've been going to her for years."

With her flyaway hair, blue jeans, and black T-shirt, "Malcolm X" dripping red on the front, Annie could have been any hip teenager from the upper West Side. She had been standing on the small unpainted porch for too long. She was ready to walk away when a six-foot woman in a purple gown wearing love beads suddenly appeared.

"I'll be with you in a minute," the woman said, leaving the door ajar and disappearing inside. Middle-aged, with hennaed hair piled high, she was drying her hands on a thick white towel when she reappeared and extended a hard pink hand.

"Hello. I'm Paula Devine. I was just finishing dinner. And you must be —."

"Annie Ryan."

"Come in, come in, Annie. How are you? Enjoying the sunshine? How's your day been?"

"I don't know," Annie said.

The palm reader led her down a tiny hallway smelling of mold into a small dark wallpapered room lit with aromatic candles. There was a table covered with lace and two straight-backed chairs.

"You're not having much fun, are you, dear?" Paula smiled.

"Not really," Annie admitted.

Paula motioned to her to sit down. "You're wise to be suspicious of me." She glanced at Annie's thin hands.

"Oh, I'm not suspicious," Annie began but then stopped, realizing the woman was right.

"Don't worry," said Paula. "It doesn't show. I know things other people don't. So Lana sent you and you are here for a reading."

"I guess," Annie said. "I mean I don't believe in it. Astrology, the occult, all that, tea leaves, astral projection. Palmistry. It's all ridiculous, isn't it?"

"Of course, but you want me to read your palm anyway." Paula laughed, patting Annie's shoulder. "I've heard it all a million times, my dear." She lit a candle on the table while Annie sat, hunched over, staring at the wallpaper covered with tiny copulating figures in kimonos.

Paula reached out and took Annie's hand. "Japanese erotica, fourteenth century, marvelous, isn't it? I had it especially hand-painted in Osaka. Don't men look just like frogs with their clothes off? Honestly, that's all I could think of every time I changed my son's pants. He's twenty-four now and in the Coast Guard. But let's get down to business. My, what long fingers," she added. "I can tell by the heart line that you are some kind of artist."

"A musician."

"Tut-tut, don't spoil my pleasure by telling me," Paula scolded. "Let's see. You are attracted to the unusual. Or do I need to state the obvious? People are your passion but not your destiny. Family is very important to you, though you have broken with your own. Your father. You don't trust him, though you should. There's separation, travel. Your mother has some sadness around her. Something she's afraid of. There's a death in the picture."

"My mother?" asked Annie, horrified.

"No, no. You have siblings?"

"One sister, Melinda. Is anything wrong with her?" Annie cried.

"No, it's not your immediate family. Ahh. There's scandal too. It's someone close by. Someone who doesn't know how important you are to him—it's a man," Paula confirmed, looking closer at Annie's delicate palm.

"Thomas?"

Paula ran her finger up and down a line in Annie's hand.

"What should I do?" Annie asked.

"You have to stick up for yourself for a change. Get out of your own way. You are your own worst enemy, child," She looked into Annie's eyes with sympathy.

"You will be terrorized and ultimately saved by your deep emotions." Paula sighed and went on. "Your test is to let them go where they will. It's not the path you're on but who you are on the path that matters."

"But does he love me?" Annie blurted out.

"Ah, the big question. Does it matter? What am I saying! Of course it does."

"He doesn't," Annie said.

"You're angry," Paula shrugged. "Remember, I'm reading your hand, not his."

"I'm angry at myself," Annie said.

Paula shrugged again.

"What about my career—am I any good?" Annie blurted.

"But that's irrelevant, dear. It's the adventure. You must persist." The palm reader's eyes caught Annie's and wouldn't let go. "If you do, that's all that matters."

She talked on about having a comfortable old age, making amends, and looking out for your own, as if she were reciting from an old script. But Annie wasn't listening. What did she care? Suddenly she felt ashamed sitting here with this soothsayer. She couldn't deny it any longer. Thomas didn't love her. Since that night at the Gala, she trusted him even less. The experience left her feeling alone, isolated. How pitiful that Lana was so drunk and stoned; how indifferent Thomas had been to both of them that night.

When Paula finished talking in her singsong voice, Annie got up to go. Paula rose too. Realizing the woman was waiting to be paid, Annie reached into her purse.

"Lana said you charged twenty," she said, handing her a bill.

"Lana? Oh, Lana, yes, Lana. I'd forgotten she sent you. How is she?" Paula folded the bill as she followed Annie out into the hallway.

Annie stopped at the door. "I was hoping maybe you could say something about her. She's not doing so well. I'm a little worried."

Paula shook her head. Was there something condescending in her look? Or was it amusement?

"I don't talk about my clients to anyone, dear. You can assure yourself of that. I only work with the person whose hand is in front of me. Tell Lana to get in touch. It's been too long."

"I will," Annie said, backing down the steps, caught up, wanting to believe, and yet not believing. She rushed around the corner and bought two slices of cheese pizza and a soft drink at Sal's Take-Out. How stupid of her to come! As if she needed an amulet to wear for an irrational and fickle future. Yet her life felt so uncertain and dangerous.

She thought of Thomas' astrology charts and how fascinating she found hers when he drew it up for her. "My moon's on your rising sign," he had said once with amazement, pulling her to him.

She had felt wonderful for a minute or two.

Stopping at the school playground across from her apartment building, Annie sat down on one end of a battered seesaw, tracing shapes in the dust with her foot while she ate her pizza. There was a phone booth at the school entrance with a handwritten sign that said, "Out of Order." The coin holder was smashed in, the cord dangling without a mouthpiece. Broken tricycles, play guns, rope and a basketball lay abandoned in the weeds and cracked cement.

Signs were posted on the telephone poles and on the abandoned building next to the school and on the fence between. "Check for VD", "Planned Parenthood Needs You", "Black Panthers Unite" and "Vote for Rockefeller" she read. A dirty man was sleeping in the doorway of the building, his matted head resting against the boarded-up door. Annie stuffed the last of the pizza crust in her mouth.

Once inside her apartment, she flopped onto her uncomfortable sofa bed and put her hands over her face. The bed creaked. A smell, ancient and crass and deep, decayed, mold perhaps, permeated this place. Why had she never noticed it before? It conjured up creepy images. That woman, Paula, holding her palm, embodied the creepiness. What had she said? Scandal, death. Whose? What was the palm reader talking about? What if it came true? Annie held up her hand and looked at the lines in her palm. How could anyone tell? What line meant betrayal, what line love? Annie put her hand up to the fading light from the window hoping to see better. When she tired of that, she got up and opened up her violin case. Practicing would make her feel she had at least accomplished something.

* * *

Lana was home when the doorman called up on the intercom to say Annie was waiting in the lobby. Lana said to come right up. Walking through the West Village, Annie had felt hot, slowed down by the muggy late summer heat, but now she shivered as the elevator door shut behind her. Lana's apartment was air-conditioned and very cold.

"Finally you came to see me! I didn't mean for you to stay away forever," Lana trilled, coughing as she puffed on her cigarette.

She wore a red angora sweater and black leather pants. Her

cheekbones stuck out. Annie was shocked at how rail-thin Lana looked, how pale without her brilliant makeup. With her black hair pulled back in a ponytail, her face appeared hollow. Deep bluish veins showed in her neck and arms. Annie couldn't help looking at the new bruises.

Lana was thrilled that Annie had brought her violin. "My very own concert!" she cried.

From the refrigerator, she took out an opened bottle of wine. Annie could smell the odor of rotten food as she slammed shut the door.

"Something to drink?" she asked.

"No, thanks. This is the piece I played for the audition," Annie said, slipping her instrument under her chin.

"I gotta hear this." Leaning against her fireplace filled with old cigarette butts and crumpled papers, Lana drank from the bottle.

Her penthouse looked worse, uglier and emptier, as if vandals had trashed it since Annie had been here last. But the ugliness disappeared once Annie began to play. The smooth tones of the opening bars of the Bruch concerto cast a spell of romance, idealism and dreams, dissolving the mess, clutter and stench of decay. Lana beat time on the tabletop with her empty bottle.

"You're terrific," Lana said when Annie lowered her bow. She wiped her eyes. "I didn't mean to cry. But that's toooo much. Really, girl, your music is beautiful. You should play at Lincoln Center with Jascha Heifetz."

"Well, I don't know about that," said Annie.

"Well, I do!" Lana retorted with an angry flourish.

"Play some Beethoven," she ordered.

Standing on the stained Persian rug, Annie played the second movement of Beethoven's Violin Sonata Number 1.

"It really needs a piano," she said, putting down her bow at the end.

"You are great!" Lana laughed. She had gotten out some grass and made herself a thick joint. "Play more!" she insisted.

Annie began playing songs from the Beatles while Lana lay down on her unmade bed, her head on a torn satin pillow.

Annie played "Michele" and then "Lucy in the Sky with Diamonds", her favorite. Lana knew all the lyrics and sang along. Her voice sounded frail. No longer did she belt out tunes in a strident Broadway tone like she had on the stage at the Gala.

By now there was a heavy smell of marijuana in the room. Annie felt stoned herself.

When she stopped playing, the day, which had been overcast, had turned into dusk outside Lana's dirty window.

"I'm so glad you came to New York," Lana sighed.

"If it hadn't been for Thomas' son, Georgie G, I would never have found Thomas," said Annie.

"I didn't even know he had a son, the bastard," said Lana. "But he never told me anything. He never did anything for me. The only reason he took me to the hospital is because he was afraid I'd die on his front step and the police would ask him questions."

"About what?"

Lana didn't reply. Annie felt alarmed and irritated. "He is worried about you. So am I," she said with some surprise, as if realizing it for the first time.

"Are you? Well, Thomas ain't worried, not about me. Who wants somebody to die on their front steps? Know what I mean? What do I care? Do I shed tears for every alley cat meowing in the gutter? Men are such fuckers. Even Ruth agrees. She's a true friend. You never met Ruth, did you? She's a colored girl from the same neighborhood as ol' Tom. The Hill District I think it's called. Do you know where that is?"

Annie nodded. "I was teaching music at the Hill House when I met Georgie G," she said.

"Oh, fuck, don't go back to that. Hell, you're here now, Annie. You're my friend, aren't you?"

Annie assured Lana she was her friend. "I went to see that palm reader across the street," she told her.

"You did! Paula, eh? How is she? I've gotta go back to her and find out what the fuck is wrong with me."

"It was weird. She talked about scandal and death, but not in my family. It was so vague. She said I didn't trust my father but I should. That I was my own worst enemy. But she could have said that about anyone. We're all our own worst enemies, wouldn't you say?" Annie stopped putting her violin away to look pointedly at Lana, but Lana didn't answer her.

"Did you ask about Tomboy?" she asked instead, beginning to cough.

"His name came up."

"Yeah? And?"

"I didn't like the way he pulled you around at the party," Annie admitted.

"Yeah. That's the scandal Paula's talking about."

"Who?"

"The palm reader. It's nothing. Do I look like I mean something?"

"I don't know, Lana."

"You look at me like I'm crazy!" Lana said, coughing and laughing at the same time.

"Well, you are so secretive about some things, making drama out of everything but saying nothing. You were really out of it that night of the gala, you have to admit."

"Was I really?"

"You were pretty insulting to me too," said Annie.

"I don't believe it!" Lana coughed more. "I must have been wasted. I'm sorry. Do you believe me? You have to believe me. Somebody has to! I can see by your face I let you down. But you won't let me down, will you, Annie? You'll be here for me. I need you."

"Yes, of course!"

Once she left Lana's place, she felt a great relief. A nagging fear remained though. Something was very wrong and too sad to even think about. Whatever Lana needed, Annie didn't have it to give.

Expectations

Your expectations have a good chance of coming true. It was right there in today's *New York Post* at the bottom of the comic section. The Horoscope for Sagittarius. That was him. Right on! Today he was going to his long-awaited meeting with Stan.

"Keep the change," Thomas said, alighting from the cab at West 34th Street. He took a deep breath and jumped to the curb, wet with a light rain.

He buttoned his white silk shirt, smoothing down his tawny leather vest. In the light drizzle, he saw himself reflected in the shining Citibank edifice before him. Damn! He admired the immaculate crease in his new bellbottoms and the shine of his black boots. The glimmer of the gold ring on his hand reminded him of the story he told Annie. The ring was actually a gift from Randy, the gaffer, who had gushed over him. Thomas took it, of course, though he was a little embarrassed accepting a ring from a gay guy. He liked the thought that he could pawn it anytime.

Your expectations have a good chance of coming true. Repeating his horoscope, Thomas spun through the revolving doors into the tall monochromatic skyscraper where Marvelous Productions had set up a temporary office. Imagine making a movie based on Othello with him as the star! A dramatic theater production would work too and would be cheaper and faster. In the vintage oak and chrome elevator, Thomas calculated his possibilities. A salary of $2500 a week to start, and after a successful run, a much higher figure—he could decide on that later. He'd get it all down in writing, guaranteed, and afterwards the option to renew the contract. He'd insist on a clause stipulating that the director must obtain his approval before making major changes to the existing script. What else?

The elevator came to a silent stop on the 17th floor and the doors slid open to reveal a mirror above a plush beige rug. He stepped out and walked down the hallway, following a young model-type wearing a polka-dot mini-dress and high-heeled sandals who disappeared into the Ladies Room.

Thomas stood impatiently in the glass-enclosed reception area of Marvelous Productions, ringed with miniature trees and emerald ferns planted in clay pots. A pencil-thin woman with a severe hairdo and tinted glasses hadn't even looked up when he explained why he was here.

When he finally sat, the chrome and leather chair was too small and uncomfortable and he drummed his fingers on the glass coffee table, rifling through the stacks of magazines. He skimmed the *Newsweek* headlines about the Soviet and US space program ending in tragedy and *Time*'s cover story about race riots striking one hundred US cities. Thomas cracked his knuckles while he glanced at the pictures, a habit he seldom allowed himself now. In some respects he was no different than that boy on the Hill thirty years ago trying to please Momma and the Man. White man, black man—it was all the same.

Leaning back in the chair, Thomas shook his leg back and forth, another habit from his days in school trying to sit still. Then he thought of those hot summer nights when he and Momma would go to the park and look at the stars over Brushton Hill. "That's you up there. A star's gonna shine no matter what," she told him. "There ain't nothing up there in that sky that ain't yours for the taking."

Thomas sighed.

"How's it going, man?" asked Stan as Thomas sat down to face the producer behind his huge walnut desk.

"I'm cool," said Thomas, crossing his legs.

"Yeah?" said Stan. "Sorry I missed you last time. I was wasted. That goddamn Mel shook me up a little at the party. If it wasn't for you, I'd say my time there was wasted."

"Yeah," said Thomas, feeling a little warm glow. On impulse, he stood up. Holding himself tall, he went over to the picture window and looked down at the New York skyline. Stan got up to join him. He came to Thomas' shoulder.

The pencil-thin woman came in with a tray of hot and cold drinks. Nodding to her perfunctorily, Stan returned to his desk as Thomas eyed her figure in the leopard maxi-skirt, the stiff pointed bra under a V-neck angora sweater. Taking a glass of water, he sat back down too.

They discussed which was the best bar on the Upper East Side, who made the last catch in last week's exhibition football game, which rock star had the biggest drug problem and whether *Fiddler on the Roof* would ever leave Broadway.

Stan crooned "Sunrise, Sunset," from the musical. "The right cast and that show would rock. I've always seen a colored fiddler on that roof." He laughed.

"Yeah, and I've always seen Shakespeare done by black folk, like what the Negro Rep did with *Midsummer's Night's Dream,*" said Thomas, sipping from the glass.

"You acted in that one?" Stan asked, picking his teeth with a gold toothpick.

Thomas nodded. He had intended to say little or perhaps respond with sarcasm, aping Stan's own faux-Western drawl, but instead he found himself wanting to please, a realization that irritated him. When the secretary had refilled their heavy crystal glasses, Thomas' with water and Stan's with bourbon and ice, Stan put his shiny black shoes on the desk and said, "So you're probably wondering why I agreed to meet you."

"Something like that crossed my mind."

Stan lit a cigarette, stroked his balding head, and inhaled. Abruptly he lunged forward in his reclining office chair.

"Who are you, Thomas Dreamer? Where do you come from?

How did you get here? Where are you going?" He punctuated each question with a puff of smoke.

Pulling down his silk cuffs one by one, Thomas sat back and clasped his hands.

"I'm thirty-two years old. I've been acting since I was seven."

In his most soothing voice, Thomas explained he was the oldest of eight, from a poor family in Pittsburgh, Pennsylvania.

"My family came from North Carolina, but that was before my time. My interest in the theater began when I performed in church, singing, acting, etc. My mother encouraged me; I have to give her credit. Without her, I'd be driving a truck, slinging hash. There were many years of amateur productions—I have all the clippings. Want to see them?"

"Na, I don't need that," Stan said, waving a fist. "It comes down to this. Are you good enough to be a gang leader who can spout gansta talk and Shakespeare in one breath? Are you able to appeal to the young white audience, not the Negroes who won't ever get to the theatre, but the white kids and their middle-class parents, the ones in colleges and the ones who dropped out? The Peace Corp bunch and the doped-up hippies with trust funds?"

Thomas pondered the rhetorical question as if he were not its object. "So we're talking the theater, not the movies?" he asked, lowering his eyes away from Stan's red face.

"Maybe, maybe not. The movie's going nowhere—it's still being negotiated. But it might work out for the stage. Mel is looking into it." Stan flung out his arm as if dismissing Mel. "Damn, you get the point."

But Thomas couldn't afford to dismiss Mel. Yeah, Mel had forgotten his roots, doling out favors like a real Southern gentleman passing out watermelons to the darkies. But Thomas had to be careful. Mel could make or break him. A few well-placed put downs in the right places—for the theater circle they all traveled in even here in New York was a small one—were all that was needed to ruin his career. Shit.

"So what can you show me?" asked Stan.

Thomas stared at him. Was this the time to recite those lines from *Othello*? He twisted the ring on his finger. Which scene was it where the Moor got annoyed with his underlings? Breathing deeply, he slowly folded his hands.

Stan was leaning over the huge desk now. His voice had risen. "Can you act like a colored Richard Burton for seven nights a week and four matinees? Huh? Huh? Or should I call James Earl Jones or Harry—that's Harry Belafonte? They'd give their right eye to have this part. I just spoke with both of them. But I'm a maverick. I don't want a big name. No, I want to make one. Are you the Othello I'm looking to discover?"

There was silence. Thomas kept his hands folded though his heart was pounding. He might as well break into a soft shoe routine like Sammy Davis, Jr. The picture of him tap-dancing around on this beige rug amused him and he smiled. He wanted to believe Stan, but he knew better. You don't want to pay the dough for those big names, honky. Hell.

"You'll get exactly what you want from me," Thomas said.

"Listen, Tom, I can call you that, right?"

"Just don't call me 'Uncle'," said Thomas.

Stan snorted. "I noticed you at the Gala. You stood out. Like your women. That one—what was her name—with the boobs and the red turban?"

"Lana. She don't have nothing to do with my acting," growled Thomas.

Stan stood up, puffing away on his cigarette as he stared out the window at the skyline of New York.

"When I take you away from Mel, and you'll come, believe me, I'll pay you more than you could ever get from that sorry play he's doing now. But I won't do that unless you make it worth my while."

"I will, better believe it."

"Yeah? Yeah. You can do something for me in the meantime. I need actors to play gangs, funky gangs. I need a whole stable of… of…"

"Niggers," said Thomas for him. How predictable white men were.

"Did I say that? Don't make me into a racist! I didn't come this far to have someone like you do that to me." Stan said, indignant. "Listen, I've bedded down with Russians at the height of the Cold War, Holocaust Jews, German Nazis, Africans, Chinese, Mexicans, even Lithuanians. Don't give me any crap. That's where Mel made his big mistake. Sorry if I'm offending a brother of yours."

"We ain't all brothers just because we have the same color skin," said Thomas. "I'm not Mel's keeper. I can't help what comes out of his mouth or what he does with his fists. I just work for him. Like you, I'm busy trying to pay the Man."

"The Man has us all by the balls," said Stan, sitting back down.

Thomas ignored that. "I don't plan to cut off my nose to spite my face, Stan. I value Mel. Playing Johnny in *No Place to Be Somebody* has given me a break I need. I don't plan to be tied down though. I have to go when I get the chance. The right opportunity and I'll take it." Thomas rose, standing over the desk, dwarfing Stan.

"Show me something," said Stan, leaning back in his seat. "Show me what you can do."

Thomas stood tall, expanding his chest and extending his arms. He let his eyes flit over the office, the window, New York outside. He was on the stage now, his stage. He had Stan's complete attention.

"Though in the trade of war I have slain men,
Yet do I hold it the very stuff o'conscience to do
no contriv'd murder.
I lack iniquity sometimes to do me service."

"Bravo!" Stan clapped.

He recited a few more lines as Stan scribbled on a pad of paper.

"It's better in costume." Thomas said when he had finished.

"I see you in contemporary dress, like *West Side Story*. Say! You could dress like Nasser's police," Stan said. "The gangsters could be Haile Salassie's goons. Hey, what about the director? There's Mel. I know you don't want a yellow-bellied honky like me directing your show, do you?" Stan grinned at his own put-down.

"A star's gonna shine no matter what," said Thomas, feeling warm with pleasure at the thought Stan had said "your show." "I'll work with any director, no matter what his color."

A little later Thomas walked out of Marvelous Productions feeling on top of the world. He rushed past the elevator and skipped down the five flights of steps, out the revolving doors. Walking fast through the mid-day Manhattan crowd, he replayed the conversation with Stan, thinking up lines he should have said but didn't, lines he'd spoken but could have just as easily have cut. Shit, he should have recited more. He knew the whole damn play now. Shit.

When Mandy passed out the paychecks later that afternoon, Thomas fondled her thigh absentmindedly. "How's it going?" he asked, putting his check in his shirt pocket. He didn't hear her reply because he was thinking of men, both white and black, Mel, Stan, and his own stepfather. They were all like trains passing through. Find was the meanest. When his stepfather came home from one of his construction jobs, he had money in his pocket too, and everything was upbeat. But then Find went out to the bars in the Strip and things got mean. Thomas could see himself leading his brothers and sisters upstairs to hide in the back closet while Find, sloppy from drink, yelled downstairs, shouting that the latest kid wasn't his, beating at Momma. They all knew what he did to her. They all saw her puffy face, her oozing eyes, the bruises on her arms and legs. Once she had a broken rib.

He called Annie before he went on that night. She seemed happy about the meeting with Stan, though he couldn't be sure. She told him she had gone to visit Lana after she got out of the hospital. "You're a wonderful girl," Thomas said.

Later, walking through Washington Square after the evening's show, Thomas savored the fall night air, the people ambling by, the rich clutter of storefronts and apartment buildings. All kinds of possibilities were beckoning. He felt like he was still onstage, rushing toward the spotlight. He hurried up the block and the next, dazed and satisfied.

Broadway

The Broadway signs were flashing red, yellow, black and white as Thomas sauntered along the street after leaving Mel's office. He was carrying a designer shopping bag. When Mel called him in earlier, Thomas had expected to be laid off. After all, *No Place to Be Somebody* was in its last week. Plus he hadn't heard a thing from Stan about his pending offer. But all that had changed as of an hour ago. Mel was extending the run through Christmas and offering the lead role of Johnny to Thomas.

Reliving the last hour in Mel's office, his chest expanded with enjoyment. He barely recognized himself in his dark glasses, black turtleneck, khakis and black leather jacket. He had just bought himself a thousand dollars worth of new clothes on credit. He'd be making good money and not paying any rent for a while. The outfit went well with his tan cowhide boots, a present from one of the girls in Wardrobe who insisted she'd pilfered them from Clint Eastwood when she was an extra on *Hang 'Em High*. He smiled, thinking of the girl and her big crush on him.

Periodically he slowed down to look at himself in the large store windows. It surprised him how good he looked in his new gear—a dark figure of mystery and allure. Hiding behind glasses, wearing camouflage, pleased him nearly as much as being on stage.

It had turned cold this past weekend and piles of brittle, crackling, multicolored leaves blew all over the wide streets of midtown Manhattan. The maple and elm trees lining 42nd Street so recently green and full with summer were thinning, blown bare by the rushing wind, the unexpected cold foreshadowing the winter storms ahead. But for Thomas even the rush of the hawk felt insubstantial compared with the fast pace of his life.

This posture of success—not for one minute did he truly feel like himself—was too good to be true. He felt like a teenager rushing back home after rehearsing *Porgy and Bess*. Any minute he expected someone to find him out, like a child caught sneaking candy from the cupboard. Mostly, he kept his enjoyment a secret even from himself for fear it should vanish. Better than drugs or food or even sex, more constant than love, was this feeling of satisfaction he was experiencing now. A man has one chance only and this was his, caused by whatever—the stars, God, Momma, or himself—what matter the reason? —And he was running with it.

An old white-whiskered man at the corner held out a torn Styrofoam cup. He had splotched torn pants and smelled of urine and alcohol. "Can you spare some change?" he asked. Thomas fished in his brand new pants and brought out a few quarters. "Bless you," said the old wino.

Dancing in and out of the crowd, Thomas continued down Broadway in a reverie, daydreaming. He felt dazed, drunk. Dreams seemed dangerous now that his were coming true. He couldn't—didn't want to—think past this heady feeling. New York City, once an adversary, seemed like a mistress he had conquered. This greatest, most cosmopolitan, most cultured of all American cities was going to be his. Born in America. Saved in America. This was a new feeling, one he had never had before, and it seemed grand and purposeful, the opposite of all the other degrading thoughts he'd had about his African-American ancestry. He was no slave, no slave's descendant; no, he was of the lineage of kings, better by far than his captors, and, best of all, now he was free.

He felt like Martin Luther King, Jr. in front of the Lincoln Memorial making his speech to 250,000 people. Free, free, free. The very word bounced off the billboards around Times Square like a huge golden basketball. Thomas shook his head. The Civil Rights Movement was a subject too painful for him to focus on most of the time. And King was in danger. Poor King. A powerful man, but a fool to let himself be so exposed. Somebody could shoot him. They couldn't let a man like him live, could they? Thomas cringed at his dark thoughts. He hoped he was wrong about King. The thing to do was to duck, hide and wait. He, Thomas, was a master at waiting. If only he could tell Martin Jr. that.

Stopping at a newspaper stand in front of a cheap souvenir store, he scanned the headlines of the *Daily News*, "Father Kills Six Children, Turns Gun on Self." Thomas moved his gaze from the headlines to the overflowing candy rack above miniature plastic Empire State buildings and Statues of Liberty. But not quickly enough. His mouth had already turned dry and his eyes beneath the dark glasses had teared up. Feeling depressed, he bought the newspaper, though he knew he wouldn't read it. He hated how men perverted, often destroyed, women and children. Men were tinged with evil, and yet he too was a man.

"Daddy? Don't use that word near me. I don't want to be no daddy, no way," Thomas said when his sisters begged him to play house and be the daddy. It made Momma laugh. She would repeat that story over and over to his aunts, her teeth gleaming white and wet. "I don't want to be no daddy that boy tell me," she mimicked. It made him angry to think she was laughing when it was the sorry truth. He hated her for that and for wanting more of him than he could possibly give. That more than anything else had kept him away from Pittsburgh.

His daddy who he never met and whose name he could not remember and his stepdaddy Find with his evil dancing in and out of Thomas' childhood, one day here, the next day gone, both taunted him with flimsy and cruel dreams. That demon role he got into with white women, the male prostitute servicing for profit, was part of that. It haunted him sometimes. Even now he didn't trust himself. Like with Annie. He wanted her, but was he good for her? He doubted it. Shit. Well, he wouldn't go there, not now.

With the money he was going to make, he could start his own theater. He'd already thought up a name, the Traveling Shoe Players. They'd play revolutionary and classical repertory. He'd have portable sets designed that could be dismantled quickly and stored in a van shaped like a shoe. They'd hit Pittsburgh every year, Cleveland, Erie, Yonkers, Connecticut. Even New York. New York had a Negro theater once Mel had told him, founded way back in 1821 and operated by free blacks, with a repertoire drawing heavily on Shakespeare. "African Grove" it was called and now they did original plays of Leroy Jones and Ed Bullins. Yeah. But Thomas wouldn't depend on ticket sales. No, he'd get grants from President Johnson's Civil Rights Administration. He'd find rich investors to back him, ask Stan and Mel. They could have a piece of the action too. Why not?

At an Automat on Broadway, Thomas bought a green salad, a banana and orange juice. He sat down at a nicked corner table, spreading out his newspaper and rifling through the sections. When he found the horoscopes, he tore out the page neatly and put it in his wallet.

He couldn't believe Mel's offer of a VIP suite at the Central Park Hilton. It had been the more surprising because Thomas had even told his landlord he was moving out, planning to stay with Mandy for a month or two until he got another acting gig. A benefactor from the Theater Department at Harvard kept the suite for alumni and other VIPs coming down from Boston, Mel said. He suggested Thomas hang out there for a while. Why had Mel been so generous? He had mumbled something about Stan and a retaining fee, keeping Thomas on the East Coast. Don't look a gift horse in the mouth he could hear Momma saying.

Now all he had to do was go back to Houston Street and gather up his clothes and toiletries. But when he got to his pad, he didn't recognize the place. It was as if he had never lived there. Even the cat had disappeared. The cheap plastic bead curtain, the stained mattress, the rusted gray pipes clanking and sputtering, all of it was garbage like those overflowing piles left at the entrance to the stripper joints on 42nd Street. Thomas began pulling the last of his shirts out of his closet. He couldn't wait to get on with his new life.

His first night at the Plaza Hilton, he took his astrology ephemeris out of his attaché case and looked up the planetary positions for today. He craved understanding, a sense of himself in this time and place, New York City, 1967. He wanted a philosophy of reason and magic with stars colliding and himself riding a streak of white fire above it all. Planetary angles to leave marks on his soul where Momma's Jesus had long since disappeared.

There was his future, a shooting star. But something dark covered it, making it hard to see. Twelve spokes in the astrological wheel, an image of order like any of the million snowflakes alighting on his eye that night of the trolley accident, December 21, 1966. The trolley accident had happened when Saturn was at 11 degrees of Taurus, the sun nearing a square of his natal Uranus. What was his part? For how much was he responsible? He struggled to encompass it all—the Impala, the cop, the ad in the paper, the Negro Rep, Annie, Lana? Would it have made any difference if he had stayed and been charged? No, he couldn't do that. Never. But it was all infinitely connected, all perfectly combined somehow. He mulled over today's planets, this year's, last year's and the meaning of it all.

He lay down on the sumptuous hotel bed covered with a rose and brown patterned satin bedspread, imagining himself as a gentleman farmer in the rolling hills of Western Pennsylvania with a garden, a house, and white blowing curtains. Snow falling on the stone chimney. In summer, rain dripping on the rose arbor outside the shining kitchen. A swing in the yard, a baby in the cradle. A girl baby. He didn't want another boy. He didn't know how to take care of a boy.

Thomas had imagined the house many times, a cottage painted white and covered with honeysuckle and roses. The house matched one from an old postcard that somebody from Momma's church sent her years ago. She tacked it to the kitchen wall behind the stove where it accumulated grease spots from the frying pan. Momma used to look at that postcard on bad days and say, "That's where I'm going to go when you all grow up and leave."

He kept that postcard in his old suitcase. Damn! He'd forgotten all about that suitcase. Suddenly he felt skittish. Had Momma thrown it out like he told her to? He must call her. But he didn't want to talk to her now. Sometime but not now.

He jumped off the bed and turned on the console TV, staring blankly at the breaking news headlining President Johnson's surge in Vietnam. Buddhist monks were being shot in front of ancient temples; peasant villagers were being blown up in rice paddies. Thomas switched to NFL Football, then a strident family sit-com, and finally the latest Hollywood game show. In the bedroom mirror, the moon's reflection shone coldly over the black, littered roofs of Manhattan. Another commercial came on with cougars leaping over Ford trucks. He had seen that cougar before in a motel room with Annie. He missed Annie too much. Damn. Thomas turned off the TV, dropping back onto the bed. His stomach felt sick.

Much later, he started awake from a dream where he was falling into Annie's open arms. He felt warm and aroused. For a moment he didn't know where he was. He felt confused. He had been traveling in a spaceship like Sputnik, but something was wrong with the controls. What was it? Damn, he hated it when he couldn't remember things. Quickly he stood up, feeling woozy and disoriented, worried what to do next.

Emergency

Lana answered the intercom. "You were expecting someone else?" she asked when she heard the surprise in Thomas' voice.

"It's just I've been calling you and you ain't been answering," he said. Gazing at himself reflected in lobby mirror, he pulled down his new felt beret over his Afro. "Just push the buzzer, Lana."

"Well, Tomboy, truth to tell I was expecting someone else too," she said coyly.

The buzzer went off. He waited for the elevator, brushing at a lone fly overhead.

Wearing a blue silk bathrobe with Japanese designs of birds, Lana opened her double-locked door. She was holding a dripping paintbrush. "Come on in, stranger. Hurry, I don't want flies in here." She shooed him in, closing the door.

"So you aren't answering your phone?" he said, unbuttoning his leather jacket.

"I'm not answering at all." she said.

He took off his beret and looked around. "You're working?" he pointed to her easel.

"This?" She held up the paintbrush. "No way."

"That was a bad scene at the hospital. So how are you doing?"

"You don't know the half of it," said Lana, tittering. She scratched her long red fingernails on her neck. Her black hair was frizzed up, held by a silvery band. If he didn't look closely, he would see little resemblance to the half-dead creature of weeks before.

"There, there. Poor Lana, she's overdoing it. Dramatizing. Just another bad actress on dope—is that what Tom-Tom is thinking?"

"I wish it were just dope," he said morosely.

"What do you care?" she laughed.

"I'm just glad you are okay."

She laughed again. Though pale, with circles under her eyes, Lana appeared upbeat. She showed him the faint blue-black marks on her thighs and stomach. "Look at how well they are healing," she said, taking his hands and placing them on her soft bruised skin.

"Yeah," he said, pulling away. Thomas surveyed the filthy room, his gaze alighting on the painting of the apricot tree on the wall above her bed. The picture always reminded him of one he'd seen in a museum. Was it a Van Gogh, that crazy Dutchman? He wished he knew more about fine art and literature. He wished he could recognize a Rembrandt or a Michelangelo like Lana could. He had loved living here just to be close to her beautiful things. Not merely pleasing to the eye or decorative, these objets d'art were tangible reminders of a life in a plane far above his. But everything was different now. Things had gone bad. Where were the authentic museum pieces, the precious Chinese vases from her father's collection, those purloined Pre-Columbian figures, the Persian rugs and Japanese lamps that used to be here? Now Lana's place was littered with old food, bottles, beer cans, full ashtrays and half-empty vials of pills. He recognized the signs. She was using again.

"I'm better. Don't worry about me. This is the last time you'll have to dirty your hands with poor Lana. Go back to your precious honky. Annie did in fact come by to check up on me. She even serenaded me with her violin. Didn't she tell you?"

At the thought of Annie, his heart dropped. Why did he miss her so bad?

Lana went on. "Ruth called your number. 'You don't see him dirtying his hands with us colored,' she said. Yeah, don't look at me like that. Ruth—from your old hometown. She's a true friend."

"Us? You're including yourself with the colored?"

"Tom, you don't get it. Everybody is colored. Everybody is Negro. We're all black. We're all relatives, don't ch'a know? 'Do not ask for whom the bell tolls. It tolls for thee'. John Donne, in case you don't know—and I bet you don't." Lana recited a few more lines from the metaphysical poet.

"Enough. I have a splitting headache," she said, falling onto her bed.

Thomas went into the bathroom. In the cabinet he found her drug paraphernalia, the rubber tubing, syringe, and box of needles. He resisted the urge to throw them out or, for that matter, even mention them. Why should he start an argument? Instead he shook out two Demerol, recapped the lid, and left the nearly full bottle on the sink. Next he rinsed out a dirty glass and filled it with water.

Lana was dipping her brush in black paint and spreading great smears over the painting of the blossoming tree when he returned.

"What are you doing?" He handed her the pill with the glass of water.

She drank it down. Then she returned to the picture, laying a thick streak of red paint over the black, covering the dandelions bleeding into the high green grass.

"Lana! You're ruining it!" Thomas cried, lying back on her bed. He put his bare arms behind his head and stared at the mutilated picture.

"But who cares? Not you." Taking her brush out of the jar, she clip-clopped over to the floor length mirror and traced a line of shining red paint on her cheek.

"Aww, Lana. Now put that down." He glared at her. "I liked that painting and now it's ruined."

"Poor Tom, have I rained on your parade?" Lana checked herself in the mirror, streaking paint on her arms and legs.

He sighed, flicking away the fly buzzing over his face. What to do? She always took him further down than he ever meant to go.

Now she was writing "Tom" and "Negro Repertory Company" on the mirror.

"Go wash yourself off like a good girl."

Lana flounced into the bathroom. He heard her go into the shower stall and turn on the water. He felt like the fly moving crazily over the smeared picture in front of him. What had Lana shouted at the Gala? He could not bear to go there now, even in his mind—it was too heavy, too shameful—but he did it anyway.

It was snowing. The street was full of ice. Joe Cop had tried to stop Thomas from running away. But nobody could stop him from running. And nobody could stop Joe from falling. Again, Thomas heard the crack of Joe's head on the cobblestones.

Was it going to involve his family? His sisters? Mamma, Georgie G? That was unthinkable. All he had done was run. Was he responsible for everything? The snow? The asshole conductor? The moving car? The stupidity and carelessness of Joe, that Uncle Tom? The terrible part was, yes, he felt responsible. And for Lana too. Hearing the shower running, Thomas closed his eyes.

The fly crawling up his hand woke him. He flicked it away. How long had he been dozing? Where was Lana? In the bathroom still? He heard the water still running. It couldn't have been long.

"Lana? Lana?"

There was no answer.

Thomas got up and pulled open the bathroom door. Hot steam clouded his vision. He wiped his eyes and looked into the shower stall. He found her naked, slumped against the dripping wall. Her eyes were blank. With Demerol? With heroin?

"Lana! What are you doing?"

"Nothing," she said.

When he picked her up, she was limp as an empty laundry bag. He wrapped her in a big white towel and lay her down on the bed.

"Lana? Are you alright? What have you taken?"

Her eyes opened and closed randomly. He attempted to revive

her, opening the window. Running back to the bathroom, he saw a torn packet of aluminum foil, an empty syringe, a dusting of white powder on the floor.

He ran water in a glass, pouring a little down her throat, attempting to revive her.

"Shall I call an ambulance?"

She mumbled something about letting her alone.

"Lana!"

"No, no," she said. "What for?"

"You're wasted, Lana. Why? Was it something I said? You know I didn't mean it."

Was she in danger? He didn't know, but he was afraid. What should he do? Could he risk calling from her room? The doorman hadn't been around and didn't know he was here. What if he was implicated in selling her drugs? What if he was traced back to the Impala?

He stared down at Lana still and lifeless on her stained satin bed. She could have been a stunning woman, a woman whose passionate nature he would always admire. But Lana was never his to love, no matter what she thought. She wasn't anybody's. It was like with Georgina. Thomas felt helpless then too.

He shook her. "You're gone," he said and began to cry. He couldn't just go. He couldn't leave her like this. She needed to get to a hospital fast.

He could call a cab—no, an ambulance. His eyes flitted around the mess in the room for her telephone. Finally he found it on a stool, hooked up to her answering machine blinking red. She had messages she hadn't listened to. They could be from him. He didn't have the time to check.

Lana was coughing. He couldn't sit around to wait until someone came for her. Besides he'd be questioned. No, he needed to get her to the hospital now. Where was her purse? Her keys?

Behind him Lana shuddered. He reached back and stroked her

head. Suddenly he thought of her Impala parked in the underground garage. Thomas searched the bedroom, kitchen, laundry room and living room. Finally, he found her purse open in a cabinet drawer among some scarves and jewelry. In a panic, he pulled everything out but didn't find her keys. Next he went through the closets, checking the pockets of all her coats. Thomas found the keys in her dirty fake fur.

In the other room, Lana was calling him in a faint voice.

"I'm coming. We're going to get you to a hospital."

Grabbing some rumpled clothing from her chair, he lifted her up. She had no energy to resist.

"Don't worry, girl. You'll be alright."

Holding up her arms, he slipped on a black sundress over her weaving head. He grabbed her foot and pulled on a gold flip-flop slipper, but she kicked it off.

"Please, Lana, we have to go."

"Go, Tom," she said.

He got her slippers on her feet. When he tried to get her to stand, but she fell against him. Again he held her up, but again she fell, a dead weight.

"I'll have to carry you. There, there. Don't worry," he said, patting her wild hair. "But you'll have to help me."

"Purse," she said.

Thomas grabbed her purse, his beret and jacket. He heard the phone ring. Lana flung out her arm indicating he should answer it.

"No, not now. There's no time. Okay, hold onto my shoulders."

After a few rings, Lana's voice kicked in on the answering machine.

"Baa, Baa black sheep, have you any wool? Sorry, you missed me. I missed you too."

Thomas reached over with Lana in his arms and turned off the machine. He carried her out the door, closing it quietly.

Nobody was in the elevator. Lana sagged, a dead weight. Her limp arms fell over his shoulders. She coughed.

"Shhh," he said. "People are sleeping."

"Sleeping," she said, "Shhh." It was a good sign that she seemed to understand he thought.

The elevator took them straight to the basement, bypassing the lobby. It was dark and damp in the garage. Holding Lana tightly, Thomas hurried, ignoring her whimpering. The Impala was at the far end of a row of late model BMWs and Mercedes. He was sweating when they reached the car. Opening the door, he laid her back on the passenger seat.

"Careful, careful," he told himself as he backed out of the parking stall, swinging the wheel toward the exit. He'd taken her other cars out many times, but not this one and didn't know how it handled. But he did remember how to exit the garage. He drove up the dark ramp and out into the sunlight. The radio was set to her favorite rock and roll station, and he turned up the dial to the loudest volume.

"Don't worry," he said, reaching over to pat her. "Talk to me, girl! Been to any parties lately?"

Each time they had to stop for traffic or a red light, he prodded her, forcing her to answer, to stay conscious. He insisted she sing along with him to the radio. He drummed his hands on the wheel with the rock and roll music and her faint mumbling wail.

Finally he pulled up to the emergency driveway of Bellevue Hospital and set the brake. Slicking back his hair and pulling his beret low over his face, Thomas jumped out and began running toward a parked ambulance.

"Hey! Hey! I need some help!" he shouted to an elderly black attendant in white scrubs smoking at the front entrance.

"There's a very sick woman in this car. She needs help right now. She took an overdose. She's wasted!"

Throwing his cigarette away, the attendant ambled toward him.

"Hurry up! This is an emergency!" Thomas shouted, rushing back to the Impala where Lana was nodding her head in the front seat.

"Everything's an emergency, son," said the attendant, reaching the car.

"Can't you all do something?" Thomas cried.

"How long she been that way?" the attendant asked, looking inside the passenger window.

"Hey man, I don't know. She asked me to bring her to the hospital. I'm just a friend." Thomas said, but the man wasn't listening. He was looking back at the ambulance.

"Get the stretcher," he shouted to the driver smoking in the front seat.

Thomas opened the passenger door and set Lana's purse in her lap. She didn't seem to notice but coughed off and on while Thomas waited for the attendants to return with the stretcher. It seemed like forever.

"Hurry!" he shouted.

Finally the men hauled the stretcher between them to the Impala idling in the driveway. Even before they finished lifting Lana up onto the stretcher, Thomas had slipped away, disappearing into the confusion at the entrance clogged with hospital personnel, slumped patients in wheelchairs and their frantic, confused friends and family.

As Thomas turned the corner, he threw his beret into a dumpster. He thought about throwing away his new black jacket too. But he liked the jacket. He didn't want to give that up. Thomas began to jog as quickly as he dared. His jacket nagged at him though. Somebody could recognize it. He ran faster, hugging it to him. He ended up leaving it on a parking meter a few streets away.

He rushed on for blocks and blocks. The sunshine had

disappeared and it looked like rain. He could have been anywhere. It could have been the East End of Pittsburgh and not Manhattan. Lines from plays he'd done and snatches of conversations he'd had years ago zigzagged in his head, snatches of random puzzle pieces he couldn't hope to fit together. Conversations he'd had or wanted to have were mixed with the rising voices of all the women he'd ever known, shattered now and overlapping: Georgina, Momma, Annie, Lana, Christine-Marie, Carlotta, the twins, and hundreds more. It began to drizzle. He was still walking in the rain when it began to get dark. He barely made it in time for the night's performance.

The lights went out. On the other side of the curtains, the audience had gone quiet. Somebody had left the Exit door opened behind him and the cool air hit him as he stood back stage alone. He looked toward the alley and the colored blinking lights of New York. He felt a cold wind, but the rain had stopped. Hearing his cue, he walked up the ramp. Sliding around the scaffolding, he burst onto the stage.

* * *

Ruth confronted him in the hall as he was on his way out of the theater. At first he didn't recognize the colored woman wearing a dark coat and scarf, her flat walking shoes making her appear smaller and older. She was carrying a brown shopping bag.

"Tom? Tom from Homewood?" she asked.

"I'm sorry, do I know you?"

"C'mon, sugar, don't play games with me now. I just come back from the morgue."

"Ruth?"

"Shit, yes, it's Ruth."

Ruth spared him nothing. She told him Lana was dead. She had died in Bellevue that afternoon. Someone had brought her in. Whoever it was didn't stick around. Her family couldn't be reached, of course. But the nurse had found Ruth's number in Lana's purse.

Ruth had to leave the post office to go down to the morgue and identify the body.

"Yeah?"

"It's too much, this shit. She must have asked this guy—whoever brought her in—to drive her to Emergency," said Ruth. "Because she came in her own car, that blue Impala."

"Yeah."

"And I had a hell of a time finding you. Like they really wanted to let me in here. I said I was your sister. You hear me? I'm your sister."

"Yeah."

"I had to identify the body—oh, she looked good, quiet too, finally!" Ruth's voice shook. "Then I went back to her place and took a look around. Yeah, Lana gave me a key. That's how I found you out."

"Yeah?"

"Your name was painted on her mirror along with this theater, the Negro Repertory Company."

"Yeah?"

"Yeah, yeah. Is that all you can say?"

She didn't wait for an answer but instead railed at him for being so hard to get hold of.

"And you think I'm the one who made her do it?" he asked.

"Not made, let. You flatter yourself. That's your trouble," said Ruth. "No, White Sugar poisoned herself for good this time."

She blamed Vern for giving Lana bad horse. But, she admitted, she knew Lana could have done herself in with anything using those dirty needles she had around her pad.

"I just wish it was your fault, Thomas. I wish I could blame someone. But she was just a rich, ragged white girl who needed somebody better than you."

She went on and on about Lana's pitiful end and his role in it all as Thomas kept backing off down the hall. He had a hard time even looking at her. Ruth's face was too painful, like all those women in his family who knew too much, raging at their men from bitterness and love. It was like Momma with her loud incessant storming at her men's failures, told not to them but to Thomas. She had confided in him, haranguing in that intimate way she could do with her firstborn.

"So don't worry none, I cleaned off the mirror before I left. I don't know why but I did. She loved you alright, but you let her go. You mean, Tomboy. You let her do it. You let her drag herself down to nothing. That's worse."

"I'm sorry," he said.

"Yeah? That ain't enough. Lana knew something she was holding over your head. You know what I'm saying?" Ruth said, setting her jaw. She held the bag to her chest.

"What?" Now they were at the exit door. He could see the alley, the wet streets, and the lights. "I gotta go now," he said.

"What? Is that all you're going to say?" Ruth shouted.

He held his arms to prevent himself from grabbing her.

"What do you want from me?" he asked.

"Nothing, nothing at all. But I got something you might want. This." Ruth shoved the brown bag at him. "Lana's answering machine. I took it with me when I left her place—after I listened to it first. I figure it was for you since you the one she mentioned by name in her last message."

Holding the bag, he watched Ruth walk away out the door and down the alley.

"Ruth!" he called out, but she didn't look back, as if she knew they'd run into each other again somewhere down the road. Whenever it was, it would be too soon for him.

Lana was dead. He felt like one of those stunned starlings frozen on the pavement back in Homewood after a freak ice storm. It was the ending of a bad play, one he never wanted to be in, but yet couldn't believe was over. He just couldn't believe it.

* * *

When he pushed the play button on the answering machine, there was a ringing noise, a high shrill buzz that hurt his ears, then Lana's falsetto voice singing the nursery rhyme he'd heard and shut off earlier that day. Still it was a shock to hear her now. She could have been right there in his room.

"Sorry, you missed me. I missed you too…"

"This one's for the Pittsburgh DA," said the baby voice. "I have a tip for you guys about that asshole who stole my Impala."

Thomas sat up in his chair before the kitchen table.

"Check out Thomas Dreamer, alias Tom Find, Joe Johnson. Oh, hell, I can't remember all his names. But you'll find him. He's a big star now. Good luck on getting your man since I can't seem to, boo hoo." The voice trailed off in a whisper.

He hit the eject button and out popped the cassette. Big star, right. Lana always could make a joke. He smashed the plastic encasement with his shoe, unraveling the tape from the spool and tearing it into pieces. The next day he threw everything in a dumpster behind a warehouse miles away. He had his unlisted phone number changed again.

* * *

After Lana died, Thomas felt himself tighten up and grow harder. He had to remind himself constantly to relax. He was always looking over his shoulder. Whenever he was out, he glanced around furtively at the crowd surging on all sides. But still he saw Lana's blue Impala everywhere, Lana grinning provocatively from the driver's seat. He saw her jumping out of cabs, or sitting across the room with a loud crowd at the very best restaurants, carrying big shopping bags, or rushing by in the West Village. Some nights he swore she was sitting in the theater. Everywhere he recognized her tipsy leer, her sexy laugh, those crazy knowing ways. Like Georgina, she tempted him all the more now that she was gone.

Sometimes it seemed as if he were free-falling after her ghost and there was nobody to catch him.

Behind him stood a group of loud excited kids. They were black, like him, wearing gray sweatshirts and tight blue jeans, white tennis shoes and red scarves around their kinky greased hair. They surged, crowding him off the pavement, oblivious to everyone besides themselves. Gesturing excitedly with their red and yellow armbands, they laughed and shouted in Spanish. Must be Puerto Ricans or Haitians. When he first came to New York, he had been impressed to hear colored people speaking in a foreign tongue. Somehow that seemed more acceptable than the street kids he'd grown up with on the Hill.

A large boy with dreadlocks elbowed him off the curb and laughed, showing his white teeth and pink gums. He was much bigger than Thomas. When the light changed, Thomas held back, letting him go ahead. Imagine Georgie G out here on Broadway. Imagine him walking beside his son. He must have grown by now. How much? He'd have to buy the kid a new outfit, more than one, and take the grease out of his hair, those natty kinks. Georgie G needed braces too. He had so much to do for his son. There was all this time to make up.

At the corner of 45th and Seventh, Thomas caught up with the teenagers, waiting for the light to change. Standing next to them was a young pretty blond woman in a black mini-suit. She reminded him of Annie with make-up. Picking up on her nervousness, the kids revved up their shouting and whistling as they jumped off and on the curb. The kid with dreadlocks shouted something at her while the others laughed and hooted. The pretty woman kept her head lowered, pretending they weren't there. One heavy kid reached out and put his hand on her thigh. Another pulled at her hair. She jumped away, a look of horror on her face, and the kids laughed.

Approaching her, Thomas touched the woman's arm lightly.

She flinched as if she'd been struck.

"Don't worry," he said. She acted as if she didn't hear him.

"Sucker," one of the kids called out.

"Asshole!" shouted another.

The light changed and the teenagers bounded off the curb. Thomas looked down at the paralyzed woman beside him. A new look—not only fear but anger.

"It's okay," Thomas said lamely, but she had already pulled away, disappearing into the crowd. Thomas realized then that the kids were talking about him. He was the sucker, the asshole.

You don't understand, he thought. I just wanted to talk to you. But there was no one to hear him, no one who would listen and he couldn't shake his sense of shame and humiliation. Thomas leaped into the busy street and hailed a taxi.

"Where to?" asked the driver.

"Anywhere," Thomas answered. "Just don't stop."

Driving by Central Park, he passed horses pawing the ground in front of antiquated black carriages filled with tourists. What had happened back there? He felt stunned. Lana would laugh. She would make him see how funny it really was. But Lana was dead. Yet he couldn't seem to shake the feeling she was close by, all around him like the approaching dark.

Funeral

Annie was reading the Fall Julliard Schedule between answering calls at the switchboard when Ruth called.

"Hi!" said Annie, surprised and pleased. "Of course I know who you are. You're a friend of Lana's." She lowered her voice in case her supervisor was in the vicinity.

"Lana's dead."

Annie stared at the blinking switchboard, too stunned to reply. Another yellow phone dial lit up.

"Lana's dead?"

"That's what I said," Ruth snapped. "Do you have a problem hearing?"

"No, no. I'm sorry, I just can't believe it."

"You want to know where she'll be laid out?"

Annie reached for the pink While You Were Out memo pad as if she were taking a message for a Metro Knife employee, as if this were any old call.

"Where?" she asked.

"The body is going to be laid out at the Parkside Memorial Chapel in the East '60s—you can look up the address."

The body? Annie put her hand to her face, uncomprehendingly. What body? What was she saying? Then she realized Ruth meant Lana's body. How could she say it like that?

"The viewing is private, for the family only, but I'm telling you anyway. I'm telling everyone Lana knew."

"Thank you," Annie mumbled. How do you know this? she wanted to ask.

"There's going to be a funeral on Tuesday at some church, St. Patrick's Cathedral I think it's called."

"A funeral?"

"Is there something wrong with your ears?" Ruth shouted. "And in case you're wondering how come I know, I had to go to the morgue and identify the body! Are you listening?"

"What happened?" Annie finally blurted out.

"She died at Bellevue two days ago of an overdose. Look, that's all I can say. I gotta go. I have to get through Lana's whole damn address book today. And don't ask me how I got the damn book."

Ruth hung up before Annie could say anything more. Hidden behind the plants and ferns around the switchboard, she held herself tightly. Her heart was racing. She felt sick. She wanted to call Ruth back, but she didn't have her number. Besides the board was lighting up again. In a strangled voice, Annie began answering calls.

Later that afternoon, she rang the Negro Rep, but couldn't reach Thomas. "It's an emergency," she told the girl answering the phone. "I'm sorry. He's not available," she was told. She called again and again, leaving messages, but Thomas didn't call her back.

She felt angry. She hadn't felt this way since she was a child. She welcomed the anger because it replaced the—what was it? The missing—yes, missing and loss like acid in her stomach that had been eating at her all her time here in New York. All that missing out on Thomas' life and longing for a place in it led to a deep well of diseased loneliness. But now anger replaced that sickness with a pure bright intense sword of self-righteousness and intolerance. Annie felt a sudden sense of conviction. Thomas, Lana, and even Ruth had wronged her. Why? For one thing, Thomas wasn't there for her. He had come into her life like a bright star, lighting her up, showing her a new world of pleasure and sex and love. She had followed him into that world, but he was not there for her. She had been under a cruel delusion, a spell, till now and it had made her raw with guilt. She assumed wrongly, oh so wrongly, that she couldn't be angry with Thomas. Why? Because of the injustice he had suffered due to his skin color. As if by being angry she was as prejudiced and as wrong as her father and mother. Moreover, she wouldn't allow herself to be angry with any man she fell in love with, because then she would be like Mother railing at Dad.

Then there was Lana for whom Annie felt a fury she couldn't name. She was dumb with disappointment, as if Lana owed her something in payment for Annie's friendship, even her violin playing. Why would she kill herself? Annie didn't understand anything about Lana. Why did she use drugs anyway? Lana had been so sick, so pathetic in her raw need to appear unique. It had to have been an accident. But Lana wouldn't make a mistake like that. She was too proud to make mistakes. Lana had to be in control, even when she was drunk. Whether it was an accident or not made no difference she decided. Annie was still angry. She was even more angry if it were an accident. In any case, Lana had lied, pretending to like the music, pretending to be friendly, while planting those diabolical insinuations about Thomas in Annie's mind like bad seeds.

Worst of all, Annie had thought Lana was her friend, not a true friend she could trust, but still her only friend here in New York. Annie felt betrayed. Lana was gone forever and Annie would never find out what happened.

She was angry with Ruth too, a woman she had never met. Why had Ruth treated Annie like her enemy when they were talking on the phone? Annie was Lana's friend too, or had been. Of course Ruth had called her, but she called everyone in Lana's address book. Annie wasn't special. How did she get Lana's address book anyway? The point was Ruth didn't think enough of Annie to explain herself. She knew a lot more than she was telling. What was it? She obviously didn't trust Annie. Well, Annie didn't trust her either.

Her anger was like a great weapon that made her purposeful and confident. Invited or not, she would go to that funeral home and tell the truth to anyone who would listen, including Lana's family. That evening after work she went shopping at Macy's and bought a dark blue suit with a tiny rag of a mini-skirt trimmed with silver buttons to wear at the funeral. She even found a sheer white blouse to go with the suit. Back at her place, she tried on the outfit, admiring her figure in her new clothes, pulling her hair up, knotting it tightly in a smooth bun. Pale and serious, she reminded herself of those filmy spirits hovering in the Hieronymus Bosch's paintings she had just seen at the Metropolitan Museum of Art.

Two days later, Annie got off early from work to go to the Parkside Memorial Chapel on the ground floor of a nineteenth-century mansion on the East Side. When she came into the large crowded foyer framed with white bouquets she was holding two pink roses she'd bought from a florist in the bowels of the subway. A bald, unsmiling man in a black suit pointed her to a big gold-trimmed book to sign. Annie backed away. Already she felt herself shivering from the frigid air conditioning permeating the place, humming above her like wasps. Annie pulled her jacket tighter. She noticed people of all ages dressed in stylish expensive clothes, wearing exquisite jewelry and accessories. Even the children, including a few toddlers, wore organdy and lace, satin slippers, silk ribbons and jeweled hair ornaments. Everyone wore light colors except for Annie, and everybody was white. There were no colored people at the funeral home. Thomas wasn't there. Neither was Ruth or Vern.

Annie drifted off to the second room where the open casket of a silvery metal had been placed on a raised platform in front of the wall. Slipping past a young woman in a pink sheath smoking listlessly, Annie stepped up to stare at the body. It was the only time she ever saw Lana dressed in white. Her thick black hair was shining around her doll-smooth face. Her perfect, full, red mouth accentuated her powdery skin and the white satin dress. She appeared to be praying. Her hands had been placed one over the other with a pink crystal rosary, silver cross face up, twined between them. Lana's beauty took Annie's breath away. She felt stunned, confused. All the accusations she'd flung at Lana during the last 48 hours dissolved. Softly Annie lay the two roses down on Lana's satin dress. "These are for you," she whispered, her eyes tearing. Self-consciously, she stepped back into the crowd.

"Where is Lana's family?" she asked the young woman in the pink sheath drifting by.

"They were here earlier, but they had to go back to Connecticut. That's what I heard anyway. Did you ever meet them? Believe me, you don't want to. Oh, I'm sorry. I'm Edith Montgomery, Lana's roommate from prep school." She held out her hand.

"I'm Annie. I met Lana a few months ago at a play. She never talked about her parents," said Annie. "But I don't think they thought very much of her. She liked her aunt in California," she added.

"They were real prejudiced, I think. You're right. They didn't approve of her lifestyle."

"Isn't that how it is?" said Annie, thinking of her own parents. She wanted to continue the conversation, but Edith was waving at a tall man standing in the open double doors and walked away.

Annie sat down on a gold and blue upholstered straight-backed chair. Two preteen girls were giggling in the corner. One was holding an unlit cigarette, the other matches. Talk of Lana and her family wafted around the room, thick with portent.

"Her brother's in Canada. Because of the draft you know. But I hear he came back for the funeral."

"I thought he was an organizer, you know, against racism and all that."

"No, he was just against the war," said a young man with long hair and side burns.

"The body was at the morgue all night. Her father didn't show up until the next morning," said a brittle socialite in a pink empire dress. "It's a shame, isn't it?"

Annie wanted to speak up and ask about Ruth—but who here might have known Ruth? Everyone was white like herself. Or were they the only names in Lana's address book? Had they received calls too? She put her hand to her throat, but couldn't speak.

"That was only the surface," said another guy wearing a flower power shirt and striped pants. "I heard she planned to go and live in a commune."

"Can you dig it!" said a balding, youngish man in skinny fitted pants, ruffled shirt and a colorful tie.

"She once told me she was proud that her great grandmother was an ex-slave who escaped in the Underground. Of course, Lana only found that out by mistake."

"It was the drugs," said a matron with a flushed face wearing apple-green silk.

"She was stoned all the time."

"Wow! That's cool."

Annie left without signing the guest book. Her head was spinning. She felt as if she had been shot into outer space and everything in her life was getting very far away. Quickly she hurried by the old white mansions, the towering brownstones, the carefully planted fall flower plots on the curbsides. She passed an old woman in a hat walking a little dog. The woman smiled at her but Annie, vacant-eyed, was too numb to respond.

She didn't feel that same anger that had fueled her before. Even her righteous attitude was disappearing like melting ice. She sidestepped the garbage spilling out of the two dented steel cans by her building and the piles of dried dog feces around the lone tree, holding her nose to avoid the urine smell in the hallway.

A wet tattered rug at the first landing reminded her of the shag rug Lana had given her. Annie bolted up the steps to the 5th floor two at a time, slamming her door, not bothering to secure the deadbolt. Another of Lana's gifts. She bet all Lana's locks were bolted when she overdosed. What had really happened anyway? Annie threw herself down on her bed and wrapped her arms over her face. Overcome, she slept by fits and starts while the moon rose above the school playground across the street.

* * *

It was the end of Indian summer, another hot muggy day, but Annie felt cold as she tiptoed below the looming white marble columns of Saint Patrick's Cathedral, the famous neo-Gothic Catholic Church dominating Fifth Avenue. She slipped into one of the many empty pews near the back. She had read the small obituary in the Sunday *New York Times* announcing the time and location of a "High Mass of Christian burial for Lana Catherine Wells, actress and beloved daughter of Mr. and Mrs. Ronald L. Wells of Hartford, Connecticut." The thought of Lana's family dispelled whatever righteous resentment was left in her. She had to find out who they were.

High above her the arched, stained glass windows gleamed like jewels. Thick red, blue and yellow glass panes outlined in solid black lead told of scenes from the New Testament, with stories and characters she recognized. She found the two Marys, Joseph, Peter and John. The main altar was covered with bouquets of white flowers, the mammoth gold cross of the dying Jesus framed by white silk. Even though she'd felt uncomfortable that the service was Catholic, sitting here now Annie experienced a familiar sense of relief, security and comfort. How she had missed this peaceful feeling. But she had come to the conclusion that faith in Catholicism was a delusion, a poor fantasy of protection and salvation at the expense of freedom. What had Lana thought? She realized Lana and she had never talked about their backgrounds or their religion. It was taboo, more so than racism. Yet they might have shared something important, something that would have made a difference. Maybe Lana would still be here.

There were about twenty people in the cathedral, built to seat 2,500. She looked around to see if she recognized anyone. Thomas? Vern? They weren't here. Ruth? Except for the color of her skin, she didn't know what Ruth looked like and nobody here was black. A middle-aged woman two rows over and across the aisle looked to be that palm reader, Paula. She wore a burgundy pants suit and a large flowery hat over her blond, frizzy mane of hair. Could she have foreseen this horrible end? Why didn't she? Annie waved, attempting to get her attention, but failed.

She squinted, trying to make out Lana's family in the front. There was a single row of five people—she counted them—sitting stiffly in the first pew on the right. On impulse, Annie rose from her seat and moved up, sliding into a pew a few rows back and across the aisle from the family. A very thin middle-aged woman sat closest to the aisle wearing a black silk dress, jacket and a large black hat. She held herself precariously, her shoulders covered by squared shoulder pads, her eyes hidden behind sunglasses. Beneath a broad-rimmed hat sloping down over her face, her perfect blond hair was coiffed into a neat beehive. This must be Lana's mother. Next to her was a big bald portly man with a crumpled face, bags under his eyes, a big nose, and flushed cheeks. This must be her father. Beside him was a young man, his long black hair in a ponytail, wearing a psychedelic shirt and bell-bottoms. Her brother? Holding onto his arm was a young woman with straight long brown hair parted in the middle and a little girl wearing a pale organdy dress with ruffles. His wife and child?

Lana's mother was holding a rosary, dabbing her cheeks every so often with a hankie. When the young man in the ponytail turned around, Annie saw a hint of Lana in the way he cocked his head. Was he grinning at her? Stoned? The woman next to him featured the latest mod look from London: a mannish black jacket and maxi skirt, white textured stockings, and white go go boots with tassels.

The giant organ began to play, filling the cathedral with

Schubert's *Ave Maria.* Everyone turned around to look as six handsome young pallbearers in St. Laurent suits carried the closed silver casket slowly up the center aisle. Did Lana know these men? Were they her family too? White roses surrounded the podium around the main altar where they laid the silver casket down.

The liturgy seemed strange and diminished spoken in English. She realized with some surprise that she was sorry that Latin was no longer used. And why wasn't it? Oh, yes, Pope John XXIII had modernized the mass to make it more relevant to the people. There was more singing in church too—even popular protest and folk songs. Things had changed. She remembered how she had teased her mother about how they could now eat fish on Fridays. Mother retorted she was going to continue to serve fish anyway. "Do you think fish on Friday is going to save your soul?" Annie had said.

She had been kneeling with the others but now she sat back in the wooden pew for the sermon by—she checked the program she'd been given in the vestibule—His Excellency, Father Tim McBride. The priest was a spry man with wavy brown hair and a clear high voice who read the 23rd Psalm and a passage from John. Although he confessed he didn't know Lana personally, he spoke about the great loss to the world of the death of one so young. He mentioned Lana's vivacity, her sense of humor, her love of life, all of which would be sorely missed. But he doesn't know anything about her, Annie thought with gloom and dismay. He was either ignorant or lying. Which?

At the Offertory, a young man with long hair in army fatigues came out from behind the gold curtains of the sacristy with a shiny guitar. He stood before the pulpit and, inviting the audience to join in, began in a reedy tenor voice to sing the pop hit of the Youngbloods, "Get Together."

Annie sang along, lulled by the tune and the words, but she could not help feeling Lana was being cheated. Lana was not the "brother" described by the song. She was a white woman and nobody was smiling on the person she had really been. They were all cheating, preferring the fairytale girl, the Sleeping Beauty locked in her casket to the real woman. Except for the gossip at the funeral home, there had been no upfront talk of drugs or Lana's estrangement from her family, not to mention whether she had committed suicide or not. The one exception, Annie recalled now, was that the obituary mentioned that memorial contributions could be made to the Bellevue Drug Prevention Center.

Annie stared up at the magnificent rose window over the west portal that was just beginning to light up in the mid-day sun and tried to pray. She watched the faithful Catholics walk to the altar railing and kneel to take the communion wafer in their mouths. The organ was playing a haunting Bach fugue. Her mind went elsewhere, dreaming of brotherly love with the Youngbloods.

After the final Amen, Father McBride announced from the pulpit that the internment would be at Our Lady of Angels Cemetery in Hartford. Everyone stood. Now was the time to greet each other, another ecumenical change since Pope John XXIII. Annie turned around to shake the hand of the woman in a brown pants suit who reached over the rows to grab her hand.

"I'll miss seeing you," she said. Her eyes were puffy and red.

"I'm sorry," said Annie. "But I don't believe I know you."

"No, I guess you don't. You came to see Lana a few times—I live in her building. One floor down. We used to go to a palm reader together. I noticed you coming by recently. I looked out for her, you see, especially at night. She was so lively. Such a waste of…" her voice trailed off. She clutched Annie's fingers.

"I miss her too," said Annie.

As the organ boomed, the pallbearers sprang to attention, lifting high the closed casket containing Lana's remains. In their hands, it shone beneath the rose window like a strangely shaped bomb or bank vault. Carefully they carried it back down the aisle.

On her way out, Annie stopped at a big candle stand in the

Lady Chapel. Kneeling, she fished out a quarter and put it in the offering slot. "I'm sorry, Lana. I wish we were still friends," she whispered, lighting a candle. An usher offered her a holy card showing Saint Anne blessing her daughter, Mary, big with child. On the other side were printed Lana's birth and death dates along with a prayer to St. Francis.

She was still holding the holy card in her hand when she stopped outside on the steps of the cathedral. Squinting from the sunlight, she looked across the street and saw Thomas. He was all in black and he was watching her. Purposefully she walked down the steps, jaywalking across the street, ignoring the drivers in their shiny black and silver late-model cars honking and screeching to stop.

"Hey, Annie, how are you? What you been up to, babe?"

He appeared thinner, more seductive behind his black sunglasses.

"I'm okay," she said, coming up to him.

"You look more than okay, sweetheart. I'm sorry about Lana."

She lowered her head.

"There, there. Don't cry. You couldn't have done anything. Nobody could," he said, choking like a small animal being strangled.

"She was sick, using," he said. "She was trying to drag me down to her level. If you only knew."

She remembered Lana taunting Thomas with a nonsensical nursery rhyme on the stage at the party. What was that all about? Lana had tried to tell her. Or had she?

"Why didn't you come inside the church?" she asked.

He shrugged. "I can say all my goodbyes from right here."

"Did you get my messages?"

"Yes. I'm sorry. I should have called you. I just couldn't deal with it. If you only knew. I really hated having to deal with her drug habit and all that. She was trying to trap me. I should have gotten away from her long before I met you."

Annie felt confused. There were so many secrets. Feeling a fury she hid even from herself, she mumbled how beautiful Lana looked at the funeral but Thomas wasn't listening.

"Sometimes I wish you had never come to New York," he was saying. "Not for me, oh, you brought me nothing but luck, but you should have never gotten involved with Lana and now this."

She felt like she was being punished, like one of those china dolls with the twisted wigs she had played with too hard and broken that Mother used to throw into the cardboard box in the cellar. Headless, armless, legless. She was one of those very dolls. This is how it feels to be dead. To be Lana.

Thomas was talking about Lana's life with drugs and Annie pretended to listen, but actually she was in a desert, a wide endless desert that stretched to the foot of a mountain. She couldn't begin to climb it, couldn't even get a foothold. There seemed to be no way out of the desert and no way up the mountain. There was nothing to console her. She loathed herself for feeling hopeless.

Across the street a procession of funeral cars with little white blowing flags on the dashboards was parked in front of Saint Patrick's, their motors running. She watched as the pallbearers deposited the casket in front of the cars where the hearse was parked.

"Thomas, I want to ask you a question. What is the secret? Lana told me you had a secret."

"Where did that come from? I don't know what you are talking about." He sounded scared and that surprised her.

"I told you I went to visit her after she came out of the hospital," she said.

"And?"

"And she said you had a secret." Annie giggled self-consciously, putting her hand over her mouth as if it were someone else's.

"She was probably on something, out of her mind," he said.

"No, she wasn't. But I could tell something was wrong. She looked sick."

"Let's talk somewhere else," he said. "When can I see you? Are you doing anything now?"

"I have to go back to work."

"What about tomorrow? Tomorrow's my day off," he said.

"I don't know."

"You're putting me off," he said.

"I'm sorry."

"I'm here for you," he said, opening his arms wide. "Don't forget."

But you're not, Annie thought, pushing away her desire to reach for him.

In the subway on her way back to work, Annie made a list of all the things she wanted to do. Once Julliard started she would have little free time, since she planned to keep her job and work part-time. But there was the Cloisters, Coney Island, and the Museum of Natural History she had to see. MOMA too. She felt excited at the prospect of the coming months. Like a fast moving cloud, Thomas was disappearing from her thoughts and Lana too.

Beethoven

From across West 74th Street, Annie saw Dad standing alone by the entrance of the Little Italy restaurant where they had agreed to meet. In his dark gray business suit, white shirt and tie, he seemed small and vulnerable. She realized she had barely ever seen him in public places without Mother. Annie had been amazed when he called to say he was coming to visit. Dad had suggested meeting at the restaurant, a place he recalled eating in years before. With his back to her, Jim Ryan stared at a menu inserted in a little glass box beside Little Italy's arched doorway.

"Dad!" she called out, extending an arm. The word "Dad" reverberated across the busy street and dissolved into the blaring noise. All of New York shriveled before the one word shouted into traffic. She was a child again and she wanted to throw herself at him.

The late afternoon sunlight crawled up the buildings on the east side of the street. Crossing over, Annie came up behind him. "It's me, Dad."

He spun around on one heel. "Annie," he said gruffly, extending his arms and turning his pursed lips toward her.

Dad's eyes were all squinted up behind his wire-frame glasses as he kissed her on the lips, a kiss so quick she didn't feel it, only the brush of his neat moustache, the heat from his face. The shock of seeing him here in New York took on another dimension, moving from her eyes to her gut. Flustered, she glazed his lips with hers and then looked down at his well-worn polished shoes. Almost immediately he let go of her shoulders, dropping his arms.

"So, you're here. Good. Let's go inside," he said abruptly, hurrying her into a narrow dark foyer like so many of the Italian restaurants Mother and Dad had taken her to in Pittsburgh.

In the dim light she could make out the walls covered with wine bottles laced with twine skeins.

"Table for two," Dad said, summoning the waiter, a tiny grizzled man dressed in a white starched coat that reminded Annie of the clinic doctor. Annie blushed at Dad's loud tone, taking her back to the times as a teenager she'd been embarrassed by her parents. Now she followed behind him, as if she were still a little girl. In the fake candlelight, the waiter led them to their table. Annie kept her eyes on the back of Dad's wrinkled suit coat, his small balding head, the white shirt collar beneath the fleshy ruddy skin of his neck, as if to memorize what he looked like. Yet even if she had been blind, she would have known him.

"Thank you," said Dad, nodding to the waiter who pulled out a velveteen chair at a small oval table set with two white plates, tall glasses, large red napkins, and shiny silverware. Annie sat down. The waiter stood by impassively, his arms folded over his chest.

"This is my oldest daughter," Dad said, addressing the waiter who had turned away to pour water into the red glasses. Sitting down, Dad went on, smiling drolly at Annie. "She lives here, not I. Oh, no. I'm from Pittsburgh, Pennsylvania. God's country. She's going to show me the sights."

"Oh, Dad, don't pretend you haven't been to New York!" Annie said lamely.

"Huh? Oh, your Mother and I were in New York. That's true. There was our honeymoon, of course, but that was during the war. Boy, that was some trip. It was hard to get here, I'll say, even though we had a car, we couldn't drive it—gas rationing, you know." This last he said to waiter holding out two gold embossed menus. "Mother and I came by train. I recall we stayed a few blocks from here. Beautiful weather. That was the spring of '43. Every tree in bloom, cherries. Beautiful weather," he repeated to Annie as she watched the waiter slip away.

She nodded just as quickly as he spoke, as if they were both on a record turned to a faster than normal speed.

"Now that I recall, they weren't cherry trees," said Dad. "You only see cherry trees in Washington D.C. Of course, I'm not absolutely sure, but I doubt we saw any cherry trees here that year. Do you have cherry trees in New York?" he asked the waiter who had returned and stood silently by, tablet and pencil in hand.

"No, it must have been Washington," said Dad. "Your mother and I saw Toscanini conducting at the Met—the old Metropolitan Opera House, not this new one, I forget the name." Dad swung his arm out in a dismissive gesture.

"Lincoln Center," Annie said.

"What? Oh, is that it? Anyway, on with my story, in case you want to know more." He laughed self-deprecatingly. "Toscanini played Beethoven's *7th Symphony*. I can never listen to that piece without recalling the concert. We stayed at the Hotel Hanlery. Let's see, where would that be?"

Dad fished a map out of his suit coat.

"Let me look," Annie said.

Rapidly he unfolded it. Reading upside down across the table, Annie tried to see the names of the Manhattan streets. She remembered how they read the Chopin score on Dad's birthday. Was it only six months ago? It seemed like a lifetime. Dad ran his fingers up and down the miniscule blue and red lines of the map. They were long and bony, deep-veined, with tiny black hairs protruding from the skin. Annie put out her hand to hold the map too.

"We're right here, Dad."

He followed her finger with his own. How alike the shape of their hands were. She unwrapped the silverware from the red cloth napkins, feeling nervous, barely noticing the waiter lighting the candle on the table. Did they want drinks before dinner?

"I'll have scotch on the rocks," said Dad. "What'll you have, Annie?"

"A glass of red wine, please." She smiled, enjoying the feeling that Dad was treating her like an adult.

"Give her the best," Dad said, smiling.

"Oh, Dad," she whispered.

The waiter brought their drinks. They each ordered spaghetti with meat sauce and a salad, unimaginative choices compared to the elegant seafood pasta specialties. Dad explained to the waiter, as if in apology, that he was a creature of habit and strange foods didn't interest him much. Taking a sip of French wine, Annie began to breathe easier.

"I'm so glad you came, Dad."

"Are you now?" He took off his glasses, wiped them, and put them on again.

"I must have seen you do that a million times," she grinned. After all, Dad was so familiar, so dear, sitting across the table. He looked gracious, cultured, appreciative, dependable, all the qualities lacking in her life since she had moved to New York. Even the shine of his glasses, the line of his receding chin, appeared refined and tasteful.

"So, how have you been, Annie?"

"Fine," she mumbled, looking down. Then she looked up. "Honestly?" she asked.

"Of course."

"I'm lonely."

"Yes, I can believe you are," he answered, pursing his mouth as if to stop himself from saying more.

Annie held her breath too. She didn't want to take chances now, especially not with her father. But still she had the strong urge, almost a temptation, to abandon her restraint and tell all, confess and receive absolution like the nuns promised, and Annie herself believed as a young girl would happen at the sacrament of Confession. But back then she never knew what to say. What were her sins? By high school, Annie felt only humiliation at making up sins to confess. "I lied five times." "I said a bad word." "I had impure thoughts." The priest on the other side of the confessional revealed nothing, leaving her to her lies, her imagination now soured with guilt.

"And what about you? How are you doing?" she asked, taking a sip of wine.

"Oh, working too hard. But I can't complain. Well, actually, I could, but what's the point? Nobody listens," Dad chuckled, as if recalling a joke known only to him.

"I'm listening," said Annie, crossing her feet in their blue leather sandals. She had just bought these new shoes. They matched her blue suit, the same suit she'd worn for Lana's funeral.

Dad sipped his liquor, pursing his shapeless pink lips together in the faintly prissy way that used to irritate her and would now if she allowed it to. But she would not, oh no. Annie was determined his visit would be nice, better than nice.

"Remember how we all used to sit at the kitchen table, Dad?"

The watch on her wrist, a graduation present from him, caught the light from the small candle flickering in the red glass.

"We each had our place. Melinda and I. You sat across from me, Mother on your left, though sometimes she was at the end of the table so she could go back and forth into the kitchen."

"That's so. Speaking of Melinda," said Dad. "She's just got another job. Working at Horne's. Brings in a little money to help out with expenses."

"It's great if you can stand working retail," Annie said, thinking of her abysmal experience one summer selling ladies dresses in Gimbel's basement. "I hoped Melinda could come visit too."

"She's tied up," Dad said. Noticing her look, he continued, "We all have to make our way, Annie. I know you don't like to think of these things."

"Oh, no, I do," she protested, her voice getting higher. "I

didn't mean she should give up her job. I was thinking she could come around Labor Day, before school started. I work too, Dad, or did you forget?"

"I recall she has plans to go to Lake Erie with her friends, Donna and Charlene, around then," said Dad, ignoring her question.

"Hmmm, yes," Annie said, figuring her sister probably had other plans. Donna and Charlene were good foils whenever Melinda wanted to spend time with her boyfriend.

"Remember when we went to Lake Erie the summer I was twelve? I climbed a fence and fell. I had five deep cuts up and down my arm, but this one on my wrist is the only one that made a permanent scar," she said, showing him her wrist.

"Is that so?"

"Don't you remember?"

"I suppose so."

But Dad didn't even look at her wrist. Annie felt dismayed, even offended.

"Is Mother okay?"

"Okay? I suppose you could call her that. She decided not to come. It was too much for her." Dad licked his lips.

The waiter arrived with a plate of antipasto, a basket of bread and a little dish piled with pats of butter. Dad took up his fork and began spearing the salad, his eyes fixed on his plate. Annie busied herself buttering the bread.

"I saw in the paper that Bernstein's at the Lincoln Center," he said.

"I saw that too! He's conducting Beethoven's *Piano Concerto in D Major.*"

"It's tonight." Dad snapped his fingers for emphasis. "Wouldn't you know, Rubenstein's playing. Should be good."

"Yes!"

"Beethoven's Concerto in D is one beautiful piece of music,"

Dad went on. "I heard Rubenstein many times on the radio of course and on records. I recall one winter he came to Soldiers and Sailors Memorial. I got tickets—oh, months in advance. But the weather was so bad I couldn't get there until after the intermission, and he had already played. Ahh, here comes the food." He smiled with enthusiasm at the waiter balancing the heavy tray.

Meticulously Dad rolled the spaghetti strings around and around on his fork. He dipped the fork into a splash of dark red sauce and brought it to his opened mouth. After each bite, he dabbed at his lips with the napkin. Annie could barely eat.

When Dad finished, he placed his fingertips on the table edge and sat back on the red velvet chair, the soft folds of his skin drooping into his neck, his thin soft face a blur beneath his mustache and glasses.

"How is your job coming?" he asked.

"Fine. It's fine. I'm keeping it. Part-time, of course. I applied for a student loan, so I won't be needing to ask for any money from you."

He didn't answer. Candlelight flickered over his hands on the folded napkin. She couldn't see his face. Annie felt herself growing colder, more distant.

"I must seem pretty distracted. You know, sometimes I don't know what I'm doing," she said. "It's hard to explain. A new friend I made here in New York just died from an overdose of drugs. She is—was—an actress, older than me, and she had everything you could imagine going for her."

"She took drugs? Now why would somebody do that?" Dad wrinkled his forehead.

"That's just how I feel. I can't understand why."

"Death comes soon enough," he said. "Life's too short as it is. You blink your eyes and it's gone. That actress—was she what is called 'a swinger'?"

Annie nodded, feeling embarrassed by Dad's question. Still it was so much easier talking to him about Lana than about herself. Eagerly she recounted the few details she'd heard from Ruth.

"Lana knows—knew—a lot about music. Just before she died, I went to her penthouse and played my violin for her. She had been in the hospital, but she was out. That was the last time I saw her alive."

As she talked on, the shock speaking about Lana's death began to fade. The time she'd spent with her dissolved into the air like the swish swish of a child's swing. The truth was she could barely remember what Lana looked like now.

"It's not right for a girl to end up like that," said Dad, smacking his lips in consternation.

"But everyone experiments with drugs nowadays." Her voice sounded complaining, frantic to her ear.

"Annie, people just don't do these things. It's like shacking up with a Negro."

Annie panicked. All of a sudden they weren't talking about Lana, but about her.

"Sure you hear about it," Dad continued. "But it's only for show to shock people. Is that what you want? That's not what Mother and I raised you for." Dad extended his hand as if summoning Mother to his side.

Annie swallowed, forcing herself to go on. "Did you ever feel like you had to do something no matter what the consequences, Dad?"

"I can't say I ever did," said Dad. "Everything has consequences, Annie."

"Maybe I made a mistake going to see Thomas, but I didn't make a mistake coming to New York."

"You always thought you knew better than anyone else," he said bitterly.

"But it's not like that at all. I don't think I know better. You don't know me. Me. It's me I'm trying to understand, Dad. If only you could understand," she choked, swallowing the last of her wine. All her arguments were disintegrating like ashes.

The waiter instantly reappeared to refill her glass.

"So hurry up with your dinner," Dad told her, refusing another drink for himself.

"Why? Are you leaving?" Annie cried. She couldn't bear to have him go this way.

Motioning for the waiter, Dad pulled a little white envelope out of his jacket pocket and laid it in her hand.

"What's this?" Annie said.

"Two tickets to the concert tonight. I picked them up at the hotel. I don't suppose you want to go."

"Oh, yes! I do!"

"Then we've got to hurry." He motioned the waiter again. "The concert starts at eight."

"Oh, Dad," Annie's lip quivered. "Thank you."

Clutching the tickets in her hand, she followed him out of the restaurant. There she looked off into the street, hazy with early evening light, half-smiling, as Dad walked out into the traffic.

"Taxi, taxi," he shouted, summoning a cab.

"Get in," he motioned to Annie, when one pulled up. Dad got in beside her and slammed the door. "Lincoln Center," he told the driver.

The Beethoven concert was wonderful, even better than she could have imagined. Afterward Dad bought her double chocolate cake with ice cream at a small café facing Central Park. He insisted on accompanying her in the taxi to her apartment on 96th Street.

"Dad, you have to come up and see my place, please?" Annie asked, getting out of the cab.

"I'm beat. I'm going back to the hotel and get some sleep. My plane leaves at noon tomorrow."

"Oh, that's okay," said Annie, a wave of disappointment overtaking her.

"I'm sorry. But, say, why don't you come for breakfast at the coffee shop in the lobby?"

"I will." Annie leaned over to hug him. Her father wiped her mouth with a kiss.

"I'll see you tomorrow, Dad." Annie said, laughing as she shut the taxi door behind her. That was when she saw the tall dark figure waiting. Annie took a few sideways steps, her stomach clenching. She didn't want Dad to see she recognized the man outside her building. She waited until the taxi sped away before turning toward Thomas.

"What do you want?" she asked.

"Hey, babe, what's happening?" he said. "I've been waiting a long time for you."

Wings

Two by two he flew up the dark stairway after Annie, grabbing onto the scuffed wooden railings as he climbed. He remembered Georgie G climbing the stairs at Momma's and smiled at the thought that now he could make plans for his son to come to New York! Now he could do so many things! He'd invite the whole family. Everybody. With each step, Thomas calculated how much the tickets would cost.

Absorbed in thought, he passed Annie on the stairs. Where would they stay? He'd have to move. Maybe he could get a two-bedroom in Soho or a loft on the West Side near Central Park or a pretty brownstone in the '70s near the Museum of Natural History.

Breathing hard, he waited for Annie on the top floor. A naked bulb burned above him in the narrow hallway smelling of disinfectant, mildew, and cat urine. He was too keyed up he realized, wanting to share his good fortune with her.

"You don't seem very happy to see me," he said, standing behind her as she fumbled for her key.

"It's just late, that's all," she answered in a faraway voice.

Maybe she'd found somebody else. Bemused, Thomas watched Annie struggle with the multiple locks.

"Hell, girl. You paranoid or did something happen here I should know about? Was this place broken into or something?"

"No, nothing happened," she said, finally opening the door. He followed her in, making sure to lock the door behind them.

Annie turned on a Japanese paper lantern hanging from the ceiling, slid down on the sofa, and grabbed a pillow from the pile of bedding at one end. She kicked off her shoes.

"Annie, love, I know it's been a while," he began, looking down shyly. "But you know me."

"Do I?" she answered. Her eyes clouded over. Maybe he shouldn't have come, should have left and not waited around. Thomas felt exhausted.

"I hope so," he said. Taking off his new hi-collared Regency jacket, he hung it carefully over the one chair by the table.

She held her thin, light body at an angle, curling up her feet under her. How attractive. He had forgotten.

"How long are you staying?" she asked a little too lightly, putting him on guard.

"For awhile. Is that okay?"

She looked at him. He walked to the front window and pulled the curtains tight.

"Maybe I'm paranoid. This isn't Pittsburgh, but still, I like my privacy. Have you started Julliard?" he asked, glancing at the Sunday Times on a small table.

"A few weeks ago," she said, leaning around to watch him skim the Theatre Arts section.

"Cool." He checked out the rest of her place. "How's it feel to be a full-time student again?"

"Like I have a purpose," she giggled, as if just realizing it.

"Nice place. I didn't notice much that other time I was here. Annie, it's been crazy. But things are going great for me right now. Mel is planning to do *Othello* with an all-black cast. Othello will be played whiteface, the opposite of the old racist minstrel shows. I have a good chance at the lead. I wasn't going to mention it because, you know, lots of times these things don't work out."

"Oh, Thomas!"

He relaxed, buoyed up by the lift in her voice. "Of course, I'd get professional coaching on the Shakespeare and all."

"Oh! I know you'll get the part!"

He felt her admiration fill the tiny room like the roar of applause. Recreated for Annie, mirrored in her eyes, he became even happier than when Mel told him of his prospects.

"We should celebrate. Do you want a glass of wine?" she asked, getting up to take the Chianti from the shelf.

"No thanks, just water."

"Oh, yes, I forgot. You don't drink. It's really late," Annie said, yawning as she slipped back on the couch.

"Are you're telling me to go?"

"I'm just tired. My Dad's here."

"What? Your father? In New York? That was him in the cab with you?"

She nodded.

"And here I thought you found yourself an rich sugar daddy." Thomas laughed.

"Dad took me to the New York Philharmonic tonight at Lincoln Center. I'm meeting him for breakfast at his hotel tomorrow."

"So he finally gave you some love," said Thomas, smiling.

"He did? Yes, I guess he did."

"Yeah. It's about time, don't you think?"

She laughed and began to tell him about the dinner at the Italian restaurant. She spoke in those endearing short breathy half-sentences he loved to hear, making flighty birdlike motions with her arms and hands.

Sitting beside her, Thomas drank her in: the pale skin, blue eyes, soft mouth, the weight of her body, small round belly rising and falling, thin shapely legs. The faint odor of sweat and cunt. He took her hand in his.

"Damn, girl, you look good to me."

She curled her fist in his open palm, as if appealing to him to share it with her. Their eyes met. On her face was a peaceful alluring expression he had never seen before.

"Why are you looking at me?" she asked.

He shrugged. "I don't know. You are a beautiful woman. What are you thinking of anyway?"

"I'm thinking of my father," said Annie.

"You could bring him to the play. Tomorrow's the last day."

"But he's leaving tomorrow."

"On second thought, I don't think your daddy would warm up to a colored play with me in it."

He saw a look of pain flit across her face.

"I'm sorry," he said, stretching out his long legs. He wanted to take her in his arms, undress her and lick those tiny pink-tipped breasts.

"Come here, baby."

"It's late," she said, inching over toward him.

"Naw, nothing's too late in this town."

She giggled.

"It's been a long time," he said, motioning her onto his lap. He took her between his spread knees gently like he might a precious vase.

Feeling her weight, her closeness, Thomas sighed with pleasure. He enveloped her, gently smoothing his finger up and down her inner arm. They kissed.

"I guess you better go," she said after a while, half-balanced on his knees.

"And here I was just about to ask if I could spend the night," he said, kissing her again.

"Oh, Thomas," she whispered.

"I was going to say I love you," he said.

"I don't understand. Why would you tell me that now?" she asked, pulling away. "We don't even see each other anymore."

"Because I feel love for you. Look, Annie, my life isn't my own. I'm being torn every which way."

"What does that mean?"

He stood up. "Why do I think something is wrong here?"

"Don't treat me like a child," she said. "I'm not a child."

Those big blue eyes accused him. He shook his head,

uncomprehending, feeling the old familiar impulse to leave.

"Annie, my luck won't last forever. I got to run with it." Standing there in her cramped place, Thomas' heart beat fast. It was nearly midnight. He'd been anxious to see her, but now? He could just leave, check in on Vern and tell him the good news. Vern was always up. Or he could look up that hippie doctor in the East Village who knew Bob Dylan. Yeah, why not check that dude out. But, no, he was here. But why couldn't she make it easy?

"Can't we just lie down?" he asked, pointing to the bed.

Annie gave a little laugh of embarrassment.

"Why are you laughing?" he said. "You want me too. I can tell. I know you, girl."

She bowed her head as if in acknowledgement. He pulled her against him.

"Don't," she said, pushing back.

"Still too much for you?" he asked.

"Thomas, we've gotten so far away from each other."

"But now we're close."

"How close?" she asked. "This close, or this close?" She let go of his hands, stepping away.

"Come on, Annie, it's too late to play games."

"What's wrong with games!" she cried, falling back onto the sofa. Leaning over her, Thomas knelt and placed his hands around her hips.

"Do you know what I was thinking?"

"No," she said.

"I was thinking of the first time we met. You thought I was a star, remember? You were wrong and I loved you for it. You were just a little girl then. Now you've grown into a woman. Hey, baby, don't give up on us."

"Is that what I'm doing?" she said, choking up.

"Looks like it," he said.

Unbuttoning her blouse, he began to trace her breast with his lips. He fell onto her, stroking her fine straight hair, rearranging the beads around her neck, kissing the thin pink scar on her arm, the inside of her thigh. Gently he slid his hand inside her underpants, cupping and stroking her as he pulled them off.

Now he was bringing her hand to his hard penis. Unbuckling his belt, he loosened his pants and unzipped his fly. Now he was inside her. How easily he penetrated her. The honey, the drone of love, the brutal sweetness, her cry when she came, his groan, their hearts beating against one another, the flight of love's wings up and up. Oh, how it blinded him! All of it was there and gone so quickly.

"I'll be back," he told her and then Thomas left.

Othello

The opening of *Othello* in April 1968 was postponed after the assassination of Martin Luther King, Jr. Mel liked to remind the frustrated cast that all this political drama was free publicity, not a bad idea in the long run. But that line didn't play well. Fearing an empty house or a wave of riots resulting in a police lockdown, Stan and his backers hinted at pulling out altogether. How long could they wait for the anger to subside and police brutality to de-escalate Stan asked? In June after Robert Kennedy was shot, the show was reframed in a full-page ad in the Times as a tribute to two great fallen leaders. From then on the theater was packed. *Othello* was still a hit now after five months, consistently sold out, and a full house was projected through next summer.

A list of fans and members of the press who had called lay on the red-lacquer table in Thomas' dressing room. During intermission, he glanced over it, recognizing some of the names. He averted his eyes from the heavy black phone with its silver circular dial nearby, as if by looking at it, he might cause it to ring. Later, he thought. I'll deal with this later.

Better yet, his agent could check on it. With Stan's backing, he'd gotten an agent, a small Jewish ad man from Brooklyn who also represented James Earl Jones. The agent had set him up with a wealthy husband and wife investor team who wanted to back him for a run in the Catskills next summer. They'd invited him to their mansion on a big lake the same week King was killed. It was to have been a fundraiser. A few jive-talking Black Panthers showed up too. When the opening was postponed by the assassination, Thomas stayed on at the mansion, chilling out with the Black Panthers until they went home to California.

In retrospect, all this success seemed easy and effortless.

Setting aside his armor and doublet from Act One, Thomas put on his red robe over his tights, winding the heavy gold sash twice, and knotting it loosely. Outside the small dressing room window, the afternoon sky had turned gray. He took out his stash of dope. He'd started smoking weed again. He needed to relax. His hemorrhoids had come back; he hadn't had them since he was in Pittsburgh. As Thomas rolled a joint, he listened to the soft howl of the wind. It sounded like those voodoo chants Momma sang in the basement when she was ironing the clothes of the white folks she worked for in Point Breeze and Regent Square. He'd make sure Momma never had to do ironing again.

He would get himself a house painted white with honeysuckle and roses, with trees around it that Momma could stay in, a place where he could grow his own tomatoes and corn. He'd make sure every one of them seeds grew. He wouldn't waste nothing. Shit, he should get back to Pittsburgh to see his family. Shit, he hadn't had a day off except for Mondays since the show started.

"Hey, Dreamer!"

Automatically slipping the unlit joint into his robe pocket, Thomas spun around to greet Jovan, the hulking actor from Trinidad who played Iago.

"How's it going, man?" asked Thomas, glancing at Jovan dancing up and down in the doorway like a boxer ready to get into the ring.

"Can't complain," said Jovan, snapping his fingers. His eyes flitted over Thomas. Like most actors, they had an unspoken pact between them to keep things light and friendly, never sharing intimacies, except for that day Martin Luther King, Jr. was murdered and Jovan found him crying in his dressing room. Thomas didn't even know where Jovan lived, or if he was gay or straight.

"You be mellow tonight alright," said Jovan, pointing to the thick joint sticking out of Thomas' pocket.

"That's for after the show," grumbled Thomas. "Gotta keep my act together now. One of you might try something."

"Hey, brother, we got the same master," Jovan said, slapping the air as if swatting a fly.

"Yeah, yeah, I know," Thomas muttered as Jovan feigned to throw a few punches and then walked off. Thomas wondered what it felt like to play Iago night after night. Whatever happened to Iago after he was led off to prison anyway?

After he finished rolling the joint, he put it under Lana's turban on his high red dresser, the same turban Lana had pushed on him the night of the gala. Nobody would ever look there for dope. Poor Lana, nobody will look for her again.

The intercom buzzed, "Dreamer, five minutes."

"Coming," he growled, taking a last critical look in the mirror. Smoothing his sideburns, he bounded out, slamming the door shut.

Jane Byrne, this evening's Desdemona, was racing up the backstage steps as Thomas hurried down.

"Hey, how's it going?" he greeted her.

"Terrible. Can we talk after the show? I don't know how I'm going to get through tonight."

He nodded, automatically holding out his arms. In the middle of a divorce, Jane was generally in tears when she was not performing. Like most white girls, she acted like she was sleepwalking. She didn't seem to know what she was doing and let herself be knocked around. Why men have to be so cruel? That's what Momma would say. He smiled, thinking of her.

"What are you laughing at?" Jane asked, pulling away.

"I'm kind of busy tonight. How about tomorrow?"

"But I have to meet with my voice coach at eleven," she crooned, leaning on his wide shoulder.

"I'll call you."

"Promise?" Jane squeezed him. Thomas squeezed her back.

All the actresses in the cast counted on him to listen to their problems. If he disappointed even one of them, he sometimes feared he might lose everything.

"Gotta go," he murmured as he heard his name called again.

Thomas ran down the steps and up the ramp behind the stage. Standing off by himself, he began his own private ritual, the one he did religiously now before each entrance. Closing his eyes, he clasped his hands and silently called up the members of his family by name, as if he were an Indian chief evoking the spirits from the height of some great mountain, saying prayers or chanting.

Each night when the curtain went up, there was Momma behind him, Georgie G, Georgina dragging her red dress, his incarcerated brothers Lorn, Richard and John, the twins, Carlotta, Christine-Marie and Old Man Find, whiskey bottle in hand. Then came his ancestors, those white sharecroppers from North Carolina, and the slaves from West Africa. His Cherokee grandmother. Her father, a chief, it was said.

Othello—a man too proud to be jealous, too passionate to be discerning, too incredulous to be wise, too loyal to be compassionate, too flawed to love—Thomas played him like a joke, poised on a tightrope of self-conscious parody, mimicking the white stereotype of the black man. Throughout the first act, he moved fast as lightning. His lines crackled like sparks flitting over the stage, like delicate cliff swallows darting crazily. Desdemona's father, Brabantio, stopped him dead center and accused him of witchcraft. Thomas ridiculed him, at the same time pandering and affecting to swallow the old man's oily words while showing him the mirror to the fool he was.

"O'beware my lord of Jealousy," Iago crooned, pointing to Thomas' crotch, half-giggling as he kissed him twice on the mouth. Thomas rolled his eyes at Jovan and toward all those other jealous lovers roiling beyond the stage. There were so many familiar faces below the footlights—each one sweating, grinning. How the audience, panting below him in the darkness, loved his jive. They were spectators hungry for blood. He built his own performance from their lust. See the blue eyes. See the brown. Play to them. He held out the rose Desdemona gave him to the audience so they could smell the sex in it too.

The heat gathered and made him wilder. But he slyly tempered his rage, teasing the audience as he swatted at the dust motes in the stage lights. He had a job to do and he was about to do it—kill the woman you love, the woman who loves you. Oh, Georgina. Oh, Lana. Oh, Annie. They had all gotten away from him. He intended to send Annie a ticket to the rushes, but that thought had gotten away from him like so many others. He was just too busy. Or was he? It was just as well. He wasn't good for her.

Iago made his path easy. Like eating sugar candy. Betrayal came easy Thomas realized with a flash of recognition. It amazed him how the women in the audience loved seeing Desdemona smothered to death, each one dying to be crowned in daisies, branded as the victim of a jealous love. You couldn't ever spoil it for them. Lana decked out in her painted obscenities like a queen in her robes. Georgina laying daisies on the upholstered seat of the abandoned car after they had sex for the first time. He'd had Carlotta place daisies at her grave the day Georgie G's mother was buried.

It was the last act now and Desdemona, asleep in her bed, was ready to be sacrificed. Around murderer and victim bright torches burned, lighting his way to commit the heinous act. Desdemona lay still, cradling her flowered head in the blue sheets. He pitied her as much as he loved her. She had no choice but to offer herself to the executioner. She had kept her fingers in the honey jar too long, that's what. It had always been dangerous for white women to have sex, especially with a black man. What's more, Iago had framed her perfectly for the slaughter.

Thomas paced the ramp around her bed, his voice rising. "Poor wench!" he moaned. Damn them, the victims. Had Brabantio known his daughter, Desdamona, too well? "Naked abed and not mean harm?" he had asked rhetorically. Did Annie's father know her too? Had Lana's? Did they all mean harm in their fathers' eyes?

Oh, but Thomas smothered her gently. It's just another day and Desdemona's dead by his hands. By your hand, boy. Why men have to be so cruel? Momma was right. All men gives you is trouble and a wet behind. As for his brothers, all they knew was violence, how to kill. Even John, his best-loved brother, betrayed him when he followed Lorn and Richard into petty crime, another family of black men crippling themselves with drugs and booze deadly as Iago's envy.

With Desdemona dead, now it was time for him to grieve and then die by his own hand. Another betrayal. Damn Shakespeare. Each night when Iago was being led off in chains, Othello pleaded with him. Why had he done this? Why had he lied? Why had he set up Othello to murder his beloved wife? What was this jealousy?

"Demand me nothing," Iago snarled in reply. "What you know, you know. From this time forth, I never will speak a word."

Iago was cruelty incarnate, a man who hadn't said a true word to Othello. What a part to play, this pitiful, cruel, impotent man whose only passion was to destroy what he wanted for himself—success, trust, and love. And yet—The most powerful and true fell before him—Othello, Desdemona, even Emilia, his kind and honest wife.

Othello never questioned Iago about the handkerchief, the only evidence of Desdemona's alleged betrayal, till it was too late. Thomas wouldn't make that mistake. He wouldn't wait till it was too late. Was it too late? He both despised and envied Othello, in the end merely a fool who stabbed himself when he found out the truth. Was Thomas any better? What was the truth he couldn't see?

On stage, he was still fleeing. He felt crazed, mad with confusion.

Where did Othello come from? It was said he came from Venice, but he was also a Moor—from which country?

"It is the cause, it is the cause, my soul," he railed over the bowed Desdemona seconds before he smothered her. But those were just mad words of a crazed man. Finding cause was no more, no less, than cutting your own tongue out with your own knife.

The play was almost over now. Face them all, boy. Everyone wants to see you cry, boy. We paid our money. Do it where we can see, boy. One Wednesday night performance, twenty-seven dollar seat.

Damn, even on stage, his hemorrhoids were bothering him. They had gotten worse these last weeks. The price of making it, of having money in the bank. And yet how he loved the power, the control.

Tragic dramas were so popular, the basis of the soaps on TV. And Thomas' role was to act them out. This was what he did to save himself from cops like Joe, from prison. He was in this as a respite from life, from himself. All those nights he played Othello to save himself.

Tonight the audience refused to let him go. Thomas took one long bow after another. And another. Clapping on and on and on, they couldn't get enough of him. He felt devoured and yet free. Bowing deeply over and over, he received their homage with a silent, immovable face.

After his final bow, Thomas was rushed away. Seeing the hired security guard standing at the stage exit, he knew tonight would be another night where it was not safe to go back to his dressing room. The guard motioned him toward the fire escape, flanking Thomas as he ran, robe flailing, through the alley and up the narrow dark steps to the adjoining building. They had devised this alternate route last week after a girl from the Bronx cut out a patch of his hair while the *Daily News* was photographing him.

Thomas had learned to distance himself from his fans and not intervene. A hippie couple he'd befriended had attacked him after a free matinee in Washington Park. At first abjectly adoring, the man had turned mean when Thomas turned down his offer to take acid in the East Village. Then there was that student from Harvard who had threatened to sue the Negro Rep when Thomas didn't return the original screenplay he insisted Thomas had been sent and had promised to read.

Tonight there was more commotion in the hallway now that the police had arrived, "Added Protection" for the upcoming holidays. Thomas looked down the steps of the fire escape to see the fuzz leading somebody away. More shouting. More scuffling. Thomas paused, reluctant to leave. The shouting persisted. Other police were holding somebody who was shrieking his name, "Thomas, Thomas!"

"Another crazy kid," mumbled the guard, holding out his arms to protect Thomas from the crowd gathering below them.

"Yeah," Thomas answered, forcing himself to keep his eyes lowered. It was harder to ignore people when he looked into their eyes. But still he saw the boy kicking, thrashing and biting. Then he heard a high bawling. Thomas' gut twisted as he recognized who it was.

"Shit." Thomas broke with his bodyguard and ran back down the narrow metal steps where the cops were holding the kid down.

"Let him be!" he shouted, rushing toward them. "He's a fan of mine."

"Some fan you got, Dreamer," said one cop as Thomas grabbed for Georgie G.

Thomas tried to lead his son away but Georgie G pulled out of his grasp, running back down the alley. He returned, dragging an old suitcase.

"Hurry!" Thomas shouted, pointing him up the fire escape

into a long hallway of small dressing rooms.

"How the hell did you get here, boy?" Slamming shut the door, he pulled his son by his shirtsleeves.

"On the bus," Georgie G cried, eyes wide with excitement and fear.

"Where are the others? Where's Momma?" Thomas hugged and shook him at the same time.

"I come by myself!"

"You little fool. What's the matter, boy, you look like you seen a ghost."

"I had to come," gasped Georgie G.

"Anything wrong back home? Everybody all right?" Thomas held the boy's skinny shoulders.

"Yes, sir! Karlene, she getting married."

"Did you play hooky from school?"

"No! School's out for vacation. I…I took some of the money you sent and bought a Greyhound bus ticket. I been looking everywhere for you. I couldn't find you! They said there wasn't no Thomas Find nowhere."

"Who said that?" Thomas blurted out, holding himself back from overpowering the boy.

"Everybody. The police. Everybody. I been out on the streets all week looking everywhere, everywhere. It's been the shits. I couldn't find you for the longest time!" cried Georgie G.

"You been sleeping on the streets?"

"No! At the bus terminal. I go back there every night."

"You some kind of fool, boy. How'd you find me anyway?"

"I saw your picture on a big sign in Times Square! It was telling about the show and where it was and all. I just followed the streets till I got here."

"What's this?" asked Thomas, pointing to the battered suitcase, though he knew what it was.

"It's yours, the one you left behind," said Georgie G.

"Why the hell you bring that nasty thing?"

"You wrote Momma about it so I thought you wanted it. You do, don't you?"

"Hell, boy, where you get that crazy idea? And how come you reading my mail? Did you open it too?" Thomas shouted.

"No, sir."

Seeing his son flinch and shrink into his blue frayed lightweight jacket, Thomas softened. "You got that guitar I paid for? You got one, didn't you?"

"Yes, sir!" White teeth flashing, Georgie G's face broke into a big smile. "I'm playing in a concert."

"Yeah? You taking that new guitar all the way downtown to the Hill House?"

"Yes, sir. We practice every Tuesday and Thursday."

"You walking?"

"Sometimes I take the bus. There ain't no more trolley cars running."

"I know what I'm getting you for Christmas, boy. I'm buying you a bike!" Thomas put his arm around him. "You eaten anything yet?"

"No, sir."

"Come on, let's go somewhere. I got a wad of dough."

The crowd had dispersed when Thomas led Georgie G back outside. He was still hanging on to the suitcase. There was still a security guard by the exit door who hailed a cab.

After a dinner of meatballs and spaghetti, two T-bone steaks, baked potatoes with butter, a green salad Thomas insisted on ordering, double-chocolate sundaes, and six cokes, he took his son to the eleventh floor of the Central Park Hilton.

"Damn!" said Georgie G, standing in the gold and red brocade elevator, the dilapidated suitcase between them.

"Damn!" he cried again as Thomas turned on the light switch illuminating his suite. He fell backwards onto the king bed and watched while Thomas changed into a T-shirt, jeans and jacket.

Thomas led Georgie G through the lobby, nodding to the obsequious bellboys, and out the revolving glass and chrome door to an ancient bellhop who immediately hailed a taxi.

A dark man in a white Sikh turban drove them around Manhattan in his Yellow Cab.

"You see that name out there?" Thomas asked, pointing through the taxi window to the *Othello* marquee blinking above the theater.

"Yes, sir," said Georgie G.

"Spell it out."

"D-R-E-A-M-E-R."

"That's right. I'm Thomas Dreamer now. The police was right. There ain't no Thomas Find in New York. Find was a no account, a nigger, you understand?"

"Yes sir."

"And he's gone. Gone for good. You understand?"

"Yes, sir."

"Don't call me that. Call me Dad."

"Yes, Dad."

Thomas told the cab driver to take them to the Statue of Liberty. They went on a night cruise all around the New York harbor while the taxi waited, meter ticking. Then they drove uptown to the Empire State building, though by then Georgie G had fallen asleep in the corner of the back seat. Not wanting to wake him, Thomas had the taxi driver cruise through Central Park, stopping for a long time in Columbus Circle behind the horses harnessed to their empty black-topped carriages, their magnificent heads lowered in sleep too. Finally Thomas ordered the cabdriver back to his hotel where he handed him five one hundred dollar bills.

"Keep the change," Thomas said, causing a slow smile to break over the cabby's long bleak face.

Momma cried when Thomas called to say Georgie G was safe. Listening to her, he felt a pang of remorse and loneliness. She used to cry that way for him. His own son had replaced him in Momma's heart.

The next day, after a breakfast of eggs and pancakes and an even bigger lunch at the Automat on 42nd Street, Thomas arranged for Georgie G to see *Othello* at the Sunday matinee.

"How'd you like the show?" asked Thomas afterwards. They were back in his dressing room. Georgie G had on the new brown-checked bell-bottoms Thomas had bought him at a specialty store on the East '60s.

"Fine," Georgie G mumbled.

"Just fine?"

"I couldn't believe you was my daddy, no sir. I didn't understand what you was saying, but I'm gonna learn what them damn words mean, you better believe it."

"Yeah? You gotta stay in school for that."

"I will, sir, Dad. Hey, where you get that red bathrobe?" Georgie G's voice went shrill, making Thomas laugh aloud. When Mel popped by to congratulate him on the performance, Thomas introduced him to his son.

"Well, ain't this a surprise! I had no idea you had family around! You got yourself a fine boy," Mel said, causing Georgie G to light up with embarrassed pleasure.

They had another expensive dinner on West 44th Street and Georgie G fell asleep looking at *The Avengers* while Thomas went to a socialite's party on East 55th. It was a relief to no longer be the token black celebrity, what with the SDS presence.

A day later he put Georgie G back on the Greyhound bus to Pittsburgh.

"This is for a new bike, hear?" he said, stuffing a wad of bills in his son's jacket pocket.

"Yes, sir!" cried Georgie G, disappearing into the bus.

Phone Call

Thomas took the old suitcase out of the closet where he had thrown it. The lock came right open. There were bundles of letters, neatly folded official papers and pictures, including one of Georgina and Georgie G as a baby. She had sent the photo while Thomas was stationed in Korea. It was wrinkled and the edges torn from all the times he'd taken it out to look at it. There was a supply of fake driver's licenses, several medals, and a black cap with United Negro Way Boy of the Year, 1949, printed in white. There was the discolored bloodstained shirt, the dirty pants and torn coat. The handcuffs too.

Shivering, Thomas slumped down on his king-size bed and fitted a handcuff over one wrist, then the other. He felt confused, shattered. All he knew for sure was that he was glad he'd not opened this up with his son around. He couldn't face Georgie G with this shit. Damn Georgie G. Damn. But it wasn't about his son, none of it. What was it about? He loved his son, but he couldn't be with him for very long. He couldn't raise him, or could he? Too much pain in that. Pain and regret, guilt too. Yep, he'd been trained well. He never saw his birth father and old stepdaddy Find beat whatever stood in his way. Thomas flinched, remembering the blow against the wall the night before Christine-Marie was born. Random violence, fear and prison had been in store for him. There was that cop falling, hitting the cobblestones, to remind him if he forgot that. Joe Uncle Tom Cop.

Thomas sat there for a long time, holding his shackled hands in front of his chest as if to pray. He felt evil, like a collaborator.

"Joe," he cried. "Joe, Joe."

But maybe Joe wasn't no Uncle Tom. Amazing how the thought cheered him, lighting up his depressed state. He had to talk to Joe, that's what. Thomas would explain everything so Joe would understand. After all, he and Joe were alike, just two black men. But how would he find him? Where was Joe now?

One very long, very cold day just before another big assault of the Vietnam War, he put in a call to the Pittsburgh Police Department. In his most distinguished voice, Thomas said he had some important information for Joe.

"Joe? Who's that you say?" asked the dispatcher with a thick Pittsburgh accent.

"Joe, the cop. You know."

"There are a lot of Joes."

"Joe's a colored cop. I believe he was involved in the trolley accident around Christmas, 1966."

"Oh, you mean 'The Rut', Joe Walker," the dispatcher said. "Hey what did you say your name was?"

Thomas hung up for the second time, cold sweat dripping down his face, but at least now he knew Joe's name.

* * *

Before the show that evening, Thomas picked up the hotel phone and asked for Information. He learned there were 21 Joseph Walkers listed in the phone book in Pittsburgh, Pennsylvania. He figured he could tell by the addresses which ones to call, but the operator wouldn't share that information, so he took down all the numbers and began with the first one.

"Good evening, my name is Thomas Dreamer and I'm looking for a Joe Walker who was a member of the Pittsburgh Police force."

Ten calls later he was nowhere. Four people hung up on him before he could finish his first sentence.

"I'm a friend of Joe Walker, one of Pittsburgh's finest. You know where I can find him?"

He hung up on anyone who spoke with a foreign accent or in a cultured, educated voice. Putting a handkerchief over his mouth to muffle his own perfect diction, Thomas softened his voice, slurred his words, reverting to familiar shit-talking. "Hi there, how you doing tonight?" He took time to listen to their stories, laughing with them, and telling stories of his own.

Finally he reached a woman with a brother by that name who just might be in the police force.

"Why you want to know 'bout Joe anyway?"

"Joe's a friend of mine I need to find real bad. Can you dig it?"

"Is he in some trouble?" she asked, suspicion tightening her drawl.

"No, no way." Thomas explained he was calling from New York City with some important news.

"Joe don't know nobody in no New York. He's sixty-seven years old and in a wheelchair," the woman replied, slamming down the phone.

Then he called an old man named Joe E. (for Edward) Walker who had a nephew by the same name who used to be a cop.

"I'm looking for the Joe Walker who would have been working out of Homewood, East Liberty and Wilkinsburg. It would have been almost two years ago, around Christmas of '66. Man, I really need to reach him."

"He's dead," said Joe E.

"Dead?"

"Yep, he died in the line of duty."

"He died?" Thomas swallowed. "When?"

"Around Christmas," said the old man.

Thomas was speechless.

"What a shame, what a shame," said Joe E., slurring his words.

"Does he have family?" Thomas asked, attempting to get him to say more, but the old man seemed to have lost interest and his voice trailed off.

When Thomas thanked him, the phone line was already dead.

Was this his Joe? Was Joe really dead? Was this all? He couldn't stop now.

The next day Thomas called the Pittsburgh Police Administration Office, repeating his question over and over to impatient clerks. Finally he reached the Homewood-Brushton switchboard.

Thomas identified himself as a relative of Joe, desperate to tell him about a family emergency. This time he was put on hold for a long time. Finally a cop picked up the phone, a Sergeant Mahoney, "Who's this?" barked the sergeant.

"A relative of Joe Walker."

"Your name?"

Thomas mumbled something.

"What? What do you want?"

Thomas' heart was pounding. When he opened his mouth to speak, no words came out. He couldn't go through with this. He hung up.

If Joe were dead, it would be in the papers. He could go to back to Pittsburgh and look through the microfiche in the Carnegie Library. Or maybe the New York library would have a record. He could do that sometime.

On a very cold overcast day, Thomas took the subway to Harlem and dumped out the contents of his suitcase in a graffiti-covered construction site, the girders plastered with old Civil Rights posters. He lit one match after another until everything went up in smoke. A few homeless Bowery bum types stood to watch. No cops came by, or if they did, they didn't stop. No fire truck sirens screamed. The suitcase itself was too big to risk torching, so on his way back to the subway, he threw it into a moving garbage truck. Oversized jaws gaping, the truck chomped up the empty suitcase with the other refuse.

Othello would not have done any of this. No, he would never have been so afraid that he had to burn up his suitcase. He would have taken charge, vanquished the cops, and stopped in his own flight for the fallen Joe. He would have taken Joe to the hospital. He would have stuck around. He would have been honorable.

But, like Iago, Joe hadn't been upfront with Thomas. He hadn't said a single true word to him. He had poisoned Irish against him, setting Thomas up. Yes, Joe Walker had laughed at him. Joe had been suspicious, calling him an "uppity nigger." He thought Thomas stole the Impala. He didn't believe Thomas' story and called him "boy." He was the one who had handcuffed Thomas and forced him into the back of the police car. He had insisted on taking Thomas in. He wouldn't listen to Irish who wanted to let Thomas go. Joe had made it impossible for Thomas to do anything but run.

Thomas admitted it. He hated Joe. But worse, he hated the Joe inside himself. When he came up to street level, snowflakes had begun to fall, but Thomas' face was already wet with tears, railing at the character he was forced to play against.

* * *

Night after night as Thomas played his part, Othello became more tortured, crying more than he raged. His white face was streaked, the makeup dissolving with his tears. The audience cried with him.

Thomas was rolling a joint during intermission when he heard a tentative knock on his dressing room door.

"What is it?" He slipped the marijuana under a towel and began touching up his makeup for the fourth act.

"I'm sorry to interrupt you," said Lynda, Mel's latest assistant, entering hesitantly, "Your mother called."

"Momma! That's impossible." He wiped a white smear from his nose, and began to reapply the paint, careful not to disturb the dark purple circling his eyes. He looked over at Lynda in her ruby-colored skirt and matching sweater. "Sure it isn't some other colored woman?"

Lynda shrugged. "Hey, I'm just telling you what she said. She said she was your mother and I was to tell you to call home as soon as you got this message. How would I know if she was your mother?"

Glancing at the clock on the wall, Thomas slid off his stool. "I'll need to use the phone in your office." He looked at her pointedly. "Privately."

"Go ahead. Nobody's in there now."

Wrapped in his cloak, Thomas hurried down the back hall. He dialed Momma's number with trembling hands. Carlotta picked up the phone at the first ring.

"Thomas?" she gasped.

"What's wrong?"

"It's Georgie G," Carlotta sobbed.

"What about him?" Thomas cried.

"He got hit by a truck riding his new bike."

"How bad?"

"I don't know. Bad."

"How bad? Goddamn it, quit that blubbering. Tell me. He's alive, isn't he? Tell me, Carlotta!"

"Momma's at the hospital now."

"And?"

"It happened in front of the A&P on Penn Avenue. His face, oh, it's all smashed up, his foot, a bloody mess. His leg twisted in the bike spokes. His guitar got broken. Oh, Thomas! They said he's unconscious. Somebody from the supermarket recognized him in the street and ran over to tell us. An ambulance took him to the hospital. Christine-Marie went with Momma. They followed the ambulance in a police car. I had to stay here 'cause of the kids. Momma said she'd call, but she hasn't called yet."

"What hospital?"

Carlotta thought it was Pittsburgh Hospital. She wasn't sure she cried; it could be another. He told her not to worry and that he'd call the hospital, but as he hung up he realized he had to be on stage in two minutes. There was no time.

That night as usual the applause was deafening. With each bow he took, he saw Georgie G lying on the streets of Pittsburgh. He just couldn't do this no more he thought as the curtain finally closed. Something had to change.

Back Home

As the plane jerked and bumped through the clouds, Thomas watched the stars and moon, just past full, from the tiny window. The flight from Newark to Pittsburgh would be barely 45 minutes long in good weather, but already it felt longer. On his right, the window was filled with tiny spots of color, Christmas lights decorating the houses all over suburban New Jersey. Over there was the skyline of New York City. He might have been able to see the lights of southeastern Pennsylvania if they had not been climbing above the clouds so fast, trying to get above the turbulence.

The scene below appeared as if viewed through a snowy glass ball mirroring the speed and confusion of recent events. Thomas was surprised at how quickly Mel had agreed to him taking time off after hearing of Georgie G's accident. His understudy, a huge ebony actor from the Belgian Congo who had studied with Sir Lawrence Olivier at the Old Vic, stepped in immediately, playing Othello with an impeccable English accent that Mel insisted would win over even the die-hard critics.

Despite his fear for Georgie G, Thomas was lulled into a reverie by these thoughts and the hum of the moving plane. Imagined scenes of comfort and cheer with his family flitted by like the clouds merging and separating, barely distinguishable from the darkness outside his tiny window.

A youngish woman sat across the aisle from him smoking. Her full red lips made concentric circles on the cigarette she held in one manicured hand. She was dressed in the style of Jacqueline Kennedy and wore high black leather boots. Makeup covered her face and her sandy hair was perfectly curled behind her ears, also like Mrs. Kennedy's, though now the style was no longer popular. Neither was Jackie, Thomas thought. Must be her marriage to the Greek tycoon, Aristotle Onassis a month ago, just two weeks before the election, an election that left Tricky Dick Nixon the new president-elect.

He noticed a box marked Bloomingdale's wedged beneath the woman's stocking-covered knees. A fur coat hung loosely over her seat. Thomas wondered if it were real or fake and wanted to touch it. The coat reminded him of Lana. Lana hated fake. If only, if nothing. Give it up, he told himself. It was what it was. He sighed, turning his head away from the smell of the smoke that reminded him of Lana too. Lana, I forgive you. I hope you've forgiven me, he thought though he couldn't believe it.

Suddenly the plane lurched and the fur coat fell to the floor. Thomas leaned out into the aisle to pick it up. The woman turned around, meeting his eyes, hers cold and blank. Without acknowledging him, she took the coat with one hand and turned away, her ringed hand fingering the glowing cigarette. "Bitch," he thought, watching the end of the cigarette flicker and wane, singeing the fur on her sleeve. Was it fear and loathing or desire that filled her eyes? Lana would have grinned seductively. Annie would have smiled, maybe. Thinking of Annie, Thomas felt the usual sorry-assed pang of longing. The women he'd been with since her were just one-night-stands. He shouldn't have let her go like he did. Why had he? He couldn't remember now. The seatbelt sign went off and then on again. A stewardess appeared offering drinks. Thomas asked for tomato juice.

He had not told Carlotta he was coming. He had not been able to get any information from Pittsburgh Hospital. He held his head in his hands.

Soon the TWA plane began jerking and bouncing as it came down through the cloud cover over the pale brown rivers, over the faint brush of bare trees he couldn't see but knew were there, over the miniature box houses of river towns in the valleys skirting the western rim of the Allegheny Mountains. The snow gleamed. Flames bloomed from the steel mills like vaporous roses. The sky shone pink. Soon the sun would go down behind the hills toward the West beyond the point where the Ohio River began. Thomas closed his eyes. When he opened them, the plane was just landing on the dark tidy snow-swept span of the runway. He jerked forward in his seat as the wheels touched the ground.

"Watch your step," cautioned the stewardess as Thomas stood at the open cabin door in his new Chesterfield coat. Across the snow spread the main terminal building of the Pittsburgh Airport. Ice made the steps very precarious, the stewardess warned. Looking at him quizzically, she asked, "Have you flown with us before, sir?" He nodded as he wrapped his red lambs-wool scarf around his neck and stepped carefully onto the ramp.

He hailed a taxi, thinking it would be quicker than the Hilton airporter bus, but with the heavy rush hour traffic, they barely moved on the two-lane road twisting through the South Hills toward downtown Pittsburgh. It took over an hour to reach the Fort Pitt Tunnel. Coming out of the tunnel, he saw to his left the Duquesne Incline, Pittsburgh's only remaining cable car railway, climb slowly up and down the stripped hillside above the Monongahela River. 'NOEL' was, spelled out on the top of the KDKA radio tower. There was the H.J. Heinz plant advertising 'Pure Food Products' on the lip of the Allegheny and the Gateway Clipper inching its way up the icy river. On the Fort Pitt Bridge, an ambulance, lights flashing, passed the taxi on the wrong side, siren screaming.

He told the taxi driver, a clean-shaven college student with a Pitt baseball cap and shoulder-length hair, to head east on the Parkway. Ahead were the outlines of bare trees on barren hills. Now came the bridges and ravines, the neighborhoods unfolding before him. He felt as if he knew every bend, every hill, even the awkward wooden houses stacked above the railroad tracks. The taxi moved from the fast to the slow lane and then back again. Heat coming through the vents under his seat warmed his legs and feet. He felt sleepy.

They got off at the Boulevard of the Allies. Since he had left, the neighborhoods had shrunk, curling into themselves like old fruit. The Pittsburgh streets were narrower, the buildings more ramshackle and rundown. The hillsides dipped brown and wrinkled.

On the way through Oakland and East Liberty, the taxi passed blocks and blocks of gutted houses in yet another redevelopment project abandoned after the riots following Martin Luther King, Jr.'s death. Through the cab window, he searched the flat black expanse. There was Penn Avenue where he had walked with Annie that icy February afternoon of his audition nearly two years before. There was the flashing Nabisco sign on the corner where he stopped to wait for her. She had been angry about something. He should know what, but he had forgotten. Where was she? New York? Pittsburgh? He didn't know that either. Maybe she had come back home for Christmas. Thomas's head ached and his mouth felt dry.

It was snowing when they reached Pittsburgh Hospital. Slipping the driver three twenties, Thomas told him to wait. Taking his suitcase, he pushed the heavy glass doors and hurried into the overheated lobby full of people. Carefully placing his suitcase on the floor, he approached the receptionist, a small pale woman with gold-framed glasses.

"I'm looking for my son."

"Just a moment, please. There are other people waiting in front of you."

"This is an emergency. He's been badly hurt."

"You'll wait your turn like everybody else."

But when finally she got back to him it was only to say she couldn't find Georgie G's name on her roster.

"He's here!" Thomas leaned over the counter, his voice breaking.

The woman retreated. "Just a moment, if you please!"

"He was in an accident, hit by a truck yesterday." Thomas lowered his voice. "His grandmother should be with him." After checking her roster again, the pale woman made a phone call, cupping her hand over her mouth while she talked so she could not be overheard.

"There's a Georgie G Beemes admitted yesterday," she said over her shoulder, hanging up the telephone.

"Beemes?" said Thomas, regaining his composure. He smiled. But of course, Georgina would have given Georgie G her last name. All these years and he'd never thought about it. She must have told him. He had never even seen his son's birth certificate—or his report card. He felt chastened. "Where can I find him? Which way?" Thomas pressed.

"Room 224," she said off-handedly, pointing toward a sign marked "Intensive Care."

He rushed down the dull fluorescent-lit hallway, ignoring the nurses in their white outfits and the attendants in their green scrubs staring at him. What did they see anyway? A black man in a camel hair coat and alligator boots. His wool scarf from Scotland was still wrapped around his neck.

Heading through the half-open door to the hospital room, he came upon a slight form in a raised bed attached to blinking medical equipment. Except for the shape of the small brown head, Thomas wouldn't have known it was Georgie G. Electrodes were stuck to the boy's shaved head and wires led from his skull to a monitor. His eyes were closed. He was wearing an oxygen mask. A tube was attached to one arm, another to his stomach under a white sheet. One leg was suspended in a stirrup, the other in a big cast. Thomas walked over to the chair at the side of the bed.

"Son," he whispered, leaning over.

"Georgie G, it's me. It's your dad."

He put his fingers around his son's limp wrist and watched the red choppy line on the monitor above him go up and down as the unconscious boy breathed heavily. He sat down.

Time passed very slowly as Thomas sat in the chair holding Georgie G's hand. In a while a nurse came in to check the boy's vital signs. She didn't have much to say except that the doctor would be by tomorrow morning.

When he finally stood up to go, he felt numb, with no real thoughts, no good ideas, no feelings except dumb panic at his boy's injuries.

"I'm going now, but I'll be back," he said. "I've always wanted to be here for you but I haven't. I've been running, afraid my whole life, guilty, ashamed. I hate it. I'm not going to do that anymore. But I don't know how to stop. No, that's a lie. I do. I just have to do it. But you have to grow up and be a man. You have to live—for me. You're strong, boy. Stronger than me. I know that."

When Thomas left the hospital, he found the student driver waiting in the taxi in the driveway, a heavy odor of pot permeating the cab. He gave the driver directions to the Homewood precinct.

"You mean the No. 5 precinct in East Liberty," corrected the kid. "There isn't any Homewood precinct. I used to drive people from there to bail bonds," he explained.

"Right," said Thomas.

On the way, they passed his old neighborhood. From the back seat, he could see the moon. Except for the Christmas lights, the houses were dark, made darker by deep lowdown snow-covered branches of the fir trees and large hulking white bushes fronting the rows of identical rundown houses. Cats scurried out from under rusted, dented cars and disappeared under different rusted, dented cars. The muffled silence in the cab mirrored the eerie scene outside. A large spruce covered with blue lights blocked his view of what lay ahead.

The precinct was a one-story brick building on Penn Ave dwarfed by a large concrete parking lot filled with police cars smeared filthy with dirt and smog. Everything was covered with a film of iced snow. Thomas walked up the steps and pulled open the door. Inside, the room was poorly lit and freezing despite the noisy radiator blowing in one corner. There was a row of torn plastic chairs lining two walls and on the other side of the counter a thin man in a blue shirt and pants was sitting at a wooden desk covered with papers. He had a red nose and a black mustache and wore a black wool cap that said 'Pittsburgh Pirates'. He was yelling into a phone.

Putting down his suitcase, Thomas stood waiting at the counter while the clerk shouted into the mouthpiece. A hallway led to a back door with a cracked glass window reinforced with wire meshing. Two cops came through the door in heavy coats and boots, hats snow-covered, stomping and swearing. They disappeared through a closed door, but not before the beefy, red-faced one glowered at him.

"What the hell!" The clerk slammed down the phone, glancing in Thomas' direction. "Who the hell are you?"

"My name is Thomas Dreamer. I'm here to find out what happened to Joe Walker, a cop on your force who was on duty two years ago this Christmas."

"Joe, the Rut?"

"That's him."

"And why do you want to know about Joe?" The man's eyes narrowed as he looked Thomas up and down.

"Because I was with him that night."

"Yeah?"

"Yeah." Thomas clasped his hands together, revealing the white cuffs of his silk shirt beneath his coat.

"Then you should know what happened to him."

"That's why I came, to find out."

"Where you say you from?"

"I didn't. I'm from New York City."

"And you say you were with Joe Walker that night?"

"Yes."

"Joe was fatally injured in the line of duty. Now if you was there, then you would know this. Walker's dead. Does that surprise you—what you say your name was?"

Forcing himself to breathe out, breathe in, Thomas answered, "Thomas Dreamer."

"Yeah, yeah. Look, I don't have time for this crap," the clerk interrupted, standing up and stretching. He stopped abruptly, as if hearing Thomas' words for the first time.

"Leonard!" he shouted down the hall. "Leonard!"

The beefy cop with the pink face stuck his head out a door. "Yeah?"

"Get your butt out here. Somebody's here from New York City to talk to you about Joe, 'The Rut'."

"No, shit," bellowed the cop, as he sauntered in, tightening his heavy gun belt. "I thought that case was benchmarked for good."

Kicking open the latched counter door, he bore down on Thomas.

The Stinky-Shoe Man

When Thomas came back to Pittsburgh at Christmas and gave himself up, at first everybody lay low, carrying on as if it were business as usual. But things began to get better after they brought Georgie G home from the hospital.

"Here he comes! I see Thomas!" cried Georgie G, wrapped up in heavy blankets. He was parked next to Momma on the couch in his rented wheelchair, his leg in a big old cast, facing the small black and white TV.

They all watched as Thomas, dressed in black, stepped out of a police car and walked up the steps to City Hall flanked by the cops and some impressive-looking bodyguards in suits. There was talk of him being charged with assault on an officer, with escape while in custody, even of murder charges. The case was still being reviewed, having been benchmarked, that is, put on low priority after the MLK slaying because of riots and more pressing problems.

"Pigs," said one of the twins.

"Hush, I want to hear," said Momma.

"Weren't no fools sitting in the back seat of that Impala that night," commented Carlotta, sitting herself down in front of the TV too.

A gaggle of press followed Thomas shouting questions, their cameras flashing as the newscaster announced the actor had been released on one-hundred thousand dollars bail put up by an anonymous donor reputed to be a New York socialite with ties to Castro.

The newscast was interrupted by a cigarette commercial.

"I never seen a thousand dollar bill," said Christine-Marie, watching a movie actor light up a Camel on the TV screen.

"Fool!" cried Carlotta. "There ain't no thousand dollar bills."

Now the newscaster went on to say that Andy Warhol, famed Pittsburgh artist, had sold his Coca Cola bottle painting in order to retain a well-known criminal attorney from San Francisco for Thomas.

"When we going to see him?" asked Christine-Marie.

"We'll see him one of these days. Don't worry," answered Momma.

"He be in hiding," said the other twin.

"I'm all right," Thomas told Momma when he called later that night. "It's going to be okay. You'll see. I'll be home when I can."

A few days later Thomas appeared on the eleven o'clock news speaking to a gathering that had rallied outside the county jail, the same corner where 3,400 National Guard and Federal troops had lined up after Martin Luther King, Jr. was killed. The camera was at his back but they could hear him clearly.

"I came back to Pittsburgh to make amends for Joe Walker," he said.

"Hot damn!" said Find, coming in the door, holding a brown bag covering a cheap bottle of Mogen David. "Why he have to open his damn mouth?"

There was a paragraph or two in the Post Gazette about Joe Walker, a rookie of six months and one of Pittsburgh's first Negro cops, nicknamed "the Rut" because he liked to drive in the infamous ruts and potholes of the city. Joe had been pronounced dead at the scene without ever regaining consciousness. On behalf of Joe's family, the Pittsburgh Police Union and the Homewood Baptist Church hired a legal team to investigate his death, resulting in allegations and counter allegations.

Karlene cut out the feature about Thomas that appeared in the *Pittsburgh* magazine the next weekend. Momma taped it to the refrigerator. Thomas' poverty-stricken childhood was contrasted with his rise in the theater. "My heart is with Joe Walker's family whether or not I had any part in his untimely death," he was quoted as saying.

After that, pictures of Thomas' family appeared in all the papers. They were cut out and put on the refrigerator too. There was a close up of Georgie G, his leg in a cast, holding an electric guitar. The caption underneath explained the Jewish Anti-Defamation League had donated the guitar when it was learned Thomas' son was a victim of a traffic accident. There were shots of his mother in color, a wide, impressive, unsmiling woman in a dark coat and hat. "I always prayed he'd do the right thing," she said. Pastor Beemes, a "close family friend" said, "Jesus made Thomas Dreamer the man he is today so that He could forgive him. If Jesus can, so should we," words that were repeated by the influential pastor of the Homewood A.M.E. Zion Church. Another shot showed Thomas holding a baby with blond curls. The caption read, "We are all one family looking for justice," from a speech he made at a rally of about three hundred people in front of Murphy's 5&10 on Homewood Ave. Amazingly, the crowd disbursed without violence. Students from Homewood Junior High sent a banner with "Get Well, Georgie G" painted in their school colors that Carlotta hung from the ceiling.

"That's a relief," said Thomas, who was home now, back from where he wouldn't say, even though Georgie G kept asking. The word got out and Momma's house was deluged with visitors, some nice, some nasty.

"Hey! Did you see this! Don't I look the fool?" Karlene held up the *Pittsburgh Courier*, the weekly newspaper of the black community. There was a big picture of Karlene cutting the wedding cake with her new husband, Lloyd, a recent inductee into the Marines and soon to be deployed to Vietnam. She showed that picture to everyone who stopped by.

Outside the Pittsburgh Court House, college students from Pitt led a march of black folk and others carrying signs that said,

"Let My People Go" and "Cops and Rats Breed on the Hill." When the Black Panthers came to town, Thomas was invited to a private meeting with them and the Mayor at the Mayor's Office. "I came back to Pittsburgh to make things right," he said. "I've learned something we all find out sooner or later. The freedom we want is inside, not outside. It doesn't come from the color of our skin, no matter who is pointing the gun." He ended with, "You can kill the dreamer, but not the dream," paraphrasing Jesse Jackson in response to Mayor Richard Daley's crackdown at the Democratic Convention last summer. Momma repeated what Thomas said to her sisters calling from California, after having seen him in the San Jose nightly news.

The Carnegie Tech Drama department staged a benefit of Leroy Jones' plays to underwrite Thomas' continuing court expenses. In the program, Mel Manning of the Negro Repertory Company was quoted along with the Hollywood impresario-turned Broadway producer, Stan Marvelous, who insisted that, "Dreamer is a world-class star on stage and off, shining bright in the dark night of racism."

When he wasn't in court or dealing with the press, Thomas spent most of his time in the upstairs bedroom with his son watching TV or talking on the phone to New York. He told Georgie G he felt like he had an angel at his back.

"Who is it?" asked his son.

"I don't know, fool," laughed Thomas. "It's just hanging out here watching you hop around in your cast, looking at reruns and eating Momma's cooking."

The whole family began to treat Thomas in the old way, like he was one of their own again. One night the twins brought up the Stinky Shoe Man. "Be the Stinky Shoe Man again!" they shouted, lunging at him.

"Awww."

"Be the Stinky Shoe Man!"

"Go on!"

"Aww, why I want to be that sorry-ass skinny boy sitting in dirt outside his house in Pittsburgh?" asked Thomas, but he was poised already for the part, assuming the actor's stance.

"Here come the Stinky-Shoe Man!" he announced. "He so skinny. His legs are two brown sticks in the dirt. It's summertime and he's wearing torn shorts his Momma cut from old blue jeans and some big old shoes he found in a garbage can behind the alley. He's waiting, knowing that sooner or later them kids are coming by."

"That be us," said Christine-Marie.

"Don't interrupt," Thomas said, poking her lightly. "Okay, where was I?"

"He's waiting."

"Yeah. Finally he sees the kids peeking around the corner or maybe they're hanging from the chain link fence where Lasher Brothers Demo piles their flat tires. But he pretend he don't see them, he don't look up.

"Carlotta be leading the pack. She wearing some long dragged down sundress torn at the hem. There's John behind her with his long brown face like a horse, always breaking into tears after he done something wrong, wanting his brother to fix things up for him."

"Here he comes! Here comes the Stinky-Shoe Man."

They shrieked as Thomas brushed himself off and put one foot into a stinky shoe, then the other. Carefully he tied up the laces. Now he came after them, clomping and flailing his arms, while they rushed backwards into the tiny bathroom screaming.

He did this a few more times.

"That's enough," Thomas said finally, sitting back down.

"You right about that. Who's ready for dinner?" Momma chimed in from the kitchen.

Nobody knew where he went some nights. He never stayed

any place more than a few days. He had to move out, he told them. He needed his space. Yet he didn't move. Thomas felt strangely safe and protected at Momma's, far away from all the publicity that was being generated with him at its center. His story may have taken off, but he didn't seem to need to.

The Connecticut Connection, as the press named Lana, dissolved quickly as neither her father nor anyone else connected with her family would agree to testify regarding a stolen Impala. A Pittsburgh Press editorial questioned Thomas' confession, maintaining his agent had confessed it was all done as a publicity stunt.

One day he went to Western Penitentiary to see his incarcerated brothers. Richard wouldn't look him in the eye but Lorn broke down and cried. Thomas held a news conference afterwards, proclaiming the prison a manhole to hell, a rotten stinking system without justice or forgiveness.

It was rumored the prosecution didn't have a case. Then the autopsy report from December 23, 1966 surfaced, performed by the Pittsburgh Police's internationally-acclaimed doctor two days after the incident. It showed the caused of Joe's death to be myocardial infarction, commonly known as an instant heart attack.

The assault charges had to be dropped when Sergeant Ron E. Mahoney, the other cop at the scene of the accident, couldn't identify Thomas from a row of look-alikes. It didn't help that Mahoney was no longer on active duty either, having been implicated in abetting racketeers on the North Side.

The story dragged on through the New Year, what with the preliminary hearing being cancelled, and the low profile Thomas kept on the advice of his lawyer. Thomas was now facing only the lesser charge of escape while in custody.

The day he was to have been charged, a sit-in was staged at the all-black Millville High School on the North Side. There was a riot on the Hill and a case of suspected arson at Schenley High where Thomas had graduated. The trial, if there ever were one, would be postponed while the prosecutor tried to have it moved from Pittsburgh to Harrisburg where there was less chance of a biased jury.

Georgie G who was still in the upstairs bedroom convalescing, his leg in a cast, wanted to know why Thomas had gone to all this damn trouble turning himself in for nothing.

"I got to see you, didn't I?" said Thomas. He was listening to Jimi Hendrix on the new turntable.

"But are you gonna stick around now you here?"

"Maybe."

"Maybe ain't good enough," said Georgie G.

"You're right, it ain't."

Thomas was thinking about Mel and Stan who, citing the success of *Hair*, let it be known they were eager to go forward with a plan to produce *Othello* abroad at the foot of the Parthenon. That was fine with Thomas. After all, Eldridge Cleaver had gone to Algeria.

Waiting for him was a plane ticket to the Bahamas via Miami and from the Bahamas to Greece. They even got him a Swiss bank account and a suitcase full of new clothes, one with no handcuffs and no fake IDs.

"You should check out the concert at the Hill House. I'm gonna be playing my guitar," said Georgie G.

"When is it? Maybe I will. It sounds like a good idea. That reminds me, I got one more thing to check out."

"What?"

"Don't worry, boy. I'll be back. You tell Momma. And don't look like that. I ain't gone yet."

River Road

Annie was very carefully hanging the last of the four stockings over the fireplace when Melinda pointed Thomas out on the Channel 2 news.

"Isn't that the actor you were involved with?" her sister asked.

"What?" Annie stepped back from the decorated mantle to look over at the TV. Handel's *Messiah Oratorio* was playing in the background on the record player.

"More news regarding Thomas Dreamer, noted Shakespearean actor originally from Pittsburgh and now appearing on Broadway," blabbed the Channel 2 broadcaster, a bland young man with a crew cut in a blue suit and red tie.

"Oh, my god! Oh, my god!" Annie cried, slumping into the armchair.

Stunned, she watched Thomas being hurried down a crowded corridor in City Hall. Serious, subdued, he exuded a calm, yet powerful presence, once or twice looking into the camera with an open vulnerability even the newscaster commented upon.

"I can't believe it," she said finally.

"He's so cool," said Melinda off-handedly. "I can't believe you don't know. It's been in the news for over a week."

Melinda sat down next to her in the matching armchair. "The accident, the dead cop," she continued. "Well, that happens all the time. That's no big deal. What's really shocking is Thomas Dreamer turned himself in. He could end up in jail for life."

"What are you saying, Melinda? What dead cop? What accident?" Stunned, Annie looked at her sister, then back at the TV.

"Thomas Dreamer, previously known as Thomas Find, turned himself in last week for allegedly causing fatal injury to a Pittsburgh policeman, Joseph Walker, during a dispute following a minor traffic accident two years ago," reported the newscaster.

"You didn't know?" Now Melinda looked shocked.

"No." Annie said, even as the conversation with Lana came back to her. So that's what Lana had been talking about. Lana knew. Poor Lana. She had secrets too. A chill slithered up Annie's back.

There on the TV screen was Thomas speaking at a rally about justice and everyone being one family. Her feelings smoldered as she stood up to smooth out the red felt stockings hanging over the cold fireplace bricks. Annie was dumbfounded, shocked. After all the time and distance between them, things fell into place. Her confusion disappeared. In a certain way Annie felt complete, as if she now understood Thomas. She had come full-circle on this, her first night home from Julliard.

After Melinda's first comments, nobody ever brought up Thomas' name at home again, not even when he they saw him featured on a special program following the news. Throughout her vacation to Pittsburgh, Annie followed his story on her own, not able to articulate even for herself all the conflicting emotions she felt. Stunned, yes, yet she felt relief too. She was proud of him for coming forward, yes, and sorry, very sorry for what had happened. Why couldn't he have shared this with her? She could have comforted him. Could they have been together? Just asking that question left her raw with something close to longing, a fire she didn't want to fuel anymore and a shame. Could she have done more?

Except for the shocking events concerning Thomas, it was an unusually happy time. It snowed heavily on Christmas. The roads weren't yet plowed which prevented the Ryans from attending Midnight Mass at Immaculate Heart Church. This upset Dad the most and he was talking about driving anyway, but he had to give up the idea when he couldn't open the garage door because of the snow drifts. Even Annie was surprised when Mother put on her snow boots and suggested they walk the seven blocks to the local parish church on Greensburg Pike instead. Annie hadn't been in a church since Lana's funeral a year and a half ago and it was both unreal and comforting to sit in the warm glow of the dimly lit pew listening to the Christmas liturgy, reflecting on her Catholic girlhood with poignant nostalgia. Still she was glad when the Mass was over.

She and Mother connected in a way they never had before. Annie had wanted to learn to cook on her visit home. "If only I could cook as well as you," she said, asking Mother if she could copy her favorite recipes. Together they began to watch Julia Child, the French Chef, on Channel 13, Public Television. Julia wore big flowery aprons over her six foot, two-inch frame. The aprons were splotchy with creams and wine sauces at the end of every show and Julia didn't seem to mind it. With her cheery enthusiasm and booming, affected voice, she always made them laugh. Mother referred to Julia as "My Lady of the Ladle" from a featured story in *Time* magazine. Annie tried out a few of the easier recipes and together they served up a formal dinner of Julia's Beef Bourguignon to Dad, Melinda and her new boyfriend. It disappointed Annie she had to use canned mushrooms instead of the fresh button and cremini ones Julia recommended. But Dad pronounced the dish, "Delicious!" and even Melinda, on a diet to lose ten pounds, finished her plate except for pearl onions she never ate anyway.

* * *

The January afternoon was sunny and unusually clear. Lucky was wagging her tail even before Annie put on her old blue navy pea coat for their daily walk. As she slipped into her boots, she thought how she'd miss Lucky when she went back to Julliard. She'd miss everyone. She'd had a great visit home. At least, so far.

It felt so warm she didn't even need a hat or gloves, but she put them on anyway. The park would be wet from new snow, the fir trees hanging heavy in her path. Annie was in a hurry. Tonight

Dad and she were attending a concert at the Soldiers and Sailors Memorial in Oakland, featuring a Romanian prodigy playing Schubert's *Three Last Sonatas*. Dad was delighted Annie wanted to accompany him and had even bought expensive seats in the Dress Circle.

Lucky was already poised before the front door, alert, when through the diamond panes of glass she saw someone on the porch outside. It was Thomas. He had his back to her and he was looking away towards the street, gray with slush. He held black leather gloves. Annie stood motionless in the middle of the living room. Thomas finally turned around and rang the bell and Lucky barked. Swallowing her fear, Annie took a deep breath and opened the door.

"Hello, Thomas."

"Hello, Annie." He offered his hand. She noticed his camel Chesterfield coat and rich brown boots.

"How did you find me?" she asked, hands at her side.

"The phone book," he said. "I know the East End of Pittsburgh pretty well, remember?"

She looked beyond Thomas to the shiny white Imperial parked beyond the fur trees at the end of her walk.

"I rented it," he said, nodding.

"How did you know I'd be here?" As if they were neighbors who had just passed each other on the street.

"A hunch. Any more questions?" he smiled, but his eyes were deep, fathomless.

She turned around toward Lucky who had retreated to her carpet behind the chair. "I was just about to take my dog on a walk."

Lucky began to wag her tail.

"Don't let me stop you," he said, stepping back.

"There's no one here but me."

"You mean it's alright for me to come inside?" His smile had disappeared.

"That's not what I meant," she retorted.

"Look, I don't want to argue. I don't want this to be another missed chance. We've had too many, wouldn't you say?" he said.

"I don't know what to say," she said, brushing her hair off her face. She leaned against the open door. "I heard about the trial being moved."

"Yeah? Got permission from the judge for good behavior."

"Is it over then?"

He shrugged.

"So you think we're just a lot of missed chances?" she said, her voice wavering.

"Don't you?"

"I don't know."

"Let's take a drive," he said.

"I'll take you out later," Annie told Lucky, locking her in the house.

Thomas drove out Verona Road and along Allegheny River Boulevard to the river. It was the same but different. Sitting next to Thomas, she took in the glaze of the cold sunlight, the high water, the gray riverbank, the barren trees hazy on each side, and the stone wall where they had parked before. This is the end of the road, she thought.

He turned off, swerving onto a gravel road leading to the riverbank. The big car brushed some leafless bushes, surprising a family of quail who flew up in front of the fender. Thomas slowed to a crawl as they went over the railroad ties and stopped in front of the slow-moving sheet of icy water. He turned off the motor. Annie rolled down the window. A drab bird flew from barren limb to barren limb. She watched the bird spring and fly at random, without regard for itself. Now the bird was flying backwards, crazily alighting on rusted railroad cars and barbwire fences, cheeping wildly. She expected it to crash into a tree or one of the posts pockmarked with rusted nails, but it didn't.

"So here we are," he said.

"She knew, didn't she? About the accident and all."

"Lana? Yes, she knew. She left it all on her answering machine for anyone to follow up on."

"I miss Lana," Annie mumbled.

"Yeah. She was doing her own time long before she took that overdose. She didn't have a way out either."

"You never told me."

"I'm sorry, Annie. I never wanted to involve you in any of this."

"But," she began and then stopped, searching for the right words. Were there any? What was right? She wanted to be with him. From the beginning, that's all she wanted. It was such a painful, hopeless thought that she took herself away where she could stare down at him like the bird in the bent, bare trees.

"It was an accident," Annie said finally from a place far outside herself, the car, and the river.

"Yeah," he agreed, pulling his coat up around his neck. "It was Georgie G who brought me back here."

"How is he?"

"Getting better. I couldn't stand myself running away while my kid was in a hospital bed."

"This is such an unjust system," she said. "I liked teaching Georgie G and the other kids at the Hill House. I'm really glad he's going to be okay."

"Yeah. There's a plane ticket to Miami waiting for me," said Thomas, sighing. "From Miami to the Bahamas, and from the Bahamas to Greece. Do you know Eldridge Cleaver is in Algiers? And Stokely Carmichael is going to Africa?"

He didn't wait for her response. "Stan has arranged for a Swiss bank account for me. I have a suitcase full of new clothes. Yeah, and Mel's got a scheme to produce *Othello in the Ghetto* at the

Parthenon. It will be a musical like *Hair,* but hipper, set in Athens."

"I saw you in *Othello,*" she said.

"What did you think?" he asked after a long silence.

She shrugged. "You did great. I just don't want to be Desdemona."

"You'll never be Desdemona, Annie."

"I like the song, 'Age of Aquarius'," she said then, changing the subject.

"It's okay." He turned and gave Annie a little smile. "I'm taking Georgie G with me. You could come along too. No kidding, Annie."

From her far away, distant place, she didn't answer. What was the point now? She wanted to grab his hands and hold them to her heart. She wanted to flop like a stunned bird against the car window. She wanted to fall into his arms, feel his heat, the strength of his body forever, one last time.

"So I got this big name now," Thomas went on. "My lawyer says the judge in Harrisburg's going to throw out the case. He says I'll be acquitted or at the most, serve a month with restitution. You know, judges don't want to stir things up. The riots here were bad, lots of police brutality, the National Guard called in, arson, fires, looting, random violence. Stan loves this, the publicity. He says it's the greatest thing that ever happened. He says I'm a genius to have dreamt this up, if I did, and if I didn't, then it's pure blind luck. Everybody mighty scared to rile us niggers up after Martin Luther King, Jr."

It was what she always wanted for him, this success, and she felt an impulse to clap, as if this were a masterful performance she was watching. But her hands felt scarred, wounded.

"I know it will work out for you," Annie said, loosening her coat.

"Yeah? You really think so? Hey, let me help you," he said, lifting up her hair.

"I don't need any help," she said, pulling away.

"I guess not," he said.

Annie slumped back in her seat. Why had she said that? Something was forcing her to do things she didn't want to do. Or did she? For a long time they sat there. Everything was still, silent and lonely.

Suddenly Thomas leaned over and kissed her. His mouth on hers, his tongue pushing inside. Another missed chance? No, she couldn't let it be.

"Thomas, I want you to be with me," she said. "I love you."

"Aww, Annie, I love you too." He kissed her again and for a moment or two she felt they might make love there in the rented car, but he moved away and then she did too.

As they drove off, Annie searched the bare trees on the riverbank and the thick leafless brush on the other side of the Allegheny dusted with snowflakes. She searched the hills behind them too. What was she looking for? The land and everything on it was dumb, muted, its meaning, if any, hidden.

Before she knew it, Thomas had driven her back home. He was rolling down his window when she jumped out. The air had turned frigid. She slammed her door shut.

"Bye," Annie called out, running away down the snowy walk.

"Bye, love," he might have answered before driving off. She ran away too quickly to actually hear any reply.

After that, whenever she wanted to reach out for him, she'd think of the moment along the riverbank before he pulled away and how it might have been different, and the moment she ran from the car and how that might have been different too. She thought of the river. But finally all that too dissolved like a cloud or a wisp of smoke or the swish swish of a child's swing.

* * *

The evening before she went back to New York, Annie and her sister sat on the sofa in front of the TV while Dad read the newspaper in the chair. Melinda was knitting a scarf for her boyfriend. Mother was in the kitchen putting the finishing touches on dinner. Tonight it was pot roast with potatoes, Annie's favorite.

"Thomas Dreamer, otherwise known as Thomas Find. . ."

Nodding toward the TV, Melinda nudged Annie.

". . . was acquitted of all charges in the death of rookie police officer, Joe Walker, who died while on duty at the scene of an accident involving a trolley and a stolen car two years ago," said the broadcaster in an upbeat tone. "The judge fined Mr. Dreamer $10,000 for leaving the scene of an accident. Mr. Dreamer's attorney said he would appeal."

Melinda stopped knitting and turned her head toward Annie. "Did you her that?"

"Thomas Dreamer, the well-known Broadway actor, is presently on his way back to New York. From there, the actor is flying to Bermuda and then Athens, Greece, to pursue new acting possibilities," the newscaster intoned.

Dad harrumphed from behind the paper while Melinda continued watching her sister for a response.

"According to a family spokesperson, Mr. Dreamer's plans include having his son, Georgie G Beemes, join him as soon as the boy's injuries from a recent bicycle accident are fully healed and the school year is completed. And now for the latest in the weather."

Seeing the tears sliding down Annie's face, Melinda looked away and then went back to her knitting. Everyone was quiet during the weather report. Then Mother called them to dinner.

Epilogue

Holding my emails, I sit in the back of a row of blue seats facing the Security area of Pittsburgh International airport and watch the arrivals on the US Airways monitor. Flight 95 from New York has landed. When Thomas arrives, he will come through the Security Gate. I can't wait to see him. And yet, on the other hand, I can wait forever. I already have. Ouch, my back hurts more than usual.

He found me on the Internet. You can find anything on the web. What happened to him in the last forty years? Before I got these emails, I'd looked for his name in the theater news of whichever city I was touring in with the Pittsburgh Symphony, but I never saw it.

In his emails he says he went to Europe and the Middle East with *Othello,* with open-air performances at the ruins in Mycenae and Cyprus. He was in multi-media extravaganzas with rock stars like Michael Jackson. He was big on the AIDS benefit circuit and ended up in Paris, starting a chain of celebrity-theme restaurants. Just recently Thomas returned to New York to reignite his acting career he wrote in one email. I think he has a show on Off-Broadway. I'm so far away from the theater scene now. I don't keep up.

Georgie G lived with him abroad, going to school in Switzerland, but then coming home to Pittsburgh. He had a family and became an elementary school music administrator. Georgie G died of liver cancer two years ago. Hearing that, I emailed back quickly, letting him know that Dad died suddenly of a heart attack while I was completing my last year at Julliard.

Thomas wrote he is a proud grandfather of two little boys who live with their mother in Point Breeze.

I look around to see if there is a woman waiting with two little boys. What color would they be? But there isn't any woman with children here.

To my left is a bank of newspaper racks full of the *New York Times, USA Today*, *Pittsburgh Post-Gazette*, and the *Wall Street Journal* reminding me I rarely read newspapers anymore, preferring to get my news on the internet. The headlines highlight the recent 2008 Democratic Convention in Denver, Colorado a few nights ago. Along with over eighty thousand people in the Mile High stadium, I too heard Barack Obama accept the nomination for President of the United States.

Though I first supported Hillary, I couldn't help myself from cheering along with the ecstatic crowd. My husband was cheering too for the African-American Democratic Party nominee. We were watching CNN with our married daughter, Melinda, named after my sister, who died tragically in a traffic accident in the mid-70s. Mother never got over her death and died herself of cancer a few years later. All this seems so long ago and yet so imminent.

I felt an unaccountable rush of hope hearing Obama becoming the first African-American candidate for President. It was unimaginable forty years ago that this could have happened.

Barack Obama is such a thin elegant man. He has a quickness, a litheness to his movements I hadn't noticed watching him in the primaries. He held the audience with his listening as well as his words, with his stillness, in the motionless space between his gestures and his words, not unlike Thomas. It's like the nation has fallen in love. Will Obama be our next President?

The Security Gate opens and I force myself to look. There are quite a few African-Americans hurrying through the turnstiles. I only have eyes for the elderly men and quickly dismiss a muscular man in a tan jacket, an overbearing gentleman walking with a cane. He's not the one with a beard and a diamond stud in one ear either.

Fueled by the newspaper headlines, hope holds me in the

balance. All my life has converged to this present moment. I practice my speech. I will tell him I am happily married, with a daughter and a son. Of course it is not the same as if—yes, I'll say it—as if I had been with him. What would that be like? My memories of being with him in New York are like ashes after a big fire that happened decades ago. Yet the ashes are still hot.

The crowd has thinned. This is all there is. My heart drops. It is in this moment that I recognize Thomas. He is walking slowly, off to the side at the end of the line. He's even thinner, slightly hunched over, though still handsome, dark. He wears black. His hair is short, thinning, and mostly white. He is looking down as if he's not part of the crowd that just passed. There are many more lines around his eyes. His forehead is full of creases, his cheekbones gaunt above the stubble of a salt-and-pepper beard. He carries a computer bag.

At this last moment, before he sees me, I feel a rare, light happiness.

"Thomas," I call, my voice faint to my ears.

But he hears me. Looking up, he holds out his hand. I stand and walk toward him.

Margaret Murray was born in Pittsburgh, Pennsylvania, and graduated from Carnegie- Mellon University and Hunter College. She attended the Provincetown Fine Arts Work Center on an American Federation of the Arts fellowship and the Squaw Valley Screenwriters Conference on a National Endowment for the Arts grant. Margaret lives in Northern California.

CPSIA information can be obtained at www.ICGtesting.com
Printed in the USA
LVOW040830100612

285396LV00002B/1/P